THE LOVELY AMERICAN

Also by Genevieve Lyons

SLIEVELEA
THE GREEN YEARS
DARK ROSALEEN
A HOUSE DIVIDED
ZARA
THE PALUCCI VENDETTA
SUMMER IN DRANMORE
DEMARA'S DREAM
FOUL APPETITE

THE LOVELY AMERICAN

Genevieve Lyons

LITTLE, BROWN AND COMPANY

A *Little, Brown* Book

First published in Great Britain in 1995
by Little, Brown and Company

Copyright © Genevieve Lyons 1995

The moral right of the author has been asserted.

A CIP catalogue record for this book
is available from the British Library.

ISBN 0 316 87623 2

Typeset by Palimpsest Book Production Limited,
Polmont, Stirlingshire
Printed and bound in Great Britain by
Mackays of Chatham plc, Chatham, Kent

Little, Brown and Company (UK)
Brettenham House
Lancaster Place
London WC2E 7EN

*This book is for Cindy and Phil
with gratitude. And Michele.*

THE LOVELY AMERICAN

PART ONE

Chapter One

∽◦ ◦∽

It was Maytime, blossom-time, sunshiny days interspersed
with light refreshing showers and gentle breezes. Spring
blessed Dundalgan as never before, draping the old house
in apple and cherry blossom, forsythia and rhododendron
blooms. The Ardmores came out of doors, testing the
temperature, setting the white cane chairs outside, but
scattering rugs about in case of chills.

Time trembled and hardly moved. Seconds lasted for
minutes and minutes hung like hours, while the pale
primrose sun drenched the world in light.

Drifts of confetti-like petals lay in piles by the curbs and
on the driveway and under the trees which were once again
clothed in verdant masses of leaves; lime, emerald, pea and
moss, a million shades of green.

There was an undercurrent of excitement in the air,
anticipation of long summer days, tennis parties, swimming,
tea on the lawn, work-on-the-long-finger, laziness permitted
or overlooked because of the sun. There was a general
permissiveness, not tolerated in the more energetic winter
months. Warm garments were cast off. Lisle stockings were
discarded and silk or nylon substituted with a sense of
luxurious freedom and abandonment. Ankle socks became
possible. Summer dresses were delivered in large designer
boxes or picked up from the dressmaker or ordered from
Brown Thomas or Switzers in Grafton Street.

Brendan Ardmore, master of all he surveyed at Dundalgan,
did just that – surveyed his property to reassure himself that
nothing needed repairing after the harsh winter months. He
had long dictatorial harangues at his gardener/chauffeur
Rushton Byrne, blaming him for whatever was wrong, not
giving him credit for what was right. Rushton largely ignored

the diatribe, his love of the land protecting him from the unfeeling presumption of his boss.

Dundalgan was a large manor-house beautifully set in the shimmering green, purple and blue land just outside the capital and on the way to the Wicklow mountains. It stood, serenely standing the test of time, its windows sparkling in the pale yellow sunshine. Behind it swans dipped their beaks in the waters of the small river that ran through the grounds and emptied itself into the sea, which lay at the foot of the estate, glittering blue crested with silvery white foam.

Dundalgan had been the home of the Ardmores since 1820, and was built in the reign of George IV. It was financed by monies earned by the Ardmore who took advantage of the increase of trade at that time to become the major wine importer in Ireland. The firm, old and honoured, was still the source of the Ardmores' wealth.

Brendan Ardmore was a large man, every inch the prosperous man of business, full of self-importance and the satisfaction of someone who can afford to buy almost anything he wants.

Rosalind, his wife, a lady of exquisite taste and refinement, ventured out more often now that spring was here. Tea, if not yet served on the lawn, was at least laid out on the verandah, and she supervised her daughters' spring wardrobe – finer fabrics, silks and cottons – with a lighter heart than she ever felt when the winter months were approaching. Vanessa and Oriana Ardmore seemed infected with a light-hearted exuberance and only Sitric, their taciturn brother, remained immune to the pervading holiday mood. But Sitric was beautiful, a spoiled child of nineteen, a mystery to all.

The servants too at Dundalgan rejoiced in the fine weather. Cessy Byrne turned her freckled face to the sun, grateful for its warmth. Imelda, her sister, shook out the sheets and laid them on the grass behind the herb garden and scattered lavender lightly over them. Their father Rushton Byrne polished the Daimler until it shone, and Sive Byrne, his wife and the cook/housekeeper, smacked her lips and looked up her recipes for rabbit stew and lamb, strawberry galette and gooseberry fool.

That particular May was remembered forever by the Ardmore sisters as a time precariously balanced, the end

4

of their childhood and the beginning of their adult lives. Afterwards they were to date everything from that particular May. Their friends would too. Elana Cassidy, Gavin Fitzjames, Pierce Powers, Dom Bradley and the others. They all remembered that May as the dawning of maturity and the last careless fling of adolescence.

And, of course they remembered it as the month the lovely American arrived into their midst.

He did not arrive with fanfares. He never really drew attention to himself – quite the contrary – yet he was to radically change all their lives. But they did not know that then, and when they looked back he was not the first person they thought of. Except of course Vanessa.

The Ardmore girls were unaware that their childhood was anything but normal. Was it not usual to be afraid of one's Pappy and in awe of him? That's what fathers were: remote and frightening figures of authority, keeping things in order. Nothing the Ardmore girls had learned or read persuaded them otherwise and that this was not as it should be never entered their heads. Pappy was head of the household, ruler, king and God, and therefore deserving of their unquestioning obedience. Without him they would starve. Without him there would be no tennis parties, coming-out balls, dances or cocktails in grand hotels. No fashionable clothes to wear at these functions. No Daimler to drive in at a time when few owned cars. No Country Club membership, no comfort, no cossetting, no security. Pappy provided them with Dundalgan, their beautiful home on the Dalkey coastline outside Dublin. He provided them with their education in the most fashionable convent in Ireland. He paid for dancing classes, piano lessons, elocution, tennis coaching – so naturally he must be honoured, humoured, obeyed and looked up to, and his terrible chastisements accepted with grace. He was the master.

The girls – Oriana, the eldest who was twenty this exciting May, and Vanessa who was two years younger – were dutifully grateful to their father. They envied Elana Cassidy her father, Dr Jack, but they supposed that the loving intimacy that existed between these two was rare and odd.

On perhaps what was one of the most beautiful evenings that

May the Ardmores were giving a party at the Country Club nearby. It was a celebration. Oriana Ardmore had become engaged to marry Pierce Powers and the Ardmores' slide downwards had begun, though no one guessed it at the time. That evening everything seemed quite perfect.

They had taken three tables to accommodate the family and their friends and Rosalind Ardmore had spent the afternoon supervising the table arrangements, the *placements*, the flowers, the decorations, until everything met with her approval.

Vanessa, wildly jealous that her sister had reached the pinnacle of success by getting engaged, had taken refuge in her favourite hiding place in the branches of the tree by the river to write in her diary: *Oh I don't want to wait too long. I want, want, want to fall in love, marry, like Oriana, so dear Lord in heaven above, help me to find someone, quick, quick, quick. Now!*

Vanessa was also jealous because, as she told her friend Elana, Oriana would have to buy a lot of new clothes. And there was the glamorous promise of a white wedding in the near future – 'For, 'Lana, Pappy is *so* delighted at her choice that he'll give her *the* most marvellous do imaginable.'

'Well, you'll be sure to get a gorgeous bridesmaid's dress,' Elana replied and Vanessa made a face and said that she was sure Oriana would choose a hideous colour that would not suit her, and Elana said, how could she do that when the sisters were the exact same colouring, and Vanessa pushed her into the bushes and vowed she did not understand. 'You haven't got a sister, Elana Cassidy, so you can't imagine how horrid they are,' she informed her friend tartly.

The only thing Vanessa was *not* envious of was the man Oriana was going to marry. 'He's a twit, Ori,' she told her sister when Oriana said he'd proposed and she'd accepted. 'Why him?'

To Oriana's fury Vanessa sounded incredulous. She refused to answer her sister's question, but Vanessa didn't need an answer. Oriana was marrying Pierce Powers to please her father. She was marrying him because her Pappy wanted her to. Oh, he hadn't *commanded* her or anything like that, but with inexorable pressure he had put her in a position where it was inevitable.

6

'We're all counting on you, Oriana, to do the right thing,' he told his elder daughter at supper. 'And you, Vanessa, you'll be well advised to encourage Dom Bradley. A really nice young man. Very appropriate. Extremely so.'

Their father was not a subtle man and he expected to be obeyed. But Vanessa had no romantic interest in Dom. He was one of their set and she'd known him since childhood. In Vanessa's opinion he drank too much and his greatest interest in life was Rugby football.

But she said nothing, lowered her eyes and looked demure. She hoped she misled her Pappy. The big fight when he realised she did not intend to marry the man he chose for her would be horrible. She prayed that when the time came she would find the courage to refuse and not copy her sister by caving in cravenly to his overwhelming will.

Long ago Rushton had built a tree house in the old apple tree at the bottom of the garden behind the house. It was meant for Sitric. He, however, showed no interest in it and it had fallen into disuse until Vanessa discovered that when she wanted to escape from *everyone* the tree was the ideal place.

It had been a beautiful day. They had baptised the tennis court for the first time this season. She had played mixed doubles with her sister and Dom and Gavin. They'd had tea on the verandah. It had been hot and they had lazed in the hammock and rocked in the chairs and Rosalind had dozed. Dom had teased Oriana about her engagement and Gavin, who everyone knew was in love with her, sulked, swinging his leg as he swallowed his tea and munched on his sandwiches with a face like thunder. Vanessa had said she thought Oriana was potty to marry Pierce Powers and Rosalind had told her to go and wash her mouth out with soap.

The evening had crept up on them, sending shadows creeping across the lawn and the boys went home to change for the party. Dusk trembled at the edge of the gardens and tried to hide the mountains, the river shivered in the evening breeze, and Vanessa retreated to her tree. She was muttering to herself, writing in her diary and trying to compose a poem about Spring, wrestling with rhyming couplets and puzzling over iambic pentameter and syntax,

7

when she spied her sister and Gavin Fitzjames wandering out of the house down towards the river and incidentally to where she lay curled, hidden in her tree.

Gavin Fitzjames was a good-looking boy. He had a narrow intelligent face with laughing eyes. Vanessa thought him utterly charming and madly attractive. But her father did not like him or encourage his friendship with her and Oriana. He told his daughters that Gavin Fitzjames was most unsuitable. He was, like Elana Cassidy – Vanessa's best friend – unforgivably poor. He and Elana's brother were studying to be doctors and everyone knew that medical students were as poor as church mice. They both came from financially insecure families and Brendan Ardmore did not think them ideal companions for his children.

But he could not forbid their close association. Gavin Fitzjames was a member of their set and invited everywhere in spite of his father's delicate financial situation, and Brendan Ardmore could not close his doors to the young man no matter how much he would have liked to.

He and Oriana strolled down the lawn towards the river and came to a halt in the shadows under the apple tree, unaware of Vanessa's presence in the leaves above their heads. She watched them, thinking how attractive they looked together, wondering why Oriana was stupid enough to marry anyone else. She was about to let them know that she was there, but she hesitated just that second too long, and the moment passed and Oriana and Gavin began to talk, and she realised after Gavin's first words that it was too late for her to reveal her presence. They would both be embarrassed if she did. Besides, she was curious. After all, her sister had just got engaged to another man. And Oriana would never forgive her for bouncing into the middle of their tête-à-tête.

'You know I love you, don't you, Ori?' Gavin said and Vanessa knew she had been right not to interrupt them. Perhaps Oriana would see sense and tell Pierce Powers to vanish. 'I love you so much' he repeated.

Vanessa shivered. It must be thrilling to listen to someone telling you that, especially someone as terrific as Gavin Fitzjames. Vanessa had always known that Gavin was in love with her sister and she put her poem aside and hugged her

8

knees and frankly eavesdropped. She was eager to hear what Oriana would say.

'Oh don't, Gavin, don't! You know I'm engaged to Pierce. You promised you wouldn't badger me about love any more. You promised!'

Badgered? Was her sister crazy, Vanessa wondered.

'Why in God's name are you marrying Pierce? He's so feeble. *He* needs looking after. He will never be able to take care of someone like you. He panics. Why won't you marry me? You know you love me.' Vanessa nodded in agreement above their heads. Gavin Fitzjames was worth ten Pierce Powerses in Vanessa's humble opinion. 'You're just jealous, Gavin,' Oriana replied huffily and Vanessa sucked in her breath at the injustice of it.

Gavin glanced up into the tree. Vanessa could see his eyes gleaming and held her breath, hoping he'd not decipher her up there in the leafy shadows. They'd kill her if they discovered her. Then he looked down at Oriana again. She was plucking nervously at the blossoms on the branches of the apple tree.

'You know that's not fair, Oriana, don't you?' he said in an aggrieved tone. 'And indeed why *shouldn't* I be jealous and you marrying another man?'

Oriana did not reply. There was silence from below and Vanessa rolled over on her stomach, very cautiously, and peered out of the leafy hiding-place, her small face wreathed in apple blossom. 'Why, Ori, why? I always thought we . . . I imagined you cared about me.'

'Oh, but I do, I do.' There was a desperate note in Oriana's voice. 'You know I do, Gavin.'

There was another pause. Vanessa, peeping out from the tree, saw her sister's lovely face raised to Gavin. She saw him tilt Oriana's chin up as he looked down at her.

'It's your father, isn't it?' he whispered.

'Oh Gavin, don't. It's no use and you know it.'

'Doesn't he care a fig for your happiness?'

'Of course he does' – Oriana sounded defensive – 'It's just, well, he feels that Pierce will make me a good husband. He'll look after me . . . take care of me . . .'

'He's filthy rich is what you mean, and I'm not. Just because his father made a fortune . . .'

9

'That's not the only thing. Pappy said he'd be a stable, reliable husband . . .'

'And I wouldn't? Jásus . . .'

'Don't blaspheme, Gavin . . .'

'I'm studying to be a *doctor*, Oriana, not to become a street sweeper. God's sakes, you'd think I was going to beggar you. Turn you into a vagrant or something.'

'He said Pierce would *really* look after me, take care of me . . .'

'Give you baubles, fur coats? Oh Oriana, how can you be such a fool?'

'Don't call me that. Pappy is always right. And I really care about Pierce.'

She didn't sound too sure to Vanessa. Vanessa didn't like Pierce Powers and she adored Gavin Fitzjames, but then, she reminded herself, it was not she who would marry one of them.

Then a thought struck her. She sat up suddenly in the tree and it shook and Gavin looked up again. Oriana was too preoccupied to notice or she'd have guessed at once that her sister was concealed somewhere above. And Vanessa's life would be hell.

'Must be a bird,' Gavin muttered and Vanessa stared down at him.

What made her sit up with such a start was the sudden realisation that if Oriana didn't marry Gavin, he'd be available. She could snaffle him! Wow!

'I'm just a poor medical student. That's the beginning and end of it,' he was saying now, bitterly.

'It's *not* that . . .' Oriana was acutely uncomfortable, Vanessa could tell. 'Look, Gavin, Pappy told me he'd be very happy if I married Pierce. That's all he said. He didn't *tell* me to . . .'

Oh no! Nothing like that. Vanessa knew how Pappy was. The pressure he brought to bear on them all. The manipulation of her sister who tried so hard to please the father she adored. She was his favourite, conscious that she was, and that he expected her to live up to his ideal of her.

'No, he wouldn't, would he? But did he ask if you loved Pierce? Did he ask you that?'

10

'He said love had little to do with marriage.' She sounded agitated now. 'He said . . .'

'But that is ridiculous, Oriana. It's just not true. In any event, it doesn't apply to him, so how can he say that?'

'What do you mean?'

'He *adores* your mother. He's nuts about her.'

'He said he *grew* to love her.'

'Rubbish. My mother was there when they met. At the musical evening at Lady Downpatrick's.' His voice was very serious now. 'See, Oriana, I remember everything my mother told me. All the precious conversations we had. And how powerful old Brendan Ardmore dissolved into a quivering jelly in front of Rosalind Ergan. It was one of her favourite stories.' Gavin's mother had died ten years ago, leaving Gavin and his father Leonard alone and very lonely. 'She said your father took one look at Rosalind Ergan and fell for her hook, line and sinker.'

'Well I don't know about that. All I know is, he thinks it would be more suitable for me to marry Pierce, that it would be the best thing for me, and Pappy has always known what is best.'

Vanessa saw Gavin grip her sister's shoulders. Oriana's hair was a dark halo around her head. As Vanessa stared from her perch Gavin kissed Oriana on the mouth, a long slow kiss. And Oriana did not pull away.

Vanessa drew in a sharp breath. She could *feel* that kiss. She knew exactly what it was like, knew how it would taste. Yet she had no real experience of kissing yet.

'There!' Gavin said triumphantly as he let her go. Oriana just stood there and stared at him. He gripped her shoulders and gave her a little shake. 'What can I do to make you change your mind? If you marry Pierce you'll be committing yourself to half a life. Oh, he's a good sort. I'm not saying anything against him. He's a twit is all.'

'Everybody likes him, Gavin. You're being unfair.' Oriana defended her fiancé but her voice was full of tears. Vanessa wanted to jump out of the tree and *make* her sister see how silly she was being, but she dared not.

'It's just I *know* you care for me in a way you'll *never* care for him,' Gavin said emphatically.

Oriana was crying. 'Oh, leave me alone, Gavin. You're

11

confusing me. I'm marrying Pierce Powers and that's final.' And she fled up the lawn to the house, running all the way, her feet scarcely touching the dew-laden grass.

Gavin broke off a twig and flung it away from him. 'Damn!' he cried to the night. 'Damn, damn, damn.' And he too walked away, but in the other direction, down to the river where the swans floated in the twilight, calm and graceful as snowy sculptured marble. He walked along the bank where the wild thyme and cow-parsley grew, where the heron dipped, fishing lazily, and the water-voles dug and burrowed in the dark, where the bluebells carpeted the earth in a softly shimmering blanket.

Vanessa hugged herself and picked up her jotter. It should be nothing to her who Oriana married. If her sister decided to marry boring Pierce Powers, well, that was her look-out. It was odd, Vanessa thought, that Gavin didn't like him either. Of course that could be jealousy. Oriana was daft, Vanessa decided, smiling to herself in the verdant shadows. Anyone who chose Pierce Powers over Gavin Fitzjames was out to lunch. Pappy's little pet, doing what he wanted. Daft! It was *her* life after all. Still, it would take a lot of courage to fight Pappy on something as important as this. She gave a little shiver.

But it left Gavin available and that was a new and pleasant thought.

She heard her name called out. Imelda. It must be time to dress for the party.

'Miss Vanessa? Miss Vanessa? Where *are* you? Come in.' Imelda's voice floated through the blue evening mist and hung there, echoing in the dusk. 'Miss Vanessa? Where *are* you?'

Vanessa giggled to herself and slid out of the tree. 'I'm here,' she called. 'Coming!' Then she, like her sister, ran swift-footed to the house.

Chapter Two

∽∾ ⌀∾

Rosalind Ardmore sat in front of her mirror. She wore a to-the-waist pink brassière that had hooks and eyes up the back and a corset laced in front. Even women who didn't need the help of these garments wore them. Modesty insisted. It was comfortable and she was used to it, preferring it to the more modern roll-ons and up-lift bras worn by her daughters. Suspenders held up her sheer silk stockings, also preferable in her mind to the latest nylon hose from America. She was applying make-up while Cessy, the maid, tidied up the bathroom after her mistress's bath.

She wore the merest touch of Rosette Brun on her cheeks. It gave her colour and she allowed herself to dust her porcelain-fine skin with Coty powder. She used a huge swansdown puff and when she had finished her skin looked as if it had been faintly sprinkled with flour. However, she was satisfied and set about dabbing the faintest smidgen of carmine on her lips.

There was a very carefully drawn line between what make-up was permissible for a lady to wear and what was definitely not. A little too much and one stepped over the mark into unsuitability. Rosalind Ardmore knew exactly where that demarcation line lay.

It applied to perfume as well as make-up. In Rosalind's youth no lady ever wore anything other than eau de Cologne or lavender water. But now, in 1949, society in Dublin had advanced enough to permit a light spray of one of the more expensive French perfumes – Chanel, Molyneux or Schiaperelli. These were only recently available again after the war and as such were a luxury and status symbol and therefore tolerated. Rosalind now discreetly dabbed Nina

13

Ricci's *L'Air du Temps* from a cut-glass bottle on to her wrists and the hollow of her neck and she was ready for her dress.

Cessy held it very carefully over her head so as not to disturb the neatly marcelled grey hair that lay close to it, like a cap, and ended in a smooth sausage-roll across her neck. It was a style Rosalind had adopted twenty years before and never seen any reason to change. She slipped into her grey moire taffeta full-length evening gown and Cessy fastened her up the back.

'Ye look gorgeous, Mrs Ardmore,' Cessy profferred, smoothing down Rosalind's skirt while Rosalind patted the firm roll at the nape of her neck in case the descent of the gown had disturbed its neatness. Then she sat again, surveying herself carefully for any irregularity. Cessy clasped the three-row strands of graded pearls around Rosalind's neck and handed her her evening bag, her handkerchief and her gloves.

'Ready, dear?' Brendan's voice called from the landing.

'Have a cigar, Brendan, and wait for me downstairs, dear. I have to check on the girls' dresses,' Rosalind called back to him.

She looked into the long bevelled mirror on its stand and gave herself a brisk check. She did not register herself as a person, an individual. She did not see herself in her reflection. She did not look into her heart in the mirror. Rather she saw odd bits, isolated. She checked the hem-line of her dress, the fall of her skirt, the placing of the corsage at the heart-shaped neck. She patted her pearls, the curl of grey hair, the smooth cap of waves, the outline of her mouth, the *placement* of the Rosette Brun on her cheeks. She pushed back her lips in a grimace and rubbed her small teeth with her forefinger, making sure they were not stained with carmine lipstick.

'Thank you, Cessy,' she said. 'Now tidy up please.' And, satisfied, she left the room.

Cessy sat down on the stool in front of the mirror and sighed in relief. The strain was over. Mrs Ardmore had gone and Cessy could now tidy up at leisure. Rosalind was a kindly and fair mistress but she was strict and there was nothing frivolous about her. She had abundant energy and expected

14

everyone to keep up with her. Cessy had to be constantly on her guard.

Dundalgan was her home and she had lived with the Ardmores all her life. Her sister Imelda, who was a little backward, did laundry and helped in the kitchen, scrubbed and polished and looked after the Ardmore girls. Their rooms were below stairs, off the kitchen, and Cessy had known no other home since she was born.

She often wondered what it would be like to live in a little house of her own, to close the door on the world and know no one could get to you unless you let them in.

She had always lived at the beck and call of her employers, answering their bells automatically, and although she was grateful for her wages, appreciated being housed and fed and gainfully employed, she nevertheless dreamed of privacy, an opportunity to finish what she was doing without interruption, and without having to cock her ear and listen for the shrill tinkle that would summon her to Mrs Ardmore's side.

She wanted and dreamed and planned her escape. Her mother and father and her good-natured sister and brother seemed perfectly happy in their positions, happy to fetch and carry, to obey, to accept that their world would always be bounded by Dundalgan. But Cessy dreamed of oer'leaping those boundaries and although her father never ceased to tell her her position was the envy of many a young girl, she would have her dream.

It would come true. She knew that now. Paddy meant what he said. Paddy would take her to America and out of this. There would be war, she knew that, but go she would.

America! Imagine that land, that glorious place where girls wore bobby socks and wide-skirted dresses. They all had curly hair, perfect teeth, bedrooms of their own with frilly curtains. She knew because she'd seen America in the movies at the Metropole and the Carlton on her evening off. She and Paddy. Oh, how wonderful that place must be and how she looked forward to going there. What was so bad about leaving Ireland? But her Da went on and on about how the great men of Ireland – Michael Collins and Padraig Pierce – died so they could have the Free State. He bored Cessy to tears, rabbitting on about history and death

15

and freedom when all she wanted to think about were high wages, pretty dresses and the new music.

'Cessy, what *are* you doing, you idle girl, sitting there, mooning?'

Cessy started, looking up guiltily. Mrs Ardmore stood in the doorway staring at her as she sat, hands in her lap.

'You know what they say about the devil finding work for idle hands, Cessy,' Mrs Ardmore admonished.

'Oh sorry, ma'am. I'm sorry. I . . . I was thinking . . .'

'There's no reason at all for *you* to think, Cessy. Leave that type of activity to your elders and betters. Girls in your position should not think. It will give you ideas. Just get on with your work and don't mope. I cannot abide mopers.' She walked briskly into the room, her taffeta skirt rustling. 'Get me the fox stole. It's chilly out and Mr Ardmore thinks I'll be cold without it.'

Cessy went obediently to the closet and selected the silver-grey fox wrap and draped it over Mrs Ardmore's shoulders.

'There,' she said automatically. 'You look lovely, ma'am.'

'Thank you, Cessy. Goodnight. You need not wait up for me.' She went to the door and turned. 'And don't mope, Cessy. It is most unattractive.'

16

Chapter Three

Rushton drove the family in the Daimler to the Country Club. He sat in front, a tubby little man with a good-humoured face and bristling brows, smart in his uniform. He never failed to feel a thrill of pride when he put it on. He looked good in it. It was like being an officer in the army. He knew who he was in it.

The females' dresses took up a great deal of room, skirts billowing up over Sitric's knees, so Brendan Ardmore rode up front with Rushton. Sitric sat with his back to the chauffeur, his face averted, staring out into the darkness, pushing impatiently at the black lace over pink taffeta Oriana was wearing. The skirt flared up over his legs in his evening suit and threatened to engulf him.

'Leave it alone, Sitric,' Oriana pleaded crossly. 'You'll crease it.' Sitric did not reply, did not look at her, but kept his gaze stubbornly fixed on the passing landscape.

All the Ardmore family were beautiful. Rosalind had, at one time, been the belle of Dublin. She and her sister Avalan were the toast of the town. Four pregnancies and one miscarriage had thickened her waist and made her stout, but she was still a handsome woman. Brendan Ardmore was a giant of a man, big-boned, tall – massive. His head of thick silver hair grew low over his forehead but his nose was straight and his chin cut square. His eyes were a piercing blue and both his daughters and his son had inherited those eyes.

Oriana and Vanessa were beauties, everyone agreed. They were called 'the lovely Ardmores', just as Rosalind and her sister were when they were young.

Sitric too was beautiful. He had a gentle sensitive face that drove his father mad, irritating him unmercifully and leaving him baffled as to why this should be so. In his heart he sometimes feared with a dreadful tension that his son might be one of those 'queers'. He had wanted a son like Pierce Powers or Dom Bradley, a large well-built, Rugby-playing rough-and-tumble one-of-the-boys, who would share man-type jokes with him and join him in his loathing of opera and ballet. Instead he had produced this sissy, this delicately boned, intellectually inclined fop, spineless, in his opinion, and a great disappointment to him.

Sitric knew full well how his father felt – Brendan was not one to try to hide his feelings. He sat now and stared out of the car window.

The sky was a purple bruise above them and the moon hung in the velvet drape of the night sky like a lamp. 'It's a lovely night,' Vanessa whispered and Sitric snorted derisively without taking his attention from the window.

Oriana in her lace sat still beside her brother. She knew if she moved her mother would reprimand her, so she didn't budge. This was her big night, the culmination of all her hopes and dreams. The night she pledged herself to her fiancé.

'You're the star,' her mother had told her before they left Dundalgan. 'You'll be the focus of all eyes.'

Oriana wanted to look her best, but she had an awareness of herself all the time. She never became totally unselfconscious. If they should see through her, really knew what she was like, they would despise her. She knew that, so she held her breath and smiled her dazzling smile and no one saw the bewilderment in her eyes.

Oriana's expression may have been composed but her mind was as active as her body was still. If only. If only. She could still feel his kiss. Gavin's soft sweet lips on hers. Oh help! Oh help!

She could see the back of her father's head beside Rushton's. She wished he was not so insistent that Pierce Powers was the man for her. But her Pappy loved her so much and therefore he must be right. Anyhow, she knew she didn't have the nerve to disobey him and deep down she had to admit that she did not want to be the wife of a struggling medical student. She wanted comfort and Pappy said Pierce would provide that.

18

When she was alone with her Pappy she felt safe, she trusted everything he told her, believed what he said implicitly, and it seemed to her then that Pierce was the perfect choice. It was only afterwards, alone in her room, that she thought maybe, just maybe he was wrong.

She had told him once how exciting she found Gavin Fitzjames, that the strangest feelings came over her when she was with him and that, perhaps, was love.

Her Pappy's eyes had become hard as marbles and he had held her upper arms tightly between his large hands, so tightly that she had big purple marks on her arms for weeks afterwards. 'Oriana, my dear,' he had said, 'I can't tell you how that upsets me. Listen to me. Those feelings are evil. They are the devil's voice within you trying to get you to do a bad thing. Now,' smiling at her gently, 'Now, do you trust your Pappy?'

'Of course.'

'Then understand the evil and pluck it out. Tell Canon Tracey about it. Talk it over with him. And forget any thoughts of Gavin Fitzjames. He's a poor man's son, a student.'

'He's a gentleman, Pappy.'

'That may be, but he's a poverty-stricken gentleman and not to be considered as eligible for you. His father Leonard is a failure, and that runs in families. Failure breeds failure. His Pappy is not like me. I provide you with everything, eh?' She nodded, looking into his smiling eyes. 'The Fitzjameses have run out of steam. That big house is in terrible disrepair and mortgaged up to the hilt. I'm afraid, dear, that if you married Gavin there would be no more comfort for you. No nice house. No pretty dresses. So,' he sighed, 'I hate to ask you this, but I want you to promise me that you'll put all these ... unsavoury thoughts of Gavin Fitzjames out of your mind.' Of course she'd promised. But it was not easy. Gavin was always *there*. He was one of their 'set', part of the gang, and there was no avoiding him.

So Oriana tried to keep out of Gavin's way and she had succeeded tolerably well until this evening when he had been playing tennis and drinking tea. He had caught her just as she was leaving the house for a walk.

Why did he have to kiss her? What had made him do such

19

a thing when he knew she was engaged to Pierce? Her spirits fell at the thought of Pierce – stolid, reliable Pierce. A big bumbling hunk he seemed to her. Oh, he was good-looking enough and lots of girls would envy her. And, she consoled herself, he was rich, rich, rich. She would have everything in the world she wanted. He played tennis well – but then he played all sports well and, Oriana thought sourly, that was no recipe for a happy marriage.

She glanced at her sister in the Daimler. Vanessa was muttering again. She didn't like Pierce too well. She said he was weak, but Pappy had pointed out that that was an advantage.

'It means you can *lead* him, Oriana. He will be putty in your hands. Think what an asset that will be.'

Oriana wasn't too sure she understood. But her father was always right and so must be about something as important as his daughter's happiness.

But why this turmoil inside her every time she saw Gavin? Nothing she could do seemed to have any effect on her emotions. Gavin was not as good-looking as Pierce, he didn't play tennis very well and was a lousy dancer. He said he had two left feet. Yet her heart always stopped for a breathless second when he came into a room. His grin made her swallow hard and when he looked at her she felt her body flood with warmth and such a surge of such nerve-tingling excitement overwhelm her that she was helpless in its wake.

And Pappy said this was a bad way to feel. Perhaps her father was protecting her from these feelings. They certainly disconcerted her. She never felt that way with Pierce. She felt comfortable with him and slightly impatient. Not, she would have thought, an ideal way to feel about the man she was going to marry. But perhaps that was the way it was meant to be. What did she know? Pappy was wise and she must trust him. She settled back, content at the conclusion she had reached, and glanced again at her sister.

Vanessa was still mumbling something to herself. Oriana shook her head. Vanessa was off on her own track again. Oriana despaired of her sister. There Vanessa sat, sheathed in white satin, with the face of a Murillo madonna, her cloud of black hair framing an angelic face, and what was she doing? Muttering. Vanessa made a fool of herself all the time and this character trait irritated her elder sister. Last week the onlookers at the tennis club had collapsed in laughter when a thread from Vanessa's white skirt had wound itself around the tennis ball. Only to Vanessa did these things happen. She had chased the ball around in circles laughing hysterically, for all the world like a playful puppy. In the middle of a game! For at least five minutes, until eventually she had rolled on her back and managed to grab the tennis ball, and onlookers and players had applauded. Oriana was not one bit amused. She couldn't understand how her sister could make such a complete fool of herself and not seem to care.

Then the previous week, when they'd gone to the Gresham for the annual Vintners' Ball, the sisters and Rosalind sat at a table in the lounge while Sitric and his father put their coats in the cloakroom. Vanessa pulled the table towards her and the whole top came off, with everything on it – glasses, ashtray, and a vase of flowers which went into her lap. People laughed at that too and Rushton had had to drive Vanessa home to change.

Oriana knew her sister didn't do it deliberately, but it irritated her that when she made such an exhibition of herself she did not seem to mind.

And now she was muttering to herself like Sive Byrne doing the shopping list. Dear God, she was irritating.

Sitric was looking forward to his drink. A Martini. Frosted glass, ice-cold. An olive. Ah! It was the only bright and beautiful thing to look forward to in this farce of Oriana's engagement to a man she didn't love. Silly girl, blindly obeying her Pappy. No, the Martini was the only wonderful thing in the whole damn world.

Vanessa was thinking about Gavin. 'Why not? Why not? Why not? I'll get him to see me in a new light tonight,' she whispered to herself, oblivious of the others. 'I'll stun him with my exotic personality, my Purple Passion lipstick, my Schiaperelli *Shocking* perfume. Tonight I'm going to be Hedy Lamarr instead of Lucille Ball. Oh, I just wish this satin was red, not white. Crimson. Scarlet. Flame-coloured. But no. I'm in virginal white. Oh hell, how can I be a seductive bitch, a Jezebel, in white satin? Not poss!'

21

'Will you *stop* that mumbling, Vanessa, for Pete's sake,' Oriana said through her teeth. 'You're driving me nuts.'

'I'll do what *I* want, *Reverend Mother*, so I will, an' what's up with you?'

'Girls, stop at once. Your father will hear you.' Rosalind glanced at her husband's silver-grey head. It was large and square and still. Quite still. He was staring out at the road, just like Sitric.

Her look was enough. The girls glanced at their father and became docile at once. Sitric stared at his mother with wide eyes, but she avoided his gaze. Oriana forgot about Vanessa and Vanessa shrugged off all thoughts and plans and decided to have fun tonight, and wait and see what happened. It might be a little too soon, particularly after the scene she had witnessed a couple of hours ago, to move in on Gavin Fitzjames and take her sister's place. Her heart beat fast with excitement and she wondered why. This was not a special night for her. This was Oriana's night. She gave herself a little pinch as the Daimler pulled decorously up in front of the clubhouse portico.

Chapter Four

❧ ❧

The Country Club had once been the home of an English lord and his lady who, when in 1921 Ireland had become the Irish Free State, hurriedly sold the house and lands, and, certain they would be butchered in their beds, hastened back to civilisation and high society in London.

It was a gracious Georgian manor-house set in rolling green lawns, with a golf course, tennis courts, and ringed by mountains. The wide circular hall where the Ardmore family stood was marble, and the stone alcoves, once graced by statues of Venus and Apollo, had been broken through to make cloakrooms for the fashionable clientele. There was an excited buzz of conversation, the sound of the band in the ballroom playing 'Oh How We Danced On The Night We Were Wed', and happy cries of people greeting each other.

'Evening sir, madam,' O'Connell, the manager, welcomed them. 'Congratulations, Miss Oriana, I believe are in order.'

Oriana smiled, held out her hand and wiggled her fingers about, flashing the large ruby to show it off. It was at times like this that she delighted in her position as Pierce Powers' fiancée. The stone was flawless and unfailingly elicited gasps of admiration. The manager's eyebrows shot up.

'Don't be vulgar, darling,' Rosalind whispered and Oriana quickly put her hand away.

'Oh dear, there you are. I thought you'd never get here.'

Oriana smiled up at her fiancé who had come from the ballroom. He looked bulky in his dinner jacket.

'Pierce! How nice to see you.'

What an extraordinary greeting, Vanessa thought. Like he was a casual acquaintance. Certainly not a lover. My fiancé will shatter me every time he looks at me, she decided.

23

'This is the big night,' he said, rubbing his hands together. He's nervous, Vanessa thought. His hands trembled and there was a film of perspiration over his top lip.

'Everything all right?' he asked Oriana anxiously and she patted his hand.

'I'm not going to change my mind,' she said. 'Don't you worry.'

'Just like a mother,' Vanessa muttered and Oriana glared at her. 'I'll take your wrap to the cloakroom, Ori,' Vanessa told her sister and repaired to the restroom with her mother.

'God, she's a fool,' Vanessa muttered and Rosalind glanced at her daughter in the mirror as she once more checked her appearance and made sure all was in order.

'Don't blaspheme, Vanessa,' she said, shaking her head. 'You don't seem to realise that all these little sins are mounting up against you. Retribution will be expected. You won't get away with it, you know. And what would Canon Tracey say?' She sat on the stool in front of the mirror. 'Oriana is no fool, Vanessa,' she told her daughter. 'She's merely taking Pappy's advice, and you know, pet, Pappy is always right.' Her voice was calmly certain. There was no point arguing so Vanessa snapped her mouth shut and shook her head.

When they emerged from the Ladies', Avalan Rackton, Rosalind's sister, breezed into the club entrance, scattering greetings to left and right. She was a beautiful woman. She made other women jealous and men uncomfortable. She seemed always aware of her sexuality, which in Ireland was rare and unfashionable as well as disconcerting. Clouds of black hair framed a cat-like beauty, green-eyed, Cheshire-smiling.

She reached out her face to her sister and their cheeks touched first one side then the other, while both of them made kissing noises.

'Rosalind, how nice to see you. How proud you must be.' She turned around, her voluptuous body in flame-draped chiffon, a shorter dress that showed off her slim ankles in high-heeled red shoes.

'Oh God, that's exactly how I should like to look,' Vanessa muttered to herself and her aunt turned and saw her and hugged her enthusiastically. 'Dear girl. You'll be next. No doubt of it. You look sublime! Sitric! Brendan! Dear man. Handsomer than ever.' She smiled at them all, and, clasping her hands together, cried, 'Isn't this a wonderful evening! And where's the most important girl?'

'Here I am, Aunt Avalan.' Oriana returned from the ballroom where she'd gone with Pierce.

'Oriana, dear sweet girl. Congratulations! How divine. Oh, isn't that ring just wonderful! Really enormous. A trophy, one might say.' She glanced mischievously at Brendan. 'Pierce, I hope you realise what a lucky man you are?'

'Is Simon coming?' Rosalind asked nervously. One was always tactful around the subject of Avalan's husband.

Avalan's beautifully serene countenance was suddenly infinitely sad. She shook her head. 'He's not up to it tonight. He said to congratulate the happy pair for him.'

Oriana nodded. She was not really interested in Uncle Simon, the sick, the old, the less fortunate, the starving folk in Africa – not at this moment. She flitted between the ballroom and the hall in a flurry of excitement. She was like a restless butterfly.

They went inside in a group. Alphonse, the head waiter (Alphonsus Haggerty from Trim), conducted them to the tables so beautifully decorated and Rosalind set about seating her guests.

Oriana and Sean Powers were talking together. Pierce stood beside his father, a smug expression on his face, and Avalan whispered to Vanessa, 'Is she sure she's doing the right thing?'

Vanessa shrugged. 'I've told her she's out to lunch but she won't listen.'

Avalan sighed. 'Goodness, you young things are in such a *hurry*! Marriage is a serious undertaking. I hope she knows that.'

Vanessa smiled at her aunt. 'I doubt that,' she said. Vanessa adored her Aunt Avalan. She was the sum total of everything Vanessa aspired to be. Aunt Avalan always made her feel grown up and wise. She smiled now, searching for the card with her name, then looked up as Oriana squealed in delight. She hurried over to her mother.

'Look, Mother, look . . .'

25

She held out her hand and they saw on her wrist a diamond and ruby bracelet that matched the ring.

'Pierce's father gave it to me as an engagement present.'

Sean Powers, a small stocky man with a red face and grey-fringed tonsure, bristling with barely contained vitality, looked very pleased with himself. He was looking at Brendan with glee.

'Well, well, well now, Brendan, match that,' he smiled at the big man. Sean Powers had made his money himself. He had scrabbled in the scrap heaps and got himself a truck, then two, then ten, then a fleet of shiny new ones with his name writ large on their sides. He despised Brendan for inheriting his wealth from his father, although why he held the big man in contempt he could not have told you.

Brendan was not at all disconcerted. He examined the bracelet, amusement on his face, then pulled an official-looking document from his pocket and threw it on the table before him. He did not give it to the engaged pair yet. He wanted to savour his moment.

'The deeds to a lovely property in Foxrock. I've had my people look it over. The house is in perfect condition. Of course, Oriana will want to decorate it in her own *style*.' He emphasised the word. Rosalind was famous for her taste and Molly Powers for her lack of it.

'Oh Pappy! Oh, how wonderful. Oh Pappy, thank you.' Oriana hurried over and kissed her father.

He smiled modestly. 'If you don't like it you can swap it for another. But your mother has given it the thumbs up, so I imagine you'll love it.'

'Oh Pappy, I'm sure I will. Oh gosh, I'm so happy.'

'Thank you, Mr Ardmore.' Pierce shook Brendan's hand and Avalan whispered to Vanessa, 'It's like an auction. Dear God, do they realise how dangerous this is?'

'What is, Aunt Avalan?' Vanessa asked, not quite understanding.

'I mean, Vanessa dear, that your father and Sean are outbidding each other most inappropriately. And for what I do not know. Oriana's affection? Showing off? I've got more money than you? Oh, it is most distasteful.' She shivered delicately.

26

Rosalind too was embarrassed. She set about seating the rest of the party.

They were all eventually settled, ring-side, just far enough from the band to make conversation possible.

The ballroom, with its mirrored walls and cut-glass chandeliers, was ablaze with lights beneath which the tables gleamed with cutlery and glass. Banks of flowers filled the room with their scent and the smell of the flowers vied with the ladies' perfume.

The Ardmores had four tables and as Brendan and Rosalind greeted their guests, people leaned across to other tables to talk to friends, and the band played and waiters rushed here and there.

'I'm your partner at supper, monkey,' Gavin told Vanessa who blushed and tried to quiet the erratic beating of her heart. She wished grimly that he would stop calling her that silly name and think of her as a woman. Someone glamorous like Hedy Lamarr.

'No man would call Hedy Lamarr "monkey",' she told Avalan, who giggled.

'If it was Humphrey Bogart in a sarcastic mood, he would,' she replied, laughing.

The ballroom had a short flight of steps leading down to it and as her aunt spoke Vanessa saw her friend Elana Cassidy arrive with Dom Bradley, hurry down the steps and over to her. The girls greeted each other with squeals of glee. 'As if they hadn't seen each other for years when it was only yesterday they were in Fullers together, their mouths full of éclair,' Sitric muttered. 'You've just come back from India then, Elana, have you?' he enquired and Elana rolled her eyes and asked, 'What's up with him?'

She wore a dress of shot-silk taffeta in a golden-brown colour that looked marvellous with her blonde colouring. She was as fair as Vanessa was dark, tall as her friend was petite, full-lipped, warmly curved, wide-mouthed. She was a beauty but quite unaware of the fact, with a deep speaking voice and an effervescent personality.

'Look at Oriana's bracelet,' Vanessa told her. Elana hurried over and greeted her hosts and congratulated Oriana. When she returned Vanessa raised her eyebrows in query.

'It's *terrifying*! With that ring! It's gross,' Elana said. 'Over the top I think.'

'You're just jealous,' Vanessa told her.

Leonard Fitzjames, Gavin's father, overheard them. He was a tall handsome man with a thatch of silver-grey hair. He leaned across the table as Elana sat down.

'No, you're not jealous,' he told her. 'You're right! You have good taste.'

Elana looked at him. 'Gosh, Mr Fitzjames, do you think so?' She was embarrassed that he'd heard what she'd said, and for once seemed awkward.

'Don't call me Mr Fitzjames, please. Makes me feel ancient. Call me Leonard.'

Elana smiled at him and nodded. She pushed back her blonde curls and picked a cigarette from the box on the table. Leonard Fitzjames took a lighter from his pocket and lit her cigarette. 'You look enchanting, Elana,' he told her.

She laughed, delighted. 'Do I, kind sir?' she flirted with him.

'Yes. Any young man's fancy,' he replied. 'Let's dance.' He came around the table, gave her his hand and led her on to the dance floor.

Rosalind leaned over to her son. 'Ask Vanessa to dance,' she whispered.

'No, Ma. She's getting all set to dance with Gavin,' he replied, lighting one of his black cigarettes – Balkan Soubranie.

'You never dance with anyone, Sitric,' Rosalind hissed. 'It's too bad. It's unsocial and ill-mannered. Look,' she indicated her sister, 'Ask Aunt Avalan to dance. She's a wonderful dancer. A regular Ginger Rogers, and she's alone. Simon's not coming.'

Avalan heard her sister. 'Leave the boy alone, Rosalind,' she called across the table and Sitric leaned back perilously, surveying the scene through half-closed eyes.

Leonard Fitzjames led Elana on to the circular dance floor. The orchestra headlined for the evening had not yet made an appearance. In the meantime a Latin–American group from Tuam played with verve and brio, and if they were not first-class musicians, they made up for it with their enthusiasm. Leonard Fitzjames was a first-class dancer. He held Elana at arm's length and, twisting one hip, guided her into a perfect samba. He moved like silk, and, controlled and masterful, he bore her over the floor in splendid harmony with the Latin rhythm.

He's probably the best-looking man here, Elana thought, smiling up at him. For a while she gave herself completely to the utter enjoyment of following his lead. She felt inspired and excited, and when at last the dance was over she was sorry.

'God, he's a smashing dancer,' she told Vanessa, taking her seat. 'Dom comes nowhere near him. And he's better than Gavin.'

'But don't you think Oriana's ring is stupendous?' Vanessa asked again. Oriana was flashing the ring and bracelet under Aunt Avalan's nose again.

'No, I *told* you. I think it's gross.'

'Don't let Pappy hear you,' Vanessa told her fearfully.

'Oh, he doesn't frighten me,' Elana said tranquilly. She took a handkerchief from her purse and dabbed it delicately against her forehead. 'God, I enjoyed that,' she repeated. 'Your dress is heaven, 'Nessa,' she told her friend. 'Can I have it after you've worn it' – she wrinkled her pale forehead which was pearly-damp from her exertions – 'say four, no three times. I'll lend you this.'

'That wouldn't suit me, 'Lana. Goldy-brown'd be hell on me,' Vanessa said. 'But you can have this, sure.'

The girls often swapped dresses and often Vanessa, who had closets of clothes, gave Elana, who did not, her ballgowns when she'd worn them a few times. The frocks looked different on the different girls and with different accessories. It was not the done thing to wear a gown more often than three or four times and as they spent a few evenings of every week at balls and dances a lot of swapping, altering and exchanging went on among their set.

'I'm with Dom tonight,' Elana whispered in Vanessa's ear. 'And your Pa gave me such a nasty look when I came in with him.'

Vanessa nodded gloomily. 'I know. He wants me to marry him. He has it all worked out. Oriana and Pierce. Me and Dom.'

'And will you? Cave in like Oriana?'

Vanessa shook her head. 'Never!' she said firmly.

'Will your Pa mind?' Elana asked.

'He'll go bananas! But I don't *care* if he does,' she said in a low voice. 'I'm *not* marrying Dom Bradley so I'm not and that's final.' She smiled at her friend. 'I am, Elana, at the moment much more interested in Gavin Fitzjames. He's available now Oriana's turned him down.'

Elana grimaced. She quite fancied Gavin herself. She picked up the card on the table with her name exquisitely printed on it. Then the one beside it. 'Oh Lord, Dom is between us. How are we going to talk across him? We'll have to use our secret language.' She groaned and glanced at Vanessa. 'Can I switch it?' she asked hopefully. Vanessa shook her head. 'It would throw my mother's *placements* out of kilter and she'd have a fit.'

Elana shrugged. 'Okay,' she said good-naturedly, then she caught Dom Bradley's eye. 'Dom, Dom, come here! You're between the devil and the deep blue sea.' She beckoned him over, laughing at him, and he blushed furiously. He was a sturdy, awkward youth with curly hair and permanently surprised eyes. His great virtue was that he danced all the new dances like a galvanised eel.

He obediently sat, chatting and laughing as the girls teased him. There was a general hubbub of greetings exchanged, kisses, embraces, congratulations and pleasantries as they shook out their napkins and put their champagne glasses down. Only Sitric nursed his gin, scowling, isolating himself from the party.

Dom Bradley edged closer to Vanessa. He glanced around, then put his hand carelessly on her knee. She could feel the heat of it through her dress. She lifted it firmly and returned it to his lap.

'I'm not interested in you, Dom Bradley, no matter *what* my Pappy said.'

'Okay, okay.' Dom raised his hands in surrender. 'I give up. I'll not run after you any more, Vanessa Ardmore. Instead I'll run after Elana.'

Elana groaned and sighed and hung her head. 'I'm so awful, Dom, you'd never be able to stand the pace,' she told him, laughing.

'You girls are the bitter end,' Dom muttered. 'I never know when you're serious.'

Elana was watching Brendan Ardmore. The man fascinated and repelled her. He had an ice-cold charm. His eyes were frosty, the expression always remote. He hardly concealed his permanent impatience. He welcomed his guests with perfunctory politeness. He doesn't really like people, Elana decided sadly. He doesn't understand the species.

Beside him at the table Oriana hung on his every word, looking at him as if he were God. Pierce, beside his father, was sitting with a fixed grin on his face. He too looked at his fiancée as if at a deity. Elana sighed. She hoped Oriana would be happy, but she doubted it. She wondered at the power the two fathers had and what would happen to their children.

Chapter Five

⅌ ⅌

Sean Powers glanced sympathetically at his wife. Molly was, he could tell, distinctly ill-at-ease. She had never really become accustomed to social gatherings in opulent surroundings. Both of them were dogged by insecurities in this atmosphere. Especially among the likes of Brendan and Rosalind Ardmore. Their money was old and they had been cushioned by wealth all their lives. Pierce, their son, who had also been born to it, took his place in this circle by right just as he took his father's money for granted. This irritated Sean beyond belief.

Sean nurtured his money. He loved it, tended it, encouraged it to increase and multiply, and the cavalier way his son scattered it about was a source of deep concern to him.

He was a mean little man. He hated his diminutive stature, hated his humble birth, hated the slum he came from and the grim school that educated him, and most of all he hated and feared the poverty he had left behind.

He had battled to leave the slum, the ugly tenement he had called home, and he could not rid himself of a deep resentment against those like Brendan Ardmore who were born to ease and comfort. He had fought for every penny, loved every coin that passed, reluctantly, through his fingers.

For a long time he had lived in one room, dressed in the same trousers and ancient tweed jacket purchased from a stall in Capel Street. In his room at the end of each day like some character in a book he had counted his money over and over and over. He liked to feel it. He liked to hold the notes in his hands and smooth them out, tidy them up, stack them into neat piles and slip elastic bands around them.

He wasted nothing. He used candles instead of electricity,

packing cases instead of furniture. He ate little. Small, wiry, he was enchanted by the tinkle of silver, the rustle of notes.

He worked all the hours God sent. He was fuelled by an overwhelming need to acquire money, to keep it, store it, treat it gently. Worship it.

He got his first scrap-metal yard in Cabra. Molly Delaney's family lived next to it. Molly's mother, a large generous sort with eleven children, Molly being the eldest, took the scrawny urchin under her wing.

Cannily Sean allowed her to feed him, do laundry for him – anything she offered he accepted. But she was not allowed to enter the tiny office at the back of the yard where he lived.

He was good at getting others to care for him, spend *their* money, not his.

He'd moved from the slum room into the caravan that did as office, bedroom, living-room et al, transporting his sacred piles of currency at dead of night, locking them in boxes, the keys of which hung on a chain on his waist-coat and lived snugly in a small pocket just under his heart.

No one entered that caravan at the back of the yard, save himself. Not even Molly, who became his friend, his companion and eventually his wife.

Molly Delaney was amazed and enchanted by the little scrap-metal dealer. He was a wonder to her. Everything he did astonished her and his energy excited her.

She had dreamed of escape from the gruesome life she led, squashed together with her brothers and sisters in one room, living like a pig in a sty. It was a hopeless place and few escaped. Her father, a quiet man, had faded, diminished day by day, struggling as the burden got heavier and heavier, until finally he had surrendered to the engulfing pressure of eleven mouths to feed. Twelve counting his wife and thirteen counting himself, though he rarely did that. He gave up, succumbed to tuberculosis and died, leaving his wife and children to fend for themselves.

Molly's mother took in washing, scrubbed floors, did anything she could to make ends meet, and Molly helped her.

A lot of the windows in Molly's house were boarded up because of the window-tax and the families lived in near darkness. But at one side, overlooking the scrap-yard, there was a small window and Molly stood there day after day, staring down at Sean Powers hurrying about his business.

Molly saw hope in Sean. That little man was on his way to great things. She was certain of that and she decided she was going to marry him.

She made herself invaluable to him, firstly by bringing him food, looking after his clothes, helping him in a thousand little ways so that he came to rely on her. Her mam saw what she was about and encouraged her. But she got nowhere in the amorous stakes. Sean was aroused only by his money and Molly realised that she would have to egg him on to an awareness of sexuality, and then she would have him. But it could not be confrontational. He'd shy away from anything obvious.

Molly showed Sean Powers the window. She told him it was her bedroom window, through which she had first glimpsed him. Thereafter, night after night, pretending to be unconscious of his gaze, she undressed in the flickering light of the oil lamp in front of that window.

It was damp and cold in the hall, and there was always the possibility that someone would come up or down the stairs, but she was playing for high stakes and she stood there in the draught from the east wind, her flesh covered with goose-pimples, and slowly pulled off her jersey, undid her Liberty bodice, until naked, in the glow from the lamp, she revealed her womanhood to him and prayed he was watching and was affected by what he saw.

He was. Love and sex had had no place in his life till then and he was overwhelmed by the flood of feelings unleashed by the sight of Molly Delaney pulling off her jersey in the dancing shadow-filled light of the lamp. He watched fascinated as her underwear was slowly peeled off. He did not see the condition of the underwear at this remove, but caught his breath at the beauty of the proud high breasts. He was in a lather for six long months, until eventually, with encouraging innuendo from Molly and her mother, he asked her to marry him.

It was put to him, indirectly, the advantages of such a match. How frugal Molly was. How he would have someone to cook and clean for him. They made the proposition sound supremely attractive and in truth Sean Powers never had cause to regret his marriage.

He became a very rich man. By the time he was twenty-five he had scrap-metal yards all over Ireland. He had a fleet of lorries that plied the north, south, east and west of Ireland. He had diversified, although he would not have known what it was called, into all sorts of other enterprises and his money mounted and mounted until people said he was so rich no one could count all he owned.

But he could. At any time of the day or night, of the month or the year, Sean Powers knew to the last penny exactly how much he was worth.

Molly insisted on a house. At first he was reluctant. He could see no reason for allowing that much money to slip through his fingers, but Molly pointed out the value of the land and that it was bound to increase, and although he loved the feel of the cash better than the acquisition of property, he did as advised by his wife and bought himself an old dilapidated house in its own grounds in Santry and gave Molly free reign to repair and decorate it. She earned his eternal admiration by spending almost nothing yet turning the place into a very attractive dwelling. She got her brothers, labourers all, to help her and when the structural repairs were done, she and her sisters set to to furnish the place. They managed this for next to nothing, studying the obituary columns in the papers and buying up cheaply the contents of a few tenantless houses.

Later, and many thousands richer, Molly would take advantage of sales and the little markets that abounded in London when she accompanied her husband across the water on business.

Molly bore Sean a son. They named him Pierce after Molly's father, but Sean and Molly were not very comfortable with the boy. Neither of them liked children much and although they scrupulously gave Pierce the best of everything, they had never really felt at ease with him. His engagement filled them with pride and joy, and, it had to be said, relief that he was finally off their hands. He would still work in his father's business, Powers & Co Ltd, down the Quays, cheek by jowl with the warehouses of Ardmore and Son.

Sean Powers remained close-fisted. No amount of money

could rid him entirely of his fear of poverty. He hated to part with cash but he also ached to be accepted into the ranks of the exclusive and the wealthy. His inclusion gave him a sense of his own success, it reassured him.

He could buy and sell most of the people he mixed with in the social circles he strove to enter and they knew this and they welcomed him. Money opens a lot of doors. It made Sean feel accepted and he liked that. Besides, he could manipulate them and that was a rich source of pleasure to him. And now his son was marrying into the foremost family, forming an alliance with old money.

And here he was, surrounded by Dublin's highest society, being entertained in an exclusive club, courted by all and sundry. He winked at Molly and she winked back.

Brendan's gift of a house did not disconcert Sean, as he had given Brendan to believe. He, in fact, had led the other man into a carefully prepared trap. Brendan Ardmore was, in Sean's eyes, a bully and a fool where money was concerned. And he was, fatally, a show-off. The man had to checkmate anyone who made an extravagant gesture. Sean was playing his own little game with Brendan. It was called, I give you something so you'll have to go one better. Giving Oriana the ruby and diamond bracelet, which he'd had at cost price from a friend who owed him one, would he knew, force Brendan's hand. And so it had.

He smiled to himself at how easily Brendan had fallen into the trap.

Last week he had phoned Brendan Ardmore and talked about the happy couple. He'd asked Brendan if the celebration would leave him out of pocket and would he like some financial help. He knew how outraged the father of the bride would be. Sean had to smile when he thought how if the situation had been reversed and he had been Oriana's father and such a suggestion had been made to him he would have accepted with alacrity. There was no false pride in him especially when it came to money.

But not Brendan Ardmore. Puffed up with his own importance he'd rejected Sean's offer of help, protesting huffily, just as Sean had guessed he would, and so, when Sean dropped the hint the idiot picked it up immediately. 'I've splashed out, Brendan, on a most magnificent bracelet for Oriana. She deserves the best,' he told Brendan at the bar in the Country Club a couple of days after the phone call and after a strenuous round of golf which he had allowed Brendan to win.

'Sure,' Brendan had said, nodding to the bartender, only half-listening. It was a stupidity that alarmed Sean. How could a man remain on top of things when he paid so little attention to what people said? 'It will match the engagement ring,' Sean continued unperturbed.

'What?'

'The ruby and diamond bracelet I'm giving Oriana,' Sean told him tranquilly. He watched the big man down some whiskey, then continued, apparently casually, 'I nearly got them the deeds of a nice house,' he shrugged, 'but it was a little out of my reach. Financially, I mean.'

He saw Brendan digest this piece of information, and, sure that he would take the bait, changed the subject.

And now the deeds, purchased by Brendan, were in Pierce's pocket and Sean smiled to himself.

Then he frowned. He'd looked at his son and wondered for the umpteenth time how he could have sired such an imbecile. The boy was useless. He showed no talent for business. Oh, he showed up day after day at the office on the Quays, but there was no spark there, no ambition. The boy was not hungry.

He'd have to speak to him. There were only two things Sean wanted his son to respect. Molly, his mother, was the first. And money. He wanted Pierce to have the same respect for money that he had. Be fired by a desire to work for it, earn it, treat it with due homage. But Pierce Powers' only talent seemed to be spending it. He seemed unable to grasp what was required of him. He was, to Sean's horror, *careless* with it, and that was something Sean would not tolerate.

He stared at the young man who was kissing an indifferent Oriana's hand, gazing at her with adoration in his eyes, and he sighed. He should have been harder on the boy. He should have made it more difficult. He made up his mind to have a serious word with Pierce as soon as possible. Everyone else was giving him advice, well, it was time his father did as well.

*   *   *

37

Elana Cassidy was dancing with Leonard Fitzjames again. She had asked him this time. Unable to resist the lure of a perfect partner she had said, 'Please Mr – I mean Leonard, will you ask me to dance with you again?'

'My dear, nothing would please me more.' Leonard Fitzjames placed his arm around her and led her into the waltz – dip and bend, dip and bend. Oh, Elana thought, I could dance like this for the rest of my life. Round and round in this wonderful room, under the lights, the music soaring and sobbing so romantically, my body obeying my partner's commands. Light as air. Light as a feather.

She could see Vanessa, her head close to Gavin's, and she wondered would her friend, like her sister, give in to Brendan Ardmore's pressure and marry Dom? She hoped not. She hoped for so much more for her friend, and incidentally for herself. As she thought this, as her attention wandered away from the dance, she tripped over Leonard's feet.

'Oh gosh! I'm sorry,' she said. 'It's . . .'

'I know,' the older man laughed. 'Food's arrived. Go, go, eat. You don't want to bother with an old fogey like me!'

Elana looked up at him, surprised. 'Golly, Leonard, I *never* think of you as *old*,' she said, and she meant it.

He threw back his head and laughed heartily. 'Could you but know it, Elana Cassidy, that's the nicest thing anyone has said to me in a long time.'

But Elana was weaving her way through the dancing couples back to the tables.

Sitric was still staring into space as if there was a wall between him and the rest of the world. He ignored the activity all around him. Everyone else was talking, laughing, louder than usual. Excited. Enjoying themselves. Only Sitric remained indifferent and remote.

The club was crowded that night. The Ardmores and their guests were not the only ones there. The waiters opened champagne, filled glasses, rushing around, taking orders for the exotic cocktails which were all the rage.

'A toast.' Brendan Ardmore stood, clinking a spoon against his glass for quiet. He was sweating and looked irritated instead of jovial. 'A toast, to Oriana and Pierce. Congratulations on their engagement. Long life and happiness.'

Everyone raised their wide, shallow champagne glasses and drank, echoing Brendan's words. Except Sitric, who silently tipped his Martini towards them, smiling his sweet smile and drinking, then beckoning the waiter for a refill.

'Does he ever join in anything?' Elana asked Vanessa.

Vanessa shook her head. 'No one knows what Sitric thinks,' she said. 'We gave up on him long ago. We just take him as he is.'

'Your Aunt Avalan is beautiful,' Elana went on, looking around the tables. 'She's the most beautiful person here.'

Vanessa nodded. All her life she had adored her exquisite and elegant aunt. She felt her to be tragic and wonderful. But she, like Sitric, seemed magically removed from the common herd, unreachable as the moon. Vanessa sighed and turned to Elana. 'Who do you fancy here?' she asked.

Elana shrugged. 'No one,' she said. 'God, most of the boys I know bore me stiff. Still, if you decide against Gavin I might have a crack at him.'

At that moment the waiters emerged from the kitchens bearing the first course and those not already sitting down took their places. Smoked salmon, slice of lemon, brown bread and butter. They slapped down a plate in front of each guest and vanished back into the kitchen.

Pierce was drinking in his fiancée's lovely profile. 'I can't eat when you're with me,' he told her.

'Well, you're going to starve then,' she replied, ''cause you'll be spending all your time with me soon.'

There's an edge to her, Avalan Rackton thought as she nibbled her brown bread and salmon, a sharp cutting edge.

Marriage didn't fix things, Avalan knew that only too well. Love did. She was suddenly overwhelmed with sadness, pity for the young couple, for Oriana who was *not* in love with her intended, and for herself, alone here, without Simon. Her beloved Simon.

Brendan pushed his empty plate away from him. He ate quickly as he did everything.

'How's Simon, Ava?' he asked, hard on her thoughts.

'As well as can be expected,' Avalan replied with the kind of finality in her voice that indicated she did not want to pursue the subject further.

Medallions of lamb and spring peas followed the salmon

and Rosalind complimented Alphonse on its tenderness. The young people wolfed down the meal avidly, without paying attention to its rarity or texture.

'Feeding time at the zoo,' Avalan said, smiling, looking at Elana Cassidy who was gobbling her lamb, talking to Vanessa across Dom at the same time. She made the remark humorously but Rosalind put her finger to her lips.

'Lack of breeding,' she whispered. Elana heard her remark and blushed.

'Oh, don't be pedantic and snobbish, Rosalind!' Avalan cried, shaking her head. 'Vanessa is doing the same thing! It's youth, land sakes, it's being young, not who sired you, Goddammit. Have you forgotten?' She glared at her sister.

Rosalind blushed. She did not appreciate being ticked off by her little sister in front of her husband and her girls. Leonard Fitzjames leaned over to Elana and remarked, 'What you say is what you are', and she smiled back gratefully at him.

But Brendan's attention was not on his wife. He was lecturing Pierce about marriage and responsibility and Pierce was shifting about uneasily under his father-in-law-to-be's attention. Avalan could not help thinking they really were a very ill-at-ease pair, Pierce and Oriana.

Meringue and cream and strawberry purée was being heaped into glass dishes and the swing band from London came to the stand. They wore white jackets and had their hair greased down. They grinned all the time.

They struck up with 'The Darktown Strutters Ball' and Vanessa jigged her feet under the table, dying to dance. They were very slick. The clarinets and the trumpeters stood up in neat rows every so often and faced right and then left as they played.

'They're great!' Elana cried, clapping her hands. 'Pity we're eating. I'd love to dance.'

'Sen-sa-tion-al,' Dom echoed. 'Let's not finish this. Let's go for it.'

'Are you *mad*!' Elana cried. 'It's strawberries! They'll be over soon and we won't see them again till next year.'

'Well, gulp 'em down. This is my kind of music.'

There was no one on the floor. Everyone was tackling their meringue and strawberries with gusto, but most moved a foot or a knee, an arm or a head in time to the stirring jazz.

'Look, Vanessa, look.' Elana's eyes were wide, her voice soft as Vanessa followed her gaze to the entrance. 'Just get an eyeful of that!' she exclaimed, but Vanessa did not hear her. She had stopped listening. Her eyes were wide open and her breath caught in her throat.

Standing at the top of the short flight of steps to the dance floor were two of the most glamorous young men the girls had ever seen.

Afterwards it seemed to Vanessa that the lights in the room became diffused, shimmered opaquely, that the chandeliers became blurred and mellow and that that face, that lovely face, like a screen close-up, was the only image there that was sharply focussed. It was, in that instant, etched on her consciousness as the two men, totally unaware of the girls' interest in them, entered the ballroom.

'They must be film stars,' Vanessa breathed.

'Tyrone Power and Sonny Tufts,' Elana whispered.

'Oh, I'm going to *die*!' Vanessa murmured.

They were tall. Both stood straight as ramrods, military-fashion, as they looked about them. One, the blond, was bigger than the other, altogether more burly with a tough muscular frame, twinkling eyes and a round face.

It was the other one Vanessa fixed on, frozen, her eyes like saucers, her mouth open, a forkful of strawberry and meringue halfway to her lips. Dark hair, close-cropped, a wide grin with crescent dimples bracketing tanned cheeks. Blue eyes fringed with thick lashes so long she could see them from where she sat on the other side of the room.

'He's perfect. Just perfect,' she breathed to Elana.

'Which one? I want the other,' Elana whispered back.

'The dark one,' Vanessa sighed, 'is *mine.*'

'Will you two girls cut it out?' Dom Bradley pleaded. 'You're talkin' across me. It's not fair.'

The men, having glanced about them, obviously found the group they were looking for. They descended the steps and went to a table slightly to the right of the Ardmores'. They stood, as if to attention, while a middle-aged, ginger-haired man with gleaming teeth stood up, dabbing his mouth with

41

his napkin, and introduced them to the others around the table.

'Hey, they're American,' Elana told Vanessa. 'The guy with the teeth is the American Ambassador.'

'They had to be,' Vanessa said. 'They're so beautiful, they had to be.' Her only experience of American males was the movies and she thought all Americans looked like the stars.

She suddenly put her fork down with a clatter. 'Oh crumbs, Elana' – she gripped her friend's hand across the fed-up Dom – 'Mrs O'Grady and her terrible daughter are there. Look,' she squeaked, 'they're all over those guys. Oh help!'

'I asked you to cut this out,' Dom cried piteously. 'I am not a statue. I am flesh and blood and I cannot stand this.'

But the girls ignored him. 'Don't worry, 'Ness. We'll stop all that,' Elana told her. 'You'll see. Mrs O'Grady's daughter is a *joke*!'

'Listen, you girls, this is embarrassing me. I took Arabella out once. Do you mind!'

'More fool you!' Elana cried.

'How? How can we . . . ?'

'We'll think of something.'

'What are you girls whispering about?' Rosalind asked reprovingly from the top of the table where she sat with her husband.

'What are you plotting?' Gavin asked. 'I *know* that look. It bodes no good.'

'You don't want to know,' Dom said in strangled tones. 'Don't ask. Just don't ask.'

They were suddenly the focus of attention. Vanessa shifted uneasily and Elana thought quickly. 'Nothing,' she said and turned to Dom. 'Come on, let's cut a rug.'

Gavin asked Vanessa to dance. A few moments ago, Vanessa realised, she would have been over the moon at Gavin's invitation. But that was before she'd seen the lovely American.

She stood, slipped into Gavin's arms and as he led her, a little bumble-footed, around the floor, all she could think of, all she could see was the lovely American.

She knew he was American. Elana was certainly right. No one had teeth like that except Americans.

42

As she turned swiftly in Gavin's arms she could see the neat back of his head where the dark hair had been shorn, military-style, in soft waves over his skull. When he turned sideways to talk to Bella O'Grady – who was monopolising him, simpering and giggling all over him, unable, Vanessa thought, to believe her luck – Vanessa could see the curve of his cheek, the firm line of his jaw, the deep cleft of the dimple. She could just glimpse his smooth dark eyebrow and the long curled fringe of his lashes as he blinked.

'You're very quiet,' Gavin said.

'Mmm.' She hardly bothered to answer.

'Who're you looking at, 'Ness?' he asked, and when there was no reply he shrugged and concentrated on his dancing, which he found so difficult, while his partner occupied herself trying to work out how she could meet this dream man.

How to get an introduction? She had to find a way. Otherwise he was going to disappear. The thought made her feel sick. She shivered.

'You all right?' Gavin asked solicitously.

'Of course,' she answered impatiently.

How to manage it? How? Elana was gesturing to her. She and Dom were doing complicated steps with style and verve. Vanessa stared at her friend as Gavin suddenly swung her around and around. She glanced at the lovely American and saw what Elana was trying to indicate to her. The Americans were standing. They were leaving.

Elana dragged Dom over to her friend. 'We gotta *do* something,' she hissed. Dom said, 'Don't mind us', but the girls paid no attention.

Panic attacked Vanessa. 'Oh . . . excuse me, Gavin. I've got to go.'

'What?' he looked at her, astonished.

'Stop dancing, Gavin and let me go. I've got to go to the restroom.'

'Oh gosh, sorry.' He tripped over her foot and the pain stabbed fiercely. She ignored it and fled to the entrance, leaving Gavin puzzled, gazing after her.

He mustn't go. He mustn't get away.

She ran into the hallway in time to see his darling back disappearing through the swing door on to the *porte-cochère*.

A car drew up to the entrance at that moment and the two men, talking and laughing, slipped into the huge limousine and the car pulled smoothly away from the entrance and purred into the night, leaving Vanessa, foot throbbing, eyes full of tears of frustration, standing desolate in the hall.

'Oh hell. Oh hell and damnation,' she cried and stamped her foot, then yelled at the pain. O'Connell, emerging from behind the desk where the members signed in and where he was having a quiet kip while the distinguished guests were eating, asked, 'Are you all right, Miss Vanessa? Is there something I can do?'

'I only wish there was, O'Connell,' she replied a little desperately. 'I only wish there was.'

Chapter Six

⇛ ⇚

In Dundalgan in the kitchens Sive Byrne was straining the stock and making the dough for the fresh bread for breakfast. Rushton would remain at the Country Club in case he was needed or one of the family wanted to come home unexpectedly. Imelda was upstairs, collecting the dirty laundry, the used tennis whites to wash next morning, first thing. Imelda would sing Irish airs as she worked and Sive shook her head in wonderment at her youngest's innocence. Imelda didn't mind work and was perfectly happy at Dundalgan. Cessy said her sister was a bit simple but Sive refused to accept that. Innocent, yes. Stupid, no.

There was a huge amount of laundry in Dundalgan what with the girls never wearing anything for more than five minutes and going through so many changes of attire in any day. There'd be the morning outfit, an afternoon one, a cocktail dress which would not have to be laundered, but cleaned, and probably a ballgown, ditto. And the petticoats and the underwear, the tennis whites and sweaters carelessly stained by the grass, and Imelda would be expected to attend to all of it and replace everything in pristine condition in its respective place in the family's wardrobes, closets and drawers. She did not seem to mind, though she had to work most days from cock-crow to sunset to get everything done. She had also to attend to the housework and yet she went about the house with a silly smile on her face and a song on her lips.

'That girl is wonderful,' Sive murmured, but Cessy shook her head. 'Daft!' she said. 'Daft!'

'We don't have enough help here nowadays,' Sive said grumpily, echoing Cessy's thoughts. 'Not these days with the childer growed up and changing their clothes like trains.

45

'Twas different when they was in uniform at school. Gev us time. Now, it's too much. An' fer yer Da, too.'

Sive was, like most cooks, a large woman, but she was of a gloomy disposition and it was only because she was used to the Ardmores and adored Rosalind that she stayed at Dundalgan. It had been their home for so long. Brendan Ardmore she hated. He was a hard and unfair taskmaster, but where else could she and her husband and family find such positions? With all the family working under one roof. It would be a rare thing indeed, and although she had often been tempted, after one of Brendan's outbursts, to march out into the unknown, she lacked the courage to do such a thing.

She had been sent out once before, into uncertainty and danger. She had come, at fifteen, from her home, a tiny farm in Galway, and she one of fourteen children, into service with the Ergans and she had been with Rosalind ever since. She had looked after Rosalind once, as Cessy did now, when she was a young débutante of eighteen. She had been trained as a cook in the Ergan establishment and had shown a natural aptitude for it, and when Rosalind married Brendan, Sive had married his chauffeur Rushton and Rosalind's father had suggested she go into service with the Ardmores and so it happened.

At first all had been well and when Rosalind had her children Sive seemed to copy her. Rosalind had Oriana and Sive produced Cessy. Then they both had sons, Rosalind Sitric, Sive Sean, but alas baby Sean had died leaving her bitter and angry and not a little jealous. And lastly they both had daughters again, Imelda and Vanessa. Of course Rosalind had Oriana, Sitric and Vanessa in a private nursing home with professional help and flowers and champagne to celebrate the births, while Sive had hers in the bedroom in the basement that she and Rushton occupied.

When they were babies, then away at school, things had been relatively manageable. They did their work and the daughters, bred into service, took their places in the household, Imelda willingly, Cessy reluctantly.

Cessy had dreams. Sive suggested they were the work of the devil, filling her head in the night with nonsense. She decked Cessy's room with holy pictures and relics of the saints and blessed it with holy water each night, but Cessy still persisted in her fantasies about leaving Dundalgan.

She sat now, in front of the kitchen fire and her mother had to admit that she looked worn out.

'What did you say, *alanna*?' Sive asked, scooping the ham-bones from the stock to save for Rascal the German shepherd who was lying across the door asleep, having spent the day chasing rabbits off the lawn.

'I said, and I'm supposed to be grateful for this?'

'Now, me darlin' . . .'

'No, Mam. I've been at it all day, an' now, at eight o'clock, I'm wore out an' I'm expected to wait up for them an' help them to bed, an' me asleep on me feet.'

'Now don't, Cessy, there's a good girl. There's many 'ud give their eyes for yer position.'

'You'd think they'd be able to undress themselves, an' they growed women, God's sakes.'

'Many 'ud give *anythin'* . . .'

'You know that's not true, Mam . . .'

'An' it *is*, love. There's a lot o' girls out there lookin' foe work an' not that many jobs for the untrained.'

Cessy glanced around the kitchen nervously. She knew where Imelda and her father were but she checked that she and her mother were alone, just in case. This was subversive talk.

The kitchen was a huge stone-floored place full of shadows, crannies, larders and storerooms, and the laundry room jutting off. Brass and copper gleamed in the dusky light and the stove shone black as jet where Sive stood ladelling the stock.

On the huge wooden table the dough she had been pounding moments before was 'breathing' under a cool damp gauze.

'Mam.' Cessy's voice was so soft her mother nearly didn't hear her. 'Mam. I'm going to leave.'

Sive dropped the ham-bone on the floor and Rascal rose from his comatose position across the doorway and, unable to believe his luck, padded across the uneven flagstones and snaffled it before he could be stopped. He returned to his position across the entrance and began to slaver over the quite unexpected booty.

47

Sive stared at her daughter. 'What?'

'You heard, Mam. I'm going to leave this place.'

'An' where may I ask are ye goin'?'

'Away to America,' her daughter said calmly. As if, Sive said later to Rushton, she was going down the shops, or to O'Connell Street, God help us.

'Look, Mam, it's no use carryin' on. I have it all worked out, see—'

But Sive had thrown back her head and let out a banshee wail that would wake the dead. Cessy was well aware that her mother would not be so vociferous if the family were home. Sive sank into her rocking-chair beside the fire and began a long diatribe of complaint, disbelief and horror liberally larded with threats of hellfire and damnation and tears and appeals to God to witness how she and her husband had nurtured a viper at their bosoms and what had they ever done to deserve such a child.

Cessy sat calmly twiddling her thumbs, waiting for her mother's outburst to subside, which eventually it did. Curiosity got the better of her and finally she turned to her daughter and, dabbing her eyes and blowing her nose on the hem of her apron, she asked, 'An' who may I ask are ye goin' with? For there's a man at the bottom of this, I'll be bound.'

'Me boyfriend Paddy.'

Sive again was overcome with astonishment. It was the first time she had heard anything about a boyfriend.

'Who?'

'Paddy. We're goin' to America. I'm not sayin' another word. That's the last syllable ye'll get outa me.'

'Have ye thought this out?' Sive asked, a little desperately.

'Yes, Mam. We'll start a new life over there, so we will.'

'An' what will the Master and the Missus say?' Sive asked.

'I don't give a fig what they say. This is nineteen forty-nine. I'm a free person, though it doesn't feel like it, not here. I don't see how I should be made to work from morning to night an' for a pittance. No, Mam. I've made up me mind. I'm outa here. Me an' Paddy . . .'

'Paddy *who*? I keep askin' ye. Paddy who?'

'Ye'll meet him soon enough, Mam.'

48

'Do ye love him?' her mother asked.

'What's love got to do with it?' Cessy asked. 'I *like* him. He's good to me, Mam. He's ambitious, like me, so he is, an' he's got plans. He suits me, Mam.'

'All the hard work, Cessy, all the difficult times have been all right with me because I had your da. It made up for everything, Cessy, the fact that I loved him and he loved me.'

There were tears in Cessy's eyes, but her mam didn't see them. 'I know, Mam. Mebbe we'll not be so lucky. But I've no other choice. There's no way out for me except through Paddy. I've made up my mind and I'm off.'

'Well, when are ye goin'?' Sive asked fearfully, half-expecting her daughter to say she was going at once.

'Oh, not for a long time yet. Not till later in the year.'

Sive heaved a sigh of relief. Who knew what might happen? Later in the year could be never.

There was the sound of a car outside. 'That'll be your da,' Sive said. 'Don't say anything about this until nearer the time you're to leave. It's no use upsettin' the man.'

Cessy sighed, her eyes on the row of bells above the kitchen door.

'I won't, Mam,' she said.

First Rosalind's bell pealed, then Oriana's. 'Think they were helpless, they can't get undressed themselves,' Cessy cried impatiently. 'God'n I hate this job. Miss Vanessa's not ringing.'

'Imelda must be with her,' Sive remarked, and she smiled at her daughter. 'Sure ye might change yer mind,' she whispered.

'Never,' Cessy said firmly. 'Never!'

She went to obey the summons, leaving Sive grappling with her daughter's news, wondering what the Ardmores would say when they found out.

Chapter Seven

❧ ❧

Next day, the day after the engagement party, Vanessa and Elana met for morning coffee in Fullers in Grafton Street. They wanted to discuss the calamity, their failure to meet the lovely Americans or even find out who they were.

They sat in the window and watched fashionable Dublin pass by. Examples of the New Look, Dior's controversial new style, meandered past demanding attention, while the majority, still in short knee-length frocks, tippets, hats perched saucily on the forehead with flimsy veils dangling frivolously over the eyes, looked critically at the wide calf-length skirts, the wasp-waists and exotic materials with a mixture of disapproval and envy.

'It's everywhere now,' Elana said, nodding to a girl in a damson two-piece.

'I know. Mother has asked Mrs O'Callaghan to make us *modified* day-dresses, but *modified*, Elana! Who wants *modified*. I want the whole hog or nothing.'

'Well, I can't afford anything new at the moment. It's only Monday and I've spent my whole salary already. There's so much material needed for this style. Everything's going to be more expensive if it catches on.'

'It will do that, all right,' Vanessa said with certainty.

'Well, we haven't the money for that class of thing,' Elana said moodily. The difference in their life-styles bothered her sometimes. 'You've got that dress your mam ordered when you got your finals,' she added.

Vanessa's face lit up. 'Yeah! I'd forgotten that.'

'I hadn't,' Elana remarked.

'It'll arrive any day now. Oh great!' But she was thinking of the American.

She gazed moodily out of the bay window of the coffee

shop while Elana picked at her éclair. 'What are we going to *do*?' Vanessa sighed.

'About what?' Elana looked up from her plate.

'About the American, of course!' Vanessa replied impatiently. 'I've got to meet him, Elana. I've *got* to.'

Elana offered her the plate of cakes from the cake-stand. Vanessa shook her head. 'No, thanks. Can you think of anything? Any possible way?'

Elana frowned. 'Well ...' She puckered her brow. 'I dunno. We could pitch up at the American Embassy, I suppose. I'm sure they're attached there or something. Gotta be.' Elana shrugged. 'I dunno,' she finished.

'It's because you're not that keen on the blond one,' Vanessa cried. 'No enthusiasm. Oh, can't you think of *something*?'

'Well, let me see. Why would anyone go to the American Embassy?' Elana spread her hands while Vanessa looked blank. 'I mean, what reason could you or I possibly have to visit the Embassy?' she mused, then clicked her fingers. 'Of course! To visit America!' she finished triumphantly.

'What do you mean?' Vanessa asked, bewildered.

'Well, if we wanted to visit America we'd have to go to the American Embassy.'

'But *no one* goes to America,' Vanessa said gloomily. 'Very few anyhow.'

'The Costellos have been to visit their uncle. And horrible Arabella O'Grady ...'

'I couldn't *sleep* last night thinking about him fancying her,' Vanessa groaned. 'Imagine if they clicked! Just imagine!'

'Don't be soppy,' Elana cried. 'No man in his right mind would fancy Bella O'Grady.'

'Dom Bradley took her out!' Vanessa chewed the side of her mouth. 'Oh Lord, 'Lana, I've seen the most gorgeous man in the *world*, but I missed my opportunity. Elana, I want to die!'

Elana gave her friend a keen look. 'Golly! You have got it bad! You've never been like this before.'

Vanessa sighed despairingly. 'I know. Oh, we must think of something.'

'Let's go up to Merrion Square. Say we're *enquiring* about

a visit to the States. I'm good at this, 'Nessa,' she giggled. 'I'm a good actress as you know. I might want to go to Hollywood. I might have decided to be a film star, like Maureen O'Hara.'

'Holy cow!'

'Well, it's possible.' Elana thought about it for a moment. 'I might, you know.' She pushed back her blonde hair in a provocative gesture.

'What do you mean, actress?' Vanessa asked. 'You're in the Bank Amateur Dramatic Society! That hardly places you up there with Sara Allgood.'

'Well, so what?' Elana tossed her head and crumbled a piece of fruit cake on her plate. She stared out of the window. 'Those dresses are only gorgeous,' she said as a pretty girl swung by, rolling her hips under an emerald ankle-length grosgrain trimmed with black braid. 'You gotta get your mam to stake you for one like that,' Elana sighed. 'It's divine.'

'And look at the one wearing it,' Vanessa cried. 'Thinks she's a film-star. Show-off. Honestly!'

The girl in the emerald grosgrain was the cynosure of all eyes and she knew it. She swanned slowly up Grafton Street, taking her time, heavily conscious of the fact that she made all the other women look dowdy and old-fashioned.

'God'n she's full of herself – you ever see the like?' Elana was as green as the girl's dress. 'We better get ourselves one of those outfits soon or we are yesterday's garbage,' she muttered.

A dreamy look had come into Vanessa's eyes and she had forgotten the girl in green. 'So . . . when will we . . . ?' She was looking at her friend quizzically. Elana shook her head and the girl vanished into Bewleys.

'How about tomorrow?' Elana answered.

'*Tomorrow*!' Vanessa shrieked. Several ladies in crêpe dresses cut on the bias, perched hats quivering, glanced her way.

'Shush! What's so awful about that?'

'Tomorrow's *ages*! Why not today? Elana, I can't wait!'

Elana laughed. 'Jasus, have you got it bad!' she cried.

The sun streamed in through the window and the chocolate on the éclairs began to melt. Vanessa dipped her finger in the gooey covering and licked it clean. Then she frowned again. 'Let's see. When do you go back to work?' she asked.

'Tomorrow. Why?'

'I've got to try to see him today.'

'Well, I start again after the two days due to me so we'll have to. I forgot I'm not available tomorrow. I've got five more but I'm keeping them for an emergency.'

'This is an emergency,' Vanessa squeaked.

'I know. But I'm off today. Oh, heaven spare me! I'm here aman't I? I'm not *in* the bank today. I'm at your service.'

'Okay then, let's do it.' Vanessa's eyes were sparkling. 'We've got the D'Altons' party at four . . . you going home for lunch?'

'Thought I would,' Elana said.

'Okay. Let's meet in the Shelbourne at two-thirty.'

'I'll beg, borrow or steal the Ford from Da,' Elana cried. 'We can go to the Embassy then swan over to the D'Altons' on wheels.'

'Terrific,' Vanessa cried, then, 'Let's go.' She jumped to her feet, beckoning the waitress in her organdie head-dress and apron. She mooched over to their table and wrote out the bill, slowly, oh so slowly. Vanessa clicked her fingers impatiently. 'Oh, come on! It's only two cups of tea and an éclair.'

Elana rolled her eyes at the waitress. 'Don't mind her,' she said, indicating Vanessa. 'She's in love!'

The waitress sighed, cast her eyes heavenwards. 'What's the rush?' she asked. 'Whoever he is, he'll wait.'

'Not the guy I'm after, he won't.' Vanessa was rewarded by a grin, a nudge and the bill.

Chapter Eight

❧ ❧

Vanessa hurried home to change. She got a bus to Dalkey at the Pillar. Petrol was still in short supply after the war so travelling by automobile was kept to a minimum.

She sat on top and looked down on the populace, ruminating about what to wear.

What would make her look utterly irresistible to the lovely American? Her lilac crêpe? It clung in all the right places, was draped over her breast and she had her black suede Cuban heels to wear with it. But, oh Lordy, it was *old-fashioned!* Being American he'd be up-to-date. She was in competition with Paulette Goddard and Jennifer Jones. How could she hope to get his attention in an *old-fashioned* lilac crêpe? She thought of the green grosgrain and sighed. It would look sensational on her.

She glanced over at the Metropole. The film advertised was 'I Walk Alone' with Kirk Douglas, Burt Lancaster and Lizabeth Scott. How could she compete with Lizabeth Scott – blonde, smouldering, slant-eyed and sultry-voiced – in lilac crêpe? How?

She'd ask Oriana. Oriana *must* help her. But Oriana wasn't home and she couldn't tell her mother what she was up to. Her mother would have heart-failure if she knew. Rosalind would be appalled that her daughter could dream of running after a man. It should be the other way around. Oh, a little encouragement was in order, but stalking a stranger as she proposed doing would shock her mother rigid.

Also the fact that she was planning to introduce herself to the lovely American without the benefit of mutual acquaintances. No one in her mother's circle met anyone unless someone already knew who they were. Otherwise one might meet the most unsavoury people. It simply wasn't done!

Vanessa was sure they'd find a mutual acquaintance. Dublin was small. The lovely American must know someone she knew and eventually there was always the Ambassador. She did not know the Ambassador exactly, but she certainly could find someone who would introduce them.

So, she could not tell her mother why she wanted to borrow something from Oriana. However, fate was on her side.

When she got to her room there was a beautiful dress-box on the bed from Switzers. Her heart leaped when she saw it and she sent up a fervent prayer of thanks to the Lord above, His Mother, all the Saints, St Anthony, St Francis, St Philomena and St Jude. Thank you, thank you, thank you.

It was her present and it had arrived at exactly the right moment. Her mother had said she could have anything she liked from Switzers for getting her Leaving Cert. with honours. Not a fur coat, her mother stipulated. She'd get her mink for her twenty-first. But whatever else she chose she could have. And Vanessa had seen *the* dress. A wonderful sapphire-blue, silk-taffeta, and of course the New Look. It had a tight little jacket with a peplum. A full skirt, long. Revers faced with white piquet. Smashing.

It had not been available in her size and Madame Dora, the *vendeuse* in Switzers Model Gown Department, said she would order it for Vanessa but she might not have it in for a while. 'It's for Spring, madam,' Madame Dora told her in a flat Dublin accent. ''Twont be arrivin' until the Sp-er-ing, so 'twont.' So Vanessa had had to possess her soul in patience.

And it had arrived at exactly the right strategic time. Perfect, perfect, perfect.

Imelda knocked at her door. 'A box arrived for you, Miss Vanessa,' she called. 'I put it on yer bed.'

'Thank you 'Melda.'

'Are you in for lunch?'

'No. Er . . . no, I'm out.'

She could, she should have lunch with the family but she knew she didn't have the patience to sit and try to make casual conversation. Her mother would expect her to maintain the calm and control she demanded from her daughters and Vanessa knew she was incapable of a relaxed demeanour at this precise time. And eat! Who wanted food when one's inside was churning like a flour mill. Her mother would guess something was up. Her mother was very observant. And if she found out she'd stop her. Vanessa decided she'd skip lunch.

She looked at herself in the mirror. Her cheeks were flushed and her eyes glittered like sapphires. They shot fire. And they were the exact colour of her dress.

Well, that was good, but her pink cheeks were not to her taste and she determined to tone them down to a more elegant pallor with some Max Factor Pan-Stik. And in her drawer she had a forbidden cake of mascara. Although her eyelashes were thick and dark, a coat of mascara would help her with the *femme fatale* look she was aiming for.

She stuck her head out of the room. There was no one about. Pappy would be at the office. Mother had probably not yet returned from the hairdresser for lunch. Oriana was no doubt playing tennis with Pierce. Oriana loved tennis. Pappy said she'd live in the tennis club if she could. She preferred playing tennis there to staying on the court at Dundalgan. There were more partners available.

Vanessa went back into her bedroom. She stripped, pulled on her dressing-gown and, although she had bathed already that morning, she went to the bathroom and immersed herself in perfumed bath-salts and bathed again.

She got ready quickly. She did not want to bump into Oriana or her mother. When she'd finished, applied the panstick, the mascara, the Purple Passion lipstick, smoothed on her one pair of nylons, checked her seams, slipped into her black Cuban heels, borrowed a little black patent purse from Oriana's closet, clasped her triple strand of pearls around her neck and slipped into the blue sapphire, she twirled around in front of the mirror, utterly enchanted by her reflection.

The blue silk-taffeta made a sound like rustling leaves and she'd put on three lace petticoats under the skirt so that she looked like a ballerina. She gave a little waltz of excitement, then slipped on a fresh pair of white gloves and, ready for anything, ran down the stairs and out of the house.

Chapter Nine

෪ ൭

The girls stood in the hall of the American Embassy greatly marvelling at their temerity.

'Your da'll kill you if he ever gets wind of this,' Elana whispered.

It was dim and shadowy with bold shafts of sunlight slanting into pools of light on the polished parquet floor. Vanessa was utterly sure of herself. Normally she would be nervous in a situation outside her experience. She hated unknown, unfamiliar territory, but today she was superbly confident.

'Boy, you look stunning!' Elana told her when they met in the Shelbourne. Vanessa was waiting for her friend, impatient to get on with her mission. 'You look absolutely wonderful.' Vanessa knew Elana meant it. She knew she looked radiant. A core of excitement inside her kept threatening to bubble over. This day was a perfect day. This was the culmination of so much, of everything she'd hoped and dreamed.

Inside the Embassy everything was hushed.

'Like a bloody church,' Elana whispered as their heels clattered on the parquet floor as they crossed to the desk marked INFORMATION.

'Yes ma'am, can I help?' a young man at the desk asked Vanessa. He had a crew-cut and his Adam's apple bobbed when he talked.

Vanessa took a deep breath. 'I'm . . . we're thinking of, er . . . visiting America. What do I have to . . .'

'Oh, I can give you a list of what you need,' the young man said efficiently. He shuffled about with some papers, looked under a folder, then opened a drawer and pulled out a couple of printed forms. He had glasses and kept wrinkling his nose under them as if they hurt. 'Here. There you go,' he said, pushing them across to her.

'Thank you.'

Her heart beat fast. That accent! American. He was American too, but this was the first time she'd heard the accent outside the cinema. She stared at him. In which movie did he belong? The dark thriller, the PI in the lonely city? She glanced at his Adam's apple and decided perhaps not. A Western? Ridin' high in the saddle? Not that either, not with those glasses. No, a cadet maybe, marching with a big grin on his face to 'Strike Up The Band'. He was the first American she had seen close up in real life and actually talked to and she gazed at him fascinated until he became uncomfortable under her stare. His Adam's apple bobbed furiously and he pushed up his glasses and said abruptly, 'Thank you kindly, miss,' and sat down again, dismissing her.

Panic. What to do now? She glanced pleadingly at Elana.

''Scuse me. Do you have two men working here?' Elana asked the young man.

He looked up, surprised. 'We have a lotta guys here,' he replied.

'No. These, er, guys were at the Country Club in Dalkey last night, at the Ambassador's table. We, er, met them and we . . .'

Vanessa's jaw dropped. She stared at her friend in admiration. Telling a facsimile of the truth had not occurred to her. Used to lying to her father, which Elana was not, she did not think of mentioning the Club or the Ambassador to the young Adam's-apple man.

To their surprise the young man leapt to his feet again at the mention of the Ambassador and stood rigidly at attention as he gazed at Elana, an anxious expression on his face.

'Oh yes. That would be Sergeant Glenn Carey and Sergeant Billy Monks. They . . . they . . .'

'Could we see them? Is that possible?' Elana asked serenely.

'Surely, ma'am. Surely. Excuse me one moment.'

He pressed something on the telephone, spoke into it in muffled tones, then replaced it, smiling nervously.

'Can you take a seat please? They'll be right out. I guess I didn't realise you were . . .' His voice petered out.

58

There were padded leather seats along the wall and the girls sat down obediently.

'Oh holy mackerel, Vanessa, what'll we do now?' Elana whispered, reverting to her school vocabulary.

'I'll think of something,' Vanessa said, but she sounded worried. She glanced at her friend. 'He thinks we know the Ambassador,' she muttered.

'Well, I didn't *exactly* say that,' Elana replied. 'The only lie I told was saying we *met* them. But in the dictionary sense we did,' she said reasonably.

Vanessa was clutching Oriana's black patent bag. There was something hard and square inside it and she suddenly knew what it was and thought of a way out of her dilemma. She opened the bag and took out a slim cigarette case. Oriana always kept a spare case in each of her bags with a fresh handkerchief, a sachet of lavender, and a couple of bob for the ladies' and tips.

'Eureka!' she cried.

At that moment the men entered the hall.

Vanessa gasped. They were wearing white naval uniforms and they were the most beautiful creatures she had ever seen in her whole life. At least *he* was.

They looked around the hall, then at the desk, puzzled. The young man with glasses nodded at Vanessa and Elana sitting in the shadows, then got on with his work, head bent low.

Vanessa rose and hurried over. She fixed her sapphire eyes on the lovely American and never once glanced away. Near to he was even more delicious. His hair was thick and silky and his skin was clear and fresh, like he'd just shaved. His eyes were blue as the sea and that grin which creased his cheeks made her heart beat a tattoo. She took a deep breath.

'I'm sorry to bother you . . .' she began.

'That's okay, miss,'

She stared up at him, trying to catch her breath. 'Em . . .' She swallowed, then continued, 'We were in the Country Club last night, and, er, after you left, we . . . er . . .' She faltered, came to a halt, stared at him helplessly, then held out the cigarette case. 'Did you lose this?' she asked breathlessly. 'We found it and as no one else seemed to have mislaid it' – she glanced at Elana – 'We knew most people there,' she added. 'Well, we thought it might be yours,' she finished feebly.

'I've never seen eyes that blue in my whole life,' he told her, leaning forward, staring deep into hers.

'What?'

'Your eyes. They're very, very blue.'

She gazed at him and he smiled. 'Will you have dinner with me tonight?' he asked.

To her horror she heard herself saying primly, 'I don't even know your name.'

'Of course she'll dine with you,' Elana took over firmly. 'We better introduce ourselves,' she said.

'Well,' the American drawled, 'I'm Glenn Carey and this is my pal Billy Monks.'

'This is *my* friend, Vanessa Ardmore, and I'm Elana Cassidy.'

'Hi,' the dark one said, not taking his eyes off Vanessa.

'That's lovely,' Vanessa said breathlessly and when she saw his quizzical look she hastened to add, 'We say "how do you do" which is silly really. I like "hi".' She was babbling and she knew it but the American didn't seem to mind.

'Let's have dinner,' he repeated.

'I can't. Not tonight. My sister's just got engaged.'

'I know!' Elana volunteered, looking at Vanessa, 'Why don't we invite you guys to the D'Altons' cocktails?'

'Oh no! We can't do that!' Vanessa protested.

'Why not?' the American asked. 'I'd be happy to accept.'

'How'll we say we met?' Vanessa cried anxiously.

'You can say *I* introduced you,' Elana replied tranquilly. 'I just did, didn't I?' and she laughed. 'It's the truth.'

Glenn Carey was looking a bit puzzled.

'See, in this town they're very strict about how and who one meets,' Elana explained.

'Sticklers about introduction? Eh? Well, I can understand that. They're like that too in my home town,' Glenn remarked.

'Where is this party?' Billy asked, then glanced at his friend. 'Think we can swing it?'

'Sure. I said I'd accepted and I meant it,' Glenn remarked, smiling, and Billy raised his brows but said nothing.

'I just couldn't bear to pass it up,' Glenn told Vanessa.

'So where is it?' Billy asked.

'It's in Ballsbridge,' Elana told them. 'But we'll guide you there. Pick us up in the Shelbourne. Six-thirty sharp. The party's from six to eight.'

'Are you organised, lift-wise?' Billy asked.

'*Très* organised.' Elana waved at the two men. 'See you then.' She took the bemused Vanessa's elbow in a firm grip and frogmarched her out of the building.

When they reached the pavement she ran the back of her hand across her brow. 'Whew!' she exclaimed.

'Don't, Elana. They might be watching. From a window.' Vanessa was walking gracefully away down the street, not looking back.

'What time is it?'

'Three. It's only three o'clock,' Vanessa said in disbelief. She felt as if she had taken a giant step into her future. 'We were only in there for about *ten minutes*! It seemed a lifetime.'

'Ah! Love!' Elana sighed and Vanessa glared at her.

'Don't you say *anything*. You hear? Not a word or I'll kill you.'

'I promise.'

'It's too important.'

'Okay, okay. Got the message.' They walked, both girls lost in thought. There were skylarks in the trees trilling in the Green and the air held a faint scent of the sea. 'Oh it's a lovely, lovely day,' Vanessa cried, wrapping her arms around her body and smiling at the sun.

'What'll we do now?' Elana asked.

'Wait in the Shelbourne. We can have tea there. Gosh, I'm hungry.'

'Well, you said you hadn't had any lunch,' Elana remarked. 'Have you got money?'

Vanessa nodded. 'Enough,' she said.

Elana looked at her and sighed. It was always the same. Vanessa had the money and she didn't. Her thirty shillings a week salary never went far enough and she was always in financial trouble after the weekend. Well, there was nothing she could do except not go out and she wasn't about to do that.

Elana's parents were poor as church-mice and her father had been barely able to muster the school fees to give her the good education she had received in the Sacred Heart Convent where she and Vanessa had met and become best friends.

At first she had avoided Vanessa Ardmore because of her money, even though the girls were attracted to each other right from the start. She was not in the same league as the Ardmores. Her father, Dr Jack Cassidy, was a successful GP but he would insist on treating people for a pittance, often waiving his fee altogether. He also took payment in kind and his wife insisted that the cash-flow in their house was so small that it might well not be counted at all. Whereas the Ardmores had a surfeit of plenty.

Vanessa didn't have a clue what it was like to have to count pennies. She often suggested taxis, ordered drinks, went automatically to the best seats in the theatre and cinema and constantly bought lipsticks, perfume, scarves and gloves and other such luxuries that were quite outside Elana's tight budget without any thought that her friend could not possibly afford such excesses. It made their friendship very difficult for Elana. It took a lot of educating to wise Vanessa up to what it was like for the less financially fortunate.

And Elana was not sure that Vanessa ever really understood. Even now, after years of explaining and illustrating, Vanessa never really took the cost of things into account, whereas it was the first thing Elana had to think of. Could she afford it?

They sat in the lounge in the Shelbourne, nearly enveloped in a huge green sofa, and gossiped and sipped tea. Elana fiddled with a paper-thin cucumber sandwich while Vanessa wolfed down the smoked salmon.

'I'm ravenous,' she apologised to her friend. 'This is the first bite that crossed my lips since I *saw* him last night.'

'You're kidding!' Elana looked at her friend. She took in the sparkle in her eyes, the flushed cheeks in spite of the Pan-Stik. 'You've really fallen for him, haven't you? This Glenn Carey?'

Vanessa put down her cup. 'Oh yes!' she said positively. She glanced at Elana. 'I'm in a whirl,' she said, 'out of control. I've never felt this way before. Never in my life. I think I've gone crazy. They say "Crazy about you" in songs, don't they? Meaning love? Being in love. Well, that's right. Crazy is mad. I feel mad, Elana. Oh, it's so peculiar.'

'But nice?'

'Not really. I feel frightened. It's so enormous. I feel sick. Anxious and terrified. As well as sublimely happy. Like a saint having an ecstasy. You remember Mother Assumpta about St Theresa of Avila's ecstasy? Out of this world. Well, I feel like that. Oh God, it's terrible.'

'Then run away.'

Vanessa looked at her friend helplessly. 'I can't,' she said simply. 'It's too late.'

She was quiet again, watching the leaves of the trees outside the hotel shiver and shake in the breeze. The leaves were tender green, new bloomed, dancing there in perpetual quivering motion. She would be cold later on, in her silk-taffeta without a stole. Or would she? She felt numb now, and then she felt as if she had a fever. It was very confusing. She felt terribly excited. Like prize-giving day. Like waiting for examination results but knowing inside that you had done well, yet there was always the *supposing* you didn't, the 'what if', the sick little core of uncertainty and tension.

The elegant hotel lounge was filling up. The girls sat on the sofa, crisp nappery, fine china, dainty little sandwiches and cakes on a table before them. The chandelier lights were turned on and the room was full of the gentle murmur of good-humoured conversation. The gilt-edged mirrors reflected the elegant hats and fur tippets of the women, with their little veils and cocky feathers, and the rough tweeds of the men, peppered here and there with reversed-white collars of the clergy.

And at the edge of the lounge, Vanessa on the sofa with Elana, sapphire eyes glowing, her sapphire outfit ultramodern among the more reserved fashions. She gleamed with a brilliance that demanded attention, a kind of feverish excitement that she was totally unaware of.

But Elana saw it and became afraid for her friend. 'What'll your mother say?' she asked.

Vanessa shifted uncomfortably on the green sofa. 'What would you expect her to say? Old-fashioned thing!'

Her reply was tossed off carelessly and Elana knew she was refusing to think about it.

'Don't be flip, 'Nessa,' she said. 'What will your father think?'

'Oh, don't spoil it, Elana, please. I can't think about Mother or Pappy now. Please, please don't spoil things for me,' she pleaded. Then her eyes gleamed ever brighter. 'Oh look, Elana. Look.'

The two men came into the lounge and a hush fell for a moment, a second-long silence as the good-looking Americans were scrutinised briefly, then dismissed, and the buzz resumed its background presence.

Vanessa's heart nearly bounced out of her body at the sight of him strolling towards her. He moved gracefully and unselfconsciously, threading his way past the tables and over to their sofa under the window.

'Hi,' he greeted her and she smiled tremulously, not fully in control of her mouth. It quivered at the corners and her grin got stuck and wobbled.

'Hello.'

What would she do now? What could she talk about now that he was beside her?

There was an awkward silence broken only by the clink of china, the murmur of conversation, the tinkle of silverwear.

'God, this place is . . .' Glenn began, looking around.

'I need a drink.' Billy waved at a passing waitress. 'Hey, Miss, can we have two Jameson's here?'

'But sir, it's tea-time. It's not usual . . .'

'Make 'em large ones,' Glenn said and gave her his dazzling smile.

'Oh well, I suppose it's all right. But the bar's over there.'

'With some ice, if you can find it,' Glenn continued unruffled, and he handed her a ten-shilling note. 'This is for you if you succeed. Okay?'

'Okay.' She took the note, half her weekly wages, and hurried away.

'Where're you from?' Elana, probably the least disconcerted there, asked Billy Monks, and the awkward spell was broken.

'Chicago,' he said. 'Illinois.'

'Where Al Capone came from,' Elana quipped. 'Saw it in a movie. "Scarface" I think. Humphrey Bogart.'

'Edward G. Robinson,' Billy told her. 'Yeah. Fancy you knowing that.'

'Oh, we know lots about America from the movies,' Vanessa said and felt stupid. It was a silly thing to say. She saw Billy glance at Glenn and they exchanged a look. She blushed. 'I didn't mean . . .' She stumbled over her words, wanting to cry. 'What I meant was . . .'

Why had she lost her composure? People thought her sophisticated and now she was behaving like a rustic.

'I know what you meant,' Glenn was saying reassuringly. 'And you are right. People here know what the Manhattan skyline looks like from the movies. And how the West looks. All that scrub and desert. We only discovered how beautiful Ireland was when we actually came here. We'd never seen it in the movies, see. So you know more about us than we do about you.'

Billy looked at his friend in surprise. 'Oh, I thought –' he began, but Glenn interrupted him.

'I come from Wisconsin. Lived in the country all my life. I don't like big cities, not really. That's why I like Dublin.'

Elana and Vanessa exchanged glances. It had never occurred to them that Dublin was not a big city.

'I mean compared to London or New York,' Glenn amended seeing their look.

'You've been everywhere,' Vanessa cried.

'Well, not everywhere. We've been to Japan. During the war. Back through Europe . . .'

'We've never been out of Ireland,' Vanessa said breathlessly.

The waitress arrived back with the whiskies. She looked flustered. 'They're not happy about this,' she said. 'See, this is *tea-time*. And the bar's over there an' this is the *lounge* an'—'

'Don't let it get you down, honey,' Billy told her, handing her another note. 'Keep the change,' he said and, considerably mollified, she pocketed the note and left them.

'What do you do?' Elana asked after a moment while the men sipped their drinks. 'The fellow at the Embassy called you "Sergeant".'

'Yeah. I'm . . . we're in the United States Marines. Attached to the American Embassy in Dublin for a spell. Two-year stint. Then back to the good old USA.'

They slapped hands, palm on palm, and grinned at each other and Vanessa felt excluded. This was buddy-buddy stuff. They were such strangers. Never in her life before had she met men about whom she knew absolutely nothing. In Ireland, with Irish boys, she could tell from their accent which school they went to, where they came from. And if she searched long enough she was bound to find an acquaintance in common. But these men were unexplored territory and as such immensely attractive and terrifying.

'Were you in the war?' Vanessa asked. Glenn nodded.

'Sure. Tail-end only.'

'We saw some action in the Pacific,' Billy said.

'Came through Europe after,' Glenn added. 'Terrible mess.'

They were suddenly very serious. Vanessa wished she hadn't brought the subject up, but she didn't know what to talk about.

'Where we going? These people . . .' Glenn began.

'She said, Ballsbridge,' Billy said. 'Only in Ireland would a place be called Ballsbridge,' and he laughed.

Vanessa looked at him uncomprehending and Glenn cleared his throat. 'We have a car outside,' he said.

'We have our own,' Elana told them and Vanessa glanced at her.

'I go with you,' Billy said to Elana, 'and Glenn can take Vanessa. Hey, you call her Vanessa all the time? It's a mouthful.'

'I call her 'Nessa sometimes,' Elana said.

'Okay.' Billy smiled. 'Let's go then.'

'Yeah! It's seven o'clock.' Glenn was feeling for his wallet.

'No, no, I'll . . .' Vanessa held out her hand for the bill but Billy wouldn't hear of it.

'Not on your life. No lady pays when I'm around,' he announced firmly.

Glenn put his wallet back and his hand out and helped Vanessa rise. His touch was like an electric shock through her body and her eyes flew startled to his. He was looking at her intently as if he too felt something wonderful was happening. She gave him a little wistful smile and he smiled back and something, she didn't know what exactly, was, in that moment, settled.

Chapter Ten

ໝ ໙

Rosalind liked the D'Altons. They were her sort, had money, lived comfortable lives – divided mainly, like her own, between balls, dances, musical evenings, dinner parties, the Country and Tennis Clubs, and, of course, in this enlightened age, the cocktail party.

They felt themselves very modern going to and having cocktail parties. The six to eight slot had at first been frowned on and considered American and therefore not perhaps in the best of taste. However the convenience of cramming a large number of duty guests into the drawing room and plying them with exotic drinks and *canapés* instead of the more demanding, formal and much longer dinner party was very tempting and most hostesses decided the advantages far outweighed the disadvantages and they felt themselves capable of making it socially acceptable. So it was done. It was a boon not to have to spend long hours across the table feeding people you owed an invitation but did not really like.

The D'Altons, unfortunately, were childless. Had there been an available son Rosalind would, doubtless, have done what she could to pair him with one of the girls, or a daughter with Sitric.

The old friends greeted each other affectionately. Margaret D'Alton was a horsy woman, strong-nosed, big-boned and awkwardly bodied, but she had the confidence of wealth and intelligence. Her husband Jonathan was a jolly roly-poly man who found life a pleasant joke and adored his ungainly wife.

'My dear, how nice to see you,' Margaret D'Alton said to her friend now, kissing her. 'I'm so sorry we couldn't come to the engagement party but as you know we just got back.'

'How was it?' Rosalind asked.

'Oh, it rained all the time. But Kerry is beautiful and the golf was marvellous. Jonathan was happy.' She smiled at Rosalind. 'You must be pleased. The happy couple arrived moments ago and they certainly are a perfect pair. Congratulations.' She winked at Rosalind, aware how pleased her friend would be at the engagement. 'Still,' she frowned, 'I think you are very noble including that terrible Sean Powers into the family. Very brave of you, darling.'

Rosalind smiled. 'Oh, Sean is all right. His position renders him eccentric.'

'His money, you mean.' Margaret laughed. 'Where's Vanessa?' she asked. 'I thought she'd be with you.'

'I don't know,' Rosalind told her. 'She's probably with Elana Cassidy.' She caught sight of Margaret's face. 'Oh, I know Elana's not really the friend I would have chosen for Vanessa but they won't be separated.' She shrugged. 'So what can I do?'

Margaret patted her friend's arm. 'Well, don't fret. And Dr Jack is a pet. Could be worse.'

'They'll be here soon, you can be sure of that,' Rosalind said absently.

'Still, you must be delighted about Oriana and Pierce,' Margaret remarked.

Margaret was right. Rosalind was delighted about the engagement. She was very pleased with herself at this moment. She was happy because Oriana was doing what her Pappy wanted and that was a relief to Rosalind. Brendan was impossible when crossed. And Pierce Powers was a good match. He had money. Perhaps he was not dashing or romantic, Rosalind had to concede that, but that was not the important thing. He had to keep Oriana in style and comfort.

Vanessa was another matter. Oriana could be relied upon to do what her father expected of her. She was a sweet-natured girl, obedient and biddable. But Vanessa tended to be stroppy. Rosalind did not like the slang word, but it suited her youngest daughter exactly. Wayward and stubborn. Like her father. Rosalind was taken aback by that thought. It had not occurred to her before. She put her hand to her mouth and Margaret D'Alton asked her if she had swallowed something. Rosalind reassured her. 'No, no my dear. It was just a thought.'

'Oh good. I was afraid it might be an olive.'

Rosalind looked at her blankly. 'An olive?'

'Yes. These modern drinks. I never expect there to be anything *in* them and I'm often taken unawares by an olive or a cherry or some other hard little thing which nearly chokes me.'

'No, Margaret, nothing like that.'

'Ice! Ice often takes me by surprise.' She frowned and fingered her pearls. 'I'm not sure I approve of ice,' she continued. 'Jonathan says it shocks the stomach. The sudden cold, y'know. Upsets the digestion.'

She looked like a turtle with her prematurely wrinkled neck and swivelling eyes. But she was good-natured and gracious, a loyal friend who shared all Rosalind's beliefs and convictions, plus her great respect for money.

Just now her darting eyes had discovered the arrival of Vanessa and Elana into the hall that led into the drawing-room. The double doors at the entrance to her drawing-room were open wide and there, in a stunning sapphire New Look suit, was Vanessa Ardmore on the arm of a complete stranger. A very good-looking stranger with cropped hair and clothes that Margaret D'Alton could see were not at all the thing. Badly tailored in inferior lightweight material. He was, nevertheless, quite the film star with his good looks and debonair manner.

She turned to Rosalind and saw her friend was also staring, mouth open, at her daughter and her friend, who was also with a peculiarly clad young man. You might have expected it of Elana Cassidy but not of Vanessa Ardmore.

The ladies glanced at each other.

'Know who on earth it is?' Margaret whispered.

Rosalind shook her head. 'Let's hope he's one of Elana's lot. The Cassidys are dear people, as you say. But Elana *works!*'

Margaret nodded and sighed. 'I know. Poor girl!'

'And she mixes with all sorts of people. God knows where half of them come from.' Rosalind shuddered. 'All sorts of odd-bods, not *at all* the thing. Not the type of person I want Vanessa to associate with.'

'Mmm. I do know what you mean,' Margaret sympathised, glancing at her friend. She silently thanked the good Lord that she did not have any children who could cause her trouble. She and Jonathan led serene untroubled lives uninterrupted by dramas or friction. In her experience most of her friends' children, no matter how carefully brought up, did precisely that – caused trouble and worry, anxiety and stress – and she was glad that she and Jonathan were not so burdened. She had to admit that she didn't *like* her friends' children – did not, as they seemed to expect, envy them at all.

Except Oriana. If she'd had a daughter, Margaret mused, looking across the room to where that young lady hung on her fiancé's arm deep in conversation with Jonathan, she would have liked her to be a carbon copy of Oriana Ardmore. Margaret smiled. She knew her husband was asking them about a wedding present.

'The wedding's next month?' Margaret glanced at Rosalind who confirmed that, indeed, yes, the wedding was at the end of June.

'Brendan doesn't think it wise to let things drag on. He likes to act decisively.'

'Sure, why would they want to hang about?' Margaret asked. 'Once they've decided?'

Vanessa, holding the stranger's arm, had reached the two ladies. 'Mother, Mrs D'Alton, I'd like you to meet Glenn Carey. Glenn, this is my mother and this is Mrs D'Alton.'

Glenn smiled his charming American smile which had absolutely no effect whatsoever on the matrons, who examined him piecemeal.

'And, em, where did you meet Mr ... er ... Mr Carey? Vanessa?'

'Sergeant Carey, Mother. Elana introduced us.'

It was a lie, Rosalind could see that at once. She knew Vanessa well enough and the rosy tide that swept her face and left it as suddenly was proof that she was not speaking the truth. And something else struck Rosalind dumb. Horrified her. Sergeant! Had her ears deceived her? Had her daughter introduced her to a *sergeant?* Whichever way she might have jumped had that prefix not been uttered,

70

once it was attached to the young man before her he was irretrievably *persona non grata.*

Her cold eyes travelled to his face. She saw there honest, humorous eyes of bright blue. She took in with dismay the film-star good looks that would have turned any woman's head. She saw strength of character but to Rosalind Ardmore the title 'Sergeant' relegated him to the masses who were not suitable persons for her daughter to know.

Margaret D'Alton had arrived at precisely the same conclusion. 'Best nip it in the bud,' she whispered as Vanessa turned to introduce another undesirable foreigner with a wide grin and a crew-cut hairstyle. Like a convict, she thought with distaste.

And the lovely American sensed immediately their dismissal of himself and his friend – their rejection and their contempt. He said nothing and did not show by even a flicker of his long lashes that he was aware of it.

He glanced at the radiant creature, so newly met, so lovely, holding on to his arm as if he would protect her from all harm. Her trusting eyes smiled up into his and he suddenly knew he'd die to save her from one second's hurt or pain or sorrow. He touched her little hand where it lay on his coat-sleeve and her smile broadened and a blush rose into her cheeks.

Rosalind excused herself and crossed the room, gliding determinedly past friends and acquaintances, skilfully avoiding their efforts to detain and congratulate her.

'Oh, Mother, Mr D'Alton has said he's going to give us a canteen of silver cutlery for our wedding.' Oriana was dimpling at Jonathan D'Alton who smiled modestly.

'Jonathan, you are, as always, more than generous. Now darling, what are you and Pierce planning this evening?'

'Well, we thought we'd go to the Golf Club hop. We thought—'

'Darling, no. I think not tonight.' Rosalind was very firm. 'Let's you and I and Pappy and Vanessa and the D'Altons dine in the Russell. Have a little private celebration. After all, Margaret and Jonathan are your Godparents.'

The Russell restaurant, one of the best in town, was roomy and exclusive. No sergeant could afford it. At all costs, Rosalind decided, she did not want this inappropriate acquaintance to continue. Prompt action had to be taken immediately. They'd whisk Vanessa away from this *sergeant* and after dinner her Pappy would have to have a word with his youngest. Forbid her to see this man again and if necessary Brendan could go to whoever was in charge of this *sergeant*, his commanding officer or his lieutenant – Rosalind did not know much about the military, did not *want* to know anyone below the rank of major, or general even – and ask him to warn off this Glenn Carey.

And, mind made up, sure her swift action would produce the desired results, Rosalind went to find her husband and put her plan into action.

Chapter Eleven

ఴ ఴ

The river ran past the front of Avalan Rackton's home. Rackton Hall was as big as Dundalgan but not nearly as well kept. It was, if truth were told, falling into rack and ruin. The weathered granite walls were cemented with moss and lichen and great gaps between the stones were covered by drapes of ivy which concealed their crumbling deterioration.

Avalan inhabited her husband's home reluctantly. She'd much rather have a small place in France or Italy, dirt cheap now to purchase because of the war. She dreamed of warm lands, sun-kissed fields and vineyards, of terracotta-coloured houses – small, flagstoned, easy to manage.

Avalan was a sensuous creature and loved the sun. She would thrive in a pink-walled château or a small burnt-umber villa. She could see herself under a wide-brimmed straw hat draped half-in half-out of a hammock under the cypresses, sipping pale yellow wine and reading Baudelaire and Pascal.

But her husband Simon loved his Irish home and he had so little else that gave him pleasure she was reluctant to suggest moving. He'd probably do it to please her for he loved her so, but he'd be miserable and she loved him and could not bear to make him more unhappy. So they were burdened by the decaying old house, ruinous taxes and Simon's only income, a measly pension from the RAF. There was nothing she could do and so, as was her wont, she accepted fate's decree with good grace.

She leaned out of the window. The setting sun sparkled on the shimmering surface of the water. A little boat bobbed beside the dock and some seagulls screeched.

She could see Simon and McWitty, the nurse who looked

after him, near the river bend, staring out at where the herons stalked, dipping their undulating necks, immersing their heads in the river, fishing for their evening meal.

Avalan thought of what she would give her niece Oriana, what they could *afford* to give her as a wedding present. Then she thought of the wedding, the tribal ceremony. Brendan Ardmore would go over the top with it. It would take all his wife's restraint to stop him going too far. He'd chosen Pierce for Oriana and everything was going his way so he'd be determined to show off. Silly man. He'd want Sean Powers to be amazed. She giggled to herself.

Avalan pitied her sister, well aware that Rosalind pitied her. Simon would not want to go, so she'd have a hard time one way or another. Simon hated her brother-in-law though he was far too polite to show his feelings. If she persuaded him to go he'd be scratchy and irritable, and if he cried off she'd be on her own and they'd all have a go at her, asking her how he was, resenting his absence and causing her pain. People never seemed to be aware that questions about a loved one could be monstrously painful to answer.

Weddings were grossly overdone affairs, she decided, and few of the family ever thought to anticipate the inevitable let-down, the hangover, the morning-after, the disappointment, the 'is that all?', not to mention the debt, the huge bill everyone involved had to foot. Not that her brother-in-law would miss a few thousand. She envied her sister that. Financial security was such a boon, gave one such freedom, but if Brendan Ardmore was the price Rosalind had to pay for the peace of mind not having to worry about money gave one, then it was not a price she could imagine herself paying. Marriage was difficult enough, but without deep passionate love it was, in her opinion, impossible.

She sighed and inevitably her thoughts went to Simon. She had not taken her gaze from his figure in the distance in his wheel-chair. Simon, golden and young when she married him. Firm of limb, graceful as sin, Simon joining the RAF. Dashing in his uniform, a devil-may-care officer, losing his legs over France when his Spitfire exploded under a barrage of Luftwaffe bullets and he bailed out leaving his legs and their sex-life behind him.

She knew that she was supposed to be grateful that at least

74

he was not dead. She was supposed to be brave, stiff upper lip and all that crap. She ought to rejoice that he'd fallen into the hands of the Resistance, not the occupying Nazis, and that they had sent him home to her alive at least and crap, crap, crap.

She murmured that word now as she leaned on the window-frame.

'Crap! Crap. Crap.' Then she said loudly, 'Shit! Shit. Shit.' Banging her fist on the window-sill. Forbidden words. Words that would empty a room if she, or indeed Simon, uttered them aloud in company. It was simply not done.

The Gate Theatre had had a problem with Eliza Doolittle saying a similar word in Shaw's *Pygmalion*. No woman was supposed to even *know* a word like that, let alone say it.

'Shit. Shit. Shit!' she cried loudly, enjoying herself. McWitty must have heard her voice on the breeze and thought she called Simon. He looked back and waved. She lifted her hand in a return salute, giggling to herself. Poor McWitty, he'd be so shocked if he heard her. Then she cupped her chin in her palms and went back to her thoughts.

Simon Rackton had been a great lover. That was the irony of it. In the divine scheme of things why couldn't it have been her sister's husband who lost the use of his body from the waist down and had to have a nurse to clean him up? She was quite certain that Brendan Ardmore was whale-like in bed and she was also certain that her sister would be relieved if her husband had to give up what she called 'that sort of thing'.

She had asked her sister once about such matters. Rosalind's mouth had tightened, her face had turned scarlet and she had crossed herself piously. 'He performs his duty if that's what you mean, Avalan, in the procreation of children, as the Church instructs.'

Well, that spoke volumes and Avalan thought how sad it was that poor old Rosalind had never been carried away on a tide of passion when body, mind and soul melted in an unstoppable flow of love and fulfilment.

And for her it had stopped, until recently, since the Battle of Britain.

She smiled regretfully as she thought of that drum-beating period. Men marching to war to the stirring rhythm of

Glenn Miller, Benny Goodman and the Massed Bands of the American Forces. They had not informed, those posters, that propaganda, of the broken bodies and minds that would return home, nor the terrible silence of those foolhardy and brave souls who did not.

How beautiful Simon had been then in his uniform, standing straight and tall, joking nonchalantly, making light of the danger when she would have sold her soul to have him chicken out. She would have sailed a boat to Goa, to Borneo, to Alaska to have kept him with her, safe and whole. But he had gone with the trumpets and the flags and come home without his legs. And a wedge had been driven between them. Useless to try to keep things as they were. The heady romance, his great and powerful performances of the act of love-making were over and although she was his friend, his love, his dearest, he could never now become part of her, in her, united in that most abandoned union.

She had her compensations. She thought now of the firm young body that romped with her in the room in Molesworth Street every Tuesday and Friday. She wondered if Simon knew about that room and the boy in it, and guessed that he probably did. Simon was a realist. He'd said to her, when he'd returned home broken and maimed in body and spirit, 'I'm no use to you now, Avalan, in that way. But we've got to be practical about this, my darling, my dear. You must find yourself someone to satisfy your needs. No. Don't say a word. I mean it.' He had leaned forward, touching her cheek tenderly, sadly remembering their wondrous coupling. 'But don't get pregnant, my darling. I couldn't bear that.' She had soothed him. She had tried to stimulate some kind of compromise but it proved impossible, and it humiliated her crippled husband. And then she decided to reject that side of her life altogether. She lived celibately for a long time. But she was no nun and she found it very difficult.

A passionate woman, she yearned for the ardour of those years with Simon before the war. She'd had a chance encounter with an Italian which, although physically very satisfying, lacked the wonderful intensity and the sheer satisfaction love had injected into her mating with her husband. Without love the union was curiously arid and mechanical. But it was a release.

And there was the danger. This she feared above all things. So she went to London and got fitted with a coil. She hated it, but it was the only thing to do.

Simon was being pushed across the lawn by McWitty. His face was turned to the house, searching for her. He was so dear to her, so precious, his face so young, so vulnerable. Time and the pain he so frequently suffered had not marked his dear face. He looked like an eighteen-year-old boy from here. It was only close to that you could see the grey in his soft brown hair, the crow's feet at his temples, the lines on his forehead and above all the pain in his eyes.

She leaned out of her window and called to him. 'Darling! Was the walk pleasant?'

He waved to her, obviously pleased to see her. 'Yes. Great. The deer were down by the lake and we saw some pheasant in the woods.'

'We'll eat early tonight,' she called back. He nodded and she saw the sudden spasm cross his face. She'd made the remark accidently. It was what he used to say to her before the crash, when he found it hard to keep his hands off her and dinner seemed too long.

We'll eat early tonight now meant consideration for McWitty so he could clean up his patient and settle him comfortably in bed for the night and maybe make a movie by nine-thirty in the little cinema in the village.

As she watched she saw his hand drop forlornly. It was a gesture of infinite sadness and resignation and she felt herself overwhelmed by a feeling of such vast hopelessness and despair that she wanted to shout those obscenities, those four-letter words out aloud to the uncaring wind. But she didn't and with a sigh she turned away into her room and began to dress for dinner.

Chapter Twelve

⚜ ⚜

'You must not see that young man again,' Brendan said to Vanessa with great firmness. He did not shout. He did not have to.

Brendan Ardmore was not a man at ease with himself. There was a constant core of anger at his centre gnawing away at him. His parents had neglected him woefully when he was a boy. He had been an unexpected product of their later years, and as they could not think what to do with him or how to behave with him, they employed a wet-nurse and then a strict nanny who, they hoped, did. They sent him off to school with the Benedictines who, as his father was wont to put it, 'licked him into shape'.

It was Rosalind Ergan's family who picked him out for their daughter. He seemed the perfect choice and Rosalind, if she had any reservations, kept them to herself. She had been as strictly brought up in her way as he had in his, and she was used to the discipline of doing as her parents advised.

She made an excellent wife, managed the household, which ran smoothly and efficiently, helped him retain his place in society and gave him healthy children. She also enjoyed the comfort and luxury of their lives together and, if romance was missing, she had been told that romance did not last. Her sister Avalan seemed to disprove this statement but, as Rosalind told her friend Margaret D'Alton in confidence, who knew what went on behind closed doors? The two matrons nodded their heads sagely at this ambiguous conclusion.

Sitric was a great disappointment to Brendan but he never reproached Rosalind for the way she had brought him up, though he felt entitled to do so. He adored Oriana, his pet, but found Vanessa an uneasy companion. When they

78

were together they were always teetering on the verge of a quarrel.

Ardmore & Son were quality Wine Merchants, and the business had always passed father to son. In Brendan's case the management was entrusted to Patrick McCawley Jnr. Brendan's father had handed the running of the business to Patrick McCawley Snr. He had done this clearly in his will because he had neglected to educate his son into the mysteries of the family business. It was a fearful oversight, based on a totally erroneous concept that his son might try to take over the firm prematurely if he became *au fait* with its inner workings. Brendan would never have had the confidence to do such a thing. But his father could not risk such a calamity and so when he died Brendan Ardmore had absolutely no idea how to run Ardmore & Son and Patrick McCawley Snr did it for him. The problem was that Brendan never told Patrick (who guessed anyway) that he was deficient in any knowledge whatsoever and so, when his son took over from Patrick McCawley, Brendan was left with the monumental secret knowledge that everyone knew more than he did, and his major preoccupation was not to let, first McCawley Snr, and after him McCawley Jnr know the extent of his ignorance.

Brendan went into the premises in Dawson Street three times a week, sat in his office and tasted the wines, although he never went near the warehouses on Burgh Quay. He pronounced disapproval or approval as indicated by Patrick Snr, then Jnr, to the wines themselves, to bills of lading, to import/export invoices that he did not understand but gave a good imitation of grasping. He signed many cheques after due scrutiny and generally oversaw, without having the remotest idea about any of it, the financial state of the company. It made him very uneasy. Subconsciously he was always ill-at-ease. He knew, but would not admit even to himself, that he was terribly ignorant. He was afraid, a fear generated by the ambiguous position he was in. He truly believed that Patrick McCawley did not realise what that position was. Patrick McCawley, if he but knew it, had an appalling advantage over him and Brendan resented that.

Perhaps this made Brendan more autocratic at home. He certainly did not lack authority *there*. His will was law.

Now he faced his daughter, issuing an ultimatum he expected to be obeyed. He looked down at her set little face. There was a steely look in her eyes although her tone was conciliatory.

'Do you hear me, Vanessa?'

'Yes, Pappy.'

'And you mind what I say?'

'Yes, Pappy.'

'Good. Then that's the end of it. That young man is not the sort of young man your mother and I approve of.'

Vanessa wanted to argue. She wanted to scream and shout and stamp her feet, but that kind of behaviour had never got her anywhere and this was important. This was her life.

'I mean *Sergeant*! A chappie in the ranks. Oh dear me no! Once a sergeant always a sergeant! And an American! Uneducated lot, most of them. Descended from the rag-tag and bobtail, the dregs of Europe. Criminals or wash-outs most of them. Sent out of the way to the New World. You've only got to see a film to see that. They can't speak English!'

'No, Pappy.'

'Had to get English actor chappies over to make sense of the speeches. Ronald Coleman and Leslie Howard. C. Aubrey Smith. Fella, what's his name, Errol Flynn. Chaps like that. The rest, no one knows what they're talking about. Don't have to, they give 'em so little to say. Swear to God, who understands John Wayne or Jimmy Stewart? Gary Cooper? All they do is mutter and say "Gee" and "Yep" and "Nope". Couldn't be trusted to say a lot more. No, this fella is unsuitable and you're not to encourage him. You're not even to *see* him again. Not ever.'

'Suppose, Pappy, we're in the same place?' she asked. 'At a tea-dance or a party.'

'I don't think they get asked to the same places as you, my girl. And *if* they are, look the other way, dammit. Give a civilised nod and leave. *Because I said so.*'

He leaned over, his face close to hers. 'If I hear you've been seen as much as talking to him, my girl, you'll feel the weight of *that* on your backside. I promise you.' He pointed to the wall where the slender birch switch was hanging, its delicate appearance belying the pain it was capable of inflicting.

She had felt it. They all had felt it. She shivered in spite of herself. She dreaded the mention of it. She had once been terrified of it with a constant inner fear that never left her. She dreamed of it then and wet her bed and shook with dread every time she thought she might have done wrong. Now she did not feel the terror of the pain he could inflict on her, only the humiliation. It was the indignity that outraged her. Her modesty was insulted, her dignity stripped from her, and it seemed to her a thoroughly demeaning experience for both of them.

But that was what a father did and she accepted his authority and his power over her to do that to her. After all, she had a choice. If she did what he told her, and it said in the Bible that she must obey him, then nothing would happen to her. If she disobeyed him, then what could she expect? It was the way of the world.

She caught his glance now in the dark study where the beatings always took place and he began to stumble over his words at the expression he saw in her eyes. Not the usual fear he expected to engender, not the cowering anxiety he was accustomed to arousing in his children at the threat of the birch. No. There was a cold blankness, a defiance mirrored in the blue eyes of his youngest. A fierce determination that reminded him of someone, he couldn't think who.

He remembered, recently, a scene here, in this study, when his son, Sitric, threatened with the switch, had towered over him and dared his father to touch him. 'Lay a hand on me, Pappy, and I swear I'll kill you.' Sitric had grown up. He could not chastise Sitric any longer. He had let the birch fall from his hand and Sitric left the room.

And now Vanessa dared to look at him in that way. Oh, it was not to be tolerated.

'You hear me, Vanessa? I won't tolerate disobedience or lies. You know that. It is my duty. So forget about this . . . this *sergeant.*' He spoke with withering contempt. 'Put him out of your life or you'll feel the weight of my anger, and *that.*' He pointed to the cane, hanging so innocently on the wall.

She said nothing. Nodded, lowering her head so that her hair fell over her face and he could not see her fierce blue

81

gaze. Brendan cast about in his mind for something else to add, but could think of nothing.

'You may go,' he said.

Vanessa rose and left the room, the light of battle sparkling in her sapphire eyes.

Chapter Thirteen

She left the study and went to her room. Her eyes were steely but her knees wobbled under her.

She remembered the crying. Hugging herself as the misery overwhelmed her, then the physical collapse as the grief took complete hold and she couldn't keep her arms up and they hung helpless by her side while her chest near burst as the spasms shook her and her breath was gone, she couldn't catch it, couldn't make it work for her and she was choking to death. And Oriana was saying to her, why don't you do as he says? Why do you fight him? Bring it on yourself? And she didn't know.

Aunt Avalan lived with them then. She was beautiful, six years younger than Rosalind. She had often held her after her father had beaten her. She'd come to Vanessa's room and comfort her.

'Now go to your room, Vanessa, and let's hope this will not happen again.' Her father always used the same words as he hung up the birch and she left, a quivering mass of hate and terror and scalding flesh.

But it always happened again.

The things she did, her disobedience always seemed to her minor, undeserving of such harsh punishment. When she was twelve years old she had gone to Phoenix Park with Elana Cassidy who couldn't believe that the Park was forbidden her. Mr and Mrs Ardmore had instructed their daughters never to enter the park. Parks were for the *hoi polloi*, the common herd. If they wanted to wander down leafy lanes, why, there was the wood at Dundalgan. There was the river there, there was everything anyone could want. Parks were for people who had nowhere else to go, nowhere to play.

So the Park held the attraction of the forbidden for Vanessa and as Elana often went there it was inevitable that her best friend would one day accompany her. And so it happened. She had gone to Phoenix Park and they had wandered about under dark green trees in the flickering shadows, Vanessa expecting that at any moment the Wicked Witch of the East or the Big Bad Wolf would jump out at her, wondering why the forbidden territory was so tame when nothing at all happened. The girls danced in the speckled sunshine and ran down the grassy inclines, hair flying, cheeks rosy from the exertion, legs running away with them, making them feel they might, at any moment, take off and fly, laughing breathlessly all the time.

And Vanessa lost her school hat.

Her father met his dishevelled daughter on the way home *sans* hat and she told him, stupidly, panicking, frightened of the consequences if he discovered where she had been, that she had it at home and had forgotten it that morning. He had frogmarched her back to the house and demanded she produce the article, which of course she couldn't. Hence the caning. Not because she lost the hat, he told her, but because she had lied. There had been other incidents, many of them similar, and Vanessa resented them bitterly. She swallowed her outrage and got on with her life, accepting her father's discipline as the price to be paid for lies and disobedience.

The last birching she had been subjected to was only a few months ago. She had been told she could not attend formal balls and parties until after her eighteenth birthday when she officially came out. She had done that in March, but back at Christmas she had broken her father's command.

It was Elana who persuaded her to go with her to a Trinity Rag Ball. It was fancy dress and not having anything to wear she went as a bubble-bath. Both she and Elana thought it was a brilliant way out. She would not have to get a costume and bubble-baths were a new commodity on the market after the war. She wore a bathing suit and sat in an old iron tub borne by a gang of four students led by Elana's brother Dominic. They had shaken Persil into the water, the real thing being too expensive to purchase, and every now and then Dominic fanned his hand to and fro in the water to keep it frothing. She had been carried triumphantly twice around the ballroom, accompanied by wolf-whistles and cat-calls and applause, and had won first prize for originality.

Unfortunately she had made the front page of the *Evening Herald* and her father had gone berserk. The beating followed and she'd had to spend three days in bed and her period came early. After that it had not been too bad. Until now. Until Glenn.

And her father had won. She had never gone to the Park again. She'd never even thought of going to another ball against his wishes. Her coming-out party had been wonderful, and she had been Pappy's good little girl, never going anywhere or doing anything without his permission.

Until now. She clenched her fists into balls and stared at her reflection in the mirror.

Something about Vanessa irritated her father, something communicated through her eyes, something that in her terror, her dread of what would happen to her, she could not conceal. Some demon of survival, of pride, of defiance. She would say 'Yes, Pappy, yes, yes, yes' in an agony of fear and he would see the 'no' in her eyes. 'All right, my girl, if you're going to be like that' and he'd grab her ear and haul her into the study and tell her to pull up her skirt and the nightmare would begin. What had she done? Sometimes she knew and they seemed such trivial acts of disobedience, and sometimes she didn't know, wasn't sure. She understood so little, she just knew it had to be so.

She wet the bed after a beating and Cessy helped her change the sheets, but once her father found out. He met Cessy on the landing and asked her what she was doing with the sheets. This was not Monday. Sheets were changed on Mondays. She had confessed and Pappy had told them all at dinner that evening.

'Do you know what your sister did last night? Peed in her bed like a babby.' He smiled at them all around the table, inviting them to join him in mirth but they didn't. No one laughed. Sitric stared at his father with loathing. Oriana avoided looking at all and hung her head as if she were the culprit. Rosalind looked embarrassed.

Vanessa had cried out against the humiliation. 'Why did you tell them that? Oh Pappy, you're hateful!'

So she was hauled into the study again, shivering, cowardly, screaming 'No, Pappy, no, no, please, no.'

Those long afternoons, confined to her room, sobbing, hysterically crying, the heartbreaking misery she felt were made bearable by Aunt Avalan, while she lived in Dundalgan before she married Simon Rackton and moved to Rackton Hall. By then Vanessa had become hardened to the experience, toughened by it. She would always resent it, be humiliated by it, but the sheer gut-wrenching terror diminished by then and her defiance increased.

Aunt Avalan used to creep up the back stairs, the servants' stairs, and slip into Vanessa's room. Sometimes Oriana was there, sometimes not. She had had her own share of beatings but they were relatively few and far between. It was Sitric and Vanessa who suffered most.

Vanessa never talked to Sitric about how they felt and afterwards Vanessa was sorry. But by then it was too late and life had pulled them apart, and Sitric was carving his own path through the jungles of experience.

It was Avalan who comforted her. Vanessa cuddled up to her like a wounded animal to warmth. Aunt Avalan's arms were always there. Secretly. When Vanessa could not hold herself together, when her whole body rattled like castinets, Aunt Avalan crept up those stairs, putting her finger to her lips when she met Sive or Cessy or Imelda. And she would hold the child together, wrap her arms around the shivering little body and sooth her niece with a jumble of humming and lulling and murmurs and kisses and strokings and tender calming until she slept, worn out, or fell into a sort of daze.

Aunt Avalan took her out walking in the woods or down by the river. She talked about the sacred flame of life and how it must be nurtured in adversity. She talked, in general terms, about how pain can be channelled not into hatred and bitterness, but into energy. A lot of what she said Vanessa did not understand.

She knew the names of the birds and flowers and she touched them all as if she loved them, as if she cared for them every one. Her fingers were long and slim and her nails were short and she'd say, 'Ah! Look, 'Nessa, a red-start's nest' or 'See the lily-of-the-valley? Smell it, 'Nessa.

It smells of Spring.' And she would tell Vanessa tales of the flowers from the Greek legends and Gaelic folklore. About the old days when Ireland was called the Island of Saints and Scholars, and the monks in the tall abbeys sat and inscribed the *Yellow Book of Lecan* and the *Book of Kells* in marvellous jewel colours and a scroll that would turn letters into snakes or birds or gargoyles. And then Cromwell came and burned it all down and only a few of the great books were saved.

'And why did he do that, Auntie Avalan?' Vanessa would ask.

'Oh, there are some people who are destroyers,' Auntie Avalan would reply, her eyes holding a dreamy far-away look in them. 'There are people and everything they touch turns to poison. And there are people and everything they touch turns to joy.' Vanessa thought of her father but said nothing. She did not want to believe that her father was a destroyer. He hadn't destroyed Dundalgan, or her mother, or Oriana. It was only her and Sitric, and everyone knew that Sitric was difficult. Maybe it was all her fault.

'You know, Vanessa, there's a poem by Blake I love. It goes,

> "Every night and every morn,
> Some to misery are born.
> Every morn and every night,
> Some are born to sweet delight.
> Some are born to sweet delight,
> Some are born to endless night."'

Aunt Avalan looked at the swans on the river and trailed her fingers in the water. 'It seems unfair, doesn't it? But you know, 'Nessa, I believe that you can *help* yourself. By your attitude. How you *see* things. We are a marvellous race, human beings, and there's only one Mr Hitler to a million kind, loving people. So you can always escape to joy. It does not need money. All it needs is an attitude. All this' – she indicated Dundalgan, the house behind them – 'all it needs is love.' She smiled at the girl. 'See, 'Nessa, it's not being born to sweet delight or misery that counts, it's whether you waste time on self-pity, moaning about your lot, blaming others when things go wrong. That's what counts. I'd write

87

a poem, if I could, saying "Every night and every morn some bring misery to others. Every morn and every night some bring sweet delight to others." That's the important thing.'

At the time Vanessa did not understand all of what her aunt told her. She only knew her aunt brought sweet delight to her and that she loved her aunt more than her mother. Her mother spent all her time telling them how wonderful their father was. She always leaned his way as if he were her strength, her support. Aunt Avalan stood alone and proud and it seemed to Vanessa that nobody could touch her.

Then Aunt Avalan went away. She met a man called Simon Rackton and she married him. She was not reachable from that time on. Like Rosalind she leaned on Simon, but even more ardently than her sister. Simon was so handsome, so kind and they looked perfect together, but Vanessa felt lonely and resented seeing her aunt so absorbed in the man. She walked everywhere with him hand-in-hand. They touched each other constantly. They kissed and for once Vanessa agreed with her father when he told them, albeit jovially, 'Cut it out, you two. This is not the boudoir.'

Vanessa nodded vehemently when her father said this, although she did not understand its implication. She just knew she was embarrassed by their display of affection.

Avalan saw the child's discomfort and she held out her hand in her good-natured way and beckoned her niece to the swinging double chair where she sat beside Simon, gently swaying to and fro. 'And you'll be my bridesmaid, 'Nessa, won't you?' she asked, smiling. Vanessa nodded but her heart was heavy as lead.

She was bridesmaid and Avalan left Dundalgan forever and Vanessa lost her comfort. She missed her aunt dreadfully, but Avalan seemed totally preoccupied with her new husband and when they met the old strong tie was broken. They never reached the same closeness again.

Vanessa took her beatings and stopped crying and wetting the bed.

She looked at herself now in the mirror and she knew that something in her was different. It was as if the advent of Glenn in her life had changed everything. Made her somehow sacred. She remembered now her aunt's words, about being born to sweet delight. Glenn was sweet delight. Glenn made people happy. Glenn was worth a beating. Whatever she had to suffer she would. But her father would not win. Not this time.

Chapter Fourteen

   ❧❦

Afterwards Vanessa wondered if she would have clung so determinedly to Glenn Carey if her father and mother had not been so adamantly against him.

Brendan's threat to beat her, and she a grown woman, awakened in her a sense of defiance. How dare he treat her like that? It made her determined to do the very thing he least wanted her to do. He would not succeed in stopping her seeing Glenn.

But she could not have stopped even if she tried. She was addicted. Glenn was like the fruit of the poppy, once tasted an impossible habit to kick.

At first Glenn was bemused by her parents' refusal to accept him. He did not understand it. However, he had some notion of religious intolerance and decided that was the reason for their non-acceptance. He felt sorry for them in a detached way, and it never occurred to him to stop seeing Vanessa because of them.

'Why should we hide, honey? You're eighteen, after all. A woman.'

'My Pappy'll kill me if he finds out, Glenn. Please let us be careful for my sake.'

'Okay, honey, if that's what you want. But it makes no sense.'

She did not tell him about the beatings. She thought it might put him off her. She thought he might despise her because such a humiliating thing happened to her.

At first they were very careful. They met in places where they would not be likely to see any of the Ardmores' friends. This gave the added savour of forbidden love to their meetings and the element of danger only increased the intensity of their feelings.

90

Vanessa had allowed herself and continued to allow herself to fall deeper and deeper in love with the lovely American. Initially she was drawn to his glamorous good looks, then she was beguiled by his charm and excessive politeness, his foreignness. He enchanted her with his tales of travel, she who had never left the shores of Ireland, and eventually she was propelled into his arms by her father's dictates.

For Glenn Carey it was a totally different scenario. He was on tour duty at the American Embassy, warned by his superiors that while in a foreign place he represented his country and his flag. He must, they instructed him, do so with honour and respect for the people therein. It was essential he behave with propriety.

Vanessa Ardmore was not a girl he could treat casually. Her family were respected in Dublin, her father a powerful and formidable man.

And an unpleasant one. As time passed the old man's hostility began to irritate Glenn and he saw his and Rosalind's attitude as appallingly snobbish. Glenn had not expected such sustained antipathy. He was not used to it. He had been sure that he could charm his way into their hearts, but he was not given the chance. He struggled with resentment at the man's attitude and with his own desire to show the old bastard that his influence over his daughter could easily be rendered null and void. How dare he insult America and Americans and who did he think he was to wield such power over his eighteen-year-old daughter? It was partly, too, a macho desire to lock horns, a wish to win that added extra ardour to his courtship of Vanessa. Beat the old guy. Show him who was strongest.

Glenn had a girl back home in Wisconsin. She was cute, down-home, utterly perfect for him. Everything was wonderful when he was alone with her, but when he was with his pals and their girls in twosomes he hardly noticed her presence and she complained of his lack of attention. Angie hung on his arm and his every word, always agreeing with him, which sometimes irritated him and he didn't know why. She doted on him, would love him forever, but, more importantly to someone of his background and upbringing, had everything in common with him and would truly honour

91

and obey him. Like it said in the marriage service. She was nothing like Vanessa.

Vanessa, this girl was from another world. She had a cultivated background, a sophisticated life-style. She was wonderfully innocent, and she beguiled him and trapped him in a mesh of glamour.

He had not meant to get caught. He'd spent his life on a farm. He loved rural living, the seasons counted by Nature's changes, and that was one of the reasons he loved Dublin. Dublin contained the best of both worlds. Such a small capital city, yet it was full of elegant restaurants, theatres, race courses, and the parties were as glittering as anywhere in the world. It had all the amenities one expected to find only in cities like London or New York. Yet it was ringed by those magic mountains and the sea lapped its feet. There were farms ten minutes from the town centre, Nelson's Pillar. Cowslips grew at the sidewalks and the main roads petered out into boreens and lush country lanes.

It was a more equitable climate than Wisconsin. The mists and the rain kept the earth lushly productive and the Gulf Stream protected the little country like a warm cloak against extreme cold or heat. It was a seductive place. A romantic place.

Glenn Carey fell in love with the country, was dazzled by the Irish girl and tempted into a romantic entanglement far deeper than he wanted or intended, far quicker than he could have believed possible.

They had dinner in little tucked-away places. Had drinks in the lounges of small hotels. Drove into the country and spent endless evenings dining in elegant crumbling country-house hotels or sipping drinks in rural pubs.

Summer was coming and the countryside was beautiful. Glenn's hours were flexible and when he was on duty in the evening they spent the days in the purple Wicklow mountains, or by a shimmering lake, or on the hill of Howth, watching the turbulent waves ride high and crash on the coal-dark rocks. They would have tea in a cottage – home-made brown bread and jam, scones and cream, whiskey-fruit-cake, black and full of cherries, sultanas, raisins, moist and crumbling. Then Vanessa returned home and joined her family in the activity of the moment, which consisted mostly of parties for the engaged couple.

They held hands. There was about her an expectation of respect that forbade him to take what he would call liberties with her. He had rolled in the hay at harvest time with Angie, put his hand up her skirt, sucked her breast and done almost everything except have intercourse with her. That was out. It was too risky. And her Mom and Pa were friends of theirs.

It was out with Vanessa too, but so was the taking of one's pleasure in more peripheral ways. She kept him strictly in line.

In Japan, during the war, he'd had professional sex from what the guys called good-time girls but he knew to be prostitutes. It was, for him, a lonely experience. He had had erotic orgies, journeys into the realm of the senses that gave him a hard-on just to think about, but eventually that was not what he wanted. He was obscurely ashamed of these encounters. His Episcopalian upbringing, his strict parents – stricter by far in matters of puritanical morality than the Ardmores – made him uncomfortable in matters of sensual exploration. So Vanessa's modesty, her implacable assumption that nice girls waited for their wedding night, restricted their love-making to tender swooning kisses under the moon, warm embraces that stirred their blood and promised wonderful excitements but delivered no fulfilment. This did not disconcert him, but instead kept them both in a constant feverish state, desperate for each other, wide-eyed with unfulfilled passion, not able to see what was real, what they had in common, how their lives could mesh, or even if they liked each other.

They were in love. They were in a state of lunacy. It was forbidden and so it was essential.

Chapter Fifteen

ভ ঙ

'Your parents don't like me but they never really met me. How come?' Glenn didn't sound resentful, merely curious. He was stating an unpalatable fact that mystified him.

They were sitting in the Shelbourne bar on plush seats tucked away in an alcove. They were getting careless, meeting more often nearer home, lulled into a false sense of security.

It was a dimly lit place with a stilly sense of no-man's-land, discreet and secretive. People met there for assignations – married people having affairs, businessmen slinking over to the opposition. Secrets were whispered and confidences exchanged. Love was ardently pledged over cocktails for two. This was a place where weary people took time off from life to breathe a little and opt out for a short while.

Glenn nursed his Canadian Club and Vanessa sipped her gin-and-it. Conversation was whispered. They were enveloped in peace.

'Well, darling, so what? Pappy's difficult. No one knows why he does things. He just does.'

'I had a talk with Gavin Fitzjames the other day,' Glenn said.

'Oh?'

'Yeah. He said Oriana was in love with him. He told me your Pappy scuppered their romance. Stopped it dead because Gavin was poor. He reckoned your pa is more or less forcing her to marry Pierce Powers because of money.'

'Have you been talking about me and my family behind my back?' Vanessa pulled her hand away from his. He could see the anger bubbling up inside her and he hastened to reassure her.

'No, honey, no. We weren't talking. At least *I* wasn't.

94

Gavin was. I met him at an Embassy party. He asked me, was I seeing you and, like you told me, I said no. He said, "I guess her Pappy broke it up. You'd not be considered suitable any more than me." I said nothing. Then he told me about him and Oriana. He talked about it for ages. I didn't utter. He sounded sore.'

Vanessa sighed. 'Pappy's . . . difficult. He's forbidden me to see you but that hasn't stopped us. Oriana could have done the same. I'm too grown up now to do everything he says.'

There was silence for a moment then Glenn looked at her. 'Listen, honey, maybe we better cool it. They'll not be too pleased at the Embassy if they find out I'm taking you out against your father's instructions. And I don't want to mess up your family. Gee, we've only known each other a few weeks and—'

'Are you suggesting . . . I mean, are you trying to tell me, you're not interested in me, in seeing me . . .' She was stammering nervously, her face desolate. Brought up to tell the truth, she could not dissimulate. Guile was quite foreign to her – she was incapable of manipulating him, it was outside her command. And it was this that got to him. He could not bear to see her confusion so he nipped uncertainty in the bud.

'I'm crazy about you, Vanessa, you know that. But family's important. I don't wanna be the cause of trouble between you and your folks.'

'Oh, I don't care about trouble. It's my life, after all.'

Her mother had said, 'I must say I don't trust beautiful men. Being the pretty one in the twosome is the woman's job.' This was when Vanessa had asked her what she had against Glenn. Her mother refused to be drawn into discussions of rank and finances.

'Ah, so you do see how lovely he is?' Vanessa had retorted.

'I'll admit he has a certain filmic glamour. I'll give you that. But, as I say, I don't trust good-looking men. They are pursued and flirted with and that leads to mistrust.'

'But Mother, Aunt Avalan's husband is very good-looking and there is no mistrust there.'

'Simon Rackton is a different matter entirely,' Rosalind said, and refused to continue the conversation.

Glenn put down his drink. Every time he spoke to Vanessa he made further pledges. He was not sure how it happened and he was not sure he wanted this total commitment, this overwhelming love. It was too much too soon, and he sometimes felt burdened by it. Billy Monks told him he was crazy. 'Why not do it like Elana and me? We go out, we have a ball, we take it easy. She's a great chick.'

'I dunno. Vanessa comes on strong. She's so trusting. I don't seem to be in control.'

'Dumb! Dumb! Dumb! She's winding you around her little finger, making you jump through hoops. Take it easy, pal.'

'Look, Billy, I think I'm serious about this one.' He was frowning.

His friend looked at him speculatively. 'Geez, Glenn, you sure?'

Glenn shook his head. 'No, I'm not. That's the problem. When I'm with her I know I can't live without her and when I'm not I'm terrified.'

'What about Angie?'

'I know. I feel guilty as hell. I want that kind of – I dunno – peace? Safety?' He looked at Billy, pulling his tie off. 'Angie is safe. I used to find that boring, sort of. I remember one time, not noticing she'd gone home! She was mad as hell. But I'm not sure now that that isn't better than this . . . sick feeling. Everything is dangerous. Vanessa is strange and exciting . . .'

Billy hooted. 'Vanessa? Dangerous? Christ, she's an innocent. She wouldn't hurt a fly. Dangerous and exciting, you gotta be kidding!'

'No, no, you don't understand. I'm not talking about her. It's what I *feel*, you dope. The whole thing is shattering. She is *too* innocent. When I think of Bangkok . . .'

Billy whooped and slapped his thigh. 'Those were the days, old buddy. Yaahoo!'

The room they shared in the Embassy was quite small. Iron beds made it like camp, and they used the room only to sleep in or change their clothes.

'Now you're talking,' Billy continued. '*That* was dangerous. God, those girls!'

Glenn gave up. How could he explain to Billy what he couldn't work out for himself? How could he explain that this very innocence of Vanessa's was far more powerful than the lures of any *femme fatale?* All he knew was that he couldn't let go of this gorgeous girl with eyes like blue iris, even though he knew there'd be trouble if he went on seeing her.

So at the beginning he hesitated. Not for long though. It seemed he had no will power where she was concerned.

It was Spring, then Summer tiptoed in and decked Dublin in glorious raiment, and the blackbird sang. Trees, mountains, gardens burst into glorious colour and flowers bloomed in profusion. The land looked ravishing in sumptuous clothing.

And she was there, tempting him, looking into his eyes with that brilliant blue stare of total admiration. With such confidence in him. So loving.

So he too fell in too deep to climb back out. He dived into that pool of the senses where nothing extreme was asked of him, no great performance demanded. He could protest his love like a gallant or a knight of old – chivalrously, honourably, with restraint. And it appealed to him, made him walk tall. He was playing Cary Grant to her Jeanne Craine, Tyrone Power to her Olivia de Havilland. He had been cast in the role, he was not sure how or by whom, and he obediently followed the prescribed script.

She was a novelty. At home in Wisconsin Angie was like bread and butter, a stable part of his life, sure to fulfil his needs. Vanessa was cake.

And she asked nothing of him. This too was novel. He was used to girls in Japan, the East, and in Europe on the way home, eager to relieve him of the mighty dollar, or what that dollar could buy. Yankee money equalled Yankee wealth, Yankee goods, Yankee glamour.

'Got any gum, chum?'

'I'd die for nylons.'

'I'll make you holler if you give us a dollar.'

But Vanessa came from a different world where comfort was taken for granted, culture automatic and money had cushioned any hardships life might have inflicted and which might have damaged that incredible innocence. It had protected her against reality, kept her ignorant of the pain, squalor and the evil that lay side by side with the May-blossom, the dinners and dress-fittings, the opera and ballet, the theatre and the million other delights her days and nights were composed of.

Elana Cassidy knew about reality and pain. He was not sure how she knew about the worm that lurked in the apple, the skull beneath soft flesh, but she did know. Perhaps because she was not rich. Perhaps because her father was a doctor. At all events, it made her more mature than her friend and protective of her though they were the same age.

He wondered why he had not fallen for Elana. She was as pretty as her friend and much more suitable for him. She'd adapt to life in the rough. She'd travel well. Would Vanessa? He did not know, could not guess.

He knew however that he couldn't decide who he fell in love with and who he didn't. If only he could organise such feelings how simple life would be.

When necessary, Elana covered for them. As Vanessa had always spent a lot of time with her friend suspicion was not aroused when she said she was spending time with Elana. Life continued peacefully. It pleased Elana that she was putting one over on Brendan Ardmore, albeit secretly. She was aware that he had always disapproved of her even though her father was a pillar of the community, a man loved and respected. It was the money, or rather the lack of it, that Mr Ardmore disliked, the difference in their social positions, and lately Elana's work. Elana was not, after all, a lady of leisure. She had to earn her own living and he himself had helped her to get into the Bank of Ireland.

Elana let all the snobbery, the exclusivity of the wealthy set, wash over her like the tide at Blackrock. It swept away all the dirt, all the rotting seaweed, the dying shellfish, threw them back into the briny ocean where they all belonged, and she too let the petty-mindedness, the ridiculous priorities, the ludicrous assumption that how much you possessed mattered in the liking or disliking of people, be washed away, out to sea.

She was only too delighted to help Vanessa, so she lied, firmly and with authority, about where her friend was, said Vanessa was with her when she was not, did a first-rate job of keeping the Ardmores unsuspicious and trusting.

It had to end sometime. Everyone knew that – Glenn, Vanessa, Elana, Billy – though they did not face up to the inevitability. Dublin was too small and the Ardmores' friends were not fools. Also they tended to the malicious. Wealth creates jealousy and jealousy generates malice. Someone was bound to split on them sooner or later.

When the rumours started they were at first whispered. But that evening in the Shelbourne bar Dom Bradley's father, who was there with his girlfriend, saw the young couple. He mentioned it to Sean Powers, who was only too delighted to pretend outrage and shake his head about it with his wife within his son's earshot. Pierce told Oriana that her sister was seeing an American marine, a sergeant. He'd not believed it at first, he said, but he'd checked up and found that a lot of people had seen the couple here and there, smoochily close, he said.

Oriana went to her mother.

Chapter Sixteen

Preparations for Oriana's wedding were underway and there was great excitement at Dundalgan. 'No expense is to be spared,' Brendan announced grandly, so it was with the complacency of untrammelled spending power that Rosalind Ardmore set about ordering, managing, designing and organising.

They were to have a marquee on the front lawn which sloped towards the cliffs and overlooked Dublin Bay. Behind the house near the river there was to be a raised platform decorated with fairy-lights for the dancing. Flowers and flower arrangers had to be ordered and booked. Menus decided upon. Workmen employed. Extra staff brought in from outside. The servants activated to work twice as hard as usual. The minutest cobweb had to be removed, the smallest speck of dust hunted down and obliterated.

The wedding outfits had to be chosen and ordered. Oriana plumped for a Norman Hartnell gown to be ordered through Brown Thomas. Measurements were taken and sent to London. Colours for the bridesmaids were decided upon and through all the hustle and bustle Vanessa moved as if in a dream, smiling automatically, lifting her arms for fittings, nodding her head at this swatch of fabrics or that, agreeing to five different colours, one after another, and exasperating her mother and sister with her absent-mindedness. 'You'd think she was the bride,' her mother remarked, surprised at her docility.

But she was always there for the fittings and the consultations, if not mentally then certainly physically, so no one could complain. The rest of the time she seemed to spend with Elana Cassidy. 'You're just trying to get out of helping with the wedding preparations,' Rosalind said, shaking her head. Oriana said, 'You're jealous, Vanessa, and so you run away.' Vanessa left them with their delusions. The bridesmaids dresses arrived and Vanessa tried hers on, found it a perfect fit, then fled, leaving the delicate shell-pink wild-silk garment thrown carelessly on her mother's bed.

'She'll have to show you more consideration, Oriana' Rosalind said.

'Oh Mother, leave her. She hasn't had a real boyfriend since I got engaged. I think it's tough for her.'

'Well, your father wants her to encourage Dom Bradley, so I've paired them at the wedding. Hopefully something will blossom there. Wouldn't that be nice?'

Rosalind was in her element and had not time to think too much about Vanessa. The preparations were going precisely as she would have wished. The wedding would be the social event of the year. She had been given *carte blanche* to organise it and she wanted the best. She'd have banks of June roses, white and dusty pink, and arum lilies, white and white shot with pink, in profusion everywhere. She'd arranged with the Country Club to borrow their best wine- and cocktail-waiters, booked the top swing band and a string quartet that specialised in Mozart and worked mostly in Radio Eireann.

She decided on the menu, after much thought – Dublin Bay prawns, *fois gras*, roast duck breasts *en gêlée*. Fresh strawberries, raspberries, and the Monument Creamery would make the cake.

Rosalind often contemplated with a certain amount of complacency her position in life. She was a success, there was no doubt about that, and she wished the same heights could be reached by her girls. It was all she wanted for them.

She had married Brendan on her father's instruction. The first years had been difficult, there was no denying that, but her mother had been there to steer her through the turbulent times just as she would be there for Oriana and Vanessa. If only Vanessa did not mess up her life by falling in love with someone unsuitable. Rosalind shivered. Vanessa was, she knew, quite capable of losing her head and making a hash of her life.

One needed to marry one's own sort. Same manners, same tastes, same cultural background and financial position. The last was vital. Girls like Oriana and Vanessa did not know how to make a cup of tea, let alone boil an egg, but they knew how to decide a menu, organise a dinner and run a large establishment competently, instructing servants and establishing good relationships with them. They had never held a Hoover in their lily-white hands or wielded a dish-cloth or a dustpan and would not know how to starch a collar or polish a table to save their lives. No, ordinary life in a semi-detached was not for her girls. They would marry out of their class over her dead body.

So it was with alarm that she heard the rumours about Vanessa and the American. Malicious little asides about Vanessa 'snuggling up to Embassy military staff', 'a sergeant or something like that', 'In the Marines, did you ever', 'In the back bar at the Bailey'. Rosalind did not appreciate the seemingly innocent queries. 'Is Vanessa going to follow in her sister's footsteps to the altar? And become an Army bride?' 'It's great to see your daughter cementing Irish–American relations, Rosalind, in more ways than one!' took her by surprise and dismayed her. And then Oriana told her that gossip was rife and, in fact, it was brought home to her that Vanessa had flagrantly disobeyed her father. It was not something she had expected, for the girls were not in the habit of defying Brendan.

They had, she knew, been brought up strictly, just as she had, and there was the ever-present birch, slim and lethal, hanging on the wall of Brendan's study, a constant reminder that he expected to be obeyed. Rosalind hated the birchings, but felt it was the only way to keep discipline. The end justified the means, and it was, unfortunately in this modern climate, necessary. Family values must be preserved at all costs. Fathers in their wisdom supervised their children and did what they had to do to see that their offspring were biddable, respectful and well-mannered. Whatever had to be done to make sure the result was successful and the children prospered had to be done, and if tears and upsets were the outcome, hopefully they learned their lesson and the exercise need not be repeated.

Rosalind had always obeyed her husband. After all, she'd promised, taken a solemn vow to do that at the wedding service. Love, honour and obey. Oriana would take the same vow in a week's time in the little church down the hill, and hopefully, one day in the not too distant future, so would Vanessa. To the right man. Definitely not this American sergeant, no matter how good-looking he was. As she had told Vanessa, she did not trust good-looking men, they didn't last, didn't mature well, and in her opinion their good looks usually made them conceited.

When Oriana told her about her sister and the gossip all over the town Rosalind decided, after careful consideration, that before she spoke to her husband she'd have a sharp word or two with her daughter. She would reiterate life's rules and regulations to Vanessa, explain yet again what was expected of her and what would make her happy. And there was no shadow of doubt in Rosalind's mind that the lovely American would most certainly not be capable of that. Then and only then, if Vanessa still continued to be hot-headed, would she have to tell Brendan and deliver her daughter over to the inevitable consequences, much as it pained her. It was, Rosalind was quite certain, her bounden duty.

Chapter Seventeen

ᔆ ᔆ

Rosalind's boudoir was full of sunlight. She liked bright rooms, was unafraid of scrutiny, and calmly accepted the ravages of time on her face as part of the inevitable process.

She had moved out of the master bedroom with great relief. She had submitted to what she thought of as the degradation of coupling – surely the most humiliating experience a woman had to endure – with fortitude and resignation. She could not understand how God, who made the flowers and the trees, could invent such an obscene method of procreation. It baffled her. Couldn't He, she often thought, have managed a more artistic way of implanting the seed of life? Couldn't He have thought of something more beautiful?

Brendan, to give him his due, didn't inflict himself on her too often, and after the birth of Vanessa and a terrible miscarriage a year later they both called it a day with relief. Rosalind, satisfied that she'd done her duty, told her husband, quite casually, that she thought of decorating this room as her boudoir. He understood and acknowledged that his snoring was not conducive to a good night's sleep, and so the matter was settled.

She sat now on the pink and gold brocade chaise, ankles neatly crossed, before dressing for dinner. She had a couple of small varicose veins and the doctor had told her to rest them. She had asked Cessy to send Vanessa to her.

Vanessa's heart sank at the summons. Her mother rarely sent for her and when she did it was serious. She guessed it was because of Glenn.

'Don't worry, Miss 'Nessa. 'Twill be about your bridesmaid's outfit, I expec',' Cessy reassured her when she saw the expression of panic on Vanessa's face.

She met her brother on the stairs. Sitric's pale face wore its usual blank façade, but he remarked as she passed, 'You're for it, 'Nessa! Better brace yourself.'

She glared at him and stuck out her tongue, but it unnerved her nevertheless. Her brother was usually completely unaware of what went on in his sisters' lives, and if he knew something then it certainly meant trouble.

'Oh shut up, Sitric,' she growled at him.

'No, but listen.' He leaned nearer to her. 'Don't let them beat you, 'Ness. Don't. You've got a right to happiness. We all have. Only *they* think they know where that lies.' He tapped the side of his nose. 'But they don't, do they?'

She shook her head at him and continued on upstairs to her mother's room.

Her mother's face was not at all welcoming and her tone was cold. 'Sit down, Vanessa.'

Vanessa sat on an elegant little pink and gold Sheraton chair.

'Sit up straight. Don't slump,' her mother instructed. She was aware of how severe she sounded but she wanted to nip this whole thing in the bud. She dreaded the canings, although she felt she had to approve of them if all else failed. But she did not want the situation to develop to the extent where Brendan's intervention was necessary. So she sounded as harsh as a Reverend Mother.

She did not beat about the bush. 'Vanessa, what is this nonsensical gossip about you being seen with this . . . sergeant?' she asked, then as Vanessa began to shake her head negatively she held up her hand. 'No. Please don't insult my intelligence by denying it or I'll have no alternative but to hand you over to Pappy.'

'Oh no, Mother, please don't . . .' Vanessa gulped. She found it difficult to continue. The thought of the birch made her feel sick.

'The whole of Dublin is talking . . .'

'Oh Mother, I doubt that . . .' Vanessa swallowed. She felt ill with apprehension yet she knew she had to fight her corner.

'Don't take that tone with me, young lady. Dotty O'Grady told me Arabella saw you both in the Royal in Bray. Canon Tracey said you were in the Gresham, and Dom Bradley's father saw you in the Shelbourne. Sean Powers told Pierce, who told Oriana, who told me.'

Vanessa hated her sister in that moment. Why didn't she keep her mouth shut?

'Is that all they have to talk about? My social life? They can't have much to entertain them if all they can do is gossip about poor little me.'

'How dare you, Vanessa. That is *not* what I would call it . . .'

'Then Mother, with all due respect, what would you call it?'

'I'd call it concern for your happiness. It is perfectly normal to be interested in your friends' doings and to remark on having seen you and I'm perfectly sure no malice was intended. Except perhaps on the part of the O'Gradys. Canon Tracey in fact said how well you looked.' Her voice became dry. 'And that you seemed in great form.'

Vanessa took a deep breath. 'I'm sorry, Mother, I didn't mean to be flip.'

'I'm going to ask you, Vanessa, to give me your word, on your honour, never to see that young man again. This cannot go on. You must see that. And it is a sacred vow you are taking. A promise. To me. I'll expect you to keep your word.'

She looked at her daughter. Vanessa's blue eyes were blazing so fiercely that Rosalind was taken aback. It was an expression she could not fathom. Nothing in her life had moved her to feel even half the passion that lay mirrored in her daughter's eyes. It frightened her, the depth, the intensity she saw there.

'Mother, I cannot make you a promise like that. I simply cannot.'

'Even when you know what the result will be?'

'Even then. I love him, Mother. I love him so much.'

'Vanessa!' her mother blazed. 'Don't you dare—'

'That is, *we* love each other so very much and there is nothing I can do about it now. It's too late.'

'That is just not possible. It is not appropriate. It is outrageous.'

'But, Mother, it is so.'

'Your father forbade you to see him.'

106

'Well, Mother, I disobeyed him. I'm eighteen after all.'

'Your father will be very angry, Vanessa, at your disobedience.' Rosalind spoke quietly now. It was a matter for her husband. It was out of her hands.

'Mother' – Vanessa sounded wistful – 'Couldn't you explain to Pappy that I love Glenn with all my heart? That I'll never love anyone else? Couldn't you, Mother?'

Rosalind's eyes flew open. Her daughter's passion disturbed and disgusted her. She stared at Vanessa, almost with distaste. 'What would you know of love?' she asked coldly.

'I know what it feels like to know you cannot live without someone,' she replied fervently.

She knew as she spoke that it was useless. Her mother would not speak to her father. She never crossed him. She believed he was like God. And Pappy would not change his mind even if Rosalind did plead her daughter's case. Not in all her life had she ever known her father to change his mind about anything. She had never known him to admit he was wrong.

Her mother shook her head and sighed. 'I'm afraid not. Oh, I don't know what's to be done.' She swung her legs off the chaise and leaned forward. 'Couldn't you give him up? He'll not make you happy, dear. He's a stranger with foreign ways.' She was pleading with her daughter. This was her last chance. 'Life is difficult enough as it is, marriage can be hard, but at least you'd be here, near your own kind if you married Dom, or Jimmy McDowell or Barry Sheridan.'

'Oh Mother, they're idiots! They're—'

'I meant one of that crowd. I don't suggest you marry any one of them specifically, but someone *like* them. Darling, have you *thought* about this? Does this sergeant know you cannot boil a kettle? Does he know you have never cooked a meal in your life? You'd have to leave Ireland. Go to America, to strangers in a strange land. Have you *thought* about it?'

Vanessa hadn't. She had not given a moment's reflection to the future and what it would all mean, what it would be like for her. She had never thought beyond her next date with Glenn. She had been too dazzled to think rationally about the future. If Glenn Carey had asked her to stand up as she was and follow him from her mother's boudoir out into the wide world without anything of her own she would happily have done so.

Rosalind stared at her daughter. It was too late, she could see, to effectively stop this avalanche of feeling Vanessa was experiencing. She had never felt such emotion in her whole life, and now as she looked at her daughter she was not sorry. There was such pain there. Her child looked so vulnerable. So intense. So ardent. She knew she'd lost.

She wondered briefly what it must be like to be so passionate. She knew a moment's heartsickness. She had paid for her comfortable serenity by refusing to go down that path. Had she missed much? Was the bargain fair? She'd never know. 'I'll have to tell your father,' she said with a resigned sigh and Vanessa nodded. So be it.

Chapter Eighteen

⁓⁓

The antique study clock ticked loudly. A shaft of light fell on Brendan's desk but his face was in shadow. She could see his eyes glittering in the dusty shade. An Ardmore ancestor had bought the clock in London, a great ugly-looking thing that took its place between the full-length portrait of Alastair Ardmore – a dour man, thin-lipped, thin-faced, thin-haired – and Brendan's head and shoulders.

'Your mother tells me that you refuse to give up this sergeant.' His voice was soft as silk, little more than a whisper.

'I can't, Pappy.'

'What do you mean?' The voice became harder, then with dawning alarm: 'You're not . . . ?'

'No, Pappy,' she replied angrily, forestalling him. 'No, no. He's always treated me with the utmost respect.'

'Respect! You call it respect when a man takes you out when your father has forbidden it? That's not what I call respect.'

She said nothing. There was silence for a moment. Her heart beat fast. She had that sick feeling in the pit of her stomach. Her hands were folded in her lap. They shook.

'You disobeyed me miss,' Brendan told her coldly. 'You were warned.'

She didn't want to cry but a sob shook her. 'Please, Pappy,' she implored, 'please don't beat me. I'm a grown woman. You don't know how humiliating it is for me . . .' She faltered to a halt.

'That is precisely why you get what you deserve. If it did not humiliate you it would be useless. Ineffective.'

'But, Pappy, it . . .'

He wasn't listening. He stood and took the birch off the wall. He flexed it, holding one end in each hand.

'Over, then.'

She bit her lip. She was sweating now and she could smell her fear. Brendan sliced the air once or twice with the birch.

'You can still change your mind. This will not happen if you promise you'll not see this sergeant again.'

The birch sang a little on its path through the air, made a little whispering, sighing noise. Brendan waited.

She shook her head. 'I can't, Pappy. I'd be lying if I promised.'

He nodded at the desk.

She was wearing a pleated Goray skirt and a pale blue cashmere twinset. She stood with her face to the desk, her back to her father, and bent over. She gripped the hem of her skirt and pulled it up over her head. Her whole body shrank in embarrassment and shame.

Her panties were plain. She had not put on her silk and lace cami-knickers or any frilly underwear for the last few days, expecting this. She wore lisle pantaloons with elastic at the thigh, but that did not now make her feel any better. She felt utterly defeated, humiliated, debased.

Her head lay on the blotting paper on her father's desk and she could smell it. She squeezed her eyes shut as the birch sliced across her buttocks. She could hear her father grunt as he raised the cane and brought it down again and again with a singing swish on her quivering flesh.

She did not at that moment feel the pain. That would come later, but now, all she wanted to do was die. To disappear. To dissolve into the atmosphere and not be there any more. Please God, let it be over quick. She pressed her face into the blotting paper. It was damp with her sweat.

He was breathing heavily now, the cane's rhythm had quickened and she knew it would soon be over.

When at last he dropped the cane she could feel the throbbing begin. It felt like burning knives slicing her behind. She hastily pulled down her skirt and with as much dignity as she could muster went to the door.

'You are confined to this house until further notice,' her father said huskily as she reached the door. 'You understand.' It was not a question.

'Yes, Pappy,' she whispered and left the hateful room.

Chapter Nineteen

∽ ∾

Vanessa was young and healthy and she recovered physically quite quickly, but inside, in her soul, darkness flooded. She was filled with hatred and resentment. Like a poison it seeped through her, colouring everything. She knew that if she didn't see Glenn she'd go mad. Only he could restore her sanity. Only he could heal the pain her father had inflicted.

One of the worst things about this kind of incident was that she felt lowly and degraded for a long time afterwards. She felt worthless, a cowering victim too feeble to fight her own corner, guilty of all the sins under the sun. Disobedient to her parents. *Mea culpa, mea culpa, mea culpa.*

Glenn rang but they said she was indisposed. Elana phoned twice a day and was told that Vanessa had a cold. Then Glenn arrived at the house where Rushton met him and said, as instructed, that he was not welcome there and Miss Vanessa did not wish to see him. So did Elana, who guessed what had happened.

Vanessa had told her friend about the beatings. Elana had not known what to say. She could not put herself in Vanessa's shoes, having no experience to compare. Dr Jack was the kindest of men and she could not imagine him committing such an act. It smacked of Gothic Victoriana, Mary Shelley or Byron or someone of that ilk. After all, it was the forties. They lived in the modern world. How could a father behave so? She could not understand. Jack Cassidy hated even to squash spiders and gave gentle consideration to all living things, treating every human being as sacred.

Elana told Glenn her suspicions. His face paled, his eyes hardened and he looked sick.

'I can't believe it,' he told Elana. 'That's monstrous.'

112

'I know,' she said sadly. 'Old-fashioned, huh? I hate Brendan Ardmore. He's a bully and one of these days he'll get his come-uppance.'

'But are you sure, Elana? That he could do such a thing?'

She nodded. 'He's done it before, oh, lots of times when she disobeyed him. I've seen the scars. And he told her not to see you and she went ahead and did. Pierce Powers says he told Oriana about you two meeting. Being seen places together.'

'The little squirt. Oh boy, oh boy, you'd think I was some kind of geek!'

'He's insular,' Elana said. 'That's the kindest thing to think. You know Glenn, the Ardmores really believe they are the bee's knees, top of the pile, sophisticated. But they're the worst kind of ignorant, narrow-minded provincials. They are, you know.'

Sitric came and whispered encouragement through Vanessa's door. 'Don't let them get to you, 'Ness,' he told her. 'Don't let him break you. Stick it out.'

'He doesn't beat you any more, Sitric, does he?' she whispered back. 'No. He can't. I suddenly realised one day when he went to get that hateful birch down that I was bigger and stronger than him. I stood up and dared him.' He laughed. 'You should have seen his face.'

Oriana came and whispered her apologies. 'I didn't mean to get you in trouble, 'Ness,' she said and Vanessa listened tight-lipped behind her door, but forgave her anyway.

She was allowed to join the family at mealtimes. The rest of the time she was locked in her room, bitter and exasperated, impatiently waiting for her release, like a prisoner.

She had taken to staring at her father at meals. It made him acutely uncomfortable, she could see that, but there was nothing he could do about it. When he barked at her to stop staring at him she blinked innocently and said she wasn't. Then went on staring.

She had done this at every meal since the beating and her father had taken to rushing through his meals and going to his study to smoke a cigar and have his coffee there immediately after dessert.

That week at Dundalgan the conversation was all about Oriana's wedding. No one mentioned the birching. No one ever said anything when one of the family was chastised – the talk was bright and general – yet Vanessa could feel everyone's awareness. Sive gave her extra helpings and smuggled cups of cocoa into her room. Cessy smiled at her and Imelda stroked her arm and understood when Vanessa pulled it away. She couldn't bear any physical contact. Not now. Not yet.

'That man is a monster,' Cessy told her mother in the kitchen.

'Now, Cess, he's only doin' what he thinks is his duty,' Sive said without much conviction.

'Well, I think he's an old bastard, that's what I think.'

Oriana looked tired. There were faint shadows under her eyes and she seemed listless. Rosalind was worried about her.

'You must get some rest,' her mother told her. 'You must look your best next week.'

'Oh Mother, I'll be fine,' Oriana replied irritably. 'But I can't refuse all the parties people are giving for me. It would be bad manners. Everybody wants to entertain us and it would be rude.' She yawned and stretched.

'Don't do that at table, darling,' Rosalind told her.

'She goes to all the parties because she's avid for presents,' Sitric said. 'Honestly, Ori, you're going to find out one day that material things are trash. They're inanimate. Dead stuff. Gosh, grow up, will you!'

'Sitric, I will not have you speaking to Oriana like that. Apologise at once.'

'Why should I? It's the truth.'

Brendan glared at his son. There was loathing in his eyes. 'Apologise, Sitric. Now.'

Sitric shrugged. 'Oh all right. Anything for a quiet life. Sorry Oriana. Will that do?' He glared back defiantly at his father who lowered his eyes and rose and left the table.

Rosalind sighed. 'I don't know what's happened in this house. We used all to be so happy. Now Vanessa is in disgrace, Oriana looks like death and Sitric, you are impossibly rude to your father and it will not do. Honour thy father and thy mother, remember? Oh, what's come over you all?'

Sitric grinned, 'We grew up, Ma, and found out Pappy is not like other men.'

114

Rosalind stared at her son with dislike. 'I'll not discuss this with you any more, Sitric. You have no right to speak like that. I'm going to my room. Tell Sive to bring me my coffee there.'

The wedding presents began to arrive. There was a long table in the music room groaning under the weight of silver, china, lamps, toasters, cutlery, linen, nappery, Turkish towels and a little pile of envelopes containing cheques.

Strangers with notebooks, tape measures, trugs containing beddable plants wandered about and were bumped into in the gardens or the hall. Fairy-lights appeared in the trees and around the fountain and the gazebo.

The bride's dress, veil and coronet were laid out on the bed in the guest-room alongside the bridesmaids' pale pink frocks, gloves, rosebud Juliet-caps and delicate grosgrain court shoes.

Vanessa moved through all the excitement in a dream. She was absent-minded, fully occupied with thoughts of a man whose smile made her heart beat too fast and whose kiss made her melt. She spent all her time selecting and discarding plots and plans to escape and meet her love.

Sitric seemed preoccupied too, but then, as Rosalind said, he was rarely any other way.

'He knows what he's supposed to do, Mother, doesn't he?' Oriana asked, exasperated by her brother's indifference.

'He's an usher. He knows. He's done it lots of times.'

'He doesn't *look* as if he does.' Oriana glared at Sitric across the table but her brother seemed unaware of the conversation about him.

Finally, after the longest few days Vanessa could remember, she sent Cessy to the phone in the pub down in the village, Glenn's number and a threepenny bit clutched in her hand. Cessy telephoned the American Embassy and asked for Glenn. When he came to the phone she told him that Miss Vanessa would meet him in Jury's, beside the Bank of Ireland in College Green that evening at nine o'clock.

Glenn found his hand shaking when he replaced the receiver. The thought of his little love, hurt and frightened, beaten by that bull of a man, had made him sick and angry.

115

He did not know exactly what he could do, but he was certain about one thing: Vanessa Ardmore was going to be his bride. If that was the only way he could take care of her, then he'd marry her.

Chapter Twenty

❧ ❧

Vanessa changed into her blue New Look two-piece, the suit she'd been wearing when she first met Glenn. Sitric turned the key for her. She sneaked down the back stairs, through the kitchen, putting her finger to her lips as Aunt Avalan used to do as she passed Rushton, Sive, Cessy and Imelda. They pretended not to see her.

She escaped, creeping past workmen and gardeners toiling away in the dusk, and hurried down the driveway, wobbling a little on her high heels. It was easy.

When she reached the gates she saw the car and his anxious face peering through the windscreen. He had parked there, keeping watch for her, and her heart leapt within her.

She flew to him. His elbow hit the horn as he pulled her into his arms and the sudden loud blare made her jump, then laugh with relief.

'Oh honey, dearest girl, are you okay? Oh honey, I've been so worried, so worried.'

'Oh my darling, my darling, my darling.'

She held him close, touching his face as if he'd been away for years. He held her as if she were a fragile piece of china, a hurt bird.

'Oh honey, is it true? Did he hurt you, my pet, my love? I can't bear him to hurt you.'

They kissed, ardently, passionately, vowing their love, reiterating their dedication their words tumbling over each other. They held on to each other, wanting never to let go, until at last caution prevailed. She saw Pierce's little red roadster come over the hill to Dundalgan.

'It's Pierce Powers. He told on me. We better go,' she said to Glenn. 'Please, let's go.'

'The schmuck! I wish I could get my hands on him.'

She was frightened and that alarmed Glenn. He started the engine, turned the car around and drove back towards town.

'I thought you mightn't have transport. That's why I came,' he explained.

'I'm glad you did. Pierce would have seen me on the road and taken me home. He's a pain. All he wants is to please Pappy.'

She slipped her arm through his and laid her head on his shoulder as he drove down the leafy roads into the city. The mountains shimmered purple and mauve in the dusk and the birds were shrilling their night chorus. The lights were beginning to glow and glimmer in the falling darkness. Vanessa loved the feel of his jacket under her cheek, the smell of his cologne.

With one hand he took two cigarettes from a pack of Strand and passed them to her.

'Light,' he said, pushing the little lighter in the dashboard. It made a click when it popped out. She put the cigarettes between her lips and pressed the little electric curl to the tips. She puffed until they were lit then passed one to him. She did not smoke much, though most people did, but she needed one now and she inhaled gratefully.

Glenn was curiously tense and silent. He said nothing until they had parked the car in College Green and descended down into the bar in Jury's Hotel. They sat side by side in the gloom.

He ordered drinks. He took the cigarette from his lips and she saw his hand was trembling, his knuckles white.

'Darling,' she said anxiously and covered his hand with hers. She had never seen him upset. Usually he was relaxed and smiling. 'What is it?' she asked.

'Did he really do . . . that?' he asked in a tight voice.

'What?' She knew who he was talking about, knew what he meant, but she was reluctant to have him speak about something so shameful. She would have preferred to blot it out of her memory, forget it ever happened. If she could.

'That your father . . .' he hesitated and she hoped he'd change the subject, drop it, let it go. But he didn't. 'Elana says your father beats you.'

There was a tightness around his lips which he pressed together in a line. She looked at him anxiously. 'Would it make a difference? To us, I mean? Will you love me less?'

He swore under his breath and glared at her. 'You believe that? You could even *think* that? Gee honey, you know . . .' He was not sure what he felt. A turmoil of emotions churned within him: rage and pity, protectiveness and an intense desire to kill fought for ascendency in his breast. He controlled his rage, found to his horror there were tears in his eyes.

'Let's get married,' he said.

Her face broke into a rapturous smile. 'You serious?' she asked.

'Never more,' he told her. 'I got to get you out of there. I'd like to give him a sock in the jaw. Let him know what it feels like.'

'He thinks he's doing his duty,' she told him. 'After all, he's my father.'

Glenn shook his head. 'That's not a father's role. He should protect you, not threaten you. I'll save you from any more of that sort of stuff,' he said gruffly.

He took her hands between his and kissed the knuckles one by one. They smelled of Lux toilet soap – soft hands, hands that had never worked, and for a moment he felt a shiver of fear. A farm in Wisconsin!

'Golly, Glenn, yes. Yes. YES! But Pappy and Mother'll never allow it.'

He was frowning. 'It's barbaric that he . . . that he could do that.' Glenn could not put into words the violence done to her. It sickened him, outraged him that anyone could lay a violent hand on this precious, vulnerable creature whose big blue eyes were overbrimming with love for him. He wanted to protect and guard her, save her from any more pain.

'You can't go back there,' he said.

'I've got to. It's Oriana's wedding on Saturday.'

'I don't want you to go back there,' he said decisively. 'I don't want you near him ever again.'

She held on tightly to his hand. 'Listen, Glenn, he won't do it again, yet. Not now. Not with the wedding. But he'd murder me if I missed the wedding and it wouldn't be fair to Oriana.'

119

'Suppose he finds you're gone? Tonight? Suppose he goes to your room and—'

'He won't. Our rooms are on one side, his on the other. Mother might find out, in which case she wouldn't tell him until after the wedding. She doesn't want to spoil it either. But Pappy won't go anywhere near us tonight.'

'Oriana will tell him. Elana said she told him—'

'No she won't. Not just now.'

'Listen, Vanessa, I won't let you back there if you have any fears that he might . . .'

'No, I'm sure he won't. Not just after he . . . punished me.' He groaned and pressed her hand to his forehead. 'No,' she reiterated, 'we have to wait until after Oriana's wedding. Don't you see? It would spoil the most important day of her life for her. I couldn't do that to her. After Saturday, my darling, I'll do anything you say.'

He'd been thinking and nodding, seeing it her way.

'After Oriana's wedding then.' He glanced at her. 'Can you stay over at Elana's house?' he asked. 'After Saturday? Can you stay with her?'

'Yes,' she answered, puzzled.

'Okay. Then what you gotta do, you gotta stay over at Elana's and we'll go together and tell him, your father, and your Mom we aim to get married. Ask him for his blessing.'

Her hand flew to her mouth and her eyes widened in panic. 'Are you mad? Oh no! I couldn't. You don't know what he's like.'

'Sure you could. I'm an American Marine. If I can beat the Japs I can face your father. Don't be alarmed, honey. I'll be with you. He's a bully. Men who beat women are all bullies and bullies never pick on anyone their own size.' He smiled at her. 'You got nuthin' to fear with me there. But I want to do this by the book. No hole-in-the-corner stuff for me. And don't you see, we have to give him a fair chance? Mebbe he'll change his mind. We gotta be fair.'

She shook her head vehemently. 'Oh no. You don't know Pappy. He *never* changes his mind.'

'You do what I say, okay? I want to do what is right and proper. I'll not have him say I stole you away or that we did anything dishonourable. 'Sides, the Ambassador'd have a fit.'

120

Finally she nodded. 'Okay,' she said, staring at him with complete acceptance.

'Don't look at me like that or I'll ravish you here and now,' he grinned. 'No, but I have to see about papers. Get permission. Rules and regulations, you know.'

Her face fell. 'Suppose they forbid it?'

He laughed. 'They won't,' he said. 'You're white, speak English and I love you. There'll be no trouble. Some of the guys married Japanese girls and that was difficult. The top brass made that pretty difficult. They were the enemy, mind.' He kissed her cheek. 'Then you gotta get certificates – birth, baptism, I'll let you know. But don't worry. Understand?'

She nodded. She was content. He had taken charge. She trusted him completely. Brought up to believe in the total superiority and authority of the male, programmed by her past, she bowed obediently to his commands, welcomed them, relished his masterful attitude.

Glenn told his CO that night. He told the Ambassador. He told Billy Monks. The army and the diplomats asked him was he sure, pointed out the difficulties, and when he assured them soberly that he had already given the matter serious thought they said they saw no problem and were only too happy to cooperate so that the event could be expedited quickly and without fuss.

But Billy was worried.

'You'll be best man?' Glenn asked him. 'Stand up for me?'

'Jeez, Glenn, you sure? It's a bit sudden, isn't it? What about Angie? You *sure*?'

Glenn nodded emphatically. 'I'm sure,' he said. 'I'm *real* sure.'

Chapter Twenty-one

∽ ∾

The day before the wedding, the Friday of that week, was the Annual General Meeting of the Board of Directors of Ardmore & Son. Brendan was furious when he realised the dates were so close but Rosalind had no sympathy for him.

'We'll have to alter the wedding date,' he said.

'We will not. I'm sorry, Brendan. It would cost you half a million to do that. The invitations have gone out. The flowers ordered. Everything is arranged. You've been attending that meeting all your life and you were the one who decided the date for your daughter's wedding. You should have realised.'

Which was no help at all. It left him without ammunition to blame anyone else and thus blow off steam. His blood pressure shot up and Rosalind sighed and knew they were in for stormy weather.

The morning of the AGM Brendan was intensely irritated. His breakfast was disrupted by workmen under his feet. There was, it seemed nowhere in the whole house that he could go and be assured of privacy. Someone burst into his lavatory while he was sitting on it, apologised and fled, leaving him feeling awkward in his own house.

The AGM was always the worst morning of the year for him. It was a morning he dreaded. It was the one day when his nose would be rubbed in it and he would be forced to realise the extent of his ignorance. Without allowing anyone else to see it. That was the difficult part. He had to pretend a knowledge he did not possess in front of a board of erudite and clever men. And bloody Patrick McCawley.

He shouted at Sive that his eggs were overdone. The cook, who had hardly slept with all the extra work she had to do and the responsibility of the wedding breakfast lying heavily on her mind, had to bite her lip so that she would not scream at him and get them all dismissed. It took some self-control not to let rip when he yelled at her, face red, eyes bloodshot, his anger overcoming him. She wanted to let him know how she despised him, how ill-mannered she thought him. She wanted to tell him he was a pig and a bully and he should show his servants more respect, but she kept her lips firmly sealed and said nothing, proving to herself that she was a better person than her boss.

Rosalind, who never interrupted her husband, said nothing either. Vanessa gulped down some tea and slipped away muttering that she had to meet Elana Cassidy for morning coffee in Fullers. Oriana was not up. The festivities and excitement had worn her out and she did not intend to rise until afternoon.

Sive put Sitric's breakfast in front of him with a resounding slam that made him jump, and returned to the kitchen smarting from Brendan's insults.

Brendan left the house out of sorts. How he hated this day, and as Rushton drove him to the Dawson Street offices he tried to still the fear rising inside him.

He entered the imposing Georgian building where the Ardmore & Son Wine Import Export Company housed its head office.

Patrick McCawley met him in the Connemara marble hall and together they made their way to the boardroom.

Patrick McCawley was short of stature, with wiry black and white hair, bright black eyes and bushy brows. His square face and body exuded energy and he hurried behind his employer, entering respectfully after him the great wood-panelled room filled with green leather furniture.

Brendan took his place at the head of the mahogany table. He sat beneath the portrait of his thin-lipped father, watched the six men enter through half-closed lids, wishing he were somewhere else.

Regan O'Doherty, Barry Blessington, Thomás McIlhinny, Roddy Clark, Geraghty and Vincent Laverty, the directors and shareholders of the company filed in one by one. Patrick McCawley sat beside him, a little to his right and behind. Very respectful.

Patrick McCawley, his second-in-command, handled all

the business. Besides that, he *understood* the business. He was a blasted know-all and Brendan hated him most. He was efficient, responsible and knew the business from A to Z. Regan and Barry were dilettantes who sat on the boards of several big firms in Dublin and who were really only interested in collecting dividends. They pitched up once a year for the Company report, which they hardly listened to, reluctantly taking time off from the golf course where they spent their days in gentle amusement, allowing others to make the profits. Geraghty and Vincent were a little more *au fait* with business proceeding. Thomás was a serious chap, earnest and conscientious, who crossed every t and dotted every i and queried every goddamned comma, much to the disgust of the others. Roddy Clark was an alcoholic who could be relied upon to doze through the whole boring proceedings. Patrick McCawley ran the meeting, allowing it to appear that Brendan was so doing.

As the meeting progressed Brendan wondered as he usually did what on earth they were talking about. His head was full of confusion, of unfinished thoughts jumbled together, thoughts that tumbled over each other as he raced first down one avenue, then another, never finishing his journeys, never reaching balanced conclusions. He could not seem to clear his brain, think without clutter, without a plethora of supposings, what-ifs and other arbitrary and useless speculation.

All the time the men in the oak-panelled room talked in a language foreign to him, looking to him for decisions and confirmation of decisions, seeking his authority and the final word.

He growled a bit, waved his hands, cleared his throat and looked to Patrick McCawley for guidance. It was a game he had played all his life at this office and it was more frightening than Russian roulette. Only Patrick McCawley knew he didn't understand a word they uttered, didn't understand how the business was run, never mind the subtleties of import and export ratios, export drives, dividends, investment coverage, maximum yield, and so on, and so on.

If once, just once in his life, he could have brought himself to admit ignorance, if he could have humbled himself to ask

124

for help and advice he'd have cracked the whole mystery quite quickly, grasped the component parts easily, but he could not, would not. Originally he had been too young, too green, too frightened. Now it was too late. So he found himself in this nightmare situation where he had to pretend an understanding he had not got and juggle replies and deliver ultimatums and finalise orders.

It drove him nuts. He wanted to level with the men before him but knew such a move would destroy him.

Patrick McCawley was replying for him. Brendan had leaned across and Patrick whispered in his ear, 'Reject' and Brendan repeated the word aloud.

'Reject.'

He could see how disappointed the others were and this pleased him. He liked upsetting people, it gave him a feeling of power he did not possess.

'What I want to know, what I want to know is . . .' Thomás McIlhinny was saying and Barry and Regan caught Brendan's eyes and rolled theirs heavenwards. 'Where are the figures for the Vie de France consignment?'

Brendan leaned towards Patrick in a sort of lollopping roll. The board members were used to this and sighed. Barry was puffing his cigar and Regan doodling on the blotting paper before him.

'Not available,' Patrick whispered.

'Not available,' Brendan huffed loudly, dismissing the question.

But Thomás was not to be so easily deflected. 'No, no. Cahill Ni Rahilly—'

'These bloody Gaelic names creeping into our land! Isn't English good enough?' Barry Blessington whispered, making a face and blowing out clouds of smoke.

'Cahill told me that Vie de France were making a huge profit. A huge profit. Said it was the talk of the City of London. No more Beaujolais, no more Mâcon Rouge, no more Burgundy, just Vie de France, blanc *et* rouge . . .'

'Oh get him with the jolly old Mamselle from Armentiers!' Regan joshed.

Barry shook his head. 'Come on, let's get on with it. I've got a date with a golf-ball and I don't want to be here all day.'

'Well, that's what I'm doing,' Thomás continued pedantically. He was a Gaelic speaker and a friend of Dev's and the others despised him. 'Should never have left the British Empire,' Barry was fond of saying. 'Much better to have remained with the winners. What do we want with our own piddling economy and our bloody Irish language, eh? I ask you!'

Thomás persisted. 'I want to know,' he said, 'why I cannot find any mention of Vie de France in this report, anywhere listed with the profits, and I distinctly remember Patrick here saying he was putting in for a very large consignment this time last year.'

Patrick McCawley smiled. He touched his Ronald Coleman moustache tenderly. He wore a grey flannel suit and a red silk tie. The others thought him rather slick, his hair over Brylcreemed, and, compared to the discreet leather brogues, the pure wool pullovers, the tweed jackets and cavalry twill trousers the others wore, he was a trifle flash. He was, after all, a man risen from the ranks, not born a gentleman and therefore to be excused for his execrable taste. But his propensity to the Teddy Boy fashion that was creeping in all over the land was deplorable.

'I said not available,' Brendan reiterated and Roddy Clark nodded furiously.

'Why?' Thomás persisted.

Brendan waved towards Patrick as if he was weary of such stupidity and couldn't be bothered to go on, but he would allow his minion to reply.

'The Vie de France bottles we got at Burgh Quay were part of a bad consignment,' Patrick said with finality.

'How could that be?' Thomás ploughed relentlessly on. 'Doesn't make sense.'

'Doesn't make sense,' Roddy Clark echoed. The others stared at him a moment and he glared unsteadily back at them. His voice was slurred and his hands trembled. 'Eh?' he asked reasonably. ''S what I unnerstand.'

'Oh quite so, quite so.' Patrick McCawley replied politely.

'Your girl's getting married tomorrow, ain't she?' Barry remarked and Regan nodded. 'We'll be there,' he said. 'We'll be there.'

Patrick McCawley who had not been invited said, 'Well

now, isn't that nice,' in a tight voice and Thomás McIlhinny threw his notes on the table and cursed.

Regan cried, 'Oh come on, Tom' – he refused to give the name its Gaelic pronunciation – 'Let it go. I'm sure Brendan knows what he is doing.' Brendan nodded sagely and Thomás rose.

'I'm not happy about this,' he said and went to the door. 'Not at all happy. And I have to inform you that I'm going to look further into this. I'm not going to let it slide by.' He gave Brendan a deep penetrating glare.

'Any other business, gentlemen?' Brendan asked.

Barry, Regan and Roddy all began to shuffle papers and made moves to end the meeting. Geraghty and Vincent, who seemed to have slept through the meeting, woke up and rubbed their hands together in expectation of a drink. Thomás, exasperated, finally left the room, slamming the door behind him, and the other board members went with obvious relief to the sideboard where the drinks were laid out in glorious array and waited while a pretty maid poured out whatever they wanted.

McCawley heaved a sigh of relief. Another AGM safely behind them. He saw Brendan put his hand on the maid's buttocks, saw her conceal her embarrassment, watched her slip away from the groping hand, and Patrick smiled. Things were going precisely as planned. The only hiccup was Thomás bloody McIlhinny. He'd have to make his move sooner than he'd planned all because of that man. It was a nuisance but Thomás was a ferret and once he started digging about Vie de France – and he would, never fear – he'd uncover stuff that Patrick had not thought would be unearthed for quite a while. So he'd better get a move on, escape out of this self-satisfied business where everyone lived in luxury off *his* efforts, *his* industry, *his* know-how and brains, and get the hell out of this little backwoods company in this sleepy little country and make his mark in the New World. And, incidentally, show Brendan Ardmore in his true colours, reveal him to the world as the hopeless incompetent he was.

127

Chapter Twenty-two

❧ ❧

Patrick McCawley lived in Finglas. The house was large, much too large for a bachelor and much too large to have been purchased on the salary of manager of Ardmore & Son at the money Brendan paid.

But no one ever asked where he lived or enquired what his accommodation was. No one cared. If asked Barry Blessington, Regan O'Doherty or Roddy Clark would most likely have jumped to the conclusion that Patrick McCawley had a room in the house in Finglas at the address given on his file in Brendan Ardmore's office, but they would have had no interest in doing any such research. And Brendan certainly did not show the slightest interest in the man who ran his business for him, which was perhaps foolhardy of him.

The fact was that Patrick McCawley owned the house and let out rooms in it, digs to the students in Trinity and UCD. Thirty shillings a week for a room and shared bathroom. From this, and as there were six rooms in the house, the dining room and attic having been converted and the master bedroom divided in half, he made a nice little annual income, a very nice income indeed. He needed the extra because his boss so underrated him.

All in all Patrick was a self-satisfied man and if he was a little nervous, then that was natural when the stakes he was playing for were so high.

Brendan Ardmore was an eejit and a fool and the whole house of cards was going to collapse on him quite soon. A-tish-oo, a-tish-oo, they all fall down! Patrick often laughed to himself as he sipped his Amontillado, the very finest from Spain, of an evening, and listened to the students pound up and down the stairs, laughing as they brought in a crate of stout, or hurried out to the Bailey or Davy Byrne's for a jar.

He was reminded of the nursery rhyme and would whisper it to himself and smile. They would, all of the Ardmores, fall, down, down, down. It was inevitable.

It might take time. It might take years, although Patrick didn't think so – more like weeks in his estimation – but it was inevitable. A business could not be run by someone who knew nothing about it and succeed. And Patrick McCawley was not going to be around much longer to run Brendan's firm for him.

They lived in their privileged world of wealth, secure and untroubled by worry over shipments and selection of brands and which body was fine and which was full and which was a wash-out this year. They led the life of Riley while he had the responsibility and the grief. And he was not like his father. He did not come from that breed of men who gave their body and soul to their employer, grateful for whatever was dished out to them, slaves. Oh no. What he intended to do was simply to go. Leave. Vanish. And take with him what he felt he deserved, not a penny more nor less, and leave them to drown in their own ignorance.

He could not be blamed, that was his reasoning. No one would believe how little Brendan Ardmore paid his manager. He had kept up his stupid pretence of being in charge, or having knowledge he did not possess without giving him, Patrick McCawley, the credit, the simple courtesy of acknowledgement, the prestige and salary due to him after all his years of unremitting good management. He had done the work and watched Brendan reap the rewards, watched him pretend that it was his business acumen, his canny management that kept Ardmore & Son so spectacularly successful, when all the time it was solely Patrick who was responsible.

And Brendan Ardmore never once said thank you, never gave him a pat on the shoulder and a well deserved 'Well done'. Oh, it was not to be borne.

His mother, long deceased, had always told him, 'Do unto others as they do unto you', and that was his plan vis-à-vis his boss. Brendan had used him, abused his talent, his know-how, and Patrick had made his money for him. It had increased vastly over the years, and now he intended to reverse the situation. Brendan could remain here and make his own profits.

And he'd take Cessy with him. She was pretty as a picture and feisty. She would work hard, shoulder-to-shoulder with him. She would not lag behind. The Ardmores had taught her to work hard too.

Patrick McCawley had no pretensions to grandeur. He was not looking to cut an important social figure in the USA. His interest was solely in making money and being a success in business. But he was not overly ambitious and would, he knew, be content with comfort rather than extreme wealth.

And he wanted a partner, a wife who would not mind hard work, who would not weep over the loss of her family and her exile, but would meet the challenge, as he did, head on, with canny insight and fierce determination. In Cessy Byrne he had found such a girl.

Oh, he knew he was older than her twenty years. Fifteen years older, and that was a lot, but Cessy did not mind. Cessy said that young men were irresponsible and fickle and that more than anything she wanted stability. She had committed herself to him and he was glad.

They'd go soon, Cessy and he, leave the Ardmores to sink in their own incompetence. They deserved it. At the end of the summer they would leave Ireland forever.

He was taking with him to America all the profits from the Vie de France account. No more, no less. He had run after that account, done the deal, laboured over the distribution, had in fact done all the work and he had decided that this would be his bonus, this would be his golden handshake. The name, as Thomas McIlhinny had pointed out, appeared nowhere on their books. He had expunged all reference to it. He had thought long and hard about it. He did not want to have to call himself a thief. Cessy said she didn't care.

'Take them for everything you can,' she urged. 'They've exploited you. They've never given you anything *like* what yer worth, Paddy. What yer *entitled* to. So rook 'em, I say.'

He would shake his head. 'No, Cess, no. I'll take what I think I deserve for the years since my old man died' – he squinted up his eyes through the smoke of the Sweet Afton cigarette he held, finger and thumb – 'and be modest about it at that. You know how much increase he's given me in all the years I've worked for him. I've worked for him twenty

130

years and you know how much? Five pounds! That's it. Five
bloody quid. Je-sus!'

'Is why I think you should rook 'em,' Cessy said, but he
shook his head again.

'No, Cess. Need to be able to live with my conscience.'
He stroked his Ronald Coleman and grinned at her. 'My
conscience tells me though I can offer myself that remuneration,' he added smugly, 'and it's a very large remuneration
indeed.'

He totted up very carefully the amount of money he would
have earned if he had done the equivalent job anywhere else.
He checked the total against what the Vie de France account
brought in and lo and behold it came to almost the exact
same sum. He said it was a sign. He told Cessy the amount
and her eyes flew open wide and she cried out happily,
'That'll get us to America fine and dandy and enough to
start a business an' all, Paddy. Oh, 'twill be grand. But what'll
Mr Ardmore do without ye?' she asked, not out of concern,
but out of a kind of mischievous malice.

Patrick McCawley shrugged and said, 'I don't give a damn,
love, not a tinker's curse, an' that's the truth. But,' he added,
'I think they'll go bust.'

Chapter Twenty-three

ഹ ൭

The Saturday of the wedding dawned misty. Blue and grey veils hung over Dundalgan, slid through the trees, hovered over the lakes and concealed the mountains. As the day dawned they lifted provocatively and the cowslip-yellow sun rose slowly, shyly peeping over the horizon.

The marquee was up blocking the view from the girls' bedrooms. Little flags flew like pennants from the peaks at the top of the canvas, white satin with ribbons, and small pink and white balloons fluttered in the breeze.

An army of caterers and servants in immaculate uniforms under the command of Sive and Rushton rushed across the lawn to and from the house and marquee.

'You awake?' Vanessa whispered to her sister. She had lain wide-eyed in bed thinking about Glenn, wishing it was her day, her Pappy blessing *her*, everyone excited for her. She had risen early and pulled on a jersey over her Goray and crept into her sister's bedroom.

'Mmmm.' Oriana struggled from a deep sleep. Her mother had insisted she take a sleeping draught the night before, in order, she said, that Oriana might get a decent rest and not look haggard, on this, the most important day of her life.

'I looked pale and wan on my wedding day,' she told Oriana. 'I was so excited, I didn't sleep a wink. I don't want the same thing to happen to you.'

The dress on a pink satin-covered hanger hung now on the wardrobe door. It looked like a costume for a play.

'How do you feel, Ori?' Vanessa asked. She was curious to know. She would be in the same position in a couple of weeks' time.

Oriana rubbed her eyes and sat up. 'Excited, I suppose,' she said. 'Oh 'Nessa, it doesn't seem *real*! It's like

I'm going to act a part. But I'm excited, no question about that.'

It will seem real to me, marrying Glenn, Vanessa thought.

'What about Gavin?' she asked. Oriana blushed. She looked crossly at her sister. 'What about him?' She pushed back her hair. The stylist, Monsieur Pierre, Dublin's finest (Peadar Houlihan from Naas), would arrive shortly to dress it around the wax flowers and diamanté coronet.

'Well, are you *sure*? You know, about Pierce? Are you sure Gavin is not your man? After today you can't change your mind, can you? No divorce in Ireland.'

'Honestly, 'Nessa, you're horrible.' There were two spots of red on Oriana's cheeks. 'Are you deliberately trying to ruin it for me? Are you, you little beast? I don't want to even think about Gavin Fitzjames today. I don't even want to be reminded about his existence.'

'But he'll be here! At the wedding. Gosh, Oriana, I'm really not trying to upset you, honest. I'm just hoping you're not making a mistake. It's not too late yet.'

Oriana shook her heavy hair. 'Yes it is,' she said. 'Look out there.' She pointed to the window. 'I'm afraid it is too late.' She smiled a little sadly at Vanessa. 'You must be careful that you don't miss your chance,' she told her.

Vanessa bit her lip. It was an instruction she didn't understand, as if girls had to watch carefully for a guy who would flash through and if you were not very careful you'd miss him.

Oriana looked suddenly utterly desolate. 'See, Pappy wants . . .'

'It's not what *he* wants, Oriana, it's *your* life.'

Oriana thought a moment, then hopped out of bed. 'No, no, no! It will be wonderful! Oh look, 'Nessa.' She put her arm around her sister's waist. 'They're all down there bustling about. Oh 'Nessa, it's going to be the most wonderful wedding Dublin has ever seen.'

And she was right.

They slipped on slacks and sweaters and went down the hill to the little chapel where Oriana would be married later in the day and where Father Moore gave them Holy Communion.

Communion could not be received if one's fast from the

night before was broken, so the bride and her bridesmaids usually went to the church early and received so that they could fortify themselves for the long wait until the wedding breakfast. It had been known for a bridesmaid, or worse still a bride or groom, to crash to the floor like soldiers on duty in the midday sun, overcome by pangs of hunger accelerated by the tension, the heat and the excitement. No one wanted a catastrophe like that to happen. Not today, not to Brendan Ardmore's daughter.

Rushton drove Brendan and Rosalind to the church, while the girls walked across the dew-drenched fields to eight o'clock mass. The air was chill and Oriana took Vanessa's hand. 'Oh gosh, 'Nessa,' she whispered, 'it's so final.'

'Forever and forever and forever, with *Pierce.* Are you *sure,* Oriana?'

Oriana stopped and shook the dew-drops from the branch of an oak-tree on to her face. The sweet fall of water showered on to her upturned cheeks and she patted the cool moisture into her skin.

'I'm sure,' she said. 'Pierce is sweet to me. He's dear and familiar and *he'll* not beat me!' She laughed and began to run. 'Come on, 'Nessa, race you.' Like when they were kids together. They ran laughing to the little chapel.

It had been decorated the night before. Each pew had a wide white bow and a nosegay of orange-blossom and carnations, ivy and white rosebuds.

It was cold there now, and dark, and Oriana suddenly seized Vanessa's hand, clutching it between her own.

'Scared?' Vanessa asked and her sister nodded. 'You'll be okay. You'll see,' Vanessa consoled her, pressing Oriana's hands warmly.

After Mass they walked back to Dundalgan. The lemon-yellow sun peeped over the mountains, cold and yet cheering up now, illuminating the day. They bathed and had a light breakfast in their rooms. Orange juice and coffee, toast and marmalade, lightly boiled brown eggs and soda bread. Molly Powers, Pierce's cousin, arrived with the third bridesmaid, Oriana's best friend, Melanie O'Brien. The girls ran giggling to the guest-room allocated to them and began to change.

Everybody was dressing. Rosalind in her favourite colour,

pearl-grey, a silk dress and jacket with corsage of pink carnations. Brendan and Sitric in their morning suits.

Sitric went off with Gavin to the church to organise the ushers. He whispered to Vanessa that Oriana had asked him to keep Gavin out of her way as far as possible. 'She doesn't want to see him. Not today' he said and looked at Vanessa eloquently, then shrugged.

Vanessa, Molly and Melanie put on their shell-pink crushed silk-taffeta dresses. Monsieur Pierre coaxed their hair into wondrous puffs and coils around the Juliet caps and added clusters of hair ornaments – ribbons and bud roses and delicate trails of silken ivy.

And at last Oriana's ivory satin was lowered carefully over her elaborate hairdo, which was protected with a chiffon scarf, and she was hooked and eyed into it, her long gloves drawn on, her silken hose smoothed over her long legs, her satin grosgrain shoes slipped on to her small feet and her bouquet of gardenias, camelias, tiny rosebuds and gypsophila handed to her.

Rosalind, refusing to allow the hard lump in her throat to dissolve, took stock of her daughter. Oriana looked utterly delightful and Rosalind shivered as she remembered her own wedding. The ritual dressing-up, the elaborate preparations. The handing over by the father to the new husband of the gift-wrapped sacrifice. And the aftermath of that ceremony. The hateful conquest of her body, the invasion of her privacy and dignity. And now she was preparing her daughter for just such an experience. How would Oriana fare tonight when Pierce, probably ineptly, thrust himself into his virgin bride, as Brendan had plunged into her on what was optimistically called their honeymoon?

'What's the matter, Mother?' Oriana was asking her anxiously. 'Do I look all right?'

Rosalind pushed her unwelcome thoughts away. 'You look radiant,' she said sincerely. 'Quite perfect. Now come along, girls.' She clapped her hands briskly.

Chattering like magpies, twittering with excitement, they seemed to float down the stairs. Brendan met them in the hall. He was bursting with pride and satisfaction. This was exactly what he had planned and it was gratifying that events were proceeding precisely as he ordained. Oriana was marrying into the family he had chosen for her, into power and wealth. She was doing as he wished and she was beautiful, a credit to him. His authority was supreme. What more could he ask for?

The bridesmaids and Rosalind went in the first car and he sat in the Daimler with his lovely daughter. 'I'm proud of you Oriana,' he told her and tears of pleasure sprang to her eyes. Her Pappy was pleased.

For Oriana the day passed like a dream. The sun was high above the horizon bathing the world in golden light. Flowers perfumed the air and opened gloriously under the sun's warmth. She was on her father's arm. The organ pealed the Wedding March. Pappy kissed her cheek and said, 'You are beautiful, Oriana', and her heart near burst with joy.

The bridesmaids like a flock of pale pink doves fluttered behind and around her, bending and tidying her train, reaching out to tuck a stray curl into place, fussing about her. Then suddenly they were behind her, docile, calm, eyes lowered, serious and respectful as her father led her up the aisle.

And there was Pierce. Sober-faced, though they'd drunk themselves silly last night according to Sitric. Pierce taking her hand. Dear, familiar Pierce taking her from her father. Her husband.

Chapter Twenty-four

∾ ᧍

'What are you going to do?' Elana asked her friend. They were sitting in a little rose-covered bower, watching the river sing and chortle over polished grey stones. Behind them stood the house, deserted and silent, and between them and it the marquee bounced with celebration. Across from the girls on the opposite bank a female swan eyed them suspiciously, daring them to approach, the light of battle in her beady black eyes. She was guarding her cygnets, challenging the girls to come any nearer, every now and then shaking threatening wings at them.

Vanessa shrugged. 'Dunno,' she said. 'Glenn asked me, could I stay with you for the next few days? From tomorrow, say?'

'Sure. You know you can. Daddy and Mother love you; you're always welcome, you know that.' She stared at the cygnets. They were trying to be sophisticated like their mother, but, more like clowns, they kept falling, tumbling about, fluffing out their cotton-wool feathers in comic panic.

'Ugly little beggars,' Elana said. As if she heard and understood, the swan drew back her beak and stretched out her wings and shook them menacingly. ''Course you'll be squashed as usual,' she told Vanessa, apologising. 'Not like here.' Why did she always do that? she wondered. Feel she had to apologise for the house to Vanessa even though she knew Vanessa didn't care. 'But you're one of the family' she finished.

'Oh 'Lana, I don't mind. Don't be silly.'

'Why does he want you to stay with me?' Elana asked curiously. There was a dim roar of conversation from the marquee behind them. A group were obviously laughing at a joke. Vanessa glanced over her shoulder. A lone guest, a friend of her father's whom Vanessa vaguely recognised, staggered out of the tent and threw up in the shadows outside. Swaying unsteadily, he looked around and saw them and waved cheerfully, a glass of champagne in his hand.

'Idiot,' she murmured.

The breakfast had been delicious, the food perfect and the wedding cake a work of art. The speeches had not been as dull as such speeches usually are and everyone was saying how the day had gone without a hitch, that it was the wedding of the year, if not the decade.

Yet Vanessa felt uncomfortable. She felt there was something terribly wrong but she did not know what it was. 'I want to escape,' she'd whispered to Elana who'd nodded and the two girls had crept out of the slightly over-heated atmosphere of the marquee into the cool dusk. A lot of alcohol had been drunk, a lot of food consumed and Elana sighed, remarking that the primary purpose had been forgotten.

'In all the celebration,' she told Vanessa, 'no one has mentioned love.'

'The priest did,' Vanessa said.

'But no one listened,' Elana told her. 'I was watching. Oh, how beautiful it is,' she cried and began, 'Love is patient, love is kind. It does not envy, it does not boast, it is not proud.' Elana had a lovely voice and Vanessa shut her eyes to listen. 'It is not rude, it is not self-seeking, it is not easily angered, it keeps no record of wrongs. Love does not delight in evil and ... oh, I forget the rest except the last bit, you know' – she clicked her fingers and squinted her eyes – 'And now these three remain: faith, hope and love. But the greatest of these is love. Oh, it's so beautiful, 'Nessa, it brings tears to my eyes.'

'You just fancy yourself *saying* it,' Vanessa replied tartly and they both laughed. Then Elana looked more closely at her friend. 'Hey, 'Nessa, you're crying.'

'Well, I'm moved,' she said. 'I was thinking of Glenn when you said that. And you know, you're right. I didn't remember the priest saying it. I was miles away.'

'So tell me why Glenn wants you in my house,' Elana said.

138

'You'll keep a secret?'

'When have I ever let you down?'

'Never! Well, 'Lana, Glenn and I, we're getting married.'

Elana screamed and threw her arms around her friend. 'Oh wonderful, wonderful, wonderful!' Then she looked at her friend, dismayed. 'But what about Pappa Bear? *He's* not going to like that.'

Vanessa frowned. 'Glenn wants me to stay with you. I told him about the, you know, Pappy punishing me . . .'

'Yes, I mentioned it to him. He was . . . appalled.' Elana took Vanessa's hand. 'And he's a wise guy. With me you'll be out of the line of fire.'

Vanessa shook her head. 'Just the opposite.' She took a deep breath. 'He wants us both, him and me, to come here to Dundalgan and ask Pappy for his blessing! Can you believe it? Tell Pappy, bold as brass, that we're marrying and he wants his blessing. He's absolutely barmy!'

'Wow!' Elana's eyes were wide. 'Does he know what he's letting himself in for? Has he ever met your father?'

Vanessa shook her head.

'Boy, is he in for a surprise,' Elana breathed.

'He says he's frightened of no one.' Vanessa smiled faintly. 'He's an American Marine and he wants to "do it right" as he puts it.'

Elana laughed delightedly. 'Golly, I wish I could be there, I really do. A fly on the wall. I'd give anything.'

'Shut up, Elana. It's my life you're talking about.'

'Your death more likely! He'll murder you!'

Vanessa covered her face with her hands. 'Oh don't, don't,' she cried.

Elana was instantly contrite. 'Oh 'Nessa, 'Nessa, here love. I didn't mean . . . You know I'm on your side, no matter what. Don't you?' She put her arms around her friend and held her, rocking her slightly on the arbour seat, their skirts billowing out around them.

Fairy-lights began to pop on all around, here, there in the trees, on the stand erected for the dancing, across the lawn, and the band began to play.

'The dancing's begun' Elana breathed and began to sing with the band,

'Oh how we danced,
On the night we were wed,
We vowed our true love,
Though a word wasn't said.
The rose was in bloom,
There were stars in the skies,
Except for the few
That were there in your eyes.'

Elana stood and held Vanessa in her arms and began to waltz across the lawn and the two girls sang together,

'Dear as I held you so close in my arms,
Angels were singing a hymn to your charms,
Two hearts gently beating were murmuring low,
Darling I love you so . . .'

They collapsed on the lawn laughing.

'Look, Vanessa, Oriana's started the dancing. She's opening with Pierce. Oh, it's all so pretty, 'Nessa. So romantic.'

'It looks that way, doesn't it?' Vanessa sighed.

The friends stared across to the raised platform sparkling with lights. Oriana in her wedding dress, her train over her arm, danced with her new husband, the two of them alone. They looked like marionettes as they twirled around and around on the dais.

'It's so mechanical,' Vanessa said and wondered why that thought had struck her.

The stars above them in the midnight blue sky began to come out one by one and the swan folded her wings over her little ones.

Elana said, 'You'll be all right, 'Ness. We'll see to that.'

'I hope so.'

'Come tomorrow. For lunch. It'll only be a shepherd's pie or something like that' – apologising again, damnation she thought – 'I'll get my mother to phone yours and suggest it. That'll allay any suspicions your Da might have. I'll get her to let on like she thinks she's doing your mother a terrific favour. You know, "You must be up to your neck with all the cleaning up and I'll take Vanessa off your hands for a day

140

or two" – like your mother doesn't have masses of servants at her beck and call.'

'My mother never cleaned up in her life,' Vanessa said.

'Well, she doesn't have to. Why should she? My mother wouldn't if there was any way out of it.' She smiled at Vanessa. 'Anyhow, you're very, very welcome.'

'Oh Elana, you're an angel. Will you do that for me? It would be wonderful.'

'You betcha!'

Elana nodded her head back at the newlyweds, circling, circling, circling around the dance floor. 'Where are they going on their honeymoon?' she asked.

'Paris,' Vanessa replied. 'Tonight they stay in that gorgeous hotel in Wicklow. Then Paris.'

'Oh God, 'Nessa, I'd die for Paris. Paris in the spring. It's nearly worth it to marry for that. Oh, she's lucky.'

But Vanessa shook her head. 'I don't think so. She doesn't love him, Elana. I'm sure of it. Oh, she's never said. But I think she loves Gavin.'

'God'n you're joking! Oh cripes, 'Nessa, that's *awful.*'

'She's *fond* of Pierce. She *likes* him. He's like a brother to her.'

Elana shook her head, bewildered. 'Then why did she . . .' Then understanding dawned. 'Oh help! Pappa Bear! She did it to please your Dad.'

Vanessa nodded. 'Yes. I think so. And I'm frightened for her. When all this is over –' she waved her hand across towards the marquee and the dancing area ringed with lights – 'the feasting and the dancing, what will Oriana do?'

'Make the best of it, I suppose,' Elana sighed. 'A lot of people have to do that, 'Nessa.'

'They can't have been in love. They couldn't do it if they'd really been in love.' She looked up at the skies. The stars, the moon – nearly full – cold and remote, flooded the river with silver light.

'Oh 'Lana, how I feel, I couldn't bear anyone but Glenn to touch me. I've been so lucky. And I pity my sister.'

'Well, she'll be cushioned by dough,' Elana remarked. Surrounded by security, comforts, luxuries as the Ardmores were, how could they understand the daily struggle to make ends meet? She said as much to her friend. 'You've got it all,

141

Vanessa, you and Oriana. A beautiful home, lots of money, anything you desire. Marrying a man you're only *fond* of is not the end of the world. Not to me it isn't.'

'You're wrong, Elana. Why do people think money makes everything better?'

'Because it does. Suffering in comfort is better than suffering in poverty.'

'Why do we have to suffer at all?'

Elana took her friend's arm. 'You'll never understand,' she sighed. 'I'm getting cold,' she said suddenly. 'And I want to dance.'

The orchestra was playing a quick-step now. Hogey Carmichael. 'Buttermilk Sky.' Elana sang, 'Can't you see my little donkey an' me. We're as happy as a bumble-bee.' She smiled at Vanessa. 'Let's find a couple of fellas and cut a rug, as Dom says.'

'Gavin is free now. Just think. In May, up that tree –' Vanessa pointed to the massy shadow of the apple tree in the distance – 'I thought I'd died and gone to heaven when I realised Gavin Fitzjames was free. He was available and I could have him. Now I couldn't care less.'

'I'd snaffle him for a dance, 'Ness, only he's not the best dancer in town.'

'Then Dom Bradley—'

'No, I bag him—'

'No, meany, Pappy would love me to dance with him.'

'And you must keep Pappy happy . . .'

And they ran laughing towards where all the dancers now twirled and twisted by the light of the moon.

Chapter Twenty-five

࿐ ࿐

On their arrival at the dance floor the girls could not see Gavin Fitzjames or any of the gang anywhere.

Brendan and Rosalind sat at a table near the platform's edge and beside them were Sean and Molly Powers with Pierce. He lolled uneasily behind his father and mother and Elana could tell, even from across the wide area, that there was an argument going on among the Powerses.

The directors of Ardmore & Son – Regan O'Doherty, Barry Blessington, Roddy Clark (the drunk they'd seen outside), Geraghty and Vincent Laverty – had left their wives chatting together in a bunch of brightly coloured silks, and were huddled, smoking and drinking, near the trestle table where the drinks were being served, laughing suggestively at some male joke. Thomas McIlhinny was not with them. He had greeted his friends with a serious face and a remark about Vie de France. They laughed and told him that this was neither the time nor the place and avoided him after that. This was a wedding after all, a celebration for God's sake, and not at all an appropriate place to discuss business.

A tall youth, slightly sloshed, put his arm around Vanessa's waist and led her on to the floor. Vanessa glanced at Elana and rolled her eyes up to heaven, but went good-humouredly with the boy. He turned out to be a first-class dancer in spite of his tipsiness and swung her around to the rhythm of the quick-step with proficiency. Vanessa gave her friend, watching from the side-lines, a quick thumbs-up sign behind his back and Elana moved away.

She looked back at Sean and Molly Powers. They were talking to Pierce and seemed red-faced and angry. He looked like nothing more than a guilty schoolboy rather than the bridegroom.

Rosalind and Brendan were deep in conversation with Canon Tracey and Leonard Fitzjames, Gavin's father, and were perfectly unconscious of the little argument happening beside them.

Elana circled the floor until she was within earshot.

'. . . ruin the whole thing, Pierce, if you are not careful,' Sean was saying. 'And if you mess up here, don't count on me to bail you out. I'm warning you. We're fed up, both of us, with your behaviour.'

Pierce didn't look at his parents. He had a sulky expression on his face and was staring into space.

'I'm telling you, laddie, I'll not come to your aid, wedding or no wedding,' Sean hissed red-faced at the uncomfortable Pierce. 'You got that? I mean it.'

Pierce sighed resignedly. 'Yes, Da,' he intoned.

Elana wondered what on earth they were talking about. She looked about for Oriana but could not see her. She was probably changing. It was an hour's drive to the hotel in Wicklow and the couple aimed to be there around ten o'clock. 'Just in time to want to retire and *go to sleep,*' Declan O'Doherty, Regan's son and the best man, had said in his speech, winking heavily and eliciting for this feeble remark a roar of laughter, a stamping of feet and hooting from the male guests, while the women blushed and stared at their plates.

Elana glanced at the dance floor. Vanessa was doing some complicated jiving with the tall young stranger. Pierce wandered to the bar and she could see him downing a large Scotch and demanding another.

'I keep telling him to get a hold of himself and settle down with a more realistic grasp of things,' Sean Powers was saying moodily to Molly, 'but that boy's an eejit.'

'I just hope he won't do anything silly,' Molly said weakly.

Elana was surprised by the fragments of the conversation she had heard but thought nothing of it until much later.

She wandered away from the dancing. Some of the guests were sauntering about in pairs under the stars and fairy-lights. In the marquee people still sat at the tables, which were scattered with the debris of the wedding breakfast – half-eaten wedding-cake, coffee and wine stains, cigarette

144

ash, linen napkins thrown carelessly about. Elana glanced in but saw no one she knew. Strangers, relations probably of the Powerses or the Ardmores, out-of-town friends.

Ahead of her lay the house, sleeping in the darkness. She wandered around the deserted drive, fanning herself with her hand. The star-strewn night was hot, or perhaps she was. She turned around the corner of the house where the library was. A cool breeze from the sea met her. It was like a benediction on her brow.

As she stood there letting the gentle wind ruffle her hair she heard what she thought was a moan of pain – one of the cats, or Rascal, the dog – and she glanced into the library through the French windows.

Oriana was sobbing in Gavin Fitzjames' arms. She was making those little moans of pain, clinging to him, pressed against him, her face towards Elana.

'Oh Gavin, what have I done?' she was asking piteously. 'I want you, oh I want you. Gavin, what am I going to do?'

'Come away with me now,' he told her urgently. 'Or leave me alone. I can't stand this, Oriana. You've put me through hell.'

'But Gavin, I—'

'No, Oriana, no. Either come with me—'

'I can't. Don't you see I can't. Pappy—'

'I don't want to hear about your Pappy. He'll not be in bed with you tonight. Pierce Powers will.'

'I can't, Gavin, I just can't.'

He lifted her arms firmly from about his neck and pushed her away from him. 'Oriana, I can't have this, this blowing hot and cold. You contradict yourself every minute. For God's sake, I love you. Now you tell me on your wedding day that you love me, you want me. Well, make up your mind. Come away with me now or leave me alone.'

'I told you I can't.'

'Yes you can, Oriana. Just walk out of here now with me, as you are, to my car, and we'll drive away. Canon Tracey will get the marriage annulled. Simple as that.' Gavin's voice was trembling and he clutched Oriana's clasped hands fiercely in his.

'Oh, don't you see that's impossible?' she cried.

145

'There's no reason why it is impossible. Only reason is, you *won't*.'

'Pappy . . .'

'Ach, your Pappy.' Gavin dropped her hands and turned and looked out of the window, up at the moon. He looked sad and defeated. Elana slunk away. She turned back around the corner to where the lights glowed and the music was.

She was halfway across the lawn when she saw Leonard Fitzjames approaching her. She was suddenly very glad to see him.

'Ah! My dancing partner. The very one. I've been looking for you. I simply must have a dance. Listen, they're playing our tune.'

They were indeed playing a Latin American tune, a samba, and Elana laughed. She took his hand and he led her to the dance floor.

An hour later she saw a glowing Oriana and a smiling Pierce leave in the Daimler for Wicklow.

Chapter Twenty-six

❧ ❧

Rosalind was accurate in her surmise that Pierce would botch up the wedding night. The problem was he'd had too much to drink and his fumbling efforts would have been farcical if the situation had not been so sad.

Oriana fell asleep in the romantic room overlooking a glorious lake with tears on her cheeks and the stale stench of brandy in her nostrils, her husband having ejaculated on her thigh.

The bed was a four-poster, its mattress dented in the middle due to enthusiastic usage by newlyweds. The dent encouraged them to roll towards each other and Oriana kept awakening to find her groom snoring in her face.

Eventually she arose. It was only five a.m. She opened the French window that led to the terrace overlooking the lake and, slipping on her satin *robe de chambre*, one of the many beautiful garments in her trousseau, she stepped out into the still morning. The light wavered with watery shadows, reflections of the lake. There was an expectant hush over the whole place as if Nature held its breath and she shivered in the fresh sharp air.

What had she done? The ox-eyed daisies were opening their petals and the water barely moved, sighing sensuously. The red-start cheeped in the grey dawn. Oriana drew in her breath sadly.

Last night had set the seal on their marriage. Last night had ended her hopes of happiness forever. She could still hear Gavin's voice, 'It's not too late, Ori, but if you walk away from me now it's forever. Pierce is a friend of mine and once you've given yourself to him it's over. Finished.' She smiled bitterly to herself. Given herself to him! That pathetic performance last night had little to do with love

147

or generosity. But that was what she had chosen. Or rather, that was what Pappy had chosen for her, and there was no going back now.

Pierce turned over in the bed, his snoring suddenly stilled. She didn't love him. It came to her now in the chilly dawn, something she'd known all along but did not want to face, did not dare to face with Pappy urging. She did not love her husband. She did not even really like him much. She had been Mrs Powers for less than twenty-four hours and she held her husband in contempt. And she knew why she'd blinded herself to the unpalatable fact. It was fear of punishment. She shuddered. Vanessa and Sitric were so brave. They faced Pappy defiantly. Only she couldn't. She had always been obedient to avoid the beating she would inevitably be subjected to if she didn't do as she was told. She knew she was a coward and that she would do anything to protect herself from the pain. Even marry a man *he* had chosen for her, a man she had tried to persuade herself she loved. How she hated herself for that. How despicable she thought herself.

She tried to drum up within herself a feeling of warmth for Pierce, of sympathy, understanding, but she couldn't. She could not find it in her heart to excuse him, yet she knew that it was not his fault. He deserved better. He deserved her love, her encouragement. Last night he had sensed her lack of warmth, her 'this has got to be put up with' attitude. She had not met him halfway. She had lain there cold as a corpse and let him get on with it, her eyes squeezed shut. He had not responded to her ardour, her love, for she had none to give him. She had lied when she made her vows, she had bent the truth and somehow she had expected him to change that, make something happen, awaken her love, her passion, and take her out of the false position she was in.

He hadn't. He was only human. And he was young and inexperienced. He'd made it worse. He'd proved himself inept, insensitive and crass and she despised him.

And she was stuck with him. This was Ireland and marriage was forever. She remembered Vanessa's voice. And even if she could prove anything, Pappy would not allow her to escape. This sentence was for life.

She pulled the apricot satin around her and sighed again. She'd cried herself to sleep last night, cried into her own shoulder. Pierce had fallen asleep very quickly. Or passed out. On top of her. Pushing him away, straining to get him off her she had wept, wept for her childhood, wept for the loss of her home and family, wept for the destruction of all her romantic illusions. This was not the way it should have been.

It was to have been a wonderful night, sexual love discovered and explored, bride and bridegroom united, fulfilled, and it had been a bungling incompetent wrestling match that ended in painful absurdity. Well, from now on she was going to take charge. There would be no more gauche messing about. She shook her dark hair and, gulping down her feelings of self-pity and resentment, accepted the facts of her life.

They'd make a go of it. She'd make a go of it. But she'd keep her feelings separate. Never again would she be vulnerable. Never again would she look for love. And never again would she be party to that ridiculous mating she'd been subjected to last night. If it meant no children, then so be it. She was not sure that she liked children much. She'd be in charge from now on. She'd be boss.

And Pappy would be pleased. At least that one good thing came out of all this mess. Pappy would be pleased.

The sun was rising. It hovered on the pearl-grey horizon, a blur of gold. They'd take a boat on the lake today. She liked boats. She'd tell Pierce that she'd like a boat. Pappy had given them the house in Foxrock so Sean Powers could give them the boat. She'd like a summer house, a holiday home in Greystones as well. Perhaps then she'd be satisfied.

She thought of Vanessa and for a moment the pain that shot through her numbed her. Vanessa was in love. So much in love. And it showed. Yet she was here after one of Dublin's most stylish weddings, empty and frustrated, feeling more alone than ever before.

But Pappy would be pleased. Pappy was satisfied with her and furious with Vanessa.

And she had money, as much as she wanted. At least, she thought, that was one more good thing.

Chapter Twenty-seven

⋙ ⋘

The Cassidys lived in a comfortable, semi-detached, three-bedroomed Victorian house in Blackrock. Jack and Adele Cassidy were a warm-hearted couple whose dictum in life was to allow people to be themselves. They were happy and healthy and certainly did not fuss over niceties. They gave their children the space to become individuals, did not try to mould them into a pattern or carbon copies of themselves nor try to impose their views and opinions upon them.

People said they were sadly modern, that they'd live to regret it, whatever 'it' was, but the Cassidys were a warmly united family.

Dominic, their eldest son, was in his first year as medic at the Rotunda Hospital, and Thurlough, their second son, was making his mark as a journalist on the *Irish Times*. Their only daughter, Elana, was in the Bank of Ireland, College Green. They were justly proud of their children and faintly surprised that they had turned out so well.

The children still lived at home. Adele tried to shoo them off to flats of their own, to a bedsit or digs, not because she wanted rid of them, but because she felt she ought to, but they were happy where they were and did not want to move. They were not fuelled by a sense of restriction or the need to rebel.

They welcomed Vanessa with open arms. When she stayed with them she slept on a camp bed in Elana's room and mucked in with the family. Far from feeling deprived of the luxury Elana knew she was used to, Vanessa relaxed in the Cassidy household. She felt as if a burden she had been carrying was removed from her shoulders and she could let go.

It was a rumbustious, boisterous, good-natured existence

so unlike the discipline and formality at Dundalgan and if Vanessa could have swopped she would. The ordered and strict menage she was used to gave her no feeling of closeness, of family, of being okay no matter what, while the turbulent Cassidy family home, overcrowded, untidy and servantless except for Matty, made her feel warmly part of something infinitely precious yet casually taken for granted.

'And how was the wedding?' Adele pushed the dishes from the breakfast table in the dining-room through the hatch to Elana who collected them in the kitchen and put them in the sink where Matty was washing up.

Matty, strictly speaking, was a maid of all work but the Cassidys treated her as one of the family. Tall, gaunt, she wore the innocence of a devout child around her like a cloak. She fitted into the family, grateful for their kindness. She had been a homeless orphan when Dr Cassidy found her and brought her home with him and she adored him. But then everyone adored Dr Jack. Matty did the heavy work, helped with the cooking, but her favourite task and something she looked upon as an honour was cleaning the doctor's surgery. Her whole life was a desire to please.

Jack Cassidy was a tall earnest man intent on his mission to help as many people as he could in his journey through life. Always busy he had rushed out and left them, having gulped down his cup of tea and taken his toast with him. He had home visits before eleven o'clock surgery. He was permanently busy and yet he always had time for his wife and children. Adele said that though he constantly *looked* tired he had more staying power than a plough-horse.

Dominic had gone off to the hospital, a picnic basket of food in the back of his bike with instructions from Adele to phone her if he ran out. He'd be in the Rotunda for a week on the wards and wouldn't get home until the weekend.

It was the Monday after the wedding. Sunday, as instructed, Adele Cassidy had phoned Rosalind Ardmore and asked if Vanessa could come to stay. Rosalind, unable to believe that her daughter would defy her father yet again after her chastisement, agreed. She was worried about Sitric, who had passed out down by the river and lain there all Saturday night only to be discovered Sunday morning by Rushton, damp

151

and unconscious in the dew. He had a fever along with his hangover and Brendan was outraged, his fury diverted from Vanessa for the time being to his son. So Rosalind was only too glad to have Vanessa taken off her hands for a few days. She trusted Adele Cassidy.

It was a curious relationship. The Ardmores looked down their noses at the higgledy-piggledy existence of Jack and Adele Cassidy. They turned their eyes to heaven when they saw the frayed furniture, the out-of-tune piano, the lack of any apparent orderliness or style in the family's lives. Because Dr Jack had to dash out when summoned, meals were rarely on time and often taken on the run, anathema to Brendan and Rosalind. Also they had no money, a matter for deep shame in the eyes of the Ardmores.

Yet the Cassidys didn't seem to understand that they were supposed to be embarrassed. They did not seem to comprehend that not to be able to pay your way was a sign of appalling failure.

Once when Rosalind asked if Elana would like to join the Country Club with Vanessa, informing Dr Jack that the annual fee was only twenty pounds, Dr Jack had horrified her by bursting out laughing and replying unselfconsciously, 'Not a chance, Rosalind. Haven't got it! I'm strapped for cash at the moment. Aren't we all? Twenty pounds! That's a heck of a lot. And the Country Club? Who needs it!'

Rosalind had been shocked to the very core. She had never really forgiven him for his dismissive attitude to things she thought of as terribly important, his casual attitude to that sacred commodity money. She could not understand why he loathed and never went to the parties, the Country Club, the Tennis or Golf Clubs. The whole social whirl which she saw as the marker of success in this life and which was essential to her he found trivial and did not take the trouble to conceal his indifference.

She decided he was ignorant, poor man, and unsophisticated, God help him. But for some reason she respected the family, though she was not sure why. She trusted them even though they had, in her eyes, no stability, no style, no power.

Vanessa was steadfast in her friendship with Elana. Dr Jack, everyone agreed, had integrity and worked hard among the poor, often not getting paid, which Rosalind thought foolhardy of him.

'There are those you cannot help,' she told Vanessa. 'They're lazy and stupid and Dr Jack is an idiot to waste his time on them.'

'Oh Mother, how can you say that? He does so much good, helps so many people.'

'And for nothing! Something for nothing is worth exactly that, nothing. If he insisted on being paid, those lazy louts would *have* to find work in order to settle up with him. Don't you see? As it is they take advantage and he spoils them.'

So, because of the girls' friendship the families tolerated each other uneasily. Not however to the extent of being invited to each other's parties. The Ardmores found the Cassidys' do's boring and unfashionable and not a little unsettling as Dr Jack might at any moment be called away. And the Cassidys found the Ardmores' events overwhelmingly stilted and formal and frankly a waste of time. 'A lot of people talking banalities, eating too much and drinking too much, wasting a great deal of money that could be spent helping the less fortunate,' was Dr Jack's summary of a typical Ardmore event.

So they had not been expecting to be invited to the wedding at Dundalgan, although Adele was naturally enough curious.

'It was the event of the season!' Elana shouted from the kitchen.

'The event of the year!' Vanessa cried.

'The event of the *decade*!' Elana screamed.

'Hush up, 'Lana,' Adele admonished. 'You'll wake the dead.'

'Go'n sit down an' I'll get ye some fresh tay,' Matty said. 'Go'n get owa my way, Miss Elana.'

'The style was fantastic! You'd've *died*!'

'Oh dear, I hope not. Don't use superlatives, Elana,' her mother smiled at her. 'Youngsters today exaggerate everything.'

Elana came into the room and sat at the table with Vanessa and her mother.

The room was dark. Adele constantly said she wanted to redecorate it but it was never the right time and they never

153

had, as she put it, 'a lump sum to cover the expense'. The wallpaper was wine-coloured and the table a huge heavy Victorian piece. They had all their meals here and it was a gloomy room but that did not dampen the family's good humour.

Matty brought the teapot in and some fresh cups and the women sat around the table sipping their tea and chatting. They were supposed to be doing other things, but that never bothered the Cassidys. They rolled with the flow, broke the morning and took the time to sip and talk. And this was what Vanessa loved about them. This could never, ever happen at Dundalgan.

'I bet Oriana looked gorgeous,' Adele remarked. 'She's very lovely, your sister.'

'Only divine,' Elana said and her mother shook her head. 'The perfect bride.'

'Only . . . only . . .'

'What Vanessa?' Adele prompted.

'Only I'm so terribly afraid she's not going to be happy, Aunt Adele. That wedding was a farce, you ask me. She's only trying to please Pappy.'

'That father of yours . . .' Adele began, then shrugged. She was only too aware that families defended each other, were loyal to each other even when there was discord, and she did not want to put Vanessa in an awkward position.

'That's what we want to talk to you about, Mam. That's why 'Nessa is here.'

'Well I guessed there was *something* up. All that conspiracy.' Adele looked quizzically at Vanessa. 'But if you think I'll help you defy your Pappy, Vanessa, then you've come to the wrong person.'

Vanessa's eyes flew startled to Elana, who protested, 'It's not that, Mam. We'd not ask you to do *that* . . .'

Adele raised an eyebrow. 'No? Wouldn't you just?'

'I'm afraid that's precisely what we're going to do, Aunt Adele.' Vanessa looked with an agonised face at the older woman.

'Vanessa has fallen in love with . . .'

Adele put her hands to her face. 'Oh no! I don't want to hear this. I'm not going to get involved . . .'

154

'But Mam, listen. Vanessa has fallen in love and her Pappy won't have it.'

'Well, that's his business, Elana. We mustn't interfere. Perhaps this fellow is very unsuitable.'

'You know the reason Mr Ardmore had forbidden her to see him?'

'He's forbidden her? Silly man! It's the one way to guarantee they'll . . . oh Lord, Elana. I give up, what's the reason?'

'Because he's a sergeant. Because he's not an officer. Because he's a sergeant in the American Marines.' Elana looked at her mother, defying her to excuse this unbelievable behaviour. Adele glanced from one to the other. Vanessa stared at her, her heart in her eyes, and Adele's heart suddenly overflowed with love for the two young things, so outraged, so indignant at the unfairness, so vulnerable, and she shook her head gently. They were so innocent about life, so ignorant of the hurdles they'd have to surmount, so unaware that life was *not* fair.

And that silly man, cocooned in his monied world, hadn't a clue how to deal with his lovely child.

She touched her daughter's cheek gently, then took Vanessa's hand.

'Well now,' she said. 'That does seem a trivial class of a reason to be against someone.' She looked at them, smiling. 'And what can I do about it to help you?'

Elana glanced at Vanessa and then at her mother. She took her mother's hand in hers and made a face. 'Gosh Mam, this is difficult. 'Nessa doesn't want me to tell you this, but I think you ought to know.'

'Well, what?'

'He beat her again,' Elana said. Adele stared at them. At first they thought she hadn't heard for her face was blank, devoid of all emotion. But she had heard all right. She was so full of anger that she dared not speak. It outraged every fibre of her being that that great bully should subject his daughter, his sensitive and sweet child, to such an outrage.

'Good God,' she eventually said. Then swallowed and asked, 'Who is this young man?'

'Glenn . . . Glenn Carey. That's his name.' Vanessa's eyes glowed as she pronounced the beloved's name.

'Ah, Billy Monks' friend,' Adele remarked. She saw Vanessa's surprise. 'Billy's taken Elana out a few times. He's been here. Nice man. I should have guessed.'

'Oh! Oh yes, well, Glenn wants to marry me. But he insists we do it right. He wants to go to Pappy with me and ask his blessing.'

'Brave boy,' Adele remarked wryly.

'We love each other so,' Vanessa said.

Adele looked at the intense face and raised her brows. 'That serious?'

Vanessa nodded emphatically. 'Oh yes, Aunt Adele. The minute I saw him I knew he was the one. The only man I'll ever love.'

'Well that's a sweeping statement if ever I heard one,' Adele said dryly.

'No, but it's true, Mam, honest,' Elana interrupted. 'I was *there*. I *saw*. Her eyes went wide . . . like saucers.'

'Well, I must say! However, he sounds very honourable to me. He's made of fine stuff, to insist on asking your Pappy for your hand. It's an honourable attitude.' Adele looked at the two girls. 'So, the situation is, you think you've met Mister Right—'

'I *know* I have.'

'And your Pappy has forbidden you to see him. And he beat you . . . I can't believe . . .'

'Oh Mam, you know it's true. He's done it before.'

Adele nodded. 'Yes. It's incredible, but, well, let's see. It's discrimination because of class and nationality . . .'

'Oh Mam, be serious.'

'I am.'

'And creed,' added Vanessa.

'What?'

'Class, nationality and creed. He's Episcopalian.'

'Oh, that's the worst!' Adele tutted, smiling.

'No, Mam. Be serious, please.'

Adele thought that if she took too serious a tone she'd weep.

'What do you want me to do?' she asked.

'Just be there,' Vanessa told her. 'I've a feeling things may get nasty with my father when Glenn asks him if he can marry me.'

156

'I think,' Adele supplied, 'I think your father will be furious. There'll be no holding him. He'll be outraged. He'll say no and ask him to leave and tell you to go to your room as if you were five years old. Then what will you do?'

'Well, I won't go to my room,' Vanessa said with finality. 'That's for sure. I'll leave with Glenn.'

'He'll never let you back,' Adele told her. 'Are you sure you know what you're doing?'

'Oh, I've never been more certain. I'll go with Glenn,' Vanessa told her with dignity. 'And then, that's the problem. If that happens can I come here, Aunt Adele?'

Adele looked at Vanessa's eager face. It was full of love, so vulnerable in her wide-eyed expectation. She squeezed Vanessa's hand in hers,

'Of course, my dear. You know you can. There's always a place for you here.'

And what pleasure it will give me to thwart that violent, disagreeable and silly father of yours, she thought. What great pleasure.

Chapter Twenty-eight

◈ ◈

When Vanessa returned to Dundalgan a couple of days later it was in the passenger seat of Glenn Carey's Riley, Glenn beside her behind the wheel.

They parked the car in front of the house. Vanessa took her overnight case from the back seat of the car and the two came up the front steps together.

Rosalind at her bedroom window drew in a sharp breath and put her hand to her heart.

Brendan would have a fit if that American set foot in Dundalgan. She'd have to get rid of him before her husband caught sight of him. She hurried out of her room, down the stairs, and was just in time to see Rushton, an expression of bewilderment on his face, usher them into the music room.

Rosalind stood a moment outside the door to catch her breath, then entered.

Rushton was serving drinks and Vanessa sat in an upright Sheraton chair as if she were a visitor in her own home. The American stood behind the chair, hands on her shoulders – for all the world, Rosalind thought, as if he owned her.

'Mother.' Vanessa rose but her mother waved her back into her chair.

'I think we've met.' Rosalind held out a limp hand to the American. He took it between his own and pumped it in that ghastly enthusiastic American way and Rosalind retrieved it gratefully and shook it gently. He returned to stand behind Vanessa and rest his hands once more on her shoulders.

'We've come to see Pappy,' Vanessa said and her mother suddenly realised that her daughter was terrified.

That was all to the good. Vanessa terrified would be easier

158

to manage than Vanessa defiant. The American, by coming here, had taken Vanessa's courage away.

Rosalind was wondering desperately how to get this man to leave before her husband discovered his presence when the door flew open and Brendan Ardmore stood there taking in the scene. They could not see his face. It was in shadow. They could only see the bulk of him looming and feel the vibrations of fury emanating from him.

Vanessa made as if to rise but Glenn's firm hands steadied her, restrained her.

Rosalind, seeing the gesture, thought, I've underestimated this man. She could think of nothing to say, all social graces deserting her. There were no words in her vocabulary to cover such an eventuality, no polite phrases to cloak the situation in respectability.

But Brendan had no such regard for etiquette.

'Get out of my house!' His voice was shaking and he could barely keep himself under control. But he kept his voice low, almost a whisper, which terrified Vanessa more.

'I told you, Vanessa, this man is not to set foot in Dundalgan. I mean it. Get out.'

'With respect, sir . . .'

'*Get out*! Now!'

'Sir, you *will* hear me,' Glenn also spoke quietly but very firmly. 'Then and then only will I leave.'

The lovely American was calm, Rosalind saw, and unruffled, which gave him the edge. He could pitch his voice further than Brendan's which, Rosalind vaguely surmised, was due to him being a sergeant and having to do that on the parade ground. But the tone was soft. Clear and authoritative.

Brendan had moved across to them. His presence filled the place with a palpable anger. The two men stared at each other across Vanessa's frozen form.

'Say your say, then go,' Brendan barked. He stood, waiting, not trying to conceal his impatience. Glenn swallowed. He could feel Vanessa tremble and he was afraid to take his hands from her shoulders lest she should flee. This was much more difficult for her, brainwashed as she was to obey this man. So Glenn stayed behind her chair, facing the enemy.

159

'I love your daughter, sir, and she loves me,' he said softly, simply. 'I've come here today to ask for your blessing.'

Rosalind could see her husband's face now and was worried. He looked as if he might have a fit. A heart attack. A stroke. Blood pumped under his skin, which turned almost black with apoplectic rage. He couldn't seem to get his breath and she hurried to his side and tried to take his arm but he pushed her roughly away. With enormous effort he controlled himself, breathing deeply, his strangled breaths the only sound breaking the stillness of the room. They all watched him, fascinated.

'I want you to leave now, you . . . whatever your name is.' He was staring at Glenn. 'Get out of my house now and never come back or I'll have the Gardai arrest you as a trespasser.' His eyes widened and for a moment Rosalind thought he looked crazy. 'And take your hands off my daughter,' he hissed.

But Glenn did not do as he was commanded. There was another silence. Vanessa was like a hare caught in a light that blinded and hypnotised her, staring round-eyed from one to the other. Rosalind kept opening her mouth to speak, then shutting it because she could not think of anything remotely appropriate to say. Only Glenn looked calm and relaxed.

'Come here, Vanessa,' Brendan commanded, staring at his daughter. She made another involuntary movement, but again the hands restrained her.

'Let her *go*.' Once again Brendan barked an order that was not obeyed.

'I'm marrying Vanessa with or without your consent, sir. We love each other. But I did you the courtesy of coming here to ask you for your daughter's hand . . .'

'Now *you* listen to *me*.' Brendan's voice was suddenly firm and hard and cold as ice. 'You are *not* marrying Vanessa because you are not worthy even to *touch* her hand. *She* will not marry you because *I* will not permit it. She does as I tell her. You should understand that, Sergeant. Now for the last time will you get out of my house.'

Glenn took his hands from Vanessa's shoulders. She turned and looked up at him and in that moment Rosalind knew that Brendan had lost. It was exactly the same look, a plea for guidance, a trusting query as to what to do next that she had once directed towards her father.

'Come along, Vanessa. Let's go. We did our best.'

Glenn took Vanessa's hand and she rose. Brendan took a sharp breath. 'If you leave this house, my girl, you'll never set foot in it again.'

'No, Pappy. I don't think I'd want to,' she replied sadly.

'I mean it. I'll disown you. Oriana will be my only daughter. This place will be hers and Sitric's.'

'We wouldn't want anything of yours, sir, under the circumstances,' Glenn said, not in anger, simply stating a fact.

Rosalind spoke for the first time. 'Don't go, Vanessa,' she pleaded. 'We love you. Let's talk about it, perhaps reach some compromise. Don't act hastily.'

'Let her go, Rosalind. There'll be no compromise. She's betrayed me. This family. I'll not have her under this roof.'

'Please, Brendan, don't send her away. She's our daughter . . .'

Vanessa turned to her mother, whose tears had more effect on her than all her father's blustering. 'Mother . . . please . . .'

'Let her go,' Brendan cried loudly, catching his wife's arm in a fierce grip.

Glenn said, 'Let's go, honey,' and he guided Vanessa out of the room.

'Don't come back here. Ever.' Brendan followed them into the hall, shouting after them. 'You're not welcome here!'

Rushton scuttled down into the kitchen. Rosalind was openly weeping, something the servant had never before seen. She kept murmuring, 'No, no, no, Brendan. She's our flesh and blood.'

They heard the engine start and the scrunch of the wheels on the gravel as Glenn turned the car in the drive. Brendan looked at his weeping wife, but he did not really see her. 'I never want to hear her name mentioned in this house again,' he said bitterly. 'Never.' They could hear the purr of the engine as the car drove away and then there was silence.

Chapter Twenty-nine

∽ ⊙∾

Adele was a fascinated and sympathetic audience. She sat in the front living-room with Glenn and Vanessa and listened riveted as they recounted what had happened.

Adele liked Glenn. Never able to resist good-looking men she fell for the American at first glance and determined to help the young couple all she could.

Elana was at the bank and would not be back until later.

'Vanessa will stay here of course,' Adele told Glenn.

'Oh, I'll ask you, ma'am, to look after her well. She's upset,' he said looking at her with concern. 'I'd check her into a hotel, save you the trouble, only I want her to be with friends.'

'Absolute rubbish!' Adele told him firmly. 'She's like family. Look, it's no trouble, Glenn. We've known 'Nessa all her life. We love her like a daughter.' She looked at the young man seriously. 'What are you going to do?' she asked.

'Well' – he frowned – 'I guess the first thing is to see the padre. I'll get the powers-that-be to hurry along the papers. I've already set it in motion. Then we'll get married. Rent an apartment in Dublin until my tour of duty is over. Then home to the States.'

Vanessa was clinging to him. She held on to his hand as if it were a lifebelt.

'I've taken nothing from home,' she told Adele. 'I'll have to borrow some clothes from Elana.'

She was, Adele could see, in a very distressed state. It could not have been easy for her, leaving Dundalgan like that. Just driving off from the home of her childhood.

'We have plenty of everything here, 'Nessa love,' Adele reassured her. 'Not as smart maybe as at Dundalgan, but

162

functional.' Then she touched Vanessa's cheek. 'Why don't you follow Matty upstairs and she'll sort some things out for you.'

Vanessa did as she suggested.

'You've asked a lot of her, you know,' Adele said to Glenn.

Glenn nodded. 'I want to do it right,' he said.

'She's going to find it difficult, poor wee thing,' Adele told him. 'She wouldn't be human if she didn't have a reaction.'

'I know, I know. Don't think I don't understand. But don't you see, it was necessary. Do you think I would have taken her out of there if there was any alternative?'

'No, I'm sure you wouldn't.'

Vanessa returned, carrying a fine lawn nightdress.

'You ought to let your mother know you're safe with us,' Adele told her. Vanessa looked startled.

'Don't worry, pet, it will be all right. I'll call her. If your father answers the phone I'll put it down. But we must let your Mam know. She'll worry herself sick otherwise.'

She glanced at Glenn who nodded.

'Pappy never answers the phone, Aunt Adele. He always lets Mother. He says the phone is for women's gossip. Man's talk is over a cigar and a drink at the Club.'

'Well if he *does* I'll put it down, as I said, and if it's your mother I'll reassure her that you're with me. That will put her mind at rest.'

'I want this done right,' Glenn said again. 'So no one can ever point the finger. No hiding. All above board.'

Adele smiled. 'We'll see it's as you wish, Glenn. We'll help you.'

'Aunt Adele, can we get married from your house? Is that a lot to ask? It would be a very quiet affair.'

'Of course, my dear child. It won't be a grand do like your sister's . . .'

'We wouldn't want that,' Glenn protested. 'But nice. A quiet nice kinda breakfast. Champagne. Stuff like that. I got the dough,' he told Adele. 'I'm not short of dollars. Been overseas a long time. Saved a lot.' He spread his hands. 'Nothing to spend it on.' And he smiled his dazzling smile. 'I truly don't want you to be out of pocket about this.'

Vanessa turned to him trustingly. 'It'll be okay, honey,' he told her. 'You'll see.'

'Poor wee lamb,' Adele talked to her as if she was three years old. 'You'll be safe here.' And she hustled her upstairs to bed for a rest after she had bid Glenn a fond farewell.

Vanessa was actually less upset than they supposed her to be. She had been in an unnatural state since the night she met Glenn and leaving her home and the overwhelming presence of her father appeared as a natural step towards her life with the man she loved. She had complete confidence that everything would be all right.

Billy Monks was not so sure. 'You reckon you know what you're doin'?' he asked his friend. 'You've gotta take her back home; who knows where we'll be stationed! Listen, Glenn, she's kinda grand, isn't she? Her family is swell folks, and her Pop is right. She's kinda outa our class.'

Glenn knew moments of grave doubt but he was a simple, dogged kind of guy and he was set on a course and was not going to be deflected. He'd given his word. He'd undertaken to marry Vanessa Ardmore and that was what he would do. He had a soldier's mind – the ability to take one step at a time without too much introspection or reasoning why. What had to be done would be done. There was no alternative. His job now was to get the necessary clearance and papers and make arrangements.

He was still the knight in shining armour. His sense of fair play was outraged, and Brendan Ardmore's cruelty had to be curtailed. His chivalry had been aroused. He was a knight rescuing a damsel in distress. How dare that savage beat his eighteen-year-old daughter? How dare he forbid her to see the man she loved? How dare he order an American Marine out of his house like some Victorian grandee? As if he, Glenn Carey were garbage. How dare he? It was monstrous. It was not to be countenanced and he was going to save her.

She awakened a protective tenderness within him that he understood was love. And there was, too, that tussle with the old man, that gladiatorial struggle, youth defying old age. He had said 'you can't' and Glenn muttered 'watch me'.

Elana was delighted. 'We'll sort it, 'Ness,' she told her friend that night, sitting up in bed in her cotton night-dress. 'Matty gave you my best one,' she told Vanessa, who immediately began to take it off. 'Oh no. Keep it, 'Nessa. It's just that she thinks you are worthy of only the best.' The girls giggled and talked far into the night.

'I love him so,' Vanessa told Elana. 'Oh 'Lana, I think I might die of it.'

'Well, much good that'll do you,' Elana replied. She wished suddenly that she loved someone that much. 'Mother said you could be married from here.'

'I'll have to decide what to wear . . .'

'We'll go to Brown Thomas at the end of the week . . .'

'And I'll have to cash a cheque. I don't have much money, 'Lana, and Pappy sure as hell won't give me any now.' For an instant her eyes filled with tears then she brushed them brusquely away.

'Oh come on, Vanessa, what are you tearful about? You've escaped.'

'It's not that, Elana. I'm just sad it had to be like that. I feel, well, displaced.'

'Nonsense. This has always been a second home to you. Now go to sleep and look on the bright side. You'll be marrying Glenn ever so soon and that's what you wanted, isn't it?'

Vanessa kept reaching for things that were not there. Her address book. Her make-up. Her diary. Her compact. She had the feeling that she was in a waiting room and that at any moment someone would tell her she could go home now.

'I sort of feel I'm marking time,' she told Elana.

Glenn found them a flat in Haddington Road. It was small and pretty. Two rooms, kitchen and bathroom. The furniture was basic, cheap but functional. The curtains and chair covers attractive and gay, but would horrify Rosalind. The rent was £3.30/- a week and Glenn and Vanessa were delighted with it.

If Vanessa thought it cramped she did not say so, content to let Glenn organise everything.

Neither of them even thought of moving in until they were legally married, even though they planned to be very soon. For Glenn it was a matter of doing it right. For Vanessa the idea simply never entered her head.

Chapter Thirty

⌒∽ ∾⌒

Vanessa's wedding was, as predicted, a very different affair to her sister's. There was no white model bridal gown flown from London. There were no elaborate decorations or bouquets or bridesmaids. There were no ushers in top hats. No marquee. No dancing.

They were wed at the small side altar in St Benedict's in Morehampton Road. They could not marry at the main altar because Glenn was not a Catholic. On the side altar there were two pretty flower arrangements gifted by the Cassidys and that was as much as they felt appropriate to the modest occasion.

Vanessa wore her blue New Look suit, the one she'd worn on that first day when she and Glenn met. Cessy had smuggled some of her clothes out of Dundalgan and brought them to her. Vanessa carried a small bunch of wild flowers. She wore a small blue hat with a veil just over her nose. The veil had blue velvet spots and Glenn thought it the cutest thing he had ever seen. He wore a grey suit, a white shirt and a dark blue tie.

There was a small gathering of friends around the Cassidys' dining table where they lunched off chicken and ham salad and the wedding cake which was made by Matty. On the icing she had spelled wedding incorrectly. Weding. No one told her. They drank champagne and they laughed a lot and their laughter was joyous and unconfined. Vanessa felt loved and protected.

To Vanessa's surprise Sitric dropped in. The Cassidys welcomed him and he accepted a glass of champagne.

'I came, sis. Had to wish you luck. Couldn't let the day go by without one of the family putting in an appearance.'

Vanessa kissed him and there were tears in her eyes. 'Thank you, Sitric. It is appreciated.'

'Mother would be here except for Pappy,' he told her. 'She sent a message. She said "Be happy". She told me to ask you to let her know where you are and she'll write.' He glanced up, puffing his Balkan Soubranie, filling the small room with smoke. Vanessa looked at his pale, delicate face. His eyes were, as usual, half-shut and he was dragging on his cigarette, gulping down the smoke.

'Are you all right, Sitric?' she asked when after a nibble of Matty's cake and a couple of glasses of champagne he rose to go.

'I'm as all right as I'll ever be, pet,' he told her. 'I don't like being here much,' he said. Vanessa flushed.

'These are my friends,' she said. 'Just because it's not as grand as Dundalgan . . .'

He laughed. She looked at him in surprise. He laughed again. Sitric hardly ever laughed. He took her by the shoulders.

'Oh no! I didn't mean *here*. I meant I don't like being alive. On this planet. I don't like life, most of the time. I don't like people much and I hate my family.'

'Sitric!' Tears sprang to her eyes, sudden and strong. 'How can you say that?'

They were standing alone together in the Cassidys' tiny hall. Sitric leaned against the wall, his head back, his eyes closed. 'Oh God, Vanessa, how could anyone even *like* them? My father is a monster who has birched the life out of me. My mother lets him. My sister, Oriana, is a wet who thinks Pappy is God and happily lets him ruin her life. Only you . . . dear sweet Vanessa, have any sense or courage or dignity.'

'But Sitric, all fathers have to discipline . . .'

'No they don't, Vanessa. It's a myth we've been fed.'

'Are you dreadfully unhappy?' she whispered.

'Of course I am.'

'Are you on drugs?' She looked at him anxiously, fearfully. Again he smiled. 'What a little innocent you are. No, I'm not on drugs.' He touched her chin. 'But then, I wouldn't tell you if I was, would I? I'm obsessed, 'Nessa. That's all. I'm obsessed with an impossible love that is eating me alive.'

He kissed her on the forehead. 'Now I've got to go or Mother'll have a fit. She told me to pop in and pop out.

167

Her words. She's terrified Pappy'll find out where I've been and have to punish me . . .'

'Oh no, Sitric. Not still?'

Sitric shook his head. 'No. Not since I rousted him. I turned on him, 'Nessa, as I told you, and he looked terrified of me. But, and I don't expect you to understand this, that frightened me more. I left the room, scared silly because I'd defeated my father. Sometimes I dream, 'Nessa, that I grab the birch from him, as I did that last time, and that I beat him to death with it.' Sitric rubbed his hands over his face as if to rid himself of some irritation. 'I enjoy every lash. I relish every blow. I enjoy his dying.' He looked at her, his eyes full of fear. 'That's not normal, 'Ness, is it? That's not a nice dream to have?'

'Don't do it though, will you, Sitric? It would achieve nothing.'

He shook his head again and smiled at her crookedly. 'No. He's birched the guts out of me. It would take more courage than I possess to kill him.' He sighed. 'But never mind me. You have a happy life, pet. You deserve it. You broke away, told him to stuff it. I know the courage that took.'

'Yes, but I had Glenn beside me,' she said.

'It still took more courage than I've got,' he said and kissed her again. 'Bye now.' He opened the front door and left.

It was the only sombre note in the sunny day.

Afterwards, while they did the washing up, Elana told her mother that Vanessa's wedding, though not half as grand or expensive as Oriana's, was a much happier event.

'Get away wi' you, 'Lana. You're having me on! Sure we couldn't compete with the magnificence of the Ardmores!' Adele shook her head in disbelief, certain her daughter's kind heart had prompted her to reassure her mother by wildly exaggerating.

But Elana frowned. 'No, Mam. I mean it. Oriana's do meant nothing. It was simply a display of wealth. It was cold, well, sort of impersonal. The ceremony far outweighed the *feeling*. And, Mam, I heard her tell Gavin Fitzjames she loved him that day after they'd taken their vows, after she'd married Pierce.'

Adele nearly dropped the plate, one of her best. Her eyes

were saucers as she looked at her daughter. 'Did ye now? Never!'

'Yes, Mam. Well, I'm not one hundred per cent sure she said she loved him, but she was in his arms in the library at Dundalgan, and he asked her to go away with him an' she just married. You could see she wanted to, but' – Elana shrugged – 'she didn't.'

'Where is she now?'

'In Paris with Pierce on their honeymoon, Mam.' She rested her arms on the sink and looked at her mother. 'Oh Mam, today was so different. So beautiful. Did you *see* the way Vanessa and Glenn looked at each other when they took their vows?'

Adele nodded. 'It was very moving. Reminded me of my own wedding. Reminded me of me and Jack.' Her love for her husband had not diminished over the years but rather had increased. 'They sounded as if they really meant what they said.'

'Well, Oriana and Pierce *didn't*,' Elana announced.

There was no honeymoon for Glenn and Vanessa. They went directly to Haddington Road, to the little flat that was to be their home.

A few days later Elana told her mother that she'd heard that Oriana and Pierce had returned from their month's honeymoon in Paris and set up house in Foxrock.

'Has Vanessa heard from them since they came home?' Adele asked.

'Nope. Not a sausage,' Elana told her. ''Course, Oriana had the excuse that they were in France for Vanessa's wedding. So they couldn't come.'

'Do you think she would have if she'd been here?' Adele queried.

'Haven't a clue, Mam. Oriana always does what Pappy asks and Pappa Bear said none of the family were to go.'

'Sitric did. I was surprised to see him here, I must say. He's a very strange boy. Oh Elana, all that ill-will would upset me so. I don't think I could live with it if my family was splintered like the Ardmores.'

'It's weird, Mam. Vanessa said Glenn met Rosalind Ardmore in O'Connell Street.'

'No! Just like that?'

'Yes. Bumped into her beside the Pillar.'

'Well, go on. What happened?'

'Like strangers they were. Glenn said she seemed terribly uncertain how he'd act towards her. She needn't have worried. Glenn is always polite and courteous.'

'And?' Adele was burning with curiosity. She could not imagine Elana being married to a man she had never really spoken to.

'He greeted her as if they were old friends. Asked her how she was. Mrs Ardmore was very embarrassed, but very anxious to know about Vanessa, and Glenn said he reassured her. "I'll take care of her, never fear" he said, and he added, "And remember, Mrs Ardmore, there is no animosity on my side."'

'Bet that made her think,' Adele said. 'Oh Elana, I do admire him. That was such a magnanimous gesture, the spirit of generosity.'

'He told her she was welcome any time at Haddington Road. Then he said goodbye and left her standing under the Pillar looking, he said, very forlorn.'

When Adele told her husband of the incident, Dr Jack remarked that it was easy to be magnanimous when you've won. 'He's carried off the prize,' he said. 'He's stolen away the forbidden fruit. He can afford to be generous.' Then he'd chucked her under the chin and winked. 'Don't tell me. Glenn is different. A saint. Oh Adele, you've never been able to resist a good-looking man.' And he laughed and she was glad that she had married him.

'Know something, Jack,' she said, 'I'm glad we're not rich. Everyone I know who is has the kind of problems I don't like.'

'Well, that's good,' he replied. 'I'm glad you feel that way, because we're not ever likely to be.' And he gave her that smile that never failed to touch her heart and told her he loved her.

Chapter Thirty-one

❦ ❧

Vanessa and Glenn settled into their Haddington Road apartment and things did not go at all well. There was a dismal reaction to the excitement of running away and marrying. Suddenly it was the morning after, glamour gone, reality setting in.

The first blip in the fabric of their lives was Vanessa's fear, or seeming fear, of sex.

After the wedding and the breakfast, full of love and champagne, they had come to the little apartment and all Glenn wanted was to make love to his new bride. Urgently, desperately, he wanted to have and to hold, envelope her body and soul. But she seemed stiff in his arms suddenly. He petted her, brushed her nipples, kissed her softly, embraced her gently, not too demandingly, but to no avail.

She tried to respond. She forced herself to kiss him back, to pretend she was enjoying herself, but her reactions were forced and frozen and he was not fooled by them.

'What is it, honey?' he asked anxiously.

She shook her head. 'Don't know,' she whispered.

So he released her. 'It'll be okay in time,' he said.

She felt extraordinary. This little cramped place they were in, where was it? This man, who was he? She wanted to cry but could not. She felt frozen in a kind of dream, suspended above herself and frightened.

He was a man, and suddenly unfamiliar. She wanted so much to please and was terrified that she would not. What would he say when he saw her without make-up? Would he be horrified and turn away from her in disgust? And her body. It was not like Hedy Lamarr's or Jennifer Jones'. It was, she thought, ordinary. When he saw her body, what then? No one had ever seen her naked. Well, only Oriana

171

and Oriana made fun of her and said she had fat thighs. Did other women look like her? What if she was peculiar, what then? Oh, it was perplexing and she had no answers.

Each night like a runner in a race she tore off her clothes while Glenn was in the bathroom, dived into her nightdress as if she'd reached the finishing line. Then she plunged into the double bed and lay there, insecure and confused. She'd turn to him, loving him, wanting to welcome him, but when his arms went around her and she felt his maleness near her, try as she might not to, she froze.

Glenn was patience itself. Although dismayed by the turn of events he tried to understand and did not rush things. But there was an awkwardness between them.

And during the day she was in an even worse predicament. She did not know how anything worked and there was no one to help her. She was used to Sive and Cessy and Imelda. They prepared the food and did the shopping. Faced with a bare cupboard Vanessa was totally ignorant of how to fill it, and deeply ashamed of her ignorance. And, like her father two decades earlier, she was afraid to admit her ignorance. And Glenn could not fathom what disturbed her for she would not tell him. She burst into a storm of tears in the kitchen and he could get nothing out of her. All he could do was hold her in his arms and soothe her as he would a frightened puppy and wonder what he'd gotten himself into.

'What is it, honey? What's the matter?'

'Nothing, Glenn. Nothing. I'll be fine in a minute.'

There were some shops in Baggot Street and she went there armed with a string shopping bag she had found on the back of the kitchen door. She bought tea and coffee, sliced bread and butter and marmalade, milk, eggs, cheese, biscuits and salt and pepper. It was a little local huckster shop and the quality was not too good, the groceries not too fresh, but she was proud of her achievement. It was a first step.

She was not a cook. Panic took over and she usually served the food undercooked, almost raw. This was not too disastrous when she did steak and chips. The meat was very rare indeed, but that was not a tragedy. Glenn smothered it with mustard and quite enjoyed it. But chicken was a whole other matter. Semi-cooked chicken was not at all

172

palatable. Prawn chowder with frozen prawns floating on onion-flavoured milk was worse.

Glenn took to eating at the Embassy and its environs on the pretext of work.

It was the arrival of Miss Venables into their lives that improved the situation and solved a lot of their problems.

Elana Cassidy had a limited idea of what was going on. She was aware of her friend's ignorance. She had been amazed at how little Vanessa actually knew about the art of house-keeping. When she visited Vanessa and watched her friend dithering in the kitchen with the teapot and the kettle she began to sense the depth of her friend's plight and her desperation.

'You're not sure how to make a cup of tea, are you?' she asked calmly, taking the teapot from Vanessa's hands. 'You do *not* put scoops of tea into a cold teapot and fill it with hot water from the tap. Uh-uh.' She filled the kettle, put it on the gas, and when it was boiled, scalded the pot, then put three scoops of tea into it saying, 'One for you, one for me and one for the pot,' and she poured the boiling water on to the leaves. 'Now leave it a few minutes to brew and there you have it.'

'Oh Elana, thanks.'

Elana looked at her friend's strained face. Marriage did not suit her. 'Listen, 'Nessa,' she began, but an angry flush had darkened her friend's cheeks and she looked very upset.

'Now don't start to preach, Elana,' Vanessa cried tensely. 'It's all so new. So strange' – and defensively – 'I'm doing my best.'

'Of course you are,' Elana agreed stoutly, setting a tray with milk and sugar and cups and saucers.

'They're horrid. Not real china,' Vanessa remarked. 'The apartment is fully furnished, which is just as well as yours was the only present we received.'

'Oh come on, 'Ness, you know you don't mind about that.'

'Well, Mother sent me a cheque. For quite a lot of money. And a note. It said, "Be happy darling. I'll work on Pappy." Some hope she has.' Vanessa's face crumpled. 'Oh 'Lana, I miss home so much. I miss Cessy and Ori and . . . oh, everything.'

'Come on now,' Elana said briskly. 'You're bound to feel strange at first.' She picked up the tray, 'Into the living-room with this,' she said and when they were comfortably settled on the chintz-covered sofa she turned to her friend. 'Listen, 'Ness. You know that money your Mam sent? Well, I've got a spiffing idea. Why not spend the money on a helper?'

Vanessa frowned. 'What do you mean?'

'I know a woman called Miss Venables.' Elana hurried on. 'You know how Daddy is always involved with lost souls? Well, he passed Miss Venables on to my mother, which he often does and she tries to find them a slot in life. Well, I think that your apartment might just be Miss Venables' slot in life.'

'Gosh, that's a great idea,' Vanessa breathed. Not to have to work out what was missing from the cupboards, to have someone who would help her.

'She nursed her appalling mother, a tyrant I believe. Her mother had cancer. She was one of Da's patients. Well, all her life Miss Venables has looked after her. Then she died and from the full-time occupation of cooking and cleaning and doing everything for her, she's rattling around, penniless, feeling sorry for herself. It would be perfect, don't you think?'

'But I shouldn't *need* anyone to help me, Elana. I should be able to do it all myself. Everyone else does. There's just me and Glenn and this tiny place.'

'Your talents lie elsewhere,' Elana said hastily. 'And don't try to fool me. You've never done a hand's turn in your life. You *do* need someone, better admit it.' And Elana smiled at her friend. 'You'd be doing Miss Venables a huge favour. Da is worried about her. She's lost her reason for living. When her Mam died there was nothing more for her to do. He's afraid she'll . . . .' Elana rolled her eyes and Vanessa looked shocked.

'Oh, never!'

'Well, you know, 'Ness, her life seems pretty meaningless to her now and . . .'

'Oh, all right, Elana, you've sold the idea.' She smiled ruefully. 'Truth to tell it *would* be an enormous help to me.'

Elana nodded. 'That's what I figured. See,' she added triumphantly, 'two birds with one stone.'

'I just hope Glenn doesn't mind,' Vanessa mused. But she need not have worried. Glenn didn't demur. When he came home to the sharp sweet aroma of Miss Venables' lamb stew that first day and was told his wife had employed her to help in the house, he deemed it politic to make no comment. He simply sat back and asked for a second helping.

Billy Monks ragged him about it. 'Jeez, these Europeans! A maid is what Vanessa's got to cater for your majesty's high-class tastes. C'mon! You're a hometown kid from Wisconsin and you live in a four-roomed apartment, kitchen and bath. C'mon!'

'Cut it out, Billy. Put a sock in it. If she needs this walking skeleton, she gets her.'

Miss Venables was indeed thin. Years of self-sacrifice and tension seemed to have eradicated any spark of vitality, sucked her red blood corpuscles out of her body and rendered her old before her time. She was as lean as a greyhound and she moved around the little apartment quietly. Used to her invalid mother, used to the shrill demands, she had developed over the years a self-effacing shadowy presence and she beavered about doing her jobs efficiently and quietly.

Vanessa, kindness itself, tried to put her at her ease. She admitted her ignorance and elicited an incredulous smile of disbelief covered by both hands to the mouth. Vanessa told her she needed help and the thin woman responded with generosity. She set about helping her new mistress with a will, teaching her what she had assumed everyone knew. Little by little she taught Vanessa and little by little she learned to smile. She had, when she came to them first, jumped every time Vanessa asked her to do something. Used to her mother she expected harsh treatment. It did not come and bit by bit she relaxed. She was like a little brown mouse; brown hair, brown eyes, brown clothes. She was a cowed creature who brought out the maternal in Vanessa, who made her warmly at home and helped her to laugh.

She came every morning at ten, long after Glenn had left the house. She scuttled in, slipped into an empty room and set to. She was very efficient.

When Vanessa asked her to help she decided that the best place to start was the cooking. Miss Venables taught her to make a simple stew, how to poach fish, how to cook vegetables and all the other things she was so proficient at, and about which her employer was so ignorant. It was simple food, simply prepared, but Glenn was no gourmet.

At least once a week Vanessa met Elana for lunch while Miss Venables did jobs Vanessa decided she would never, *could* never learn to do. Like cleaning the bathroom and the lavatory.

Things improved in leaps and bounds. Venny, as Glenn and Vanessa soon began to call her, her full name proving unmanageable, was a treasure. She became a pillar of strength and a mine of information and without her intervention it was doubtful whether the Carey marriage would have lasted the summer. Elana was delighted to have been instrumental in obtaining this treasure for her friend.

'Oh Vanessa, if you knew how delighted Daddy is. He was so worried about her.'

'If you knew how delighted *I* am. I'm thrilled. She has changed my life. I don't know how I would ever have managed without her.'

Sex still presented a grave problem. Their first night of passion was agony for both of them. When at last Vanessa's body melted a little in Glenn's embrace and she relaxed enough to let him enter her he found he could not, it was too painful for her. He felt like he was raping her and he stopped, unable to continue.

They were both ignorant. Glenn's experience had been limited to the Bangkok whores who had played his body like an instrument while he actually did very little. Back home on the farm, Angie had been a more than keen participator in the sexual experimentation they had indulged in before he left to fight the Japanese, although they never actually went the whole way. But it was amateur and they had learned together. He had not had to take the initiative.

When at last he managed to penetrate Vanessa her obvious agony took away any pleasure he may have felt and left him feeling guilty and ashamed of himself as if he had done something dishonourable.

She too felt ashamed; of her pain, of her lack of response. She felt she'd let him down, been inept and clumsy, that she'd failed. And she had no one to talk to. This was not

176

something Elana could get someone to fix for her. She would not talk about this to Elana, it was too personal, too private, and anyway, what would Elana know about it? She was not married.

Their relationship had been utterly romantic, charged by their differences, accelerated by the Ardmore family's disapproval, and now they found it difficult to communicate. They struggled on, aware of those differences now, determined not to allow the family a terrible victory by their failure. They struggled alone and unhelped.

And they quarrelled. 'Why do you wash yourself every time I touch you?' he asked. 'Think I'll contaminate you or something?'

'I don't know,' she'd cry, tears threatening to fall.

'Are you afraid of me? Is that it? Do you know how that makes me feel?'

How could she explain the panic within her? How could she communicate to him that though she loved him so very much some instinct implanted deep in her froze her and through no fault of her own repulsed his ardent foreplay, and that the terrible pain she felt when he tried to come into her left her terrified of making love?

One night she turned to him piteously. 'I think . . . Oh Glenn, I think I'm frigid,' she said.

'Honey, honey, don't cry. Please don't cry. We'll work it out. We'll sort it, I promise,' he said, but his heart was heavy within him and he longed for America where they *could* seek advice and perhaps get help. Here in Dublin in nineteen forty-nine there was no one to turn to, no way to get help. Psychiatrists, if there were any, were people you saw if you were nuts and to get Vanessa to go to one, always supposing they knew anything about how to unlock her sexually, would be unthinkable.

At least she'd talked about it. At last she'd admitted there was something wrong and perhaps when they returned home she could get the help she needed to sort things out.

He sighed. Marriage had proved difficult. Perhaps the big brass were right and marrying into a different race and culture put an unusual strain on a couple's chances of a harmonious life together. But, he told himself, he'd made

177

his vows. For better or worse. That's what the guy at the altar with his reversed collar had asked them to repeat after him and that's what he had promised. And Glenn Carey did not break his promises.

Chapter Thirty-two

✌ ✍

Pierce Powers looked helplessly at his wife. Oriana sat in the yellow room nervously twiddling her exquisitely manicured hands. The room was warmly gracious but neither of its occupants seemed at ease in it.

'Must you pace about like that, Pierce?' she asked impatiently. 'Ring the bell. Bennett is late with the sherry.'

At that moment Bennett, the maid, knocked and entered. She put a sherry glass before each of them on the low rosewood table. Neither of them liked sherry but it was the done thing so they did it.

Pierce in the early days after their marriage had told the maid one hot day that he'd prefer a lager and the look Oriana gave him almost froze his eyeballs. He had learned not to repeat the request, or, indeed any request that threatened the *status quo*. He knew that Oriana was terribly insecure and these routines helped her find her feet in the jungle life appeared to present to her. She had relied totally on her parents, leaned on them, and without her mother and father at her side she was lost and tentative. The only way she maintained calm was to follow strictly the routine her parents had followed at Dundalgan and this she did. Sherry at eight in Foxrock was the manifestation of Oriana's anxiety.

Pierce felt helpless. There was no way to aid her. He watched her floundering, loving her, wanting to support her, but he soon realised that this was going to be almost an impossibility. She kept him at arm's length. He had somehow become part of the enemy forces and try as he might he could not seem to mend the situation.

He had made a complete idiot of himself on his wedding night. He knew that, but then it was something that might happen to anyone. It was not an abnormal occurrence after the excesses of the stag party, the overwhelming solemnity of the wedding service, the huge carnival of the celebrations afterwards, the lectures and admonitions of the parents, the innuendos of his mates. It was all so heavy, and what was expected of him seemed awesome. She would be a virgin, he knew that, and he was supposed to masterfully deflower her even though he had no experience and totally lacked the confidence. It was not as though the idea excited him as it did some of his friends. It appalled him, filled him with dread.

Most of the fellows like himself, though they talked about it a lot, had little or no experience in the sex department. Dublin was not the place to be easily introduced to the mysteries of sexuality or gain any know-how in such matters. Nice girls did not do it. Prostitutes gave you social diseases, and most of his friends simply hadn't the courage to dip their wicks where sickness might lurk. They were careful of the girls they knew, as it simply was not done to get a nice girl pregnant, and the responsibilities connected to such a situation were overwhelming. Fast girls were few and far between and wildly in demand, so they had their pick of young bucks and always went for boys like Gavin Fitzjames or Dom Bradley, not Pierce Powers.

Pierce had made a hash of it, he knew that, but surely he deserved a second chance? She had been cool as a cucumber with him since their wedding night and nothing he could do seemed to please her. She simply did not allow him near her.

He'd bought her things. Her extravagance was phenomenal and he gave in to her, tried to outdo her Pappy. He was alarmed at his own tendency to try to buy her approval, her affection.

She took his gifts from him as if they were her right, but gave him nothing back. No love. No tenderness. No sex. He simply did not know what to do, where to turn.

She never asked him where the money came from to buy these gifts, and bought things for the house as if he had the run of the bank.

Who could he tell about his failure? His problems? To whom could he turn to for advice? There was no one. Certainly his family would not listen. Sean Powers would ridicule a man who could not keep his wife in line. His friends would laugh at him and he'd never live it down. His mother would refuse to listen to anything so embarrassing.

All he could think of doing was buying her more and more *things*. But he was running out of money and he knew his father would not give him any more. He'd made that plain. He already thought Pierce was getting more than he was worth and kept him on a salary that would not stretch to the expensive gifts he was wooing his wife with.

Pierce was not at all sure what he should do next, but he *was* decided about one thing; he was not going to let Oriana go. To him she was everything. He loved her completely. She was the reason for his existence, and he would do anything to keep her happy.

He stared at her now, at her nervous hands as she took a cigarette out of the silver cigarette case. She lit it with the matching silver Dunhill lighter. 'What is the matter, my dear?' he asked. He hated his own voice, the banal question, his clumsiness, the underlying whiney tone.

'My dear! My dear! My dear! God, you sound like your father!' She blew out a cloud of smoke and shook her head. 'You're *hopeless*, Pierce.'

'Can't we start again?' he asked in a tired voice.

'Start *again*? We never started in the first place, idiot. Oh, leave me alone, do.'

He changed course. 'I saw the new furs in the window of Swears and Wells,' he said, hating himself, not knowing what else to do. Her lashes flickered. She glanced up at him. She took a sip of sherry, swallowed it. Then sucked on the cigarette. He knew he'd caught her interest.

'Umm,' he said. 'Lovely swingback sable.' Oh God, what made him say that? Sable cost the earth. Why hadn't he said mink? Oh God, oh God, how could he rustle up what a sable coat would cost?

He was rewarded with a brilliant smile. 'Oh Pierce, a sable!'

He nodded. 'I'd love a sable,' she said.

He smiled back at her, pathetically pleased. 'Keep you snug in winter,' he said casually, finishing his sherry. He knew better than to become amorous. He'd tried that in the early days, when he'd given her something rare and beautiful and she'd looked at him with contempt and informed him

181

that she was not a prostitute. He had felt humiliated by her rejection.

'I'd love that, Pierce,' she told him now. 'I think sable would suit me.'

Bennett came in and announced dinner. She pulled open the dividing doors, revealing the table set and glittering behind them. Waterford cut-glass and Limerick lace, trimmed Irish linen, Georgian silver and the Venetian chandelier. She looked at the room with pleasure. She rose, smiled at her husband, and to his surprise took his arm as they crossed the room to the dinner table.

Chapter Thirty-three

ೞ ൦ಀ

Brendan would not have admitted it for all the tea in China but he missed his daughters. For a start his ready-made audience was no longer there. He had always been able to lecture at length about whatever he chose and they would have to pay attention. Now that they were gone the bulk of his audience had disappeared.

It irritated him that he disliked his son so much. He hated Sitric's arrogance and was uncomfortable in his presence. He could not seem to rid himself of the notion that Sitric was secretly laughing at him.

And there was something deep in Rosalind's eyes that had never been there before. Something that gave him the distinct feeling that she held him in contempt. That since Vanessa's departure she looked down her nose at him ever so slightly. He was not sure about this but he felt shaken by the discovery of this scintilla of reserve when she looked at him.

The girls had been wonderfully mute and admiring. They had been uncritical listeners to his boasting, about his success in business. He missed them sorely. Not being able to convince himself how clever he was by telling them loudly and firmly led to a terrible uncertainty within himself.

He missed Oriana most. Her total obedience to his wishes, her constant love and admiration for her father left him with withdrawal symptoms that affected his temper adversely. His fuse became very short indeed.

Sitric never said or did anything that Brendan could actually pick upon, challenge or admonish him for. So he frustrated his father at every turn. On the rare occasions that Brendan met his son's glances he recognised – or thought he did – the same contempt he saw in Rosalind's eyes. It drove him wild and his blood pressure shot up alarmingly.

And then there was the thought of that upstart American who had absconded with his daughter, stolen his youngest from him, humiliated him and stripped him of his authority.

He refused to allow Vanessa's name spoken in the house. When his wife talked of reconciliation he puffed up like a toad and told her to shut up. He forbade Rosalind to meet her daughter or have anything at all to do with her, but Rosalind refused to be bossed about like that and although she appeared to bow her head meekly and accept orders she nevertheless planned to meet her younger daughter as soon as possible and find out how married life suited her.

Brendan, meantime, feeling distinctly uneasy and full of ill-concealed irritability, wrestled with an emotional tidal wave that threatened to engulf him. He did not know that in the near future these problems would look very paltry indeed compared to the deluge that awaited him.

Chapter Thirty-four

❧ ❧

Cessy Byrne and Patrick McCawley left Ireland from Queenstown four months after Oriana's June wedding. They did not tell anyone they were leaving and Cessy, to Sive's great sorrow, did not even kiss her mother goodbye. The pair simply vanished without a trace.

Sive knew where her daughter had gone and that she'd gone with someone called Paddy. But who or what he was she had no clue. She did not tell her husband what she knew, little though that was. She was too afraid of what he might do. Years of being patient with Brendan Ardmore had taken its toll on his temper, and often these days he over-reacted with an irascibility that scared her.

When he heard the news Rushton went wild. 'What do you mean you think she's gone? Where would she go, in the name of Jasus?'

'How should I know, Rushton? All I know is her clothes is missin'. Her dress an' her winter coat an' her boots an' the skirt Miss Oriana gev her an' the little grip ye bought when we went with the Master an' Missus to Greystones that time.'

'She's gone? So she's gone?' he shook his head in bewilderment. 'An' what'll the Master an' Missus say? She's not supposed to go *anywhere* without their permission. What'll they say? They'll go mad!' His eyes narrowed. 'I *bet* there's a fella at the bottom of all this somewhere. I'll *bet*.' Sive didn't say anything at all and he looked at her narrowly. 'You sure she never said anything to you?' he asked. She crossed her fingers behind her back and shook her head.

'Jasus, I'll kill her when I lay me hands on her. When I get aholt of her she better watch out. I'll *murder* her.'

Sive didn't tell him that that was an unlikely event. She held her peace and left it to Rushton to break the news to the Ardmores, as befitted his position as head of the family. He however chickened out of taking the initiative and kept putting off breaking the news from day to day. Imelda worked double and so did Sive. They both knew they could not carry on at this pace. They had been overworked as it was with Cessy there and now in her absence the workload had become impossible. But still no one wanted to tell the Ardmores the news.

Rushton was confused by his daughter's defection. He simply could not understand why she should want to leave what he considered a wonderful position in a nice house.

Brendan Ardmore was curiously silent these days. Something much more terrible than a maid doing a bunk had thrown his precious peace of mind into chaos.

When a strange little man he vaguely recognised but couldn't name met him in the hall of Ardmore & Son instead of Patrick McCawley he knew a moment of pure panic. Then he controlled himself as the little man held out his hand. Patrick must be ill. Patrick had never in all his time in Ardmore & Son been sick, had not missed as much as one day, but obviously his spotless record was to be tarnished and that day had arrived.

The dapper little man said his name was Reginald Crosby and he informed Brendan brightly, walking briskly beside him up the stairs, that he was Mr McCawley's assistant and that Mr McCawley was not in today, had not been in all week, and what should he, Reginald Crosby, do? When Brendan did not reply he continued, 'I took the liberty, sir, me being his assistant, sir, of going to his house and there I found –' he cleared his throat and his heavy eyebrows shot up and down over his eyes – 'that Mr McCawley has gone! Vamoosed! Done a bunk!'

Brendan stopped suddenly and Reginald Crosby found himself addressing the air. Brendan stood behind him as if turned to stone. He retraced his steps a pace or two until he was once again side by side with his boss, then began explaining earnestly to the great man. This might be a gigantic jump up the ladder of promotion for Reginald Crosby and he was not about to muff it. He had watched Patrick McCawley with hopeless admiration for many years now and had become quite resigned to the fact that due to the man's cleverness and his robust health, his turn would probably never come. And here was an opportunity, suddenly and most unexpectedly.

Brendan's heart had plummeted into his boots and he was filled with an appalling dread, a foreboding that left him unmanned and helpless. Even his bullying ability deserted him. Without Patrick McCawley he was lost. He knew nothing.

'Come in here . . . er . . . what did you say your name . . . ?'

'Crosby, sir. Reginald Crosby. Mr McCawley's *personal* assistant.' Reginald bristled importantly. He had exaggerated his position, being, at best, a sort of secretary to Patrick, at worst a general dog's body for him. Patrick played his cards close to his chest and no one at Ardmore & Son knew how exactly he did his business. But Reginald was all set, straining at the leash, ready, ready, ready. It was now or never and he knew it. He also knew that Brendan Ardmore probably had no other choice.

Brendan in the meantime was wondering how much he knew.

'I took the liberty, sir, of going to Mr McCawley's house . . .'

'His digs, yes,' Brendan corrected but Reginald shook his head.

'Oh no! His *house* in Finglas. Nice big house. He bought it quite some time ago. He rents out rooms to the Uni students.'

'That a fact?' exclaimed the bemused Brendan.

'He got a loan from the bank. Told me that within five years he'd have paid them off. Renting the rooms and such,' Reginald carried on helpfully.

'Of course. Of course,' Brendan blustered. He was afraid this Crosby person might think he was not *au fait* with his assistant's affairs. 'And . . . and . . . what's the news of him? Is he sick or something?'

Reginald shook his head. Really his boss was thick. He obviously hadn't taken in what Reginald had told him.

''Fraid not, sir. Like I said, he's gone!' He spread his hands in a helpless gesture, indicating the totally mysterious disappearance of the manager.

'What do you mean "gone"?' Brendan asked incredulously, still not grasping the full import of the news. All he knew was that his heart pounded, he was covered in a cold sweat and he felt like being sick.

'He's sold the house, sir, lock, stock and barrel to a Mr Doyle from Drimnagh who is in the business of buying property and renting it out. He makes quite a nice little profit . . .' Then he noticed Brendan's colour, which had turned a dangerous brick. 'Come in here, sir,' he cried and, taking the boss's arm, he steered him into the boardroom and sat him down in a big green leather chair. 'A brandy, sir? You could do wi' a brandy, I'll be bound. News like that is certain to wind ye.' He hustled about, pouring a brandy from the bottle marked Napoleon into a sherry glass and giving it to Mr Ardmore, all the time his spirits lifting and soaring telling him he was in for a promotion sure as sure. The Director had no alternative, did he?

'There sir, you drink that an' soon ye'll be right and tight.'

'Do you know where he is?' Brendan gasped. 'Where McCawley is?' He could only see disaster in front of him, only chaos. When Reginald Crosby shook his head he groaned.

'Well sir, America, sir, is what I heard, but I can't say for sure.'

'America!' It was a furious high-pitched bellow and Reginald jumped back a pace, startled by the sudden shout. But he was not daunted. This was his big chance. Patrick McCawley often boasted about how much he knew and how ignorant the boss was. If the Board of Directors of Ardmore & Son, he often said, were unaware of the extent of Mr Ardmore's ignorance, the staff were not. *They* knew that Brendan was an ignoramus and Patrick McCawley was the real governor.

And Patrick McCawley had been fair. He had been exacting and expected everyone to be efficient, but he was fair. Which was more than could be said for Brendan Ardmore. Patrick had maintained and increased the company's financial success and its reputation. Now Reginald Crosby, armed with the knowledge of his boss's ignorance, was determined to take over from the departed manager.

'Yes, sir, America,' he told Brendan firmly. He wanted to strike while the iron was hot. Dolly, his wife told him, 'Strike while the iron is hot, Reggie,' and Dolly was nobody's fool. He twisted his hands together in an agony of anticipation.

'He's sold the house and departed these shores.' A gleam

of malice flickered in his eyes. 'He went with a maid, sir.'

'What? Who?' Brendan sputtered.

'With a maid, sir. A servant of yours from Dundalgan, I believe . . .'

Brendan stared at him stupidly. His brain refused to absorb all this information, the horrible news this cheery little man was imparting to him.

'A Miss Cecilia Byrne,' Reginald informed him.

'Cecilia? Cecilia? I don't know anyone called Cecilia.'

'Cessy, I believe she's called, up at the big house. Cessy, daughter of Sive and Rushton Byrne, sir.'

It was sweet to see the Director twist and turn under this barrage of information. This boss who did not know his name was Reginald Crosby even after fifteen years of faithful service. Wait till he told Dolly. She'd not believe he didn't know her husband's name or position. It was sweet for the clerk to see his wealthy employer cringing like the coward he was under the impact of his news and the realisation of its repercussions. Old bastard. And what was he going to do now?

Reginald Crosby took a deep breath. His moment had arrived. 'Sir, will I continue as Mister Patrick did, sir?'

For a moment Reginald's heart stood still. Mr Ardmore looked up at him, fire flashing from his eyes. But he bit his lip and said nothing. Reginald took the empty sherry glass over to the sideboard. Everything in him ached to beg, to plead, to implore on his knees the man sitting head in hands rocking back and forth, thinking his chaotic thoughts, to give him the job. Please, please, please Mr Ardmore. But he bit back his words, steeled himself not to give in to his impulse to grovel. What else can he do? What else can he do? he asked himself.

At last Brendan looked up. 'Yes,' he said. 'You'd better.' Then he paused and looked at Reginald keenly. 'You familiar with Mr McCawley's work?'

'Oh yes, sir,' Reginald assured him, lying through his teeth. And deemed it politic to add, 'He relayed to me your instructions and I carried them out. When he had other things to do.' He looked Brendan straight in the eyes. 'I was Mr McCawley's Confidential Secretary. His Confidential Assistant, sir.'

'Very well then. Get on with it,' said Brendan in relieved tones.

'At the same salary Mr McCawley received, sir?'

Brendan glanced up. 'Yes. Yes, I suppose so.'

Reginald's heart did a double somersault and he carefully replaced the glass, noting with surprise and delight that his hands were steady.

Afterwards he said it was the word 'confidential' that swung it. Where the word had come from Reginald never could figure out. That it arrived in the nick of time, out of the blue, a word he'd never used before, became a cause of thanksgiving in the Crosby household. It did the trick, as Reginald told his admiring wife, and launched him into the prestigious job of Manager of Ardmore & Son.

It was only after Reginald Crosby was in the job for a month that Patrick McCawley's appropriation of a ludicrously high salary, back-dated for twenty years, came to light. It was carefully documented in Patrick McCawley's neat handwriting, a yearly assessment deducted eventually from the Vie de France account and every penny scrupulously accounted for. It was with fear and trepidation in his heart that poor Reginald Crosby realised he was going to have to tell Brendan Ardmore about it. The messenger often got shot if it was bad news, and this news was about as bad as news gets.

Chapter Thirty-five

⤫ ⤫

Rosalind sat in her room of light. The house was so quiet, so very quiet. No one interrupted her for permission to go to a ball or a party with this or that young man. No one came for her help with zips, or hooks and eyes, or to borrow stockings or gloves or a dab of perfume. There was no distant laughter, no suppressed rumble of arguments, no flying feet, no cosy chats.

Her girls were gone and she was alone with her men, neither of whom, she had to admit – albeit reluctantly – she liked very much.

Sitric had always seemed to her a changeling. Was he real? she wondered. Did he actually exist? Or was he, as the existentialists would have it, a figment of their collective imagination?

He sat at breakfast each morning sipping black coffee and smoking one of his exotic cigarettes, his eyes slits, his head thrown back slightly as if his hair was too heavy and weighed him down. In this period of cropped greased-back hair he wore his long and it made people suspicious of him. His beautiful face was really too pretty for a boy. What was she supposed to do with him? She had asked Brendan to start him in the business, show him the ropes, but her husband either hooted at the mere idea or got ludicrously angry. Sitric refused to discuss it. He simply left the room if the subject came up.

He had an irritating ability to disassociate himself from people, places and situations, as if he inhabited another planet. He came to parties with the family, lounged in other people's rooms tilting his chair dangerously backwards, and did not ask any of the girls to dance. And what he did with the rest of his time was a mystery to Rosalind.

Sometimes he did not come home all night. His bed remained unslept in but when she asked him where he'd been he gave her a blank look and did not reply. She despaired of him.

As for her husband, she'd never really liked Brendan, but she'd managed to keep herself from acknowledging the fact all these years. After his implacable rejection of Vanessa she found it impossible to keep up the pretence. It was difficult to find justification for his behaviour.

She did not say so, but try as she might her underlying feelings showed in her eyes and Brendan felt uncomfortable.

She did not approve of her younger daughter's marriage, but family was family and to cut Vanessa so ruthlessly out of the circle of her home was both heartless and precipitate. After all, who knew how it would turn out? If it failed, as Rosalind feared it would, the two of them coming from such different backgrounds, Vanessa would have returned to the nest, Brendan would have paid the Vatican a large sum and the marriage would be annulled. Then, sadder and wiser, she could easily be persuaded to marry Dom Bradley or another of his ilk.

But not now. Not after the things her father had said, the stance he had taken. She knew her daughter well enough to know that Brendan had said and done the unthinkable and she would never trust him again. If the marriage did succeed, unlikely though that seemed, she'd be lost to them forever. Vanessa would disappear into the wilds of America and they'd never see her again. The thought of that broke Rosalind's heart. Vanessa had always been her secret favourite, Oriana her father's.

Rosalind sobbed into her handkerchief. Life was very unfair. She'd been so happy at Oriana's wedding, so proud, so successful in every way and now it had all changed.

She missed Oriana too and although she was loath to admit it she was worried about her elder daughter. Oriana was not the picture of happiness Rosalind had expected her to be. She looked pinched these days and she had hardened somewhat. Her lips, usually relaxed and soft, were now most of the time clenched in a tight tense line. Her smile had become practised, lost its spontaneity, and she had developed a new habit of twisting her fingers together.

Pierce was his usual polite self but he seemed to be under his wife's thumb and jumped to her wishes and requests with alarming alacrity. Sometimes against her will Rosalind could not help thinking that Vanessa's word for him was sadly appropriate. He was a twit. She was afraid there was something wrong and she longed to find out what it was but lacked the courage to ask outright. Oriana had never really confided in her. She tended to be fiercely proud. Any tentative inquiries received stout denials and assurances that all was well, and a show was put on whenever Pappy was present, a show that echoed with falsity. And Brendan pointed to his perfect girl and sounded off about his own wisdom. So Rosalind did a novena to the Sacred Heart for the young couple and included them in her prayers night and morning, and in her daily rosary.

She had to accept the unacceptable, try not to miss her daughters too much and come to terms with an increasingly irascible and bad-tempered husband.

And put up with an uncommunicative son who was not there very often.

'You have the cough of an old man!' Rosalind told her son. She had asked him to join her for tea in her boudoir and Sive to serve it there.

Sive had been looking tired recently so Rosalind had told her to let Cessy serve the tea. Sive had looked embarrassed.

'What is it, Sive? Something wrong with Cessy?'

Sive shook her head. 'No, mum, it's just . . .' She hesitated. 'Well, she's not here.' This was the first that Rosalind had heard of the disappearance of her servant. She frowned.

'What do you mean, she's not here? She did not get my permission to go out so how can she *not* be here?' Servants these days were very lax indeed. Sive burst into tears and Rosalind sighed. It was going to be one of those days.

'Sive, what on earth's the matter?' she asked briskly.

'It's Cessy, mum. She's, we . . .'

'Well, what, woman? What is she?'

'She's run away, mum.'

'Good heavens! How on earth did that happen?' Rosalind asked.

'I don't know, mum,' Sive gulped. 'Oh Holy Mary, mum,

I'm sorry. I can't understand it. We brung her up so carefully. Rushton an' me, so we did.'

'Where has she gone, Sive?' Rosalind asked. 'This house has run mad,' she added. 'Nothing like this has ever happened before.'

Sive closed her eyes and lied and Rosalind knew at once that she lied: 'I don't know, mum, truly I don't. She just upped and left.'

'Who is responsible for this, Sive? Is there a man in this sorry story somewhere?'

Sive lied again: 'Sure how would I know, mum? She just disappeared an' never said goodbye. I'm destroyed, mum, so I am, destroyed entirely.'

'That's as maybe, Sive, but we are the ones who'll suffer. And after all our kindness to her, is this the way she repays us?' Rosalind looked closely at the servant. 'Now, Sive, you can stop lying to me and tell me the truth.' She caught the woman's wrist in a fierce grip. 'Now tell me.'

Sive shifted uncomfortably and tried to pull away but the mistress's grasp was firm and strong. 'Tell me, Sive.'

'Well all I know, mum, is she's been talkin' about emigratin', so she has . . .'

'And?' Rosalind's grip was steel-like and Sive's wrist began to throb.

'And, she talked of a fella. You're right there, mum.'

'Who is he?'

'I don't know, mum, honest I don't. He was called Paddy. That's all I know, an' sure half of Ireland's called Paddy. That's all, mum, I swear.' Rosalind looked at her closely.

'All right, Sive,' she said eventually, letting her go. 'You should have told me. She's supposed to have our permission before she does *anything* or goes *anywhere*. Emigrate! The very idea!' Rosalind was outraged. 'Well, I hope she doesn't live to regret it. America is teeming with penniless people like her. Most of them die in poverty. I know. I saw *The Grapes of Wrath* in the Carlton.' Rosalind glanced at her servant. 'I hope Imelda is not entertaining any such ideas?' she remarked.

'Imelda, mum? Ah no. Sure she hasn't got the brain-power to figure out where America even is! No, mum, Imelda is quite happy here.'

'Well, I'm glad to hear it.' She looked Sive in the eye. 'Seems

194

we both have wayward daughters, Sive,' she said. 'Now serve tea here please.'

Sive bit her lip and rubbed her wrist. The mistress was strong, stronger than she looked. She nearly told her, those days are gone mum, but she restrained herself. Those days of asking permission to wipe your bottom have disappeared forever, mum, only you haven't noticed. Rosalind Ardmore didn't seem to be aware of the fact. What had been the practice in her mother's day was good enough for her and she saw no reason to advance with the times. Like her hairstyle she remained fixed in a former era.

Rosalind had developed a blinding headache. She realised that she had had one headache after another since Vanessa left. How fragile the family structure really was. She who had thought it indestructible found to her dismay that it collapsed under the first conflict. She sighed. She would find another girl. Ireland was full of girls desperate for a position. She'd looked after her servants well, from the cradle to the grave she'd been fond of saying, and she felt betrayed by Cessy's defection. Well, she'd let Sive and Rushton see her displeasure and make them realise how lucky they were to be in a household like this one.

'Ask Sitric to come and join me for tea Sive' she told her servant as she reached the door. Her voice was very cold.

Sitric, Rosalind told herself firmly, had to be dealt with. It was a ritual that took place about once every two months. Rosalind sent for her son and asked him what he was doing with his life.

Rosalind hated these interviews but deemed them her duty. Just being near her son made her nervous. And that was very strange. Whoever heard of a mother frightened of her own son?

When Sitric arrived he stood nonchalantly near the door as if ready to leave and she made the remark about his coughing. He hacked away constantly and the words just came out. They were not at all what she meant to say.

'Oh Ma, don't plague me,' he said impatiently. 'I can't help it if I have a weak chest.'

He had a weak chest, Rosalind had to admit it, so she changed course. 'Sitric, have you given any thought to the future?' she asked.

Sitric laughed. 'That again! Oh Ma, isn't that Pappy's job? Or is he opting out of that one too?'

'I don't know what you mean, Sitric. Don't you dare speak so disrespectfully of your father.' She glared at him. 'And don't call me "Ma". I'm your mother.'

'Are you? I'm never quite sure. You really don't like me, do you? You never did. You're uncomfortable with me. Must be something wrong with me. I wonder what?'

'Of course there isn't. Don't be absurd, Sitric. Of course we love you. You are our son.'

'And Pappy hates me. Anyone can see.'

'I forbid you to talk like that. Your father has given you everything. He's clothed you, fed you, educated you . . .'

'But, Ma, that's his *duty*. That's the very *least* he should do. A parent must do the very best for their offspring, after all. They shouldn't expect medals for what is their duty.'

Rosalind didn't like the way the conversation kept getting away from her. So she changed course again.

'Sitric, isn't it time you decided what you're going to do with your life? Everyone does *something*.'

'Ma, what can I do? I'm not fitted for anything. I'll live off Pappy's money until he gets fed up and throws me out like 'Nessa and then I'll top myself.'

He spoke lightly and she shrugged off what he said impatiently. 'Sitric be serious, can't you. Vanessa and Oriana are married women now. They have a very important job to do. They'll run their husbands' homes and soon they'll have children and that's a full-time occupation, as I should know. What will you do?'

'Ma, didn't you hear what I said? Pappy would not let me go to college. He said he didn't believe in it. Okay, so I have no qualifications. He won't let me try my hand in Ardmore & Son, so what do you propose I do? Sweep the streets? Wash up dishes? Even that I'd probably fail at. Probably break them all. Ma, I'm useless! Don't you understand? Oh Christ, what's the use!' He opened the door and slipped away from her, mentally and physically as he always did, and she was left sipping her tea.

She wondered that he knew about her being uncomfortable with him and after a moment's contemplation she shrugged. It was not her fault. She couldn't help how she felt. She sighed.

She'd have to deal with the Cessy thing, but not today. She could not bear any more worry. She was worn out with all these problems. Young people today, she decided, had absolutely no discipline at all. And where would it lead? Violence in the streets, no doubt. A slipping and sliding of morals and the inevitable corruption. Youngsters deciding to do whatever they wanted without fear or favour, never realising that the bill always had to be paid. If there was one thing she had learned in her life, it was that the bill always had to be paid. Kids did not realise how difficult life was, they did not realise that life was not fair. They were in for some very nasty shocks. Reality, Rosalind knew, could be unpleasant unless you were prepared for it. If not, there was anger, violence, resentment. The jolliest party left you with a nasty hangover unless you were careful. But youth never reckoned on that nor counted the consequences. Rosalind hoped the reckoning would not be too high for Oriana, Sitric and Vanessa, or indeed for herself and Brendan.

Chapter Thirty-six

ᴖ ᴗ

Brendan Ardmore was fit to be tied. When he reached home that night, frustration, fear, anger and a sense of his own impotence forced him to announce to Rosalind his decision to dismiss the Byrne family.

Rushton had feared this. He knew his boss, and his reactions were predictable to the chauffeur. Brendan would feel he had to sack them. He *might* have overlooked Cessy's defection, but not her defection with Patrick McCawley, and when Rushton found this out his heart sank and he guessed he was for the high jump. One of the girls in the typing pool at Ardmore's had told him the truth. The whole place buzzed with the amazing news that the manager had run off with the maid from Dundalgan. It was a sad day for the Byrnes and Rushton was sick with worry the inevitable effect on him and Sive.

So he was looking gloomy when Vanessa and Sergeant Carey came down Dawson Street as he waited for Brendan in the Daimler.

'Oh Glenn, it's Pappy's car!' Vanessa cried, clutching Glenn's arm.

'So what, honey? Your Pappy is the one to feel nervous. You've done nothing wrong. Don't be scared. Come on.'

'I should have thought. It's where the offices are. Oh, if Pappy is there I'll die.'

'Honey, don't be silly. *I'm* here. Anyhow, your Pappy isn't there. Only Rushton.' And he greeted the chauffeur with his usual friendliness. Rushton stood leaning on the Daimler, an expression of unalloyed misery on his face. 'What's the problem? How come you look so doggone gloomy, Rushton?'

'I think, sir, I'm going to be booted out.'

198

Vanessa looked astonished.

'See, Miss Vanessa, our Cessy has run off with your Pappy's manager, Patrick McCawley,' he told her.

'You say that as if it explained things, Rushton. Well, it doesn't,' Glenn said, bewildered as to how Cessy's defection had anything to do with her father.

'Well, in Pappy's mind it has,' Vanessa told him. 'He'll blame Rushton for Cessy going. Without his permission. And with Mr McCawley.'

'But that's crazy! It has nothing to do with Rushton!' Glenn was indignant.

'You know that, sir, and I know that, but try to tell Mr Ardmore . . . it's a waste of time.'

Vanessa nodded. 'Total waste. Rushton is right. Unless Mother can talk him out of it he'll blame Rushton. Oh Lord, Rushton, I'm sorry. Everything seems to be going wrong. I can't imagine Dundalgan without you and Sive and Cessy and Imelda.'

'Who's this guy? McCawley?'

'He's Pappy's Manager. Pappy relies on him. He'll be lost without him,' Vanessa told Glenn.

Glenn had presumed as much. He did not think Brendan Ardmore had either the patience or the understanding to run a business like Ardmore's and make it a success. It seemed to him that few would be happy dealing with a man whose fuse was so short and who was so inflexible, and in that business customer and buyer relationships were terribly important. No, he had never believed that it was Brendan Ardmore who had steered the firm to its huge financial success. Apparently he had been right and the guy at the tiller was this Patrick McCawley.

'Rushton, the Ambassador needs a driver. He's always had one of us on tap, but he said the other day that we'll be goin' home soon and he wants to get an outsider who knows a lot about cars. Suppose I talk to him? Eh?'

'Oh sir, I'd be that grateful, so I would.'

'I'm not promising anything, mind.'

'I understand, sir.'

Brendan seethed all the way home to Dundalgan that evening and Rushton crossed his fingers as he drove, and prayed.

When they arrived home Brendan went directly to Rosalind, almost crashing into Sitric coming out of her room.

'Good God, boy, mind where you're going,' he muttered angrily and Sitric glared at him then scuttled away.

Rosalind reclined on her sofa sipping tea. She had been feeling very lonely and was quite unexpectedly glad to see Brendan, unaware that Cessy's defection would mean much to him. She was appalled by his intentions.

'They're out! All of them.'

'Who, dear? Who are out?' she asked.

'The Byrnes. I'll speak to Rushton, to *all* of them on Saturday morning when I give them their wages. It'll be the last farthing they receive from me.'

Rosalind, dismayed at the turn of events, was naturally concerned about the running of the house. 'Dear, are you sure? Who'll cook? Who'll do the housework? Where'll we ever get a cook like Sive? She's a treasure. They're used to us now, dear, so don't you think . . .'

'No I don't. They've got to go. All of them. Bag and baggage.'

'Who'll do the housework? Dundalgan is run by the Byrnes, I just don't know how . . .'

'Sive Byrne always overcooks my eggs,' Brendan irritated her by saying.

'I cannot manage without them, Brendan,' Rosalind said angrily. It was a mistake and she knew it. Whatever chance she had had of talking him around went when she defied him. Now he would become stubborn.

'Well you'll have to! You're not going to sit there and tell me you can't replace that faithless family? Dublin must be full of cooks and maids and things.'

'Well dear, but the Byrnes suit us. They've been trained here. Servants have to be trained you know and—'

'Well you'll just have to train another set of people.'

'You won't like it, dear,' she warned him. 'Things are so comfortable with the Byrnes—'

'Are you not at all interested in *why* I've come to this decision?' Brendan asked her, heavily sarcastic.

'I expect it's because of Cessy. But we'll never have someone as willing as Imelda to—'

'You don't know what Cessy's done.'

'Yes, dear, I do. She's run off to America. That's what she's done.'

'But you don't know *who* she's run off with—'

'Dear, be calm. You'll have a stroke. That's how your father went.'

'I'm trying to tell you something!'

'I *know*, dear. Cessy has run off to America. It was probably the greengrocer's son,' Rosalind said.

'Who was?'

'Who ran off with Cessy. Sive said there was a man called Paddy.'

'*Shut up, Rosalind, and listen to me.*'

Rosalind turned a cold face towards him. 'Do not speak to me like that, Brendan. You may shout at your employees. Or the servants. Or the children. But *not me*.' She spoke quietly. 'Now, what is it you want to say?'

'*Cessy ran off with Patrick McCawley.*'

She looked at him blankly and he realised she did not know who he was talking about. Frustrated he stomped about the room.

'Who, dear?'

'My manager at Ardmore's. You have no idea how inconvenient that is.'

'Well, dear' – she could not resist a smile – 'I'm sure Dublin is full of managers you can train.'

She was being flippant and he left the room in cold fury. She did not realise that Patrick McCawley was essential to him. He did not realise that the Byrnes were essential to her.

Chapter Thirty-seven

❦ ❧

On Saturday the Byrnes were duly summoned to the study where the birch lay fallow on the wall. There would be no need of it any more. The girls were gone and Sitric had outgrown it. That was how Brendan explained it to himself. He preferred to forget that scene where his son had seized the cane and threatened his father with it.

The Byrnes filed into the library, Rushton leading, and Brendan surprised a smirk on his chauffeur's face. Well, he'd soon wipe that off. Perhaps Rushton thought he'd been called in to be given a raise. Brendan laughed to himself. That would be irony.

Brendan was enjoying the situation. Never a man to examine the consequences of his acts, all he cared about now was venting his spleen on the hapless Byrnes and ridding himself of some of the terrible anger and resentment that burned in his soul against the family who had taken his manager away from him.

They stood in front of him; Rushton, Imelda and Sive. 'Well, this is a sorry day,' he began by saying. He intended to lecture them about duty, loyalty, control over one's children ... well, maybe not that, thinking of Vanessa. But suddenly Rushton stepped forward, taking the wind from Brendan's sails.

'Tis too a sorry day, sir. We didn't know you knew.'

Brendan looked at him blankly. 'What are you talking about, Rushton?'

'We're that sorry, sir, honest we are. But Sergeant Carey got us a job at the 'Merican Embassy, Mrs Byrne an' me. Wages is good. Almost double what you pay. Mrs Byrne ...' Brendan noted she was Mrs Byrne now, not Sive any more. 'Mrs Byrne'll cook for the 'Bassador an' I'll drive an' look after the cars. An'

with the wages we're gettin' 'Melda won't have to do a tap.'
He ended on a triumphant note and Brendan stared at him
for a moment, gobsmacked. Sive said afterwards, 'Te look at
him, his mouth open like a fish, would've made a cat laugh.'
But now, in the silence following Rushton's announcement,
she just giggled nervously.

'We'll work out our wages next month, sir,' Rushton told
the amazed Brendan. 'Give you time. We're fair-minded
people.' And nodding his head, he turned and led his family
out of the room.

It was the first of the lovely American's good deeds, if you
could call them that. He didn't seem to be aware of having
done anything at all. If told he had brought prosperity and
peace to the Byrne family he would have laughed. If he had
been told that he had saved them from unemployment he
would have doubted your word. If you had said that he
enabled that family for the first time the opportunity to
live free from strife, comfortably, happier than they had
ever been, he would have shaken his head in disbelief and
returned to whatever he was doing and forgotten your words
in five minutes.

Chapter Thirty-eight

ൟ ൟ

'We met here, Mother, Glenn and me, our first date,' Vanessa said. Her eyes, her mother saw, shone when she mentioned her husband's name.

They were in the Shelbourne tea lounge sipping Earl Grey and talking, Rosalind observing her daughter carefully. She had decided on neutral ground, the better to assess her daughter's state of mind.

'And I, darling. Glenn and I,' Rosalind admonished automatically.

'What? Oh yes. More tea, Mother?'

She was acting hostess, Rosalind saw, with a new quiet grace and authority. Pouring the tea, stirring it in the pot because it was not strong enough. Offering her mother sandwiches.

But she looked strained. There were dark circles beneath her eyes and she seemed weary.

'Are you all right, dearest?' Rosalind asked.

'Of course, Mother!' Vanessa replied, too quickly, too defensively. 'I'm terribly happy.'

She did not say 'we' and in Rosalind's experience one didn't talk of being happy unless one wasn't. One *showed* it. It radiated from one, or not, and there was no faking it.

'I'm terribly happy, Mother. Why wouldn't I be?'

Vanessa thought of that day when Billy and Glenn met them, herself and Elana, here, at this table, and the men drank whiskey and tipped the waitress who didn't want to serve them. It wasn't very long ago but it seemed ages. She remembered how she felt, the rising tide of excitement, the sheer magic of Glenn's presence. She still felt that gasp of elation when she saw him, but now, she also felt such confusion. The facing of reality. Dirty socks.

She'd forgotten about laundry. She'd simply been throwing their dirty underwear and Glenn's shirts into the laundry basket, not thinking about it, of what would or should happen to it. In Dundalgan Cessy or Imelda collected it and did whatever you did with laundry, and how should she know what that was? She forgot that in Haddington Road it was her responsibility. She had never asked Venny to attend to it. It had simply not occurred to her.

'Where are my clean socks, honey?' Glenn had called out and realisation dawned. Like a guilty child she'd curled up in bed and pretended to be asleep. She heard him banging about the drawers, hoping he'd awaken her so that he could have his fresh pair of socks, but she remained resolutely comatose. She could hear him grumbling. He must have put on yesterday's, for he finally left. He would hate that, she knew. He was very fastidious.

When he'd gone Venny arrived and she seized her poor helper. 'Washing!' she cried. 'I forgot the laundry!'

'Oh, Mrs Carey, it's my fault. Oh, I shoulda thought. Oh Jasus, Mary an' Joseph, I'm an eejit I am.' The woman was in a state and Vanessa tried to soothe her. 'Calm down, Venny. Let's just get it done. Okay?' And she helped her do the washing. She hated it, loathed it, but what choice did she have?

'It's my fault, Mrs Carey,' Venny kept worrying at it. 'I'm sorry, I shoulda thought. Me Mam woulda skinned me alive, so she would.'

'No, Venny. *I'm* the mistress of the house.' She looked around the little apartment and sighed. '*I* should have known.'

'Sure you're as innocent as a newborn babe,' Venny said fondly.

How true that was, Vanessa realised sadly. Only she would call it ignorance. If her mother or Venny knew the extent of her ignorance, how they'd despise her. And if Glenn ever found out he'd divorce her on the spot. And she knew she would die without him.

Her mother looked at her now with gentle eyes, 'You're father is very upset, Vanessa. He misses you, darling, very much.'

'Oh, I'm sure he does!' Vanessa replied bitterly.

'You flouted his authority. He lost face, dear, which for most men is a terrible thing. You gave him no time.'

'Time wouldn't have changed him, Mother.' Vanessa frowned. 'Besides, in another couple of months ...' She shrugged. 'Oh, I don't know how soon Glenn's tour of duty will be over, and we'll be going to the States.' She looked straight at her mother as she spoke and saw the dismay in Rosalind's eyes.

'Does he *have* to go?' she asked. 'Couldn't you both stay a while? Give your father time?'

'I've told you, Mother, time won't fix things between me and Pappy.' Vanessa spoke impatiently. 'And Glenn has to go wherever he's sent. Oh Mother, don't you see? Pappy'll *never* change. We'd best accept that.'

There was a pause. Rosalind stirred her tea. The trees were bare outside the Shelbourne and in Stephens Green. Almost every female in the fashionable crowd sipping tea wore the longer skirts and new shape. The new fashion was not a rarity any more and women sat like bunches of flowers, skirts billowing out around them, petticoats peeping from beneath soft wool, taffeta, gabardine and grosgrain. In the corner the red-faced man on the piano played 'Blue Moon' and 'Embrace Me, My Sweet Embraceable You', soulfully and with tears in his eyes. He was very tipsy and an extremely good pianist. Waiters hurried about replenishing boiling water from the huge silver samovar on a service table.

Rosalind sighed. The world went on no matter what dramas occurred in homes across the land.

'How's Oriana?' Vanessa asked, pouring more tea, offering her mother a tiny cake.

Rosalind looked startled. 'Haven't you seen her?' she asked, surprised.

Vanessa shook her dark hair, 'No. I must admit, Mother, that I haven't telephoned her. But I thought it *her* place to phone me. After all, I'm the outcast.'

'Don't say that, dear,' Rosalind admonished gently, then, clicking her tongue, she added, 'I don't know what's happened to this family. Just last May we were the closest, most loving family imaginable, and look at us now!'

Vanessa stared at her mother in dismay. She wondered

if her mother really believed what she said and decided she did.

'People taking sides. Not talking ...' To her horror Vanessa saw there were tears in her mother's eyes.

'Don't, Mother. Don't. It will all blow over.' But Vanessa knew it wouldn't.

'Perhaps Oriana hasn't got your number,' Rosalind said with a sniff.

'Oh Mother,' Vanessa rolled her eyes heavenwards. 'Golly, it's no big secret. She could find out soon enough if she wanted.'

'Well, you be generous, you call her.'

'Maybe, Mother, maybe.' Vanessa sighed, then asked, 'How is she?'

But she knew. Her sister would be living it up. She'd not be having to do her own washing, having problems about cooking and cleaning and shopping, God's sakes.

'Well, darling, she looks a bit *strained* to me,' Rosalind surprised her daughter by replying.

Vanessa realised her mother was frowning so she must be worried. She always smoothed away frown lines and tried not to wrinkle her forehead. But worried about Oriana? Why ever would that be? Vanessa gave her mother a startled look, 'Does she? That surprises me, Mother.'

'Yes. She's sort of hardened. I can't explain it. I wish you'd see her and tell me what you think.'

Rosalind was trying to keep her splintered family from disintegrating. If she could get Oriana and Vanessa together then there was hope for all of them.

She must have realised that she'd married the wrong man, Vanessa mused. That would be it. Poor Oriana. Stuck with Pierce Powers for the rest of her life.

At least she loved Glenn. No matter how she messed things up, despite their inept sex life, she loved him. That fact was never in doubt.

As they sat there chatting with each other, mother and daughter, there was some sort of fracas outside. They ignored the commotion, concentrating on each other until Rosalind, frowning at the noise, glanced out of the window, gasped loudly and pressed her hand to her breast.

'Oh God, it's Sitric,' she whispered.

Vanessa made as if to stand, but her mother gripped her sleeve and pressed her back on to the sofa. 'No, don't, Vanessa. Don't draw attention.'

They both remained sitting, staring out of the window into the street.

The hotel doorman, in an impressive wine-red uniform trimmed with gold braid, had Sitric by his coat collar and the seat of his pants and was forcibly ejecting him from the hotel. 'Unnatural bloody little snot!' he cried, shaking the boy like a wet umbrella. 'Think ye'd get away wi' that kinda behaviour in *this* hotel? Not on your Nellie! Yiz are outa here now. Yiz are barred. Outa me sight now. Off home wi' yiz an' never let me see yer face around here again or I'll send for the polis.' And he cast Sitric on the pavement like a dog.

Rosalind looked around quickly to see if she recognised anyone, but the tea lounge was empty of friends or acquaintances. In any event, and much to her relief, theirs was the only vantage point. No one else could see what had happened in the street. No one else had a view. She looked quickly back out of the window. The boy had picked himself up. He was dusting himself down nonchalantly, his elegant beige whipcord trousers spattered with dirt. He was smiling and he did not seem at all disconcerted.

'I better go to him,' Rosalind said, rising again. 'What on earth's happening? What did he *do*?'

'No, Mother, don't.' As Rosalind had a moment ago so now her daughter restrained her. 'I don't think Sitric would like it.'

Rosalind turned to her, stony-faced. 'I don't *care* what Sitric would like or not like. I'm—'

'No, Mother. Someone might see you. You don't want to cause a commotion. Draw attention. Let him go. He looks all right to me.'

Sitric was standing in the street, swaying ever so slightly, lighting one of his black Russian cigarettes.

'And we don't want another scene,' Vanessa said. 'That doorman is rarin' to go.'

Rosalind was blinking rapidly. 'What is this family coming to?' she repeated. 'I really should see if he's all right.'

'No, Mother. Best talk to him in private,' Vanessa told her.

208

Rosalind looked at her daughter in surprise. 'My dear, you've grown up,' she murmured.

Vanessa glanced at her watch. 'I better go. Glenn'll be home soon.' She reached for the bill but her mother got there first.

'No. I'll do this.'

'Mother, we're not poor, you know. Glenn has money.'

Rosalind snorted a little and looked at Vanessa pityingly. 'Not what I'd call money,' she said. 'No, I'll treat you. You go on, dear. And remember, phone your sister. We can't allow our family to fall apart.'

Vanessa kissed her mother, rose and put on her gloves. As she left the lounge she thought that her mother was too late. The family had already broken up and like Humpty Dumpty she did not think it would ever be put back together again.

Chapter Thirty-nine

꙰ ꙰

When Rosalind went home that autumn day she was full of a helpless kind of despair. She felt as if she were trying to hold water in her hands. The lovely days when she sat with her children around the table at mealtimes, catching up on the news of parties, of dances, of gossip about friends, had gone and she now ate most of her meals with a taciturn Brendan, and sometimes, only occasionally, a remote and unreachable Sitric.

She went to visit Oriana but felt an unwelcome visitor in her house. Oriana was edgy in her mother's company. She was brittle and seemed to be avoiding Rosalind. Her mother had believed and hoped that Oriana's marriage would bring them closer together, that they could share more, but the reverse had happened. Oriana treated her mother as if she were a stranger she sought to impress.

And dear little Vanessa, Rosalind's secret pet, was hostile and defensive. Oh, she was as sweet to her mother as usual, but Rosalind knew she would not easily forgive her parents their rejection of her and her husband and the way they had been humiliated by Brendan that terrible day at Dundalgan. She was aware that Vanessa nursed, deep down, a shattering disillusionment that she'd find it hard to get over.

Rushton drove Rosalind home. He was silent and answered her attempts at polite conversation in monosyllables. She went directly to her room, telling Rushton to send Sitric to her the moment he came in.

She pulled off her soft leather wrist gloves and removed her hat. She sat on the chaise and kicked off her shoes. She felt empty and bereft, as if life had suddenly lost its meaning.

A moment later Sive came in.

'I'm sorry, mum.'

'What about, Sive?'

'About goin', mum. I didn't have much chanst to talk to ye about it an' I'm that sorry. 'Twas because we knew that Mr Ardmore was goin' to sack us. We had to look after ourselves.'

Rosalind pressed her fingers to her forehead. 'I really don't want to discuss it now, Sive. Where is Master Sitric?'

'He's in his room, mum, Mrs Ardmore. Will I send him to ye?'

Rosalind nodded. 'Please,' she said tiredly.

When Sitric arrived he was in a paisley silk dressing-gown, socks, no shoes. He was smoking.

'Put that out in here, dear,' she told him, wrinkling her nose. She emptied a delicate Limoges dish of hairpins and grips and handed it to him, then pointed to the only chair in the room. Sitric sat.

He was as slim as a willow and very like her, she thought, staring at him. Or like her before childbearing had ruined her figure. She was stout now and nothing could change that. Maybe she didn't get on with him because he was so very like her. He was fastidious, a perfectionist and he did not refrain from showing his impatience with fools. She stared now at the attractive, arrogant face and she wanted desperately to slap him.

'I was in the Shelbourne today, having tea with your sister,' she began.

'Oriana?'

'No, Vanessa.'

'How very noble of you. I thought your Lord and Master forbade conversation with dear 'Nessa.'

'We saw you,' she continued.

'Oh cripes!' It was blurted out and he seemed suddenly very young. He looked at her, wide-eyed for a moment, but recovered quickly and his eyelids drooped back over his eyes to their usual half-closed position.

'I witnessed that revolting scene in which *my* son was forcibly ejected from the hotel before my very eyes.'

'I'm sorry, Mother.'

'Is that all you've got to say?' Her voice was rising and she tried to control it. Nothing would be gained by shouting.

211

'Well I *am* sorry, Mother, truly I am.' His half-closed eyes slid away from hers. 'But it was a mistake. Alf, the barman, thought I was drunk, but as you can see, he was wrong.'

'I don't *care* what the *reason* was,' Rosalind said crisply. This was not true. She did care but she was terrified to probe too deeply, unsure what she would uncover. 'All I care about is the fact that my son, your father's son, was *thrown out* of the Shelbourne Hotel in broad daylight, into the street.'

'Appearances! It's pathetic! All you and Pappy care about are *appearances*. Not "Did they hurt you, Sitric?" Not a scintilla of criticism of that bloody doorman, his brutality, the nerve of him, manhandling me like that. Oh no! Everything as seen from the other side.' Sitric stood. 'Well, Mother, I'll not sit here and be lectured. I've had a lousy and humiliating experience and I'm exhausted.'

He left the room, left her there, defeated and bewildered, and, if she were honest, relieved that he had gone. She could not think where she had gone wrong with him. She loved her children dearly and she realised that she did not understand them at all. A feeling of hopelessness enveloped her and for the first time since she was an eighteen-year-old bride she put her face in her hands and wept.

Chapter Forty

⋘ ⋙

The house in Foxrock was a gracious detached two-storied building, with six bedrooms, a groomed and satiny lawn in front and immaculate gravel leading up to a porticoed front door.

Vanessa walked up the drive her high heels sinking in the loose stones. She had taken the bus. Glenn would have been happy to take her in the car but on the phone Oriana had made it plain that she did not want her brother-in-law in her house and Vanessa had no intention of telling him that he was not welcome. Her mother was right, she thought, the family *was* falling apart.

'It's not that I've anything against him, Vanessa,' Oriana had assured her. 'It's Pappy's orders, and – well, you understand, 'Nessa, don't you?'

'Oh, I understand only too well,' Vanessa replied dryly. She understood that her sister was still under their father's thumb, still Pappy's little girl. Well, at least *I'm* not his slave any more she thought as she toiled up the drive pulling her heels from the gravel as it sucked them in, hoping the suede would not get snagged. This was a drive for motoring up, not walking.

The door was opened by a uniformed maid who showed Vanessa into an elegant, airy living-room. The furniture was covered in pale yellow brocade and the carpet was coffee-coloured. There were bowls of chrysanthemums everywhere and gilt-edged mirrors on the walls and over the mantelpiece. The autumn sun streamed in through the windows and picked up the colour of the primrose drapes. It was a beautiful room.

Vanessa sighed. It was a far cry from Haddington Road – its furniture not her choice, not her own, a bit battered from

213

use by previous tenants, the rooms so small, the cramped space. She had been perfectly happy about the apartment until just now, when she compared, and her heart sank as she felt a sharp pang of envy.

"Nessa! Darling!' The greeting was effusive and false and at once Vanessa could see what her mother meant about Oriana. Her sister wore a full soft skirt in amber mohair and a cream angora sweater, three strands of graded pearls around her neck that Vanessa could see were real, and high-heeled tan leather shoes. She looked slim, beautiful, and brittle as angel-hair toffee.

'Sit down, 'Nessa do.' She turned to the maid who stood respectfully in the open doorway behind her. 'Bennett, bring us some coffee, please. Sit down, 'Nessa.'

She *would* have a maid called Bennett, Vanessa thought, irritated, thinking of Venny which sounded so blah, and Venables which sounded impossible! Thinking of the poor untidy Venny's looks, the straggle of hair always hanging over her eyes, her enormous red hands. Bennett was as neat as a pin, permed hair pat around her white starched maid's cap. She left the room at Oriana's command, closing the door quietly behind her.

The two sisters stared at each other. Vanessa could think of nothing to say and she was overcome with a sense of Oriana's strangeness. Oriana, usually so soft, so pliable, the muscles of her face now stiff, her hands restless. She wondered briefly how Oriana and Pierce managed in bed, then pushed the shocking thought away. Oriana seemed unwilling to meet her eyes and they sat in awkward silence. Everything Vanessa thought of saying seemed inappropriate, so she sat there acutely embarrassed, remembering how once they had not enough time to say all they wanted.

At last Bennett came in with a huge silver tray set with a silver coffee pot, delicate Spode cups and saucers, almond biscuits and assorted *petit fours*, all perfectly arranged. She moved efficiently yet gracefully and served them their coffee and helped them to the sweetmeats on tiny plates with small linen napkins delicately embroidered at the corners.

Delicate. Everything was fine and delicate, Rosalind's type of administration, and as unlike Haddington Road as the North Pole is from the Sahara Desert. Vanessa felt an overwhelming sense of jealousy and defeat.

'It's a beautiful house, Oriana,' she said when the maid had left them.

'Thanks.' Oriana still seemed stiff and formal, as if she were playing a part.

'Are you happy where you are?' she asked Vanessa politely.

Vanessa was fed up with the charade. She'd always been up front and honest, always lacked guile. So she looked at her sister in exasperation. 'Oh cut it out, Ori. You *know* where I live,' she said frankly. 'You know I'm in a tiny cramped apartment in Haddington Road. You can imagine what it is like.'

'Well, you *would* disobey Pappy. You wouldn't listen,' Oriana replied righteously. 'You can't blame anyone but yourself.'

Vanessa shook her head. 'I'm not complaining, Ori. I'm very happy with Glenn. I don't regret what I did if that's what you're suggesting.' She glanced at her sister who had averted her face and was staring at a portrait of herself on the wall. It was a new portrait showing Oriana in an elegant ballgown, her pearls around her neck, her eyes vacant, a faraway look on her face as if she was staring into nothingness.

'That's lovely, Oriana. Who did it?'

'Oh, Fitzgerald did. Yes, it's good.' Vanessa thought wistfully how it was a long time since she had worn a ballgown. 'Pierce likes it.' Oriana sounded totally uninterested and Vanessa decided that she was not happy. She felt suddenly sorry for her sister, grand house notwithstanding. But Oriana was prickly as a hedgehog and not available for sympathy.

'It's just that at the moment we can't afford this standard of living,' Vanessa explained gently. 'I'm not sure we ever will.'

Oriana's face was still turned from her sister, just like the portrait, her shoulders tight, her back stiff.

'Are you happy, Ori? With Pierce?' Vanessa ventured, hoping to break down the barrier between them.

Her sister nodded her head vehemently. 'Of course I am,' she said firmly, but her voice shook. 'I've got everything in the world, Vanessa. Everything.'

There was little else to say. Silence descended on the room and in the corner an antique clock ticked peacefully.

Vanessa opened her mouth to tell her sister about the fracas in the Shelbourne but Oriana seemed in another world, time was pressing and frankly Vanessa wanted to escape. She wanted to leave the elegant house, the evidence of wealth and ease and the look of emptiness and unhappiness on her sister's face. She wanted to go home to Haddington Road and the safety and love Glenn always gave her.

'Glenn will be home soon,' she said, rising. 'Hungry as a hunter.'

Oriana nodded but she wouldn't, *couldn't* understand. The servants would prepare the food she and Pierce ate that night and they'd wash up afterwards. Oriana probably didn't know where to find anything in her own kitchen.

'Bye, Ori.' Vanessa said, pulling on her gloves. Oriana's body was unyielding in her embrace and her cheek withdrawn swiftly from her sister's kiss. Vanessa took her leave sadly, wondering what had happened to push them so far apart.

Chapter Forty-one

❧ ❧

All the time her sister was in her house Oriana's attention was elsewhere. She had got into the habit of worrying and it preoccupied her to the exclusion of all else, a record she played in her head over and over and over. She heard the noises of the outside world only over this record, and muted by it.

She knew something was seriously wrong with Pierce, with his family and their whole situation, but she could not fathom what was the matter. An atmosphere of unease permeated everything. It baffled her to such an extent that she found it impossible to give Vanessa or anybody the attention they warranted.

It was not only in the marriage bed that Pierce Powers proved ineffectual, but in every other area of their lives. He was constantly nervous and on edge and she did not know why. He declined to talk to her about business or finance and refused to admit that there was anything wrong. The only spectacular success poor Pierce had was in the gifts with which he showered Oriana. He bought her beautiful presents constantly and for that she was grateful.

When the door closed behind her sister Oriana wanted to call her back. She wanted to put her arms around her sister and confess her confusion and her worry but Vanessa had gone believing, so Oriana decided, that she should envy her sister and feel ashamed of herself.

In reality it was Oriana who envied Vanessa, though she would have died rather than admit it. She held in her imagination an unrealistic concept of the lovely American and her sister in their romantically poor but clean apartment. It would be comfortable in a primitive way. She had never been there but in her mind it was a cross between the humble

217

peasant home Jeanette McDonald was wont to burst out of, singing, on her way to meet her Bohemian prince, and the shabby, untidy comfort of the Cassidy household which she'd always disapproved of but which had relaxed her every time she'd been there and which had inculcated in her a profound sense of well being. She had never felt this anywhere else, and the realisation alarmed her, so she quickly pushed the thought out of her mind. The sum total of her experience of houses not of the same standard as her own was sadly limited. She did not envy her sister the apartment. What she envied was her sister's obvious love of her husband. She imagined nights of unbridled passion, Vanessa clasped in the masterful embrace of the lovely American, and she sat on the arm of the chair in her yellow drawing room, tense as a violin string, looking out of the window, shivering and shaking with unshed tears.

So many little things had upset and puzzled her. What was the matter between the Powerses, father and son? Neither would tell her, neither would discuss with her what was wrong, saying that she was female and would not understand. Sean Powers was not a man to show his feelings in public, yet he was clearly at odds with Pierce. There was a scarcely concealed contempt for Pierce patently obvious on family occasions, an intense irritation between them, and she could not fathom its cause. They excluded her, leaving her confused and troubled. She'd asked Pierce but his replies were always evasive and he talked down to her in a way she found intolerable.

'Is there a problem between you and your father, dear?'

The glowering frown she had become used to, the scowl. 'Of course not Oriana, what an idea! Dad and I are the best of friends. Where you get these ideas from I do not know.' Leaning across the breakfast table. 'Look dear, you'd never understand. Girls don't. In business there are tensions all the time. Men's stuff. Dad and I are in harmony in spite of all that, never fear.'

She knew in her bones it was a thundering great lie, and if he lied to her about that how many other lies was he telling her? How many half-truths, how many evasions, what *was* the mystery? Her imagination ran riot. Was the problem business? Was it personal? A power struggle? Had Pierce

218

tried to take over the business from his father? Somehow she couldn't imagine Pierce in competition with his father. He was too weak a personality for that. So what was it then?

Was it perhaps something quite different? Another woman? She tortured herself with imaginings about another woman whom everyone knew about except herself. She plagued herself with questions she could not answer.

Her mind wrestled with vague uncertainties, possibilities which, late at night and in the early hours, became overwhelming. She had no peace, gave herself no rest, chewed over every small happening and worried in her beautiful home while she was waited on by her efficient servants and surrounded by the luxury her sister envied so.

Chapter Forty-two

ᗆ ᗄ

Glenn and Vanessa's nights were hardly satisfactory but they were gradually improving. Many was the night Glenn had been from sheer frustration on the verge of behaving with a brutality that was not in his nature. He'd had to exercise supreme patience, which also did not come easily to him.

Vanessa was like an apprehensive and nervous animal, untamed, her natural reaction to protect herself against all advances, however gentle, and she experienced such pain that Glenn was sure there was something wrong. But she would not go to the doctor. 'I'd be embarrassed to tell him,' she whispered and he resisted an impulse to shout at her not to be stupid. It took a lot of reassurance and loving kindness to unlock her reserve. Little by little, so slowly, so gently, she was beginning to relax, not be so tense. His patience was being rewarded.

She had no one to talk to and sometimes she felt lonely and lost, out on a limb with no means of comparison, no yardstick to judge whether her behaviour was normal or whether she was weird and unnatural.

Finally Glenn persuaded her to see Doctor Quinlan, the family physician. He poked about a bit, much to her shame, told her she was still a virgin as far as he could see and that she should tell Glenn to 'ram it in, get it over'. His advice to her was that she should relax and brace herself. 'Thing is, Vanessa, every woman has to go through that once in her life.' He smiled kindly. 'Only once, mind,' he told her. Then he asked her how her father was and sent her away, more confused than ever.

Glenn, exasperated by the doctor's ignorance and lack of tact, suggested she go to Dr Jack, but he was Elana's father and no amount of persuasion that the Hippocratic oath would protect her convinced Vanessa to risk it.

'I did what you said,' she told Glenn. 'I didn't want to see Dr Quinlan, but I did. And, Glenn, I *hated* it. Dr Jack will tell me the same thing. And he just *might* let it slip to Elana. He's human, after all.' She looked at him, pleading. 'Can't we just go on without you . . . you know, do it the other way?'

'You're not getting any fun out of it, Vanessa.'

Vanessa frowned. She'd never heard the word fun used in connection with sex.

'Promise me one thing, 'Nessa,' he begged her. 'When we go to the States you'll see an American doctor.'

'Irish doctors are very good, Glenn. They are very good indeed.'

'About everything else maybe. About sex, no.'

But they loved each other. That made him patient, that made her try harder, that gave them both sustenance.

They settled down. Glenn could rely now on fresh under-wear, shirts neatly ironed, nicely cooked meals and a tidy, ordered apartment. Venny and Vanessa both hummed about their work and the latter began actually to enjoy some aspects of housekeeping that were hitherto anathema to her, like shopping and cooking.

She had adapted after the first panic-stricken days to being an ordinary Dublin housewife, and she found to her surprise that the position was one which, despite her mother's dire predictions, she thoroughly enjoyed.

They were not asked to fashionable parties. How the word had got out that Brendan Ardmore did not approve of the match, Vanessa did not know. Perhaps there was a tacit understanding. At all events she was struck off the list. No more parties at the tennis club, the Country Club, the golf club. No more cocktails with the old crowd, no more inclusion in groups to go to this ball or that. Their mantelpiece remained very bare.

No one cut her. Her crime was not considered that bad. There were polite nods accompanied by cheery greetings in the street, or in restaurants, but she was not included in the social round that had been part of her life.

She minded much less than she would have believed possible. Experience changed her. She valued love more than popularity. Her father's cruelty made her appreciate Glenn's tenderness, and his company was all she needed. His and Elana's.

Some of her old friends did not turn their backs on her. Naturally the Cassidys were staunch. They had never for a moment been disloyal to her, but they had never been a real part of the social whirl, and Elana had only been involved because of her friendship with Vanessa.

Vanessa had expected loyalty from the Cassidys. It was Gavin Fitzjames and his father who surprised her, asking her and Glenn to be one of their party to various events. And Dom Bradley also included them in an invitation to a cocktail party, but he did not have the sanction of his parents.

They didn't accept these invitations. They did not want to accept hospitality they could not return. And Vanessa was afraid of bumping into her parents at any of the fashionable events. Glenn understood.

'I'd be sick,' she told him. 'I'd vomit right there in front of everyone if Pappy ordered Mother out or shouted at me or even left.'

'Then we won't go, honey. Don't you fret about it.'

They did not know that her parents were refusing the very same invitations. Glenn, however, was unaware how much she missed the friendly gatherings, the exchange of gossip and the reassuring familiarity of belonging to her own circle. She hated being ousted from her position in the group. He had never been part of it so he did not realise the extent of her loss.

Part of Vanessa's secret sadness was her disillusionment. It was funny how shallow people could be. None of them, her erstwhile friends, even knew Glenn. He wasn't Jack the Ripper. He was an American sergeant and had done nothing to warrant being ostracised. He would have brightened up their gatherings, brought a little glamour into their parties.

She was aware however that he was not rejected because of his position or personality, but rather because Brendan and Rosalind Ardmore had given him the thumbs down.

But it did not worry her excessively. She had begun to enjoy sex 'the other way', as she called it. She had begun to enjoy being a wife, sharing things with Glenn, eagerly awaiting his arrival home, talking over the day's events with him, holding his hand when they were out together, being his other half. All the little things that went to mould them together, to make them a couple, she enjoyed so much that sometimes tears came to her eyes at the wonder of it all.

Chapter Forty-three

 so ov

Glenn and Billy were recalled. Uncle Sam was gathering his sons home. The war in Europe was over and the American troops who had remained there were gradually being reduced in number. Some of them would remain for a long time but excess servicemen were being repatriated.

Glenn was ecstatic but Vanessa had very mixed feelings. The move would separate her from her family and all the people she knew, from the only town she'd ever lived in. That town had proved fickle, her friends unstable and inconstant and her family had cast her out, but she loved it and them, it was familiar, it was home. Her mother saw her secretly, her father would not speak her name, her sister was remote as the moon and still she would be lonely for them. Near them there was always the chance of reconciliation, far away, the mighty ocean between them, she would lose them surely. And she would miss Elana more than she could say. Her friend, staunch and true, would leave a gap in her life she would not easily be able to fill.

All in all the move filled her with alarm. She'd miss Dublin, miss Fullers, miss Mitchells, Brown Thomas and Switzers, Davy Byrnes and the Bailey, and of course the Shelbourne for tea.

On the other hand, she told herself, she was going to a new and exciting land. She'd meet new people, make new friends. She'd find new places to cherish, places that would go into the scrapbook of her memory to become, she hoped, as dear to her as Dublin.

And she had no choice. *Whither thou goest, I will go too.* She'd follow him through the Sahara Desert if necessary. To the ends of the earth. She was his wife.

Her mother wept. Rosalind, who was always socially correct, displayed in public an inappropriate show of emotion that was acceptable only in private. She bawled. In the tea lounge of the Shelbourne of all places.

'Sobbing openly she was,' Mrs O'Grady told Bella, her daughter, lips in a thin line of disapproval. ''Tis well for you, my girl, you didn't snaffle that fine young American you fancied. He's brought nothing but trouble to Vanessa Ardmore. Out in the pale is that fine young lady. And her mother forgetting herself enough to cry her eyes out in the Shelbourne.'

It was a sad parting. Rosalind was heartbroken. She had once again pleaded with Brendan to forgive Vanessa as she was going so far away, and what's done is done, she said. But he remained obdurate, losing his temper at the mere mention of Glenn's name.

An even sadder parting threatened when Venny went into hysterical decline after Vanessa told her they were leaving. Useless to assure her that the Cassidys would not desert her. Useless to tell her that she would not be abandoned – she was inconsolable.

'Oh missus, what'll I do wi'out ye? It's me mam over agin.' As her mam had been, according to Jack Cassidy, an unbearable tyrant, Vanessa listened to the comparison with mixed feelings. Jack assured her, however, that Venny had adored her mother, cruelty notwithstanding, and very near worshipped the ground Vanessa walked on. Venny cried on Vanessa's shoulder, leaving a damp patch on her pale blue sweater. 'What'll I do? Oh, what'll I do?' she kept hollering and Vanessa repeated over and over and assured her that she would be all right, the Cassidys would look after her.

Between bouts of weeping Venny helped Vanessa with the packing. There was little to do. They had not had time to accumulate much during their short spell in Haddington Road. There had been few wedding presents and the furniture and decorations in the apartment belonged to the landlord. So there was almost nothing to pack.

Vanessa was weary of Haddington Road. Her sojourn there had been stressful. She hated her habit of comparing it to Dundalgan or Oriana's beautiful home in Foxrock. She was fed up with the snobbery of the petty-minded, the fickleness of the social set, people who were influenced by what she had rather than what she was, and she valued now the kind of love that was unconditional and did not depend on her being perfect. She had grown up enough in her marriage to be able to assess the ludicrous standards that had ruled her life for so long, standards she now saw as ridiculous.

She would be glad to leave. Glenn's plan was to take her to Wisconsin to the farm, introduce her to his parents and leave her with them until he had organised quarters for them in the camp in Corpus Christi, Texas. It sounded wonderful to her. The exotic names of places she had heard of only through the movies, like New York. And Texas. She looked forward eagerly to the future.

Only farewells worried her. Saying goodbye to her mother, to Oriana and Elana filled her with dread.

But before she left Ireland something happened that surprised her. Her Aunt Avalan phoned and asked her out to lunch. She said she would like to take Vanessa to the Russell. Vanessa was delighted to accept.

Chapter Forty-four

⤮ ⤯

Avalan was already at the table when Vanessa arrived. She looked stunning in a black suit, her enormous eyes outlined in dark pencil, her mouth cherry-red and her cat-like eyes glowing. She held an amber cigarette-holder but took the cigarette out of it as her niece arrived and stubbed it out in the ashtray an obsequious waiter held for her.

Waiters always buzzed about Avalan, and the prosperous well-dressed gentlemen lunching in the restaurant cast amorous glances at her. Avalan had always attracted attention from men, and Vanessa thought briefly that perhaps, just maybe, such a worldly aunt might be able to help her.

Avalan was surprised by the tension in her niece's face and came to the same conclusion.

'What will we eat?' she asked. 'I'm going for the duck. It's superb here. Duck with orange. I phoned in the order this morning. Salad to start? Nettles. I adore nettles. Some spinach?'

The menu was huge. There were three waiters around Avalan and she behaved as if that was her due.

The cutlery was silver, the nappery damask. The whole place reeked of comfort and Vanessa sighed. She hated to admit that she missed this opulence, but she did.

Vanessa drew the line at nettles. She said she'd love the duck but would prefer crab mousse and toast to start.

'We'll have a Pouilly-Fuissé with the starters.'

The waiters left reluctantly, and Avalan jumped right in. 'You must know I don't go along with your family about your marriage, Vanessa. I'm only sorry I've left it so late to support you. But I've had things on my mind . . .'

'Oh, I know, Aunt Avalan, I understand. How is Uncle Simon?'

Her aunt glanced at her. 'Oh he's ... the same.' She sighed, then shook her head as if to push away some unpleasant thought. 'But I think it is terrible what your father and mother have done. I wanted you to know that.'

'Mother doesn't mean to. It's Father,' Vanessa told her.

'Oh, I know that.'

'But it's very kind of you, Aunt Avalan, I appreciate it.'

'Don't call me "Aunt". It makes me feel old. Avalan is fine.'

'Okay.'

'I married for love,' she told her niece. 'It's the only thing, my dear. Look at your mother, my sister . . .'

'What do you mean?' Vanessa asked. Avalan spread her palms upwards.

'She can't have been happy all these years, living with your father, doing as he told her. Keeping silent when she's been hurt or he's been crass or violent.' Vanessa gasped but her aunt smiled. 'Oh, it must have been very difficult. I know you can tell me to mind my own business but I've always thought of Brendan Ardmore as a bully and a man totally lacking in understanding. There, I've said it. I hope we're still friends?'

Vanessa before her marriage would have protested. Now, however, she nodded in agreement. 'Of course you are.'

'I got the feeling he'd railroaded poor Oriana into her marriage when she'd far rather have married Gavin Fitzjames, am I right?'

'Gosh, Aunt Avalan, you are. You saw through it all, didn't you?'

'My dear child, most people did. That is the irony. Your father leading the lamb to the slaughter and all society looking on in approval.' She leaned forward. 'Your father judges books by their covers and people by their public images, by how they seem socially, and that's excessively silly.' The waiters brought their first course and Avalan waved a forkful of nettles about before popping it into her mouth. 'I have a feeling,' she continued, 'that poor old Brendan is terribly wrong about his precious Pierce Powers.' She shrugged, munching her greens. 'I could be wrong, but there are rumours abroad. But there you are, my dear, I've always believed in marrying for love. That way, if all else fails, you have *something* left.'

An expression of infinite sadness crossed her face and Vanessa saw there were tears in her eyes. She thought how lovely her aunt was, how compassionate. But then, suffering did make people more understanding.

'Oh Avalan, yes. Yes.'

Since she'd married she'd received only criticism. Now this mature, infinitely admirable woman, her aunt, was telling her she'd done the right thing. Her spirits lifted and a feeling of security came over her, a feeling that everything was going to be all right.

'You see, my dear, when Simon was wounded, how could I possibly have dealt with it if I hadn't loved him?'

Vanessa thought, yes. Of course. Without love Aunt Avalan would have been without anything, living in a nightmare. They ate and drank for a while in silence. Waiters removed their empty plates. The duck made its appearance and the *maître d'hôtel* was congratulated. The crisp vegetables were served, the orange and brandy sauce, the finger bowls, the sauté potatoes, when it was all satisfactorily served they began to eat with hearty appetite. Vanessa noticed her aunt darting curious glances at her as she chewed the duck. Finally Avalan put down her fork and looked intently at Vanessa.

'My dear, what is it?' she asked, dabbing her mouth with her napkin. 'You can't fool me. I've known you since you were a baby. Something is not quite right. Tell me, dear, and I may be able to help.'

Vanessa thought of her problem and blushed deeply.

'It's sex,' Avalan said to Vanessa's further embarrassment. 'There's a red flush over your neck and cheeks and that could only be brought about by sex.' She waited while the waiters removed the remains of their finished meal. When they'd gone she returned her attention to her niece. 'This country is the blessed end,' she told Vanessa. 'Anything else it is all right to discuss, but the most fundamental thing is taboo. Everyone, Vanessa, needs advice about sex. One day we'll *all* get it. Until then we'll have to rely on having the wisdom to *ask* for help wherever it is offered. I'm offering help. Now tell me what's wrong.'

They had raspberries and cream and coffee to follow and by the time Avalan had put a Benson & Hedges into her amber holder and an attentive waiter lit it she knew all about Vanessa's failure in bed with Glenn.

'I love him so much,' Vanessa told her aunt eagerly, so relieved that she could, at last, put into words what had been troubling her for so long. 'I don't know what's wrong. I seem to freeze. And there's the pain.'

'So you're still a virgin? Is that what you're saying?'

'So Dr Quinlan said, and he told me to tell Glenn to ram it in' – Avalan shuddered – 'And me to . . .'

'Lie back and think of England? Oh God, how cruel men are.' Avalan tutted. 'Dear God in heaven, I simply can't believe it.'

'Oh Avalan, I don't know what's the matter. I think I must be frigid.'

'Oh, stuff and nonsense.' Avalan frowned. 'I think I know what's the matter. I only *think*, mind. Dear sweet child. When you go to America, go see someone.'

'That's what Glenn wants me to do. But what do you think it is?'

'It's called vaginismus. It's an involuntary tightening of the muscles that surround the vagina.' She lowered her voice. 'If anyone heard us, dear God we'd be thrown out. But, Vanessa dear, it makes sexual intercourse impossible sometimes. The vagina clams up so poor Glenn can't get in.'

Vanessa was so interested that she forgot to be embarrassed. She leaned forward over the table as her aunt explained.

'I think it could also have to do with your father and those beatings,' she finished. 'It's psychological as well. They'll fix it for you in the States.' Then she cheerfully raised her voice to its normal level. 'They're up on things like that there. So sensible. So intelligent. As if we could sweep problems like that under the carpet.' She glanced at Vanessa sympathetically. 'Poor little lamb. No one to ask,' she continued. 'We're an appalling society,' she told her niece, 'but I'll wager I'm not far out in my diagnosis. And cheer up, sweet. It *can* be fixed.' And she clicked her fingers for the bill.

Chapter Forty-five

ॐ ॐ

Glenn and Vanessa left almost unnoticed for the USA. Something so dramatic happened that their departure, a few days later, drew little or no attention from the family shocked to the core by the arrest, for embezzlement, of Pierce Powers.

It was Glenn who told Vanessa when it happened ten days before their departure.

The apartment was full of crates, cardboard boxes and cases full of the clothes her mother had brought her from Dundalgan, when Glenn came into the living-room. He held a newspaper in his hand. 'I think you ought to go to your sister, honey,' he cried. 'I think she's in trouble.' Vanessa had been thumbing through the Tatler & Sketch. She cast it aside, and, holding up her face automatically for his kiss, asked, quite calmly, what he was talking about. He told her. The news made her sit up.

'Pierce? Arrested? That's not possible!'

Glenn nodded, loosening his tie. 'Yeah. I can't think how his father'd allow it to go that far. Still –' he shrugged – 'we don't know the facts an' I guess there's some good reason. Maybe he doesn't know about it.' He plopped himself down beside his wife and kissed her again. 'But Oriana'll need support.'

Vanessa leaned her head on his chest. 'I'll phone. But if Pappy's there . . .'

'He can't eat you,' Glenn said, smiling at her, touching her face gently with his fingers, stroking her cheek. 'He can't lay a finger on you, honey. Never again. He's got absolutely no power over you. When are you going to get it?'

She squirmed a little under his words. 'I know, dear, I know,' she said, 'but it's what I *feel*. I don't seem to have any control over it. He strips me of courage.' She looked at him, surprised to see his eyes twinkling. 'What is it?' she asked.

He began to laugh, throwing back his head, showing his white teeth. 'Your father! Jeez, I'd love to see his face! His favourite son-in-law, the perfect husband, the guy who could do no wrong, arrested for embezzlement ... what'll he do about that?' He stood and gave a little skip and chuckled, 'Holy cow!'

Vanessa's eyes widened. 'Holy cow,' she echoed. 'Pappy'll go crazy.' She turned to her husband. 'Tell me all. What did you hear? Oh, I must phone Oriana.'

'Well, it appears that the perfect son-in-law has been dipping into the coffers at Powers'. He's been cooking their books, and not very well it seems. His fellow workers suspected something was going on and they tried to warn him. But poor old Pierce didn't heed their warnings.' He leaned over the back of the sofa and put his hands on Vanessa's shoulders. 'Surely he didn't need to steal honey? His pa gave him lots of dough.'

'Maybe he did and maybe he wanted too much. Oriana is expensive. Maybe he wanted to keep her happy?'

Glenn shrugged. 'Maybe,' he said. 'Any rate, they laid a trap for him.' He wrinkled his brow. 'Pretty mean thing to do, seems to me. Those people knew him since he was a kid. His father was the prime accuser. Didn't try to protect or shield poor Pierce. Well, they'd warned him and they laid a trap, caught him red-handed and he's in jail now. Behind bars.' Glenn shook his head. 'So much for your father's judgement of character,' he said. 'Serves him right!'

'Not poor Pierce!' Vanessa cried.

'No. Certainly not Pierce. I meant your father.'

'And it doesn't serve Oriana right.'

'No, honey, I know. That's why I think you should call her. Although she did have a choice. You said Gavin Fitzjames loved her and she loved him. She shouldn't have married Pierce Powers unless she loved him. It's a kinda mean thing to do to a fella.'

'It was Pappy—' Vanessa began but Glenn interrupted her.

'Your Paw has a lot to answer for. But she shouldn't have obeyed him. She should have stood up to him. After all, she's a grown woman.'

'Oh, it's all very well for you to talk, Glenn, an outsider. You don't know how it is for a woman. How helpless we felt. We had no power, don't you see? No financial power, no physical power. And we loved our father. We were taught to obey him. You don't know what it *feels* like, how frightening it can be, enclosed like that at Dundalgan with someone as big and powerful as Pappy . . .'

'You could have just walked out.'

'And go where? Oriana and I were not trained to *anything*. We were Pappy's little girls. We had no money of our own. What would we do? Sleep on the sidewalk? This is not America, we can't just leave for another town and get a job as a waitress. No one would give Oriana or me work like that. We speak wrong.'

'Well, you could have stayed with Elana Cassidy?'

She shook her head. 'Oh no! That would be terribly unfair. I'm not the Cassidys' responsibility. Oh, I could stay a couple of weeks, months even, but what then? I'd still not be trained for anything. I'd have no incidental money. Do you realise how little the Cassidys have? By your standards they are quite poor. They have to be very careful and I couldn't take advantage of them like that. Even to take a typewriting course would cost. Oh no, Glenn, you're a man. You don't understand.'

'I never thought of it like that before,' he said, chastened.

'No. Most men don't. They don't follow it through. A lot of the time there is no place to go. And you've gotta remember we trusted him. We thought that was how fathers were. We were not looking at it from the outside, we were on the inside. Oh darling' – she flung herself into his arms – 'I'm so glad you helped me to leave. That you rescued me. I'm so grateful.'

'Nothing to be grateful for,' he replied, kissing her. 'I did it for me.'

'Oh yes there is. I'd never have done it without you. Oh Glenn, honey, stop. I've got to phone Oriana. Oh my gosh, she's going to be in a state.'

Chapter Forty-six

❧ ❧

Oriana was weeping on the phone when Vanessa got through. All her barriers were suddenly down.

'Oh 'Nessa, 'Nessa. What'll I do? We're disgraced. I'm so ashamed. You remember that day you came here? Well, I knew in my bones that *something* was going on. But I didn't know what. Oh 'Nessa, it's terrible. I'll never live it down. Please come over, I need you.' She ended on a wail.

Glenn drove Vanessa over to Foxrock. He waited in the car, unsure of his welcome. 'Don't be silly Glenn,' Vanessa told him, but he wouldn't budge.

'No. I wasn't welcome here yesterday, why should I be today? It's okay, honey,' he reassured her, 'I don't mind. I can wait.'

Oriana was pacing the living-room when her sister entered and she ran to Vanessa and embraced her. 'Oh 'Nessa, 'Nessa, what'll I do? What's to become of me?'

'Be calm,' Vanessa urged, guiding her sister to the sofa. A shaft of light illuminated the yellow room and it seemed strange that the beautiful golden place could hold such misery.

'How can I be calm?' Oriana shouted angrily. 'They say my husband is a criminal. He's in Mountjoy prison, for God's sakes.' She spread her soft manicured hands.

'Good Lord, why? Shouldn't he be out on bail?' It was Glenn in the doorway. Oriana looked up at him and hiccupped. 'I came to see if there was anything I could do,' he said. 'I don't want to intrude if you don't want me here, but it seemed kinda rude, just sitting out there in the car.'

'Oh God, why should I mind,' Oriana intoned. 'I have no right to object to anything any more.' She raised her tearstained face to Glenn, and, suddenly socially aware, said, 'We haven't been properly introduced. I'm Oriana Powers.'

Glenn didn't laugh, but, perfectly seriously, said, 'And I'm your brother-in-law, Glenn Carey. How do you do? That's what you guys say here, isn't it?'

Oriana laughed, a forced little laugh. 'Oh, I'm being ridiculous.'

'Oriana, why is he in prison? Why isn't he, as Glenn says, out on bail?' Vanessa persisted. She didn't know much about the law, but for what Glenn had told her on the way over in the car.

'I don't *know*,' Oriana cried angrily. 'No one will tell me. Mother says his father won't help him. They say he was given loads of chances and now he has to pay the piper. Mr Powers insists he face the music.'

'Sounds kinda tough to me. They encourage you to marry him but at the first sign of trouble they duck!'

'And where is the family?' Oriana asked. 'Where's Pappy now? Mother says he blames *me* for Pierce's crime, whatever that is.' She caught Vanessa's hand. 'Do you know exactly, Vanessa?'

'Embezzlement, I think,' Vanessa said. 'It's in the paper. *The Independent. The Times.*'

Vanessa had not meant to excite her sister but Oriana screamed, 'The *papers*! Oh my God, oh my God. *Everyone* will know. Oh, I can't bear it.' Then she looked up at them. 'That explains it,' she cried. 'Do you know what happened to me today, 'Nessa?' Oriana looked at her sister, distracted, pushing her fingers through her dark hair.' 'Well, I'll tell you. I had a date to meet Molly Powers, Pierce's cousin, and Melanie O'Brien in the Shelbourne for morning coffee. So I go. All dressed up in my sable coat. And do you know what happened? I'll tell you,' she said, not waiting for a reply. 'Everyone cut me! They turned away when I greeted them. Mrs O'Grady and the ghastly Bella. Mr and Mrs Bradley, Dom's parents, there with Andrew Grace and Billy Quinn. They all cut me, and I sat there' – she began to weep softly, helplessly – 'and waited, and waited, and Melanie and Molly never pitched up.' She swallowed her tears. 'And I didn't know why.' Then she added angrily, 'Bloody Melanie chickened out. It figures. But Molly! Wouldn't you think

Pierce's own cousin would have the courage to brazen it out and incidentally help me? She should have called at least. Put me out of my misery. Melanie's supposed to be my best friend, 'Nessa. She should have sent me a message. So should Molly. Only decent thing to do.'

Vanessa nodded. 'Yes, they should have,' she replied.

Oriana went on crying. She didn't seem to realise she was. There was mascara down her cheeks and little white tracks through her Max Factor Pan-Stik.

'Elana'd never do that to you,' she cried resentfully.

'No,' Vanessa agreed. 'She wouldn't.'

'Why?' Oriana asked piteously. 'Why, 'Ness? Why is that?'

'She was not chosen by me because she was rich, or her family were powerful, or because Pappy ordered. I guess she was chosen for love.'

'I guess. I guess,' Oriana jeered. 'You're going all American on us.'

'Well, I'm married to one, and I'm going to live there, so I shall probably go much *more* eventually.'

'So Mother said,' Oriana remarked vaguely. 'For love, eh? Like your husband?' She glanced over at Glenn who had gone to stand by the French window, staring out at the trees. A tender look came into Vanessa's eyes and Oriana saw that look and her heart twisted within her. 'I see,' she said to Vanessa and sat down abruptly on the sofa. 'I think I hate you.' She shook her head. 'Oh, ring the bell. Let's have some tea. Or a drink. Would you like a gin, 'Nessa? Glenn, Glenn would you like a drink? Heavens, come over to the fire. It's cold! Or is it just me?' She went to the fireplace and rang a bell which peeled somewhere in the nether regions of the house. Glenn went on staring out of the window and Vanessa sat on the sofa, trying not to feel hurt at her sister's thoughtless remarks.

Bennett arrived and Vanessa noticed she had a sullen look in her eyes. There was a subtle message of resentment as she put a tray of glasses on the sideboard and left.

When she'd gone Oriana remarked, 'She's furious. An ambitious girl, is Bennett, and she's aware she'll probably have to look for another position, and a reference from a jailbird is no recommendation at all.'

236

Vanessa thought of Venny, who would happily have joined Glenn in jail if that was where he ended up. Oriana poured drinks for them.

'Whiskey okay, Glenn?' she asked and he nodded.

'Canadian Club on ice if you've got it,' he said.

'We've got everything,' Oriana said in bitter tones. 'Gin okay for you, 'Ness?' Vanessa nodded. There was silence broken only by the call of a seagull outside and the tinkle of ice on glass inside.

'Here.' Oriana handed them their drinks, looking at them helplessly. 'I don't know what to do,' she said. She shook her head, glanced at herself in the mirror as she went to get her own drink. 'Oh my God, look at me. Great balls of fire! 'Ness, Glenn, one of you do the honours please while I clean up. Oh, what must you think?'

'Nothing, you silly girl,' Glenn laughed lightly. 'Do you really think it matters what you look like right now? Get real, Oriana. Life's not about how you look, but how you *are* an' how you deal with that.'

Oriana was staring at him as if he was crazy. She glared at him a moment then turned and left the room.

'She doesn't understand, Glenn,' Vanessa told him. 'She never understood. To her life is like a cocktail party and how you look is the most important thing.'

'She's in a state,' Glenn said. 'Can't say I blame her. Must've been quite a shock.'

'Everyone cutting her like that in the Shelbourne. That's what she'd have hated most. Poor Oriana.'

Glenn hooted. 'Oh dear, oh dear, Yes, that was awful!' he mocked.

'No, dear, but it was all her friends,' Vanessa told him.

He shook his head. 'No, honey. *Not* her friends. Friends don't do that. No, they were a judgemental group of fashionable people, not friends. They are not worth bothering about.'

He sounded impatient and Vanessa smiled at him. 'You're adorable, know that?' she whispered. 'And very wise.'

He smiled back and went over and kissed her. 'No, honey, I'm not. I'm a realist. I see things as they are, not as I want them to be.'

When Oriana returned, spruced and tidied up, they

listened as she talked. She talked for hours. During that time there was no sign of Bennett. No one called. The phone did not ring once.

They let her spew it all out. How lousy Pierce was in every department including the boudoir. How his father and he were always bickering. How sure she had been that something was wrong but no one would tell her, talk to her about it.

At last she began to show signs of fatigue and her eyelids drooped and Vanessa helped her to bed. She removed her shoes and tucked the eiderdown over her and left her on the bed, her eyes closing, hiccupping from her weeping, her breathing ragged.

'I'll stay here tonight, Ori,' she whispered. 'I don't think you should be alone.' But Oriana did not hear her. She had dropped off, exhausted and shocked, worn out by the day's events. 'I'll stay with her, Glenn. Just for tonight,' Vanessa told her husband.

'Okay,' he said and swallowed the last of his drink. 'I'll go bail out Pierce. Think I ought to. He shouldn't be left like that before he's convicted. The guy's not up to jail.'

Vanessa nodded. 'That's kind of you, Glenn.'

'It's common sense. You take your time, honey, but remember we leave at the end of next week.'

'She's so alone, Glenn. So very alone.' Vanessa told him. 'I keep thinking how lucky I am with you and Elana.'

'And Venny,' he grinned at her. 'Don't forget Venny.'

'No.'

'But you must remember your sister chose that way, 'Nessa. I'm afraid she chose badly.'

'No, dear. Pappy chose badly,' Vanessa corrected him and Glenn smiled at her. 'What wouldn't I give to see his face,' he said. 'What wouldn't I just give.'

Chapter Forty-seven

꧁ ꧂

Brendan Ardmore read in the newspaper that Pierce Powers
had been arrested and was in jail for embezzlement. He read
it in the *Irish Times* at breakfast. The news outraged him
and he took out his anger on Sive. He made the mistake
of roundly telling her off because his eggs were overdone.
She took the plate of scrambled eggs, held it a moment
in her hands and stared at him, eyes glittering. Rosalind
could see she was struggling with some inner compulsion
and she prayed that she would not give in to whatever it
was. The cook lost the battle because she suddenly and
quite deliberately emptied the soggy contents of the plate
into Brendan Ardmore's lap and banged the empty plate
on the table in front of their incredulous stares, crying, 'Get
your own bloody eggs!' Then she left the room looking very
pleased with herself.

Rosalind sat stunned. She was alone with her husband.
Tears sprang into her eyes. What had happened to her
ordered household? What had happened to her family?
Only last May she had been surrounded by her children
and her servants, cocooned in happy domesticity. Now her
daughters had gone and her servants were leaving, one
daughter's husband had been arrested, the other's name
was banned. It was horrible, most horrible.

There was no sign of Sitric who was rarely at home these
days, and Rosalind sat opposite Brendan at the other end of
the table nervously twisting her handkerchief between her
fingers, trying not to give in to depression.

Brendan behaved as if nothing had happened and ignored
the eggs in his lap. He kept reading and re-reading the article
about Pierce's arrest which, of course, like Vanessa's picture
long ago in the bath, was on the front page. Not tucked away

discreetly, oh no, but blazoned all across the primary sheet where the world and his wife could read about it without even having to buy the damned paper.

Rosalind had found out earlier and was hoping vainly that her husband would not find out at home but in his club or at work. She had no intention of telling him herself and drawing his wrath down on her head. Let him find out how he would and tell *her* and she'd pretend that was the first she'd heard of it. Today was his day at the office. Let some malicious gossip-monger break the news to him there. She had no doubt there were many at Ardmore & Son who would relish the task. But she had reckoned without the newspaper.

'Are you in to lunch today, dear?' she asked.

When he did not answer she looked up to see him, ashen-faced, half-rise to his feet, his mouth opening and closing like a cod-fish. He stared at her, face contorted, holding the newspaper out with trembling hands, and fell, face first into the toast and marmalade on the plate in front of him, the eggs in his lap slowly descending to the carpet. She stared at his inert form collapsed across the table and noted in a detached way her lack of concern.

Dr Quinlan was sent for and he came to the house, bumbled and rumbled about, blustered over his unconscious friend until Rosalind lost patience with him. She sent for Dr Jack and he packed Brendan off to hospital instantly.

'It's a stroke, Rosalind,' Dr Jack told her and Rosalind, looking into his kindly eyes, wondered why she didn't give a damn. She wanted to tell the sympathetic doctor, 'Look I couldn't care less whether he lives or dies,' but she was so used to playing the part of the concerned wife she did it automatically. She wondered what the doctor would say if she told him she was indifferent to her husband's fate and decided, looking at him, that he probably guessed the truth.

They took Brendan to the Mater Hospital and Dr Jack reckoned he would be all right. 'He has a very strong constitution and he'll get over it quickly. But I recommend that he sees Gordon Collinson. He's a specialist in that field. He's a grand man, a grand man, and if anyone can pull your husband through, he can,' Dr Jack assured her. Not being at all sure she wanted him to pull through, but dutiful to the last, Rosalind accompanied Brendan to the hospital, saw him settled in, then returned home.

She decided to give herself a quiet time to think about all the happenings that had thrown her life into chaos. She had had to get a taxi, as she had travelled to the hospital in the ambulance. The taxi had smelled of stale cigarette smoke and the Dublin cabbie was voluble on all subjects, including her son-in-law. 'Jasus, the likes of him, a silver spoon in his mouth, him rippin' off his own da! Jasus! It'ud freeze yer liver, so 'twould. Janey Mac, an' his da leavin' him te rot in bloody Mountjoy, ha, ha. Well, missus, ye know what they say: only in Dublin would ye find places called Ballsbridge an' Stillorgan, an' the prison called Mountjoy!' And he threw back his head and chortled, glancing at her in the rear-view mirror. Then, seeing her stony face, he gave up and returned to his own thoughts.

When she reached home she found pandemonium. The Byrne family were collected, all their worldly goods about them on the front steps of Dundalgan. This was strictly forbidden. Servants were supposed to use the back entrance, but at that moment Rosalind had to pay the cabbie, who was staring at the house, and the motley crew in front of it, their trunks and cases piled up on the gravel, with avid curiosity.

'Will ye be needin' me?' he called hopefully to Rushton, who glared at him and waved him away.

'What on earth – Sive? Rushton?' Rosalind faltered. 'What are you doing? You know this is not allowed . . .'

'Not another minute, mum. Not another second under this roof.'

'We've had it, Mrs Ardmore,' Rushton said resolutely. 'We're going now this minute.'

'But you must work out your notice,' Rosalind protested feebly. 'And Mr Ardmore is very ill. In hospital . . .'

Sive put her hands on her hips. 'Well now, Jasus, Mary an' Joseph forgive me, but I can't say I'm that upset. He's *never*, never once been nice to me, mum. Never! Never said a kind word. An' now we have this job Sergeant Carey got us with the 'Merican 'Bassador an' we don't see why we should put up with one more insult, mum, one more night under this roof.'

'But how will I manage?' Rosalind asked tearfully.

'That I don't know, mum.'

'I can't manage without you, Sive, with no replacement.'

'You should have thought of that before, mum. You should have made Mr Ardmore understand.'

'I'll be lost,' Rosalind cried, contemplating the huge empty house.

'I don't mind staying, Ma,' the good-natured Imelda volunteered. She had been smiling vacantly at Rosalind who, looking at her, decided the girl was definitely a few bricks short of a load. She had had little to do with Imelda over the years as the girl worked mainly in areas she had no contact with.

Sive folded her arms and looked from Rosalind's helpless face to her daughter's vacuous one. 'Well,' she hesitated and glanced at Rushton who shrugged his shoulders. 'Well, provided ye don't ask her to cook. Provided she does only the work she knows, then mebbe, as it's the only place she's ever known, an' we're bound to have problems wi' her in a strange place, well . . . if you want to, 'Melda?'

She looked closely at her daughter who nodded vehemently. 'I'd like to stay here, Mam' she said. 'Don't wanna go.'

'Then remember, mum,' Sive told Rosalind firmly, 'I'll be keepin' tabs on her. She's to do what she's used to, no more, no less, an' we'll see how things turn out.' She turned to Rushton who had piled their cases on and into the Daimler.

'We're goin' in *that*,' Sive told Rosalind defiantly, 'an' there's nothin' ye can do about it. Rushton'll deliver it back an' come to the 'Bassador on the bus. He'll lave it perfect, so he will.'

'I'm sure he will, Sive,' Rosalind told her, still bewildered by the turn of events. 'And thank you for Imelda.'

'That's all right, mum, but you treat her right. No more, no less, remember. It's only because she never had dealings with Mr Ardmore that she wants to stay. He's a shadow to her, so he is. See you keep it that way or she comes home to us.'

She climbed into the big car, front seat, beside her husband. There was an anxious look in her eyes and Rosalind knew she was a little apprehensive about the future in spite of all her bluster. 'Well, come on, Rushton,' she told her husband. 'Let's go. I don't want to spend a minute more here'n I have to.'

Rushton started the engine and they drove off. Rosalind was left forlornly on the driveway. Imelda slipped her hand into Rosalind's and she did not pull away. She stood there feeling terribly lost, the maid's hand clutched in hers.

The girl looked at her. 'What now, mum?'

Rosalind fought the tears that threatened to spill. 'The laundry, Imelda,' she suggested, although she had not the faintest idea how Sive had organised the work timetable. 'Perhaps the laundry might be a good idea.' Rosalind glanced at the girl. 'And a cup of tea? I so need a cup of tea. Maybe you could get me a cup of tea?'

'Me Mam said I wasn't to cook,' Imelda said in a matter-of-fact way.

'But a cup of tea, Imelda? Just that?'

'Don't ye know how to do it yerself, mum?' the girl asked with something like pity.

'No,' Rosalind admitted. 'So you better show me, Imelda, so I never have to ask you again. *Showing* me how to do it isn't exactly cooking, Imelda, is it?'

Imelda thought for a moment, then she smiled at Rosalind. 'No, mum, 'tisn't. All right then. I'll show ye.' And together they mounted the steps to Dundalgan.

Chapter Forty-eight

೭๑ ๑೨

Rosalind went to Haddington Road to say goodbye to Glenn and Vanessa. Brendan was recovering and he still refused to allow her to talk about or see the Careys. His rude health had stood him in good stead and the doctors had watched in amazement, Rosalind with sinking heart, as he bounded back, recovering more quickly than anyone could have dreamed. But the experience had not softened him.

Rosalind told Glenn that Vanessa's father was outraged by the fact that it was he who had bailed Pierce out of jail. He was angry that Glenn had interfered, muttering that the Yanks thought that they could meddle in everyone's business.

'It was not the plan at all, Glenn,' Rosalind told him. 'The plan was that he should stew in jail for a while. Teach him a lesson. That's what his father wanted and Brendan agreed when Sean Powers told him how he wanted it.'

'Make Pierce a very angry guy,' Glenn said, 'and angry guys are dangerous.'

'Well anyway you frustrated the plan, good or bad, and now Sean Powers and Brendan are furious with you.'

'He was already,' Glenn said tranquilly. 'See, Ma-in-law, I really don't care what he is.' And he shrugged his shoulders indifferently.

'Only it's difficult for Mother,' Vanessa pointed out.

Her mother had simply arrived in Haddington Road, much to Vanessa's embarrassment. She did not want her mother to see the apartment and had insisted their meetings were in the Shelbourne or another such place. Rosalind's reaction was all Vanessa feared. She glanced in horror around the two small rooms, the kitchen and bathroom, and inquired,

'Where's the rest? Is this *all*?' in stunned tones. Then, 'Where do you put the servants?'

Before Vanessa could mumble an apologetic reply Glenn introduced Venny, who was carrying a basket of last-minute laundry from the bathroom where she'd done it to the kitchen, to hang on a clothes-horse to dry. They all collided on the tiny landing and Glenn said, 'This is Venny, Mother-in-law. She's our cook and general factotum. She's been looking after us beautifully. She is wonderful. A first-class cook.'

Vanessa looked at her husband in surprise. Speaking like that about Venny was out of character. Then she saw what he was up to.

'Cook!' Rosalind breathed. 'Cook.' She forgot all else when she heard that word. Her head shot up and she scrutinised Venny closely. 'Why are your eyes red?' she asked.

'I bin' cryin', mum,' Venny told her.

'Why?'

'Mr Carey and Mrs Carey are goin' to America. I don' know what will happen to me,' she wailed and disappeared into the kitchen.

Rosalind had been having great trouble replacing Sive and Rushton. At the moment with Brendan in hospital the absence of Rushton was not the catastrophe it could have been, but Sive was a different matter. Sive was sorely missed. They had tried to replace her but the girls and women who came to Dundalgan were either totally ignorant and would have to be trained from scratch, or they wanted a fortune for their services.

'Oh yes, Mother-in-law, Venny is a very capable cook.' Glenn twinkled at Rosalind who glared at him.

'I do not like your choice of title for me,' she told him.

'Sorry, Mother-in-law.'

'Venny nursed her mother for many years and it appears her mother was very bad-tempered. She's used to –' Vanessa hesitated – 'people being a bit sharp with her.'

'But she'll write and tell me if she's not happy.' Glenn looked anxious.

'Don't worry, Glenn. I'll see she is treated gently.'

Rosalind followed Venny into the kitchen where she

announced that she wanted her for a week's trial period as soon as Vanessa and Glenn left for America.

'I'm sure it will work out satisfactorily,' she told the ecstatic servant. 'Mr Ardmore is a very difficult man. He'll roar at you a lot, but you must not pay any attention to him.'

'Ach, sure that's the least of my worries, mum,' Venny cried, delighted at the turn of events. 'Sure'n I don't have te listen, do I? I never listened to me Mam.'

'As long as Mrs Ardmore likes your cooking and you can ignore Mr Ardmore's temper you'll be hunkey-dorey, Venny. Only you must not tell him you came from us. He'd go mad.' And Glenn winked at Rosalind. 'He doesn't like me, see.'

'Then he's daft, sur,' Venny cried, 'an' not *worth* listening to.'

Rosalind said a sad goodbye to her daughter. She felt numb and dispirited and a great hopelessness overwhelmed her. 'I'll include you in the rosary every night, dear,' she said as she hugged Vanessa. 'And I'll work on Pappy. In the end he'll give in.' She drew a ragged breath. 'Now don't let them bully you over there in that heathen land. And don't begin to say hi and okay and call men guys or chew gum or anything like that. Promise me?'

'Oh Mother!' Vanessa cried, half-laughing, half-crying as they embraced. 'I promise, Mother.'

'I love you, pet. I'm just sorry things turned out this way.'

'So am I, Mother.'

'But you are happy?'

'Yes, Mother, of course I am.'

'He has a nasty habit of showing your father up,' Rosalind remarked, looking at Glenn who stood in the kitchen doorway talking to Venny.

'Who, Mother?'

'Your husband. Glenn.'

'Oh yes, Mother.'

'Oh, my dear one, I'll miss you so much. You must write often.'

'I will, Mother. And I can phone.'

'Put it down if your father answers,' Rosalind abjured.

'Okay, Mother.' Rosalind glared at her and Vanessa clapped her hand over her mouth. 'Sorry, sorry, Mother. I will. I will.'

And they had gone. Disappeared out of Dublin as if they had never been.

Afterwards when people talked and gossiped, putting everything together piece by piece, they wondered about the lovely American. They decided, some of them, that he was a saint, as Venny put it, a walking saint, that it was his sweetness, his goodness, his desire to help others that had solved so many of their problems. There were quite a lot of people who believed this. Pierce Powers certainly did. He had been abandoned by all who knew him and Glenn had rescued him. The Byrnes too spoke of him with awe and gratitude.

'He worked quietly, like the good Lord, not letting people know what he did, never letting on,' Venny would tell anyone who would listen. 'He helped everyone, so he did.'

Others were sceptical. It was accidental, they said. He just happened to be passing when whatever the problem was arrived and he simply dealt with it. They admitted that he saw with clarity what had to be done. Outsiders often saw what people involved could not.

Or was it, yet others speculated, a huge stag-like struggle with Brendan Ardmore? An American combatitiveness and a determination to win, however deviously. He was canny, they said, and swift, and at each turn it was Brendan who had been the loser. Oh yes, he knew what he was doing all right. He was making a complete fool of Brendan Ardmore.

Some said that he might not even have been aware that he was defeating the man who had insulted him, insulted his country, treated him like an outcast and an inferior. Some said the American Marines programmed you to win. It all might have happened subconsciously. Jack Cassidy thought so. Or not. Who would ever know for sure?

PART TWO

Chapter Forty-nine

⊷ ⊶

Sitric drove the MG fast along the river bank. He was nearly up to eighty. The wind blew his hair from his forehead, which was wet with sweat. One of his hands rested lightly on the wheel while the other held the cigarette he was smoking elbow resting on the windscreen.

Sitric was charging into trouble and he knew it, but he did not care. If anyone had told him he was like Brendan Ardmore, his father, at this moment, he would have hooted in derision. Yet they had many similar character traits. Sitric possessed his father's habit of acting heedlessly on an emotional impulse and not thinking through the consequences.

Back from hospital Brendan was suffering, squirming and fretting under the horrible inevitability that his ignorance of the business was to be revealed. Ardmore & Son were going to find him out. He was going to be shown as a fool to the world, and his world was Dublin. Then there was the hideous fact that he had been wrong about Pierce Powers. Added to that he missed his daughters. He had flown off the handle with Oriana, inferring she was somehow to blame for her husband's crimes, and now she would not speak to him. And he secretly realised that he had behaved precipitiously with the Byrnes. Dammit, he missed Rushton more than he would have admitted and realised that if he'd given himself time to think, if he'd weighed up the pros and cons of the case, he'd never have sacked the family.

Brendan had acted hastily and now his son was doing the same. He had been told not to go where he was going yet he was driving there at the speed of light, bullheadedly determined.

His affair, begun that Maytime a year ago when all the

world was young, was in deep waters. He called her his life, his love, his woman, his child, his mother, his beloved, his whore, his sybarite, his Princess of Babylon, his she-tiger, his pussycat, and other titles too exotic to utter except in the throes of passion. But now he was angry. She did not want his total love, she said. Passion, yes. Erotic adventure, yes. Dalliance, yes. Love, no. What could he do? He was realistic enough to know that it was rare indeed for a young man of nineteen, in the year of grace 1949, to find himself a mistress who initiated him into the arts of erotic sex and steered him through the difficulties of youthful passion, educating his taste, refining it, experimenting with and developing his sexuality. How could he *not* fall in love with her? That's what he wanted to know.

From that first kiss, last May, under the trees, he had been her slave, her lover, her adoring acolyte. She, summer-garbed in transparent voile, like gossamer, on the swing in the woods at Dundalgan, had been silent witness to his precipitate entrance into the glade, his tears, his helpless sobbing against the old chestnut opposite the swing.

He had not seen her. He had been overwhelmed by some cruel remark made by his father and had run out of the house and down here to his favourite spot to release the anguish pride forbade him to in the house where his father might see. She had been sitting on the swing watching him as he beat his head against the gnarled trunk of the tree, smashed his forehead against the tough bark, crying salt tears of frustration and humiliation.

Her legs were bare and open, her hands between them holding the seat, her face glimmering in the green shadows, her voice calling to him, like a dove, soft and cooing. 'There, there. There, there. It's going to be all right.'

He'd turned and saw her there like a wood-nymph, staring at him wide-eyed. She looked too, curiously expectant. She told him afterwards that she had known there was only one way she could heal him and it surprised her as much as it did him. There was that something in her gaze that, to his initial horror, made him suddenly desire her. She'd seen it, her eyes widened, then narrowed, and she'd whispered, 'Ah!' Softly, slowly. Then she'd held out her arms and said, her breath short, 'Come here,' and he'd walked slowly forward

252

and she'd pulled him close, between her legs, her hands on his arms, until his hard centre was pressed against her soft one with only the clothes between them.

Still, he was afraid. Was this a dream, here in the verdant shadowed wood, a wild unbelievable hallucination?

'Pull them down,' she whispered against his ear and he knew she meant his tennis shorts. But he didn't want to stop pressing against her, did not want to separate his body from hers even for a moment.

She understood. 'It won't stop,' she said, smiling.

Everything she did inflamed and excited him, and he did as he was told.

She opened the buttons down the front of her dress, quite calmly, and took off her brassière, then her panties, and he watched her, fascinated, and all the time his manhood grew and she stood there before him, naked, perfect in his eyes, an enchanted creature of woodlands and water and earth and sky.

She said, 'You have a wonderful body.'

He gulped and hardened, stimulated by her admiration. But what to do now?

She guided him. She sat back on the swing and opened her legs. 'Come here,' she said again. 'Let me guide it home. Home into me. Here. Like this. I'm ready. You're ready. Into me, oh God, into me.'

He could not plunge into her without wanting instantly to come, but she did not let him. Not until later. She played with him, her muscles tightening and letting go, tightening and letting go, again and again, around him while he cried out and his voice joined the chorus of wild creatures in the wood.

'They're all doing this,' she said as they fell soldered together off the swing and he mounted her, trembling with excitement, his orgasm on the brink, a tide of shivering nerves agitated into screaming pleasure. Then she pressed his buttocks with her hands, lifted her legs around his waist and cried, 'Now, now, now, now, now!' And he let go. Completely, flooding out, releasing a tide of such acute sensation that he thought his body would explode.

He had never known, never experienced anything like the peace that followed. His problems seemed to shrink in her arms, vanish in a puff. Who cared about a father's cruelty when soft arms enfolded him? Why did it matter if he felt stupid and awkward in front of his family when her body wrapped itself around him? She was balm to him, she was a healer. She was his love.

It had gone on from there. He could not stop. He was obsessed by erotic thoughts of her night and day and he was indefatigable, a measureless lover. And she could not get enough of his young, priapic body, she who had been starved for so long. When he was with her they indulged in all the games in the world. They were locked together in a sexual fixation that absorbed and completely preoccupied them.

His appetite, as Shakespeare said, increased by what it fed on and he fed on her constantly.

So he fell in love. Fell deep into that pit where nothing else existed except her, where the view was blocked out and nothing else could be seen, where there was no reality except her, Venus of his soul, his senses, his very core. Useless for her to forbid him. Useless for her to tell him she loved another. He had fallen down into the abyss and there was no climbing out.

Never come to my home. She'd told him, time and time again, and as in all things he had obeyed her. But now, after last night, no – two whole days and nights without her, with no explanation as to why she did not come to the apartment in Molesworth Street, he was going to disobey her. He was on his way to her home.

He knew full well he shouldn't, but he could not think rationally about the consequences of his acts, how disaster could follow.

'Never, ever disrupt my private life, Sitric, or you are history,' she'd said.

'My family thinks I'm on drugs,' he'd told her.

'Well, in a way they are right. I'm the drug,' she'd said.

'Then what if I got withdrawals?' he'd asked. 'And came and knocked on your window?'

'I wouldn't open it,' she said with a finality that chilled him.

'I know you don't sleep with him,' he told her. 'You couldn't.'

'That's not your business,' she'd said, turning her back. 'And what do you know about it anyhow?'

He *had* felt drugged all year. At Oriana's wedding, sitting looking at her, trying to feign an indifference to match hers, smoking, smoking, desperately hoping to contrive a meeting away from prying eyes. Not succeeding because she didn't want to. Always, always she led, he followed.

He supposed that was normal practice under the circumstances. A married older woman with a young man, but he came to resent it. Why did she always have to be in charge?

Then, last week, she'd missed one of their nights together. Distraught, he waited for her, walking up and down, up and down, pacing, pacing in a lather of indecision. She never came. Never sent a message.

This week she'd not shown up at all. Nearly out of his mind with worry and panic he'd finally had enough waiting, and, jumping into his little red roadster he decided he could not tolerate the anxiety any longer and headed in frustrated anger and against her specific orders to Rackton Hall.

Chapter Fifty

c✎ ✎ɔ

Simon had been ill. He had suffered a severe increase in pain. It had become acute and agonising and McWitty advised the specialist. But the specialist who knew about Simon's case and was familiar with him was in England, so Avalan set about chartering a light aircraft and arranging to transport Simon to London.

She was deeply concerned about her husband. It broke her heart to see him whimpering, crucified under onslaughts of pain that left him exhausted. Teeth chattering, clutching her hand until he bruised its delicate skin, he writhed in agony while she and McWitty looked on helplessly.

Sitric was the last person on her mind at this moment. He was the icing on the cake and as such she could well live without him.

It had been absorbing and fulfilling, their love affair. At first the excitement was all important. Teaching him all that Simon had taught her. Inventing new things. Shutting themselves up in the flat in Molesworth Street and giving themselves over to an erotic idyll without shame or barter or conditions. It had been doubly exciting to play games with the family, deceive them, listen to their hypocritical clap-trap, their moral poses, their righteous self-justification while they behaved so mean-spiritedly about poor Vanessa and Oriana. Especially Brendan Ardmore, a man whom Avalan really despised.

Brendan was glib, quoting from the Bible, but Avalan noted he chose only the parts that suited him. It seemed to her that Christ promoted love rather than gain, that He did not waste much time on sex, seeming to spend much more energy urging his followers to be kind and love one another.

McWitty came into her room and told her that her nephew was there. An expression of annoyance crossed her face. 'Show him up, will you and go to Simon,' she told the nurse. 'The plane will be here from Collinstown in half an hour.' She looked into the crumpled, ugly face of the nurse. 'You'll stick with us, McWitty, won't you?' she asked and a look of relief crossed his countenance. 'Oh yes! I'd like that very much. I was hoping you'd suggest it. He's a dear man is Mr Rackton, a very dear man.'

'It's not going to be pretty,' she said.

The nurse bowed his head. 'I know,' he replied. 'But I have a loyalty, Mrs Rackton. I don't want to leave him until ... until ...'

'Until it is over,' she replied, nodding. 'No, I understand.' She turned her back and sighed. 'Well then, that's settled. Go, get him ready for the journey.'

'Will I give him the morphine?' McWitty asked and Avalan nodded.

'If he'll take it. You know what he's like. He's afraid that the hallucinations will get worse ...'

At that moment Sitric, unable to wait a moment longer, burst into the room. McWitty nodded to her and left, saying, 'I'll attend to everything, Mrs Rackton, don't you worry.'

When he'd closed the door behind him she turned angrily to Sitric. 'What on earth are you doing?' she asked him. 'How *dare* you come here!' But he'd thrown himself at her feet, his head in her lap, sobbing. 'I didn't know where you were. What happened? I've been desperate ...'

'Oh Sitric, get up. Heavens, boy, suppose someone came in?'

'I don't care if they do. Let the whole world know. See if I care.'

'Ah, but *I* do, Sitric. And it's against the *law*. What we're doing. Consanguinity, or incest, or something. You don't want to end up in jail like your brother-in-law, now do you? Making headlines? And for a crime like that?'

'Wouldn't that shock the pants off Pappy!' Sitric cried.

'It would kill him,' Avalan said.

'Terrific!' Sitric rubbed his hands together. 'That would be just wonderful.'

'You don't mean that, Sitric, not really.'

'Yes I do. I'd love to see him dead at my feet. I'd kill him if I wasn't so cowardly. I've wanted to so many times. When he used to beat Vanessa I used to fantasise about how I could murder him slowly.'

'When you look like that, Sitric, you look horrible. Stop it at once.'

She lifted him up firmly by his elbows, desiring him suddenly and fiercely, shocked by the realisation of her urgent need. She smiled at him and pushed his soft hair back from his damp brow. 'There now, sweetness.' She spoke softly, as if he were a child. 'Simon is very, very ill. That's why I did not come. He's in great pain and my place is at his side.' She patted his arm. 'I know you are grown up enough to understand this, so you must leave me now.'

'When will I see you again? I die without you.' His voice was anguished.

'When Simon is better.'

'But—'

'No buts. Simon was brutally maimed, Sitric, defending our freedom. I must go now.' Oh Christ why? Why did my husband have to care about the liberty of others? We were not threatened here in Ireland. Why did he have to offer himself up, a human sacrifice? Why Simon, oh why? What made men do it? The thoughts crowded in her mind as they always did and she wanted to break down and weep in her lover's arms, weep about her broken husband. 'And he needs me. His wife. You must understand that. I have to go. I *want* to go.' She sighed and touched his lips with her fingers. He kissed them while trying to protest. 'No, no, don't say anything. There's a plane coming in a few moments. To take him to London, to see the specialist. Now you must leave. Please. Go.'

He went. There was no way he could argue with her without sounding callous. Unhappy, hurt, feeling acutely superfluous and aware of the secondary place he took in her life, he left Rackton Hall, got into his little red car and drove back to Dundalgan.

Chapter Fifty-one

∽ ∾

Pierce Powers was found guilty but his sentence was light. The judge decided he should pay back what he had stolen from his father's company. As he could not do that in prison, his Honour said, he was going to put the young man on probation.

Privately the judge resented the fact that the case had come to court at all. It was, after all, a family matter. He felt that it should have been dealt with in the family home. Surely a man should be able to sort out his son's dishonest behaviour? And the boy seemed a rather feeble type, not at all belligerent or bellicose. But he did not say any of this. Sean Powers was too powerful and was one of his Honour's golf partners.

In the event he still antagonised Sean, who snorted angrily at the sentence and stomped out of the courtroom. Sean had wanted his son to go to jail. Oriana, looking fetching in a wide-brimmed black hat, burst into tears though she was not sure why. She was relieved, however. It was a definite social disadvantage to have a husband in prison, but she could not decide whether being on probation carried an equal stigma or not.

The press had a field day. The whole affair had begun to take on the aspect of a young man's persecution by a stern and unbending father, and the tide of public opinion began to turn against Pierce's father, Sean Powers, who was after all a vastly wealthy man cruel enough to allow his son to be publicly humiliated, and, seemingly, quite eager to see him sent to prison. That, the general public and the press decided, was unnatural.

Pierce was at once offered a job by his father's rivals, Murphy & Callaghan. Gleefully, Mr Brewster Callaghan came

259

to Pierce and told him he had an opening in the counting house for just such a young man. The press seized on it and to Sean Powers' fury the headlines screamed, RIVAL TRUSTS SON THAT FATHER CONDEMNS.

Brewster Callaghan hated Sean Powers and acted out of malice. He did not trust young Pierce but was fairly confident that the boy would not get up to his thieving practices so soon after the court case. He was very frightened, Brewster could see that, and in any event he had no intention of keeping him on the staff for very long. He would have fun, though, in the meantime, showing Sean Powers up, having a laugh at his expense. He crowed to the papers that he thought Sean Powers a Victorian father, cruel and unkind. He turned a benign face to the photographer and said he could not treat a child of his like that and in common decency he was employing Pierce Powers so that he could pay his father back what he owed him. 'For he'll demand every penny from his son,' Brewster said. 'Every blessed penny.'

Surprisingly, in Dublin, where a certain laziness prevailed (most people decided they would act, planned to do it, then forgot about it) a lot of customers actually left Powers & Co, and crossed to Murphy & Callaghan. Brewster was ecstatic, Sean Powers incensed.

Oriana was disgusted and confused. There was no blue-print as to how she should behave. Pierce came home and a sort of silent fury simmered between them.

'How can you *face* people?' Oriana asked him one evening at dinner.

'Well, what else can I do?' he shrugged.

She had no answer. Money was short and she did not know how to budget. She did not *want* to know. She carried on as if nothing had happened and the bills poured in and Pierce had no way of paying them. He tried talking to her, but she would not listen. 'I don't want to talk about that. Money! It's not my concern. It's *your* job to pay the bills, not mine.'

'But, Oriana, I'm on a low salary now. We can't *afford* to live at the rate we're living.'

'Well, too bad! I can't help it. You'll just have to work harder, won't you? I can't manage on less.'

Oriana's constant whining since his disgrace was getting on his nerves, and her refusal to face facts angered him.

He had been humiliated in public, arrested, bailed out by a brother-in-law he did not know, ostracised by his family and tried in front of scandalmongers and gossips, then a judge had dressed him down but given him a way out. He was tired of it all. He wanted to get on with his life and make the effort to pay his debt. But with Oriana that was impossible. She neither stood by him nor would contemplate cutting expenses. She was getting money from her family, he guessed, or using her own. But it could not go on. The bills were mounting, the money they were spending was way beyond what was coming in and only a miracle could save them. There was no possible way they could go on living at the same standard but Oriana did not seem able to face this fact.

'It's all such a disgrace, Pierce,' she cried. 'Bennett is leaving. I've got to find another maid.'

His heart sank. 'Can't you manage without a maid, dear?' he asked.

She looked at him incredulously. 'What do you mean?' she asked, in a dumbfounded way, unable to grasp the concept. 'What on earth do you mean?'

'Vanessa didn't have a maid. Not one like Bennett. She had help. Couldn't you manage with help?'

'Don't be ridiculous, Pierce,' she replied, sounding very like Rosalind. Then frowning. 'All my friends are cutting me. It's terrible. Oh, why did I ever marry you?' And she burst into tears and fled to her room.

It was like that a lot in their house these days. Since their wedding night Oriana had acquired the habit of treating Pierce contemptuously, and since the court case with derision. He slid further and further away from her. He'd been so hell-bent on marrying her, he realised, because he was jealous of Gavin Fitzjames and he had been egged on by his father. He had thought he was a hell of a guy taking her away from Gavin, but he had awakened to the fact that she was a stranger. He did not know who she was and was not sure that he wanted to. So he stopped conversing with her. He kept his peace. He became silent and lonely.

What he was discovering, to his amazement, was that at Murphy & Callaghan, because he was under scrutiny, because he could not cut corners, because he wanted to let them see how wrong his father had been, he worked hard and effectively. He found he enjoyed being honest and above-board. He was enjoying doing things the right way. And he was efficient. He was good at his job.

He would have liked to share this discovery with his wife but she was not interested. For the first time in his life he was working for himself, and although it was for a paltry wage, nevertheless he was making a success.

But Oriana was light worlds away, resenting their position, their slipped social standing, their shame, their lack of money.

And Oriana began to think morning, noon and night about Gavin Fitzjames.

Chapter Fifty-two

လ ၛ

'Do you love me, truly?' Elana shifted her weight and snuggled up closer to Gavin on the rickety sofa in the Cassidy living-room. Tucked into the crook of his arm she took a deep breath and asked the question she was so afraid of asking. 'Do you love me truly?'

''Course,' he replied.

It was not the reply she wanted. She sat up. 'But *truly*, Gavin, truly? Do you love me a lot?'

''Course,' he said again. There was a pause. 'Has your Dad got a skeleton somewhere?' he asked. 'One I could borrow? Oh, I s'pose Dominic would be using it,' he decided.

'Oh Gavin! I'm trying to find something out.'

'So am I.'

'Do you love me?'

He turned to her. 'Sure I love you, Elana Cassidy. Lots and lots. Madly. Now, has your Da got a skeleton Dominic is not using, or could he lay his hands on one so I could practise on it? The lads have removed ours from the hospital for some prank or another.'

'Oh fuey!' She threw a cushion at him and gave up.

He was always the same, flippant and casual. Try as she might she could not coax the declaration of undying love from him that she needed to calm her fears.

She was afraid that he still loved Oriana. He never talked about her or for that matter showed any interest in the court case. When gossip raged all around, Gavin Fitzjames kept his mouth shut. He sounded noncommittal when she talked of the Ardmores, curt when she talked about Brendan, and there was no emotion in his voice when Oriana's name cropped up.

Which it did. There was avid interest in the court case.

263

Elana wrote to Vanessa, keeping her abreast of the news from Dublin. She reported the guilty verdict, the judge's sentencing and Pierce's employment by Murphy & Callaghan. Vanessa replied that Oriana had written, but her letters were full of complaints about Pierce and their situation and she could not make head nor tail of what was happening at home. Elana asked Gavin if he knew how Oriana was, as Vanessa was worried about her. It was a sort of a test to see how he would react. But he did not take the bait – he simply shrugged and said, 'I expect she's all right. She's got her nice home in Foxrock. That's all she ever really wanted.'

'Won't she lose that? To pay back what he owes? Won't they take it away from them?' Elana asked.

'No. The house in Foxrock is in Brendan Ardmore's name. So it can't be taken away from her. Though how they're going to keep it up I don't know. Brewster Callaghan is not paying Pierce much.' He thought a moment. 'It's funny, Elana, but I earn more than Pierce does now and my prospects are better. Poor old Brendan Ardmore! That must be a bitter pill to swallow.' He turned to her then. 'Oh Elana, why talk about it? It has nothing to do with us.' And with that she had to be content.

Elana missed her friend dreadfully. It was shortly after Vanessa left for America that she began to go out with Gavin. They had, they realised, a lot in common.

He had bumped into her outside the Bank of Ireland.

'Oh I didn't realise . . .'

'That I worked here?' she said defensively. 'Oh yes. I do. I'm a working girl.'

He'd smiled at her, that wonderfully sympathetic grin which had turned a lot of female heads. 'Well, I'm a working boy too,' he said.

The rain was bouncing off the pavements, sleeting down in rivers to the gutters, sweeping away the last of the autumn leaves. Windscreen wipers busily sliced across car windows, and people held their umbrellas in front of them like shields. Elana licked the rain from her lips and smiled at him. 'I know. My brother Dominic talks about you,' she said.

'I suppose because we only meet at those posh parties we've got into the habit of thinking of each other as the idle rich.'

She laughed and nodded.

'Would you object if this working lad asked you to the Ballsbridge Tennis Hop Saturday night?' he asked. His hair was plastered to his skull and he kept blinking the water from his eyes.

'I'd love it, Gavin,' she said.

On that first date they'd talked about his set. 'They've always treated me like a second-class citizen,' she told him. 'I never really fitted in. They only accepted me because of Vanessa. Not like you. Born to it . . .'

He smiled. 'Well, that's as maybe. We may have been born to it but we couldn't keep up. We've got no money and you need money, you need loot to keep pace with that lot. And if they only tolerated you because of Vanessa they were fools.'

'Now Vanessa's gone I never see any of them,' she said ruefully.

'Fair-weather friends,' he said. 'Pa said even poor old Brendan and Rosalind are not seen around any more. I think they're afraid they'll be snubbed.'

'Gosh, Gavin, it's so stupid! Who cares about all that stuff? Who really cares?'

'*They* do. They make their own rules and they expect you to abide by their code. They feel they're doing you a big favour by including you on their list of desirables. They think that's the most important thing in life. Some of them would die if they were scratched off the list.'

'Is your Pa like that?' Elana asked. She didn't know why. She thought of Oriana's engagement and wedding, thought of the tall man dancing so beautifully with her. She said as much to Gavin.

'Pa? No. Pa treats it all very lightly.'

'Life was a fairy-tale when Oriana married Pierce,' she said. Then continued, knowing she should drop the subject. 'We thought then that life was a fairy-tale and we *must* have a happy ending. Marriage.'

'God, marriage is the *start*, not the finish.'

'I know that *now*, but we didn't know it then. Oriana didn't know it.' She looked at him but his eyes were blank and he did not reply.

They had begun to date regularly since then. Elana had written to Vanessa telling her about Gavin. Vanessa wrote back saying, 'I'm so happy for you. But watch out for

Oriana. Now that Pierce is disgraced, and, God forbid, has very little money, Oriana, if I know my sister, will be very miffed, and knowing her she'll be looking for a handy shoulder to cry on.'

Elana also told Vanessa what Gavin had said about her mother and father and Vanessa replied, 'I'm sorry to hear that Mother and Pappy are not seen out and about any more. They enjoyed the social whirl so. Mother's written to me and she sounds fine. I *know* she's lonely, but Oriana and I had to leave home sometime. Pappy, she tells me, has made a spectacular recovery but has not been himself since the stroke. Whether that's good or bad I don't know. He doesn't go into the office as often as he used to, but, she says, he has a wonderful manager called Crosby who keeps things in order for him.'

Vanessa was not too forthcoming about America. Everything there, she wrote Elana, was swell. The food was swell. The gang (Glenn's friends) were swell. The folks back home (Wisconsin where Glenn's family came from) were swell. Either, Elana decided, Vanessa was utterly content and in a state of bliss, or she censored the reality, cutting out the bad bits and concentrating on the good. Like everyone, Vanessa was probably experiencing ups and downs.

So Elana and Gavin became a pair. They slipped into the habit of going everywhere with each other. But Elana knew that the love she felt for Gavin was not the kind that made her heart beat fast or put stars in her eyes. She remembered Vanessa, the way she had looked when she saw Glenn, the way her face was transformed every time she talked of him. The way she glowed. Gavin was more like an old friend. She liked his kisses, his caresses, the way she liked strawberries and cream or champagne. She liked his company. She felt at home with him, comfortable with him, but wondered, wasn't there more? They slipped into the habit of assuming they would be with each other at all the parties and events they were asked to, and for Elana there was in this a slight irritant. It was as if she was already an old married woman. But then, she argued with herself, what more do I want? I have a man who loves me, is kind and sweet and good to me. Why should I look for anything more?

Chapter Fifty-three

❧ ❧

'KALAMAZOO, I've got a girl, in Kalamazoo, Don't want to boast, But I know she's the toast of Kalamazoo-oo-oo-oo.' They sang together in the car, American songs, American swing, laughing.

The open road before them, the green fields of Wisconsin behind them. They had left his family – mother, father, aunts, cousins, uncles, sisters, brothers, a multitude of relations – Vanessa had to admit, with some relief.

His family had overwhelmed her. There was such a thing as too much kindness and they had swamped her with hospitality and wildly intrusive friendship. They greeted her with an instant familiarity that had kept her in a state of acute embarrassment ever since they arrived in Wisconsin from New York.

New York had been magical. On their very first day there Vanessa went to Park and 64th Street and saw a Dr Abrahamson. He had been recommended by the medical officer from Glenn's unit, who had made the appointment for Mrs Carey before she had arrived in the States. There seemed no embarrassment at all about this and Vanessa could only marvel at a society that freely discussed such intimate subjects so matter-of-factly. On a sunny winter day Vanessa rang Dr Abrahamson's bell and he changed her life.

It did not happen all at once. Her time in New York seemed to her largely spent in doctors' waiting rooms. Dr Abrahamson had recommended that she see a psychiatrist, an obstetrician, a female psychologist, a paediatrician and they all promised that they would make things easier for her. And they kept their promises.

She had minor surgery. She was given exercises to do. They talked to her about her feelings for her father and advised

267

therapy. In the end it appeared that Avalan had been correct in her diagnosis. It also appeared that everyone in America wanted to help her. It seemed to her that that was what Americans were all about. They helped family, friends, the populace at large, everybody. They all wanted to help you.

She was cossetted through her surgery. The medical staff, Dr Abrahamson, Mr Morgan the surgeon, the nurses all conspired to soothe her and make her happy and her recovery was a complete success.

She was very soon out and about and doing tourist things in the city of skyscrapers. The tall buildings, the canyons of sparkling shops that made Aladdin's cave look second-rate, the crowds of people both frightened and fascinated her and she clung like a limpet to her husband as he showed her the sights prior to taking her to Wisconsin to meet his family. It was a holiday for them and she felt closer to Glenn than ever before, but the surgery was still healing and they did not make love.

While they were in New York they ate in drug stores and delis. It was all very exciting and Vanessa took to the American way of life eagerly and with only a few reservations.

She grew tired very quickly of the junk food. She ached for one of Sive's well planned meals, fresh vegetables and fruit. Glenn was always making do with hot dogs or hamburgers or mighty club sandwiches on the trot, and at first she found it fun. But the novelty soon wore off and she longed for the discipline of three meals a day and small portions.

But she had no reservations about the American people. Everywhere, in the streets, in the stores with their pleasant greetings and friendly approach, she found herself welcome.

Glenn's family, however, was a culture shock. Though she enjoyed meeting them she was relieved to leave. They swamped her with kindness. They overwhelmed her with their welcome. Their constant attention intimidated her but they did not seem to notice. She found it quite impossible to remember all their names and the names of all their friends.

The farm was delightful. Set between fertile fields of corn, surrounded every couple of miles by other small holdings, everyone knew everyone else and they were only too eager to embrace her into their midst.

They stayed with Myrna and Boo, which was short for Robert. Myrna and Boo were Glenn's Ma and Pa. They lived in a rambling ranch house, whose walls seemed to Vanessa thin as tissue. But perhaps, she had to admit to herself, she was being abnormally sensitive at this particular time in her life. She felt the entire house shook if she sneezed. The whole family wandered in and out of each other's rooms and she was constantly starting up in alarm as she accidentally came upon another Carey drifting where you'd least expect them to drift. Once when she'd thrown herself on the little bed in Glenn's room sighing with relief, his brother Clark (after Gable) suddenly emerged from under the bed unconcernedly muttering something about a mouse.

She wanted so much, now that she had recovered from the operation, to spend uninterrupted time alone with Glenn. She was in a fever to explore that whole sensual world, forbidden to her before, if only she could manage to find some privacy. She wanted to fix that part of their lives that up to now had been beset by frustration and unfulfilment. But in Wisconsin it seemed impossible – there was never a moment, day or night, when they were alone. Boo, a farmer and the father of eight, the third of whom was Glenn, and Myrna seemed sublimely unconscious of their need. Myrna would call them to meals from the kitchen, confident that everyone, no matter where they were in the house, could hear her. Vanessa gave in with good grace. Love-making would have to wait.

Boo sat in his rocking-chair on one side of the verandah and Eli, *his* father, sat rocking on the other side. There was a verandah all around the house and there was always someone rocking. Myrna told Vanessa that sometimes, in the summer, they sat there all night. 'They set there, content, grumblin' about the weather, or the crops or such-like. An' those ol' chairs creak. Disturbs my sleep,' Myrna said, not seeming to notice any irony. Glenn and Vanessa's room overlooked the verandah and Vanessa's inhibitions were magnified.

And on top of it all Glenn himself was curiously reluctant to fondle her in the bedroom he had occupied as a boy. It drove Vanessa to near wild frustration, but it was, Glenn told

269

her, his childhood bed and it froze him up. 'Now you know how I felt,' Vanessa said.

The walls were hung with pennants, pictures of baseball teams, groups of uniformed men, Marines, his smiling face always somewhere in the middle, a clear picture of the history of his life.

'I grew up in this room, honey, lived here till I left for Japan,' he said when she turned in towards him, thinking, if we keep very quiet, maybe, maybe it will be all right.

'I don't know, honey. It just doesn't seem right here.'

And to her annoyance he turned from her and fell into a deep peaceful sleep, and all she could hear was the squeaking of a rocking-chair going backwards, forwards, backwards, forwards. She ground her teeth in frustration and reflected that for farmers, living close to nature, they were obtuse. Dim really.

The countryside, however, enchanted her. The lush greenery. The cornfields, the sunflowers for oil, the blueberries, the little clapboard houses, white or brown, and the converted brick-red barns. It was all so vast and seemed to go on forever. They stayed through the autumn and then it snowed. The world was a shimmering white fairyland, but the old men, mufflered, coated and booted, cocooned in wraps, still sat out on the porch and rocked.

Then they had to move on. There was news of a possible conflict in Korea and Glenn was recalled to base camp, in Texas. Glenn proposed to drive her there, let her see the American countryside. The trip turned into an idyll.

In the car, after fond farewells, they sang 'Kalamazoo' and 'What Did Della Wear Boys (She wore a brand New Jersey)' and all the American songs about places in the USA like 'California Here I Come', 'Chicago', 'My Old Kentucky Home'. They sang as Glenn drove his Buick through white blanketed fields.

As they travelled South, staying in motels on the way, the snow vanished and the sun came out. The motels all had single beds, like in the movies, and Glenn, bushed from driving all day, fell into them and was almost immediately asleep. Vanessa sighed and tried to get comfy in her narrow bed and curbed her impatience as best she could.

Then they reached Texas. Once more the fields stretched

out before them in the sun and Vanessa pushed up her skirt over her tanned legs as they drove and knew she could not wait any longer.

'Please, honey. Stop the car.'

'What?' He was beating 'The Yellow Rose of Texas' on the car wheel and whistling it through his teeth.

'Let's try now. Oh, now.'

Eyes widening he looked at her incredulously. They were bang on the highway. He glanced left and right about him and seeing nobody, pulled the Buick under some trees and began to kiss her, murmuring, singing in her ear, 'Oh I want you, I want to, my mouth wants to, my lips want to, my legs, my arms, my hands, my . . .'

'Say it,' she whispered and he did in her ear, his hands on her breasts, between her legs, and she opened to him, feeling herself offer the lovely moist centre of her being, welcoming, receiving and embracing him.

It was the most wonderful feeling she had ever had and she gasped in surprise at the sudden activity of her nerves, the wild clamour they set up, the fierce sensitivity they welcomed him with.

She felt him spurt out inside her and though she did not come with him she had relaxed enough to be able to enjoy it and marvel at the wonder of it and realise what it could be like. A man and his wife.

Two days later, shouting out in the most overwhelming spasm of release, she had her first orgasm.

'There, honey. I told you it'd be good,' Glenn whispered in her ear.

'Oh Jesus! That's the understatement of the year!' she said.

Glenn laughed. 'It's not that big a deal,' he said.

'Oh, but it is,' she told him, then whispered to herself, 'Mamma, what you missed.'

Chapter Fifty-four

తళ ౖత

Reginald Crosby was beginning to wish he'd never accepted
the position of manager of Ardmore & Son, much less
suggested it himself. One year after his official appointment
he was floundering in very deep water indeed. It was not that
he was incompetent. Far from it. It was simply that Patrick
McCawley had been a genius. Reginald Crosby hated to
admit it, but it was the truth. Patrick had been born with
flair, and ability. He'd been handed the gift of management
at birth and was instinctively brilliant at his job. It was not
a question of learning. He'd always known.

He had been capable of complete control of the men he
was in charge of. He had their respect. He forgot nothing,
was able to memorise numbers and amounts down to the
last decimal place. He could add, subtract in his head with
lightning speed, spot a mistake at a glance and he knew how
much, down to the last bottle, everyone had ordered, what
they owed, who was a reliable 'pay in advance' customer, who
would pay eventually, and who to avoid because they would
not. He knew how to flatter the Ardmore salesmen, who to
encourage, who to bully, who to sack. But more than this he
instinctively knew what the customers would want and what
they would not. What would sell and what wouldn't.

Reginald Crosby, though a hard worker, conscientious
and thorough, though he toiled night and day until his
wife threatened to leave him, had not been gifted with
that talent. He was panicking. The returns were appalling
and showed a huge deficit. Patrick's expertise in a radically
changing market was badly needed and Reginald did not
know for the life of him what to do.

He knew he'd be held responsible, yet he had done
nothing to be ashamed of. The simple fact was that when

he examined the situation, what he saw before him was a market place suddenly flooded by fine French, Italian and Spanish wines selling directly and much more cheaply than his firm, leaving importers like Ardmore's out in the cold.

On the body of war-torn Europe the land was recovering and the French, Italian and Spanish were foraging for trade with a cut-throat ferocity that took Reginald Crosby's breath away, leaving him perplexed and without a clue what to do about it. He would have been all right if business had proceeded as it had done these past years, peacefully expanding and steadily increasing. Even if trade had decreased somewhat he could have coped. It was this terrifying change in the market that alarmed him and left him helpless. He wondered if indeed his respect for Patrick McCawley had perhaps blinded him to the man's humanity and perhaps even *he* could not have solved the dilemma. True he had broken new ground. True he had overturned old prejudices against fine old wines in favour of paddy, malt, stout or Guinness. True he had actually helped to make wine fashionable in a land of whiskey and porter. But this was different. Ardmore's had never had much competition from outside before and under this onslaught Reginald was flummoxed.

Everything seemed to be going rapidly downhill, gathering momentum as it slid. Even the salesmen were letting him down. A hard-drinking group, easily managed by Patrick, they seemed to have all turned into raving alcoholics overnight. Or had they always been? He wished he knew. They were, at this moment, bumbling about the provinces in an alcoholic haze, half-heartedly selling Ardmore's stock. He could not seem either to control or inspire them, and they were not bringing home the orders needed to keep Ardmore & Son afloat.

And the buck stopped with him. There was no one to turn to. Brendan Ardmore would blame him, trounce him, turn him out without a reference, and finally not know what to do himself. Ardmore's would go under and that would mean Reginald Crosby would be known through the land as a failure.

He wanted only one thing and that was impossible. He wanted to be *told* what to do. He needed guidance.

He talked it over with his wife.

'You've got to ease up,' she told him. 'You'll kill yourself, duck.'

'But I don't know what to *do*,' he replied. 'Patrick McCawley'd know what to do. I simply don't.'

'Well,' she suggested with mind-boggling simplicity, 'why don't you write and ask him?'

He was astounded. He hugged her and set about finding where his former boss had ended up.

First he'd tried the Byrnes. He arranged to meet Rushton in a pub off Grafton Street.

The chauffeur greeted him civilly. Brushing froth from his moustache he extended a hand and asked Crosby how he could help him. 'I didn't think for a minit youse was just wantin' to converse wi' me,' he told Reginald, 'so spit it out, what yer after.'

'I'm lookin' for Patrick McCawley, 'Reginald informed him without preamble.

'Patrick, is it? An' what ye want him for? Spyin' for the polis, are ye? Tryin' te get him back here te face the music, is it? Well, good luck te him, I say. Ye'll get no help from me, so ye won't.'

Reginald shook his head. He was very uncomfortable in the shadows of Nearys pub. Sitting there on the green plush, pinned against the wall by the large man thirstily gulping his stout, Reginald, a fastidious little person, felt threatened and somehow furtive. As if he was doing something wrong. 'No, no,' he protested his innocence, 'I do assure you all I want is his help.'

Rushton looked at him sceptically. 'Says you!'

'No, no. I need him.'

'Oh's that so? You assure me, all you want is his help!' He mimicked Reginald's voice, making it sound very grand. 'Well, let me tell you, fella-me-lad, anythin' to do with the Ardmores is bad cess, y'hear. Bloody bad cess.'

Reginald was not discouraged. Part of his failure as a businessman lay in his inability to see the large picture. He ferreted single-mindedly down minor boreens while Patrick McCawley studied the road-map. But that quality helped him now.

He telephoned Dundalgan and asked to speak to Sitric. Someone there answered and seemed unsure who Sitric was.

So he hung up and telephoned again in the evening and he got Rosalind. Grateful she would not recognise his voice he asked if he could speak to Sitric and Rosalind asked who this was, and he mumbled something inaudible and she said no, she did not know her son's whereabouts and put down the receiver.

He finally telephoned the American Embassy and spoke to Sive. She proved chattier than the others and told him that Sitric sometimes had a drink with his aunt in the Arts Club on a Tuesday evening and he was often there. 'I know, sir, because that was where he was when Mr Ardmore had his stroke. They couldn't find Master Sitric, and I was told to run him down. That's where I got him in the end. In the Arts Club.'

Reginald thanked her and phoned the Arts Club. A voice told him that yes, Sitric Ardmore was usually there on a Tuesday evening. 'It's quiet then. He likes it quiet,' the voice told him. Reginald made a mental note to try to speak to this chatty man when he went to the club as he seemed quite happy, even eager, to give out information.

On the Tuesday Reginald went to the club. It was a little dingy but wore its tattiness with the pride of an old whore, unashamed of the thousand wild nights that had left their mark on her appearance. It had a welcoming atmosphere and even for Reginald, who was after all a stranger, it embraced and projected a feeling of familiarity. He told them he was a guest of Sitric Ardmore and they let him sign in. There was a semi-circular bar at the end of a long green-carpeted room. The carpet, although newly hoovered, was patterned with old beer and wine stains and dotted with cigarette burns where people thoughtlessly ground out their fag-ends underfoot.

'Evening, sir. You a member?' Behind the bar a large moon-faced man with a florid countenance, huge handle-bar moustache and ears that stuck out from his head like wings asked him the question with a grin. It was the same voice he had spoken to on the phone.

'No. I'm meeting a member though.' He slid on to a high stool at the bar. The man leaned on his elbows and looked at Reginald speculatively.

'Oh's that so? And who might that be?'

'Sitric Ardmore,' Reginald replied.

275

''Nough said!' the barman smiled. 'What'll it be?'

'Tio Pepe, please,' Reginald said and the man grimaced and poured the drink.

'You telephoned, didn't you?' the man asked. Reginald nodded.

It was gloomy outside but still daylight. The lights were on in the room and the heavy green velvet drapes were half closed. This seemed to give the room a Dickensian cosiness, the feeling of a refuge from the dingy world outside.

Reginald sat and sipped. The only other person there was an elderly grey-haired poet of the city, dozing drunkenly over an open *Irish Independent* he was not reading. He looked as if he had been there all night. Probably he had, Reginald decided with a fastidious wrinkle of his nose.

The barman was curious about Reginald and he had something on his mind. Reginald decided to give him the opportunity to air whatever it was. He smiled at the man.

'You know the family well, sir?' he asked, encouraged.

Reginald moved cautiously. 'Well,' he hesitated, 'I work for the father.' He cast a glance at the ceiling, indicating whatever the barman wanted the look to mean.

'Know what you're sayin', sir. Right old bastard he is.' Then he glanced cautiously at Reginald. 'Some of us think,' he added, covering his back.

'Sure.' Reginald nodded in agreement. The barman looked relieved. He did not want to lose his job. There was another pause while Reginald sipped his sherry and the barman polished glasses.

It was a depressing evening. Reginald could see the drops of rain chase each other down the windows.

'Know him well?' the barman enquired casually. It could be very boring behind the bar all day. 'Master Sitric? The son?'

Reginald shook his head. 'No. He more agreeable than the old man?' he asked.

The barman hooted. 'Nice? He's so nice he's havin' a thing with his *aunt*!'

There. It was out. The barman's eyes glittered with unhealthy excitement. This was what he wanted to tell Reginald. This was the information he was bursting with.

'Everyone knows it, sir. The whole town. They come in here. A bloody disgrace, I say. They can't keep their hands off each other. They're wicked! Tony Blatch, he's one of the barmen up at the Shelbourne, said he'd had to have young Sitric Ardmore thrown outa the hotel. Know what he did, sir, in a Catholic country?' Reginald shook his head. 'Well, sir, an' I dunno how to tell you this.' Reginald waited, patiently. 'He's sittin wi' his auntie in the bar at the Shelbourne an' he suddenly shouts, "I don't care who knows" an' he –' the barman lowered his voice, his tone salacious – 'throws his leg over her. Sits astride her and kisses her. There in the bar, God help us. Full view. People object, sir. It's a respectable city, not London or Hollywood, where all sorts of obscenities occur. In the streets, they tell me! Oh no, sir. Not here. We don't like that sort of thing in Ireland, do we sir?'

He was in full flow now. Reginald nodded every now and then and the barman continued, 'They put the heart across me every time they come in here, sir. But I keep me eye on them. There'll be no obscenity here, sir,' he finished robustly.

Reginald reflected that this man probably dealt with helpless and aggressive drunks every night and saw no obscenity in that, but he said nothing.

'She's old enough to be his mother, sir,' the barman added, and gave a feverish little laugh. 'God'n' she could be. She's his Mam's sister. They're a disgrace, I say. A dirty disgrace. She should be put in a convent and he should be –' he made a snipping gesture in the general region of his crotch – 'you know.' Reginald shook his head negatively. 'Cas-ter-a-ted!' the barman mouthed silently. He glanced at the door and his expression changed. He said in a phony voice, 'Can I get you another, sir?' Then he muttered under his breath, 'He's just come in, sir.'

Reginald turned around and saw a tall, lean, handsome young man with soft longer-than-fashionable brown hair, sleepy eyes and a black cigarette in his mouth. He was glancing around the room as if searching for someone.

Reginald got off his stool and advanced. The young man looked startled, as if he'd been attacked in some way, as Reginald approached him.

'Sitric Ardmore?'

'For my sins, sir,' the young man said, showing even teeth,

the eye ones pointed. This gave him a dangerous look, a greedy look.

'I'm Reginald Crosby. Your father's manager.'

'I'm glad *someone* is managing him. I never could.'

'I mean I'm manager of Ardmore & Son.'

The young man pushed his hair back impatiently. 'I *know* what you mean. Although I thought Patrick McCawley was Pappy's manager.' He frowned. 'But didn't he run off with one of Mother's maids, one of our servants or something?' He looked keenly at Reginald and spread his hands. 'I'm joking, Mr Crosby. Not a very good joke I admit, but still a joke.'

'Could I buy you a drink, sir? I need to talk to you.' Then catching the bartender's eye he added, 'Privately, sir. It's a matter of some importance.'

Sitric shrugged indifferently. 'Don't call me sir. I'm not your sir. You are probably much worthier than I am to be called sir. And let *me* get *you* a drink.' He called to the bartender, 'The same again for this gentleman, Bill, and my usual, over here please.'

He chose a table at the back of the room under the window. The table, like the carpet, was pock-marked by cigarette burns and discoloured rings of stale alcohol.

Bill brought the drinks, giving Reginald a reproachful look, then left them.

'Now, er, Reginald, isn't it? What's the problem?' Sitric pushed back his hair again and Reginald realized it was a mannerism of his. 'Though I have to warn you that I'm not much good at problems with the business. I've never been allowed to, er, dabble, as the boss's son. So what can I do?'

Reginald plunged in feet first. 'I'm afraid the business, Ardmore & Son, is in terrible trouble. Terrible difficulties, sir . . . er . . .' Reginald floundered. Sitric threw back his head and laughed loud and long. He seemed to Reginald to be delighted and the unfortunate manager suddenly realised that he was not going to get any help here.

'Call me my name, which is Sitric,' the young man told Reginald when he'd stopped laughing. 'Oh gee, oh gosh, oh glorious day! Pappy's hit bottom. Oh great!'

His voice on the last phrase had become hard as granite.

He leaned across the table. 'Terrible difficulties ... how terrible?' he asked.

'Disastrous sir,' Reginald said.

'Disastrous as in irretrievable, or disasterous as in a bad way now, but recoverable? Or only a slight hiccup?'

'Recoverable, sir, but only just and only if attended to at once.' For a moment hope flickered in the manager's heart. But it was short-lived.

'Well, if I were you I'd let him drown,' Sitric said calmly. 'I'll bet he doesn't pay you half of what you're worth? Well, sit back, sir, and watch him go under. I would if I were you.' He looked at Reginald. 'It happened because Patrick pissed off, right?'

'Yes, sir. And I want to find him, so I thought you might be able to help?'

'Ah! So only Patrick can put it right? Yes?' Reginald nodded. 'Well, let me tell you that I don't know where he is and even if I did I wouldn't tell you. Nothing, Mr Crosby, would give me greater pleasure than to see my father destroyed.'

'Not even if you too are made penniless in the process, sir?'

'No. Not even then. I don't really care about money and all that.' Reginald noted wryly that it was always the ones with money who said that. He'd never heard a poor person express such a conviction. 'You're looking, Mr Crosby, at a man who cares very little whether he is up or down, lives or dies. It is a matter of total indifference to me.' He was sipping his drink, which appeared to be a Black Velvet. 'I have one completely absorbing passion. This passion is not smiled upon by the general public and is fairly hopeless. So I assure you what happens to my father's business is of no possible interest to me.'

Reginald thought of what the barman had told him. Sitric looked at him, smiling faintly through half-closed eyes. 'I cannot have what I want, Mr Crosby,' he continued, 'so you see, if you are looking for help from me, not only can I not help you, but I *will* not.'

He tossed back the remainder of his drink and stood. With old-world courtesy he bowed to Reginald, turned on his heel and left the room. The barman watched him and then watched as Reginald followed.

It had occurred to Reginald that he had spoken to Sive only to ask Sitric Ardmore's whereabouts. He got a tram to Dalkey and walked up to the estate, wondering what would happen to it if Ardmore & Son went bust. The trees hung their heads in the rain and seemed to be weeping. A couple of seagulls cried out like angered harpies and the mountains were swathed in grey mist.

He had been told Imelda Byrne was still in employment there. He went around the back and asked to see her. She was very forthcoming.

'Me Mam doesn't know where me sister is,' she told Reginald. 'She's gone to 'Merica with Patrick. She's that anxious, sir, but see, Cessy's man is worried about the polis. That's what Mam says. You best talk to me Mam.'

So he went to the American Embassy and saw Sive. Sive was only too happy to help him but unfortunately, as her daughter had said, she didn't know where Cessy and Patrick were.

'He's afraid that if we know where they are one of us will let it slip and the polis will find out. If Mr Ardmore decides to issue an arrest order, who knows, the FBI might return him here and he'd be sent to prison.'

'But that's ridiculous, Mrs Byrne. The FBI wouldn't be interested in Patrick McCawley.'

'You know that, Mr Crosby, and I know that, but try persuading Patrick. Oh no! He won't listen.' She cocked her head sideways and looked at him cannily. 'He phones us. But he never says where he is. That's what you want to know, sir, isn't it? So why? If not to have him arrested, then why do you want to know where he is?'

Reginald told her he needed advice about the business. Then he asked, 'Does your daughter write?'

'Yes. She's a good girl, Cessy.'

'Where do the letters come from?'

'I don't know, sir. I'll get an envelope, you can look.'

She produced a crumpled pack of about twenty letters, well-thumbed, each one in its envelope. He examined them, and close scrutiny provided him with the information that the McCawleys had started in Philadelphia and ended in Chicago where the last letter had been posted.

Sive, who had been keening a little over her lost daughter,

wiped her eyes. They were sitting in the kitchen of the American Embassy. 'I'm happy here, sir,' she said, 'but tell the truth I miss Dundalgan.' She glanced around the large immaculate place. The pretty dishes, blue and yellow, neatly arranged on the shelves, the shining copper hanging from the walls, the polished brasses, the wood, the wonderful amenities of refrigerator and washing machine. 'Yes, I know' – she read the expression in his eyes correctly – 'it is perfect here. Like an advertisement, isn't it? But I was *used* to Dundalgan. And the family were all together. Cessy was with me and Imelda. We were very happy and we didn't know it.' She smiled at him sadly, wiping a tear from her cheek. 'Do we ever know when we're happy, sir?' she asked. 'Do we only realise it after it has gone?'

Reginald Crosby was not interested in happiness. He was only interested in saving his hide, in not finding himself jobless. 'If he telephones you again, or she does, er . . . ?'

'Cessy, sur. Cecilia McCawley now. With a babby. Little Meg. I'm a granny now.' She threatened to become overcome again and Reginald hastily rose to go. He was, he knew, useless at consoling large, distressed females.

'If they phone you will you mention I called? Reginald Crosby?' He wrote his name and his number on a small piece of paper from his notebook and shoved it into her hand.

'He'll be frightened. He'll think you are looking for him for Mr Ardmore.'

'Then you'll have to tell him I'm not. Tell him I need his help. Tell him I can't do it alone. Just tell him to contact me. He can take any precautions he likes.'

'I will, sir,' she assured him but he did not think she grasped his message. He left her there, sitting in the immaculate kitchen of the American Embassy in floods of tears.

Chapter Fifty-five

⤙ ⤚

Reginald had nearly lost hope when his wife came up with her second spectacular idea.

'Why don't you contact Vanessa?' she asked. 'After all, she's there, in the USA. She might know where Cessy and Patrick are and if she doesn't her husband might be able to find out. Get a private eye, like Philip Marlowes. They're three a penny in America. Anyhow, Vanessa's husband is in the American Army or Navy, I heard, isn't he? They'd be bound to be able to find out for him.'

Reginald was delighted with his wife's perspicacity. 'Don't know what I'd do without you, duck,' he told her. 'If women could run businesses, I'd get you in to help me at the office. Maybe you could make a better fist of it than me.' She laughed at him, at his sauce. Her, the boss of an office? What next!

So he wrote to Sergeant and Mrs Glenn Carey c/o the American Marines. Posted it to the American Embassy in Dublin, asking them to forward it, and crossed his fingers.

In the meantime things went from bad to worse. The AGM was postponed because of Brendan Ardmore's health. Reginald Crosby was very relieved about this and wondered was it only Brendan's health that made him put it off, or was he too afraid? He must be terrified, now that Patrick was not there any more to shield his ignorance. A date was fixed for the following September.

Reginald felt he was losing his mind. He could not sleep. He could not rest. He could think of nothing but the mess, the financial ruin that Ardmore's was plunging into and was totally unaware of. Only he knew. Only Patrick could help.

At night, that long hot summer, he wrestled with the bedclothes, fought with the pillows, tossed and turned, dozed off only to have nightmares and wake with headaches of such intensity that opening his eyes proved painful beyond belief.

His wife said, 'You'll have to resign from Ardmore's. You can't go on like this, duck. You're killing yourself.'

And when at last he'd almost decided to take her advice, that perhaps it was the inevitable course of action, a letter plopped on their doormat. A letter with an American stamp. A letter from Vanessa.

Chapter Fifty-six

❧ ❧

Vanessa wanted to go home. Glenn realised it almost at once in the camp in Texas. She'd been so happy on their visit to New York, content with his family in Wisconsin, ecstatic on that passionate journey through the wild west countryside. Camp Neuson at Corpus Christi, Texas, she hated. It terrified her and she had cause. The whole place, the women there, dampened her spirit, defeated her in a curiously insidious way. She lost her vitality and her sparkle.

The camp was army-oriented, naturally. It was military, and it was peopled by tough macho men and their tough wise-cracking wives. They were as foreign to Vanessa as if they came from Mars. She who was used to admiration and love, close friends and a very gentle and modest way of life, was suddenly surrounded by tough cookies, as Glenn called them. Women who were streetwise and knew the ropes and thought her wide-eyed innocence a hoot. They thought her uppity and were convinced she thought she was better than them, which was, in fact, the furthest thing from her mind.

They did not like her much. The most important thing in the camp was conformity. It was essential for anyone who wanted to be happy there. You *had* to fit in. Everybody was expected to be like the others, like the same things, like to *do* the same things, eat the same foods, enjoy the same pastimes. Above all to learn the same patois, the slang that identified them as a group, and isolated them from the rest of mankind. And Vanessa found this almost impossible.

They held slumber parties, and morning, bring-and-buy and Tupperware gatherings. They had cook-outs and ate popcorn at the one movie house on the grounds. They gave drinks parties and got very drunk and did and said silly things which they told each other about the next morning

284

amid hoots of laughter. She felt awkward and out of it. She'd never been drunk in her life.

No matter how hard she tried, Vanessa was *per se* an outsider. Her cultivated Irish accent they heard as English and it sounded hoity-toity to them so they felt uncomfortable around her. Her clothes, so much more formal and sober than theirs, seemed out of place among the shorts and tee-shirts they wore, and the flamboyant, slightly gaudy party dresses they wore made her look as if she was doing a Grace Kelly number. So they told her. Even the slang they used was incomprehensible to her, and though they often took time to explain the joke, or what they meant, she could see it bored them to do so and they just as often left her in ignorance, not bothering to enlighten her.

And Glenn was partisan. He understood the guys, their horsing around, their joshing, their chauvinistic attitude. He understood the wives' mistrust of the stranger in their midst, understood their casual cruelty, their lack of understanding. His heart bled for his sensitive young wife. She tried so hard. She worked at it for his sake, but he was one of them.

What happened in Camp Neuson drew them closer together than ever before. Their sex-life, so wonderfully satisfactory now, so absorbing, lured him away from 'the boys' as nothing else could have.

If she had criticised his buddies and their wives and remained cool and aloof and sexually arid it might have been a different story and it was probable she would have lost him in Camp Neuson. But she tried so very hard to fit in, never complained, tried to be agreeable to the other women in the face of their indifference, and she had become, since that day on the highway in the Buick, an ardent and passionate lover whom he could not get enough of.

There were rumours abroad about Korea, and Glenn was becoming disenchanted with the Marines. The drum-beating, the encouragement of violence, the playground tactics of 'Zap, you're dead' seemed to him, after real combat, a trifle silly. He began to realise the extent to which it was necessary to be brainwashed before he could, in reality, become, on order, a killing machine. And he might be called upon to become just that, once more, in Korea. He had had,

285

he realised, enough of fighting. Army life was losing all its attraction.

And he missed Ireland. To his everlasting surprise he missed the good-natured wit, the slower pace of life. He missed the soft purple mists, the long evenings in the pubs, drinking slowly, telling yarns, swapping adventures.

And he missed the concerts, the plays, the intense cultural activity he had been almost casually drawn into, although he would never have admitted it. He began to hate the aggression all around him. It was inherent in everything he heard, everything that was taught them, everything they chatted about on the camp. He reached for peace.

So when Reginald Crosby's letter arrived via a very circuitous route they were both ready to crack under the strain of pretending they were just swell. They both felt miserable.

Billy Monks came to see them. He'd left the Marine Corps and was back home in Oklahoma working in his Pa's haulage business.

'I never said, old buddy, but I got fed up with the killin',' he told Glenn, voicing what Glenn had been thinking but so far had not put into words. 'Couldn't see why I should shoot some little yellow guy I never met and didn't know piss-all about.'

And when Glenn looked up sharply he continued, 'Oh, I never *said*. I know that I'd be considered unpatriotic if I did. It's a shooting offence.' He grinned at Glenn. 'And I'd have looked like a sap.'

Glenn nodded in agreement. 'Just as I felt,' he said. 'But I thought there was something wrong with me. Those little fellas we killed, our enemies. We were taught to hate them. Hate 'em all. Geez, can't hate a whole race. Must be some nice ones. Stands to reason. An' now it's over and we're making friends all round again. Don't make sense.'

Billy nodded his head in agreement. 'Sure as hell don't.'

They felt guilty there, in the mess, talking like this. It was treason.

'World War Two,' Glenn whispered, 'I thought, is humanity culling its own species?' He shook his head. 'Doggone little fellas, seemed more like toys to me!'

Billy nodded, throwing back the last of the cold beer in the sweating can. 'Sure were. Kept thinking, each of them was as scared as us, had families like us.'

'I kept it to myself though. Din even want to *think* it. Sayin' it aloud be like terrible disloyalty.'

Billy glanced about as if he thought the CO might suddenly materialise in the mess.

'Well, see now, Billy,' Glenn said slowly, running his hands through his thick hair, 'I've heard I might be sent to Korea.'

Billy shook his head and clicked his teeth. 'You want to go through that again?' he asked.

'Well, Billy, like I got this idea. See what you think, ol' buddy.'

'Shoot.' Billy went to the refrigerator and got himself another can. He held it up to the barman who nodded. He ran his hands over the cool sides of the container. It was hot in Texas.

'I'm thinkin' of goin' back to Dublin, Ireland.'

Billy scratched his head. He wanted to laugh but Glenn's face was awfully serious. He decided to keep his mouth shut and listen.

'See, 'Nessa is miserable,' Glenn told him. 'Oh, it's not her fault. She's gone all out to make friends, fit in, but you know these places, Billy. You understand.'

'Sure as hell do. Have to conform. These women are like a wolf-pack, huntin' together. An' the guys, Glenn, is why I left. One of the reasons. It's all how tough you are. That's all that counts. Fella strains his guts out so's another fella thinks he's a tough guy. Some ambition. It all seems so silly when you've been out there, in the fightin'.'

'Nothing they teach you prepares you for the reality,' Glenn said sadly. 'An' to hear them josh about it here, hear them revvin' the guys up, I just couldn't work up enthusiasm no more.'

'So?'

'Well, with that and the chicks being so mean to 'Nessa –' he looked at Billy – 'Oh, she's never said a word, never complained, but I just know, see. Well, I got this letter and I have an idea.'

'What idea?'

'Well, I think I just might go get back to Dublin by September and save Mr Brendan Ardmore's business for him.'

Billy did a double-take. 'Je-sus Glenn, you a sucker or

something? What you talkin'? He's the guy, correct me if I'm wrong, cor-rect me if I got the wrong end of the stick, but he's the guy who treated you so bad. Wouldn't let you marry Vanessa, right? He's the old bastard insulted America. Spit on our flag, good as? Am I right or am I?'

Glenn nodded. 'Sure are,' he replied. 'But the old guy is in deep shit, Billy. I mean deep. He's up to his neck in the stuff. Near to drowning. It's sink or swim time.' He glanced at his friend. 'See, I figure I can make 'Nessa happy. Save her father and the family from ruin. Show 'em I can do it and cut myself a piece of the action at the same time.' He flashed his perfect teeth. 'Nothing's for nothing, old buddy, right? I'd ask a take of the profits. A mighty large take.'

'What makes you think you could do it?' Billy asked. 'What makes you so sure?'

Glenn frowned and shrugged. 'Don't know. Just feel it in my bones. The case this guy puts' – he tapped the envelope he'd taken out of his pocket – 'an idiot could turn it around.' He grinned. 'If they looked at it from the *outside*. He can only see from inside. Blinkered vision.' He raised his voice to its parade ground level: 'An idiot could do it, provided he had a will of iron and could put the fear of God into men's hearts.'

Billy laughed. 'And,' Glenn added slowly, softly, 'it would make 'Nessa happy.' He gave his friend what Billy thought of as his blue look, when he almost closed his eyes and they seemed like indigo pebbles, so intense his expression. 'And that, old buddy, is about the most important thing in my life,' he said.

288

Chapter Fifty-seven

❧ ❧

Reginald Crosby was ecstatic to receive a reply from Vanessa, and if he was floored by the contents, he felt relieved of the full responsibility for the position Ardmore's was in.

Something might be saved from the mess, all might not be lost. That was the promise. But for Reginald the fact that Sergeant Glenn Carey was going to deal with the situation was what took him off the hook and helped him once more to sleep the sleep of the just and innocent.

Glenn Carey was coming to Dublin to look into things. Miss Vanessa's husband said, in his own letter to Reginald, that he'd got in touch with Patrick McCawley in America. The Marines, he said, could find anyone if they set their minds to it. He'd talk to the former manager 'so highly praised by you, Reggie', sound him out, and maybe persuade him to help with the dilemma.

Reginald Crosby did not appreciate the diminutive of his name – it smacked of familiarity – but there was nothing he could do about it now, and the relief he felt swamped any feelings of hurt dignity.

'He wants to handle it himself, duck,' he told his wife, worried in case he had done the wrong thing.

She put his mind at rest. 'Let him, pet, let him,' she told him. 'He'll be in front line of battle. He can face the enemy. You just stay a mite behind, quiet like. It's a position that suits you and we should all stay in the position that suits us best. Let him draw the fire from you.'

They had followed the war with maps pinned to the wall and strategy fascinated her. He saw the analogy and it struck him as plain common sense. He felt more hopeful than he had in a long time, though he could not think what Sergeant Carey could possibly do to rectify the situation.

Glenn wanted the accounts, or copies of same, to be sent to him to study. He asked Reginald to send him data at once, as if that was something Reginald did, all the time, just like that. I ask you, he said to his wife that night, sending accounts to America. All the way to the United States.

But he sent them, sent a full account with explanations about the market, justification and reasons for falling sales and orders and declining profits. He sent a breakdown of all that had happened before and since Patrick McCawley had left the firm with instructions to Sergeant Carey to contact the man himself about anything he did not understand as he was the only person in the world who knew the firm inside out. 'For you and I, sir, with the best will in the world, with the purest of motives, cannot mend this sinking ship without his help.' He finished thus and Glenn smiled to himself as he set about meeting this remarkable man.

Chapter Fifty-eight

୶ ஒ

When Glenn found the McCawleys' whereabouts in Chicago he applied for leave of absence, packed a grip and took Vanessa to the windy city to talk to Patrick face to face.

He'd resigned from the Marines in the way he had of acting decisively when he'd reached a decision. It was quite a common occurrence these days, now that the world war was over. A curious change-over was happening in the American Forces. Men who'd known combat were leaving on pension when they returned and a new young breed, jealous of not having seen, as they put it, 'real exciting action' were joining up. There was no shortage of young bloods eager for battle to take the place of combat-weary veterans.

The Corps did not make things difficult for him, far from it. There was no place for men like him, disenchanted with action, soured by the real thing. The Corps demanded, needed total dedication and anything less was a liability. So they bid a friendly farewell and hustled them away as soon as possible before their attitude could infect the men.

Vanessa was ecstatic. She had tried so desperately to be what they wanted her to be and failed so miserably. When Glenn told her the situation she was completely taken by surprise.

'But, honey, I thought, I thought . . .'

'I know what you thought,' he told her. 'You were bustin' a gut so hard to please you never noticed that I was miserable too.' He turned on his side and leaned on his elbow, looking down at her.

Her hair fanned out over the pillow, a cloud of jet. She no longer tried to cover her breasts with the sheet and she had her hands clasped behind her head, smiling up at him. He could see the delight in her eyes at the possibility of going home.

'Will you mind being plain Mrs instead of a military wife?' he asked. He had been very proud of his rank, his uniform, and he had never understood that for her it meant nothing. There was no glamour for her in being married to a Marine. But she did not tell him that.

'Oh darling, need you ask? Oh, but what will you do? We can't just do nothing.'

'Well, that's the beauty of it, baby. I think I've come up with the perfect solution. That letter you got from Reginald Crosby, you know?' When she nodded he told her the plan.

She stared up at him, mouth open. 'And why would you want to help Pappy when he treated you so badly?' she queried when he'd finished.

His eyes narrowed. 'Well honey, it's funny you should ask that. Everyone does. Sometimes people get all righteous and they can't see the wood for the trees.'

'What do you mean, darling?'

'How can I explain? Well, it's like, once, in the east we were liberating these Brits and Aussies from this prison camp. It was at the edge of this jungle, a terrible place, hot, steamy, riddled with disease.' He lay back as she had been, hands clasped behind his head, and she leaned on her elbow and looked down at him, her chin resting on her hand. He very seldom spoke to her of those days and when he did she listened breathlessly, feeling privileged to be allowed into that part of his life.

'Our guys had every inoculation under the sun but they were fallin' like flies. Malaria mostly. Dysentery. Jeez, it was bad. Our company got smaller an' smaller an' when we got to this prison camp there were these little yellow bastards shakin' in their shoes, an' the Brits and the Aussies shouting and cheering us. An' the CO orders us to shoot these guards. And we obeyed. An' I never could understand why. All of them, the English, the Australians and us, all of them wanting to annihilate the enemy. Me, I was furious.'

'Why?' she asked, staring at him, trying to make the connection.

'Sure, shoot the commander. Sure shoot the ones in charge. The prisoners'd been tortured. They'd been degraded. The emotion was understandable. But, see honey, those little guards, the guys who did the obeyin', they coulda worked for *us*. They could have been a great help gettin' us outa there. Getting us back. Guiding us through the jungle. They knew it like the back of their hands. That's what the Romans woulda done. Utilised the enemy. And that's what I'm going to do with your Pappy.'

He grinned, the grin that twisted her heart each time he smiled at her. 'You know what I'da done with those guys? I'da got them to *carry* us, piggy-back.' He laughed. 'I would, honest. Anyhow –' he became serious – 'what I'm saying is it's not going to get me anywhere, wasting time hating your Pappy. But now see, I set up the Ardmore company, turn it around, everyone's happy. We've *all* gained. Just because your Pa gains too is sure as hell not goin' to spoil my parade.'

Still she didn't fully understand. She was a person who relied on loyalty and taking sides and she could not grasp the generosity involved nor the detachment. Emotional detachment. But she didn't care. She was so happy with him, so totally in love, and now, to top it all, she was going home.

She laid her head on his chest. She could feel his dog-tags next to her cheek and the long beautiful line of him against her. She'd become familiar with every part of him, every sensitive bit, nerve and pulse, every scar, all of this beloved body, from his thick thatch of dark hair to his crooked little toe. Everything about him excited her. Every time he came in her she felt like a sacred vessel, the receptacle of his love and passion, and now this flooding into her womb while she cried out her orgasm had borne fruit.

She was pregnant.

He whooped with joy when she told him. He was so gallant with her, so proud, so possessive, so pleased. 'Well that puts the lid on it,' he called. 'We're out a here.'

In the last weeks of their time in Camp Neuson they were happy. It was strange, Vanessa thought, that everyone suddenly began to become more friendly. It was as if now that they were going, the wives, from what motives she could not guess, wanted to show her they were good old girls, all together in a club, sisters under the skin. They gave parties

293

for Glenn and herself, and perhaps because now that they were leaving, because she didn't try, didn't care what they thought of her any more, she enjoyed the revelry, enjoyed the banter and the teasing and for the first time felt herself part of the gang.

In the middle of the farewell parties they went to Chicago. They found it hot and bustling, a beautiful town, proud of its architecture, boasting the highest tower in the world, its wide boulevards alive with activity. Bargains abounded. The slogan 'No sale is ever final' was born in Chicago.

The people were friendly and all down State Street where they were staying in the Palmer House Hotel, brand-new stores hustled to take trade from the more permanent, fashionable Marshall Field and Carson Pirie Scott.

Vanessa was in seventh heaven. 'I'm having a facial, a manicure and a whole new wardrobe,' she told Glenn, who smiled and told her, 'You have yourself a ball, honey. I got a lot owin' me from the Corps. But first, business.'

In Chicago they met with Patrick McCawley. Vanessa could not place him, but when he walked into the lounge of the Palmer House Hotel she suddenly recognised the face. Once or twice she had met him in Ardmore & Son when she had been invited in to see her father, sit on his knee and be shown off.

He hadn't changed much. He'd been then a man of medium build with canny eyes and flash clothes and the smile of a shark. She looked at him now as he crossed the lounge and thought he had not changed. He was quite sure of himself, quite relaxed in the opulent surroundings, not fazed by the obvious prosperity and wealth of the clientele of the famous hotel.

He had become American, Glenn could see. Slick in his choice of clothes, flashier even than he had been, brash rather than stylish. He chewed gum with nonchalant ease and held a cigarette out sideways in his hand. Glenn smiled to himself as he remembered Dublin and his own clothes when he'd first arrived, similar in material, if not in style, to what Patrick McCawley was wearing now. It was a slippery kind of synthetic fabric that was hard-wearing and did not crease. But Glenn had become used to the quiet elegance of Irish tweed and Irish linen, the softness of cashmere and lambswool and the luxury of pure cotton. Now he did not know how he could ever have been happy with the more convenient, man-made fibres that had seemed so attractive before.

Patrick strode across the crowded lounge. A black was tap-dancing outside and they could hear him sing 'Darktown Strutters Ball' which Vanessa remembered being played at Oriana's wedding. It seemed so long ago now. Long ago and far away, another time, when she'd been so ignorant, and so very innocent.

'Miss Vanessa?' Patrick McCawley enquired tentatively.

'Sure.' Glenn leapt to his feet. 'This is my wife.'

'How do you do?' Vanessa said, then apologetically, 'Sorry. Here I'm supposed to say hi.'

Patrick laughed and shook their hands. He sat down in the chair Glenn indicated.

'They played that tune at my sister's wedding,' Vanessa said. 'We were just saying . . . Ireland seems so very far away.'

'Your sister's wedding?' Patrick said. 'Oh, we weren't there.'

'Why ever not? Didn't Pappy invite you?'

Patrick laughed. 'Oh Lord, no. He'd never have us anywhere near the family. We weren't good enough.'

Vanessa said nothing. Patrick hesitated, then said, 'Sergeant Carey, why did you . . .'

'Glenn, please. Call me Glenn.'

Patrick's eyes widened. 'Bit informal, eh? Still, you're American. It helps.'

'I find it helps me to remember I'm human. Stops me from getting too arrogant.'

Patrick grinned at him, warming to him as everyone did. Vanessa smiled to herself as the Irishman looked at her.

'I met you, twice only I think, when you came into the Ardmore offices, after I'd taken over from my Da. Your Ma brought you in. She was wearin' a mink an' a diamond on her finger worth enough to buy up the Congo. And there was me, runnin' the whole shebang, three quid a week.' He shook his head. 'I'm not regrettin' what I did, not for a minit. I'd do the same again, I promise you. It was rotten pay, an' I only took what I thought I

295

deserved. So if you think I'm going to say I'm sorry yer wrong.'

'We're not apportioning blame, Paddy,' Glenn told him. 'All that's got nothing to do with me. But as we told you in the letter, Ardmore's is in trouble an' we want your advice.'

'Well now, that news doesn't surprise me in the least. And it doesn't break my heart either, sorry Miss Vanessa. 'Bout time I say. Maybe now they'll realise my value. That man –' he glanced at Vanessa – 'I know he's your father, miss . . .'

'Stop calling her miss. She's Vanessa to you now, Paddy. This is nineteen fifty, not Victorian times, an' we're talking partners here.'

Patrick McCawley looked amazed. 'Geez! You're crazy,' he said. 'Old man Ardmore knows fanny, beggin' your pardon, miss, about the business and he's not about to admit that. Ever.'

Vanessa agreed. She nodded at Patrick and looked at her husband to enlighten him.

'Not unless we force his hand,' he said.

'How can we do that?'

'I gotta plan.'

'I hope, sir, Glenn, that it doesn't include me. I'm happy here. Doin' all right. I've no intention goin' back to Dublin, get myself arrested.'

'Would you like to go back if you could?' Glenn asked. Patrick nodded. 'Yeah,' he said. 'Oh, I'm happy enough here, but it's not home. And Cessy, the missus, she misses her family something shockin'. She's awfully homesick. An' where we are, it's not the best place to bring up childer. It's the city, sir, er, Glenn. Not the green fields of Ireland.'

'You needn't fret,' Glenn told him. 'You'll not be arrested.'

'How can you be sure, sir? I'd not survive jail. I'd die there.'

'Trust me.'

'That's what Mr Ardmore said when I took over from my Da. "Trust me, my boy, I'll see you right".' He snorted. 'What a rotten joke that turned out to be.' He rose and held out his hand. 'No, Glenn. Sorry, but no thanks.'

Glenn didn't take his hand. 'Sit down, Paddy. You haven't

heard my plan yet. At least listen to that. We've come a long way to talk to you about it.'

Patrick McCawley sat down. Running a going concern, he had discovered, was a whole different ball-game to starting from scratch. Being an intelligent man he had decided to stick with what he knew. Wine. He had the contacts in Europe and there must be thousands of wine-drinking emigrants here in the USA. It had seemed a cinch, but it was not. It wasn't as simple as that.

The Chicagoans were not yet into wine. The Italians, the Germans, Spanish and others were learning new customs and adapting to the American way of life. They worked eight-thirty a.m. to nine at night, sometimes longer, and the siesta and the carafe of vino, the long suppers in the gleaming, were things of the past. They went to ball-games now, slugged their beer from frosted cans, ate on the job instead of having long lunches under the bougainvillaea. They didn't want to know wine.

They would. Eventually. He was sure of that. Some day they would want the finest on their tables, because they were ambitious. America was the land of opportunity and they would want to keep up with their neighbours. The troops coming home from Europe were bringing a new concept of cuisine with them. But it took time and Patrick didn't have the financial security to wait. There would eventually be a fortune to be made, but waiting took money.

He had promised Cessy a good life and he was going to give it to her come hell or high water. Heck, he'd promised *himself* a good life and he was greedy for it. His savings and the money he had paid himself from Ardmore's had been spent on a nice little clapboard house, painted white, with baskets of geraniums hanging from the stoop and a vegetable garden in the back. What he hadn't realised was that the house was in a fairly rough neighbourhood and Cessy, unused to any other home but Dundalgan, was continually nervous there. Gangs patrolled the street, their menace veiled but palpable.

The rest of the money had set him up in business but it was very slow. Very slow. Snail's pace if he was honest. So he listened to Glenn Carey.

'Sit still a minute, Paddy, and listen to me. If you decide

no, after you've heard what I have to say, I'll leave you in peace and say no more. But hear me out.'

Patrick McCawley decided he had nothing to lose and maybe, just maybe, a lot to gain. He sat back and listened.

Chapter Fifty-nine

❧ ❧

Simon returned to Rackton Hall on a stretcher. The specialist shook his head and squeezed his eyes tight-shut to cut off the tears that threatened to slide out of the corners and would be inappropriate in front of the man's wife. He was sick and tired of botched or makeshift jobs performed under near impossible conditions in the goddamned obscenity that was called World War II. He was tired of trying to put together the bodies broken by man's inhumanity to man. He was tired of the hope that blazed forth from the eyes of those that loved these brave, bewildered and ruined men, the hope he knew he'd have to shatter. He was very tired of their bravery. He was very tired of expected miracles and he was very tired of trying to patch up others' mistakes. The men he dealt with had been ill for a very long time. Would be until they died.

He did not blame them, those surgeons on the battlefields in makeshift tents, those doctors armed with little else but their expertise and morphine. He didn't blame those amateurs who glued a man or a woman together any which way they could, risking their lives while so doing, in order to smuggle them out of a danger zone or occupied territory, or away from mortar attack, bombs or gunfire. He doubted he'd do better in their place. But the clean-up job was grim.

He wanted to spend time with people who had a chance, people with mundane illnesses. With broken bones, appendicitis, with rashes, coughs, measles, mumps, and 'Good morning, Mrs Grattan, what can I do for you today? I see you've got little Tommy with you. How is he?' 'He's got a nasty cough, doctor, and my varicose veins are killing me.'

Avalan looked at him and nodded. She said nothing. She was one of the few who understood, one of the few who faced the terrible truth about their loved one with bravery and understanding, and he was tired of her sort too. They broke his heart. He gave her the prescription for the morphine and, not saying anything – for there was nothing to say – they strapped Simon's decaying body on the stretcher and left. They were taken by ambulance to the plane and came home.

At home, in the weeks that followed, Simon was in constant pain and his eyes pleaded with her. Like the wild duck she had nursed at Dundalgan, those eyes begged her, 'Let me go. Set me free.' She couldn't bear it. She wanted so much to breathe life and vitality back into his poor broken body. The man she'd fallen in love with was in there somewhere, but buried deep, and he recognised her memory of him and was heartbroken before her.

Let me go. Set me free. She knew he wanted her to help him go, quietly, with dignity. She knew the pain was gathering momentum and that the bouts of abject terror would become more frequent in the face of fiercer pain and that the morphine was becoming hallucinatory and frightening.

She was, anyway, in a losing battle, a battle that could not be won. She knew that but she could not meet the demand in his eyes. She was a life-sustainer. Her every instinct was geared to survival. She had always nurtured life, breathed hope and courage into dying things, people, plants, animals. All nature. To do the reverse was something outside her capacity.

McWitty was in the same position. To help Simon in that way was against all his instincts. They stared at each other, helpless, knowing what Simon wanted, unable to meet his eyes, aware neither of them could do what was needed.

When, a week after her return from London she went to Molesworth Street Sitric was waiting for her.

'Jesus, I've been here for weeks,' he cried, falling on her like a beast of prey, into her neck, his sharp teeth sinking into her soft flesh like a vampire. 'Weeks and weeks, waiting, waiting.' Kissing her. Devouring her. 'I've waited in agony.'

'No, no, Sitric, don't talk of agony. You don't know the meaning of the word.'

He stared at her, eyes wild. 'Oh, I do. I do. You drive me mad. Oh, my darling, my darling, my darling.'

She didn't answer but threw back her head and, as avidly as he, pulled him to her.

They moaned in lust and love for each other, tasted each other like starving travellers suddenly finding an oasis in each other, reviving dead limbs, inert nerves springing to life, greedily consuming each other.

'I can't do without you any more,' he told her when at last they fell apart. But not completely apart. He couldn't bear that and had to hold her hand, throw his leg over her hips, touch her lest she might disappear. 'You are killing me, Avalan. I'm dying for want of you.'

'Oh Sitric, my darling, my lamb, I'm here now. I'm with you. I'm part of you.'

'Never leave me again. Never.'

'Oh, my love. Simon is dying.'

'I don't care about Simon,' he said. 'No. You must not expect me to. It's asking too much.'

'Well, I love him. He was my youth. My husband. Whether you like it or not, my dear, I love you, but I love my husband too.'

'Then you can't love me.'

'I've read this book,' she sighed wearily. 'I know every page. We've been over it and over it. Don't do it, Sitric. It's a waste of time and energy. I'm tired, can't you see? I need you to keep me alive.'

He noticed for the first time how exhausted she looked and he relented.

'In any event what can we do?' she asked in a tired voice. 'I'm your aunt. The Church would excommunicate us. We'd be social outcasts and might have to go to prison.'

'We could run away to Italy. Or France. No one will know who we are. We could idle our time away in the sun, looking at wondrous ruins, drinking warm wine in olive groves.'

It was so exactly her own dream that she gasped.

'What is it?' he asked.

'Don't ask me now, Sitric,' she told him. 'Just hold me, hold me, never let me go.'

Chapter Sixty

⤶ ⤷

When Elana discovered that Gavin was running to the house in Foxrock every five minutes, she was, at first, sick, then very, very angry. She was a forthright, honest person and the thought of deception disgusted her. She had trusted him, thought he would play fair.

It began, as these things do, with excuses on his part for breaking dates, and she, like a fool, did not twig that anything was amiss. Afterwards she realised that what hurt most was the fact that she had been so easily duped. She had accepted his excuses. He was always busy at the hospital, she knew that, but once, when she remarked to Dominic, her brother, who was in the same hospital, that the work load must be getting him down, he had looked at her in astonishment and replied that they had been very slack of late and what on earth was she talking about? She said that Gavin had said they were very busy and he had looked at her sceptically and said that Gavin must be hallucinating, that they'd been twiddling their thumbs up at the Mater, thinking that the population of Dublin must be the healthiest in the world.

That evening Gavin phoned her and said he couldn't make the movies, he was 'Busy at the hospital,' she finished for him.

'Yes, 'Lana, how'd you guess?' He sounded quite serious, unconscious of her sarcasm, very sincere, so that if she hadn't spoken to Dominic she would have been utterly convinced by him.

Furious, she went that evening to Foxrock, Oriana Powers' house, without hesitation, and sat in her little Ford roadster – the boneshaker, her father called it – and waited, hating herself, hating what she was doing, unable to stop herself, quite certain Gavin was going to pitch up there.

A half an hour later, lo and behold, who should drive up but Gavin Fitzjames, bold as brass, sweeping around the gate-posts and up the drive, jumping out of his Humber without a glance behind. He stuck his finger in the bell, automatically, without having to look, and after a few minutes the uniformed maid opened the door and he disappeared inside.

Elana was shocked. Although she had suspected he was seeing Oriana, the actual evidence chilled her to the bone.

She did not think that finding out would matter that much to her. After all, she had prepared herself for it. Right from the beginning she had been sceptical. That little voice inside her had kept her uneasy. She'd been afraid in her heart that she was second choice. However there was always the possibility that she was wrong and she wanted, oh so much, to be proved so. It was the finding out that she was right that hurt, that felt like a blow in the solar plexus, and she felt ill sitting there, slighted and degraded. She felt bad too, as if she was the guilty one, spying on him. That's what his mates would say. They'd blame her, not him, saying she shouldn't have trailed him, that she shouldn't have been suspicious, that it showed lack of faith and that girls should trust the men they were doing a line with, not follow them around sneaking on them. She'd brought it on herself, that's what they'd say. Never mind she'd been right not to trust him. Never mind she was correct in her suspicions. They'd put her in the wrong willy-nilly. Goddammit, she *felt* in the wrong.

She rested her forehead on her hands, clenching the wheel with vice-like ferocity and let the pain sweep over her – and the rage. Tides of fury and agony overwhelmed her, then receded, then another onslaught, like a fever.

She saw the lights go on upstairs in the Foxrock house. Not daring to think, forbidding her imagination to take over, she let the wheel go, shook her hands to loosen them, then reversed the car and drove home.

She followed him several times after that to the house in Foxrock. When he called her, breaking a date, she would be as pleasant as pie. She'd say, 'Oh, it's all right Gavin. Sure. I got girl-things to do. I *know* how busy you are.' In such a sweet voice that she felt sick. Then she'd get in her car and drive to Foxrock, sit outside Oriana's house, and sure enough he'd arrive soon after if his car was not already there.

He never noticed hers. He was that confident. He never once twigged that she sat there, watching him prove himself a liar and a fraud.

The rest of the time, when they were together, he was so normal as to make her doubt her senses. He'd hold her hand, kiss her, murmur sweet nothings, tell her the news of his day. It was to her a deep impenetrable mystery how anyone could lie like that. He seemed unworried by anything in the world, serene and at peace. The only thing she noticed was that sometimes he seemed excited, as if he had an absorbing secret he could not bear to share.

She did not know what to do. No one had prepared her for such perfidity. She was sure she'd lost him and yet she could not bear to tell him to go, to get rid of him, to accept the fact of his infidelity. She invented reasons, bizarre and silly reasons as to why he was at the house in Foxrock, why he lied to her. Oriana was giving him the sex Elana could not, being unmarried. Obviously therefore he was enthralled by her, caught in her meshes. She was a married woman. She was not a virgin any more so she gave him sex, and like any young and lustful man he was caught in a web of sexual favours.

One night in his car, in desperation, she more or less offered herself to him.

'I'll do it with you, Gavin, if you like. If you really want, I'll do it with you.'

He'd pulled away. 'No! What kind of fella you think I am?' he asked, looking shocked. 'What kind of girl are you anyway, Elana Cassidy, that you'd say a thing like that? Think it, even? I thought you were a lady.'

Elana rushed home in tears. She was confused and bewildered and disgusted both with herself and with him. She felt the end of the world had come.

She crept into the Cassidy house. It was around twelve o'clock and she didn't want to disturb anyone. But her father met her in the tiny hall. One look at her face made him shake his head and beckon her to follow him into the front room. It was used as his study, there being nowhere else for him to use.

She did not want to go with him. She wanted to escape, to be by herself.

'No, Da, I'm tired, I—'

'The hell you are,' Dr Jack said firmly. 'In there, my girl, and no nonsense out of you.'

He was whispering, not wanting to awaken Adele, who was over-worked and got so little chance to rest.

'Now sit down there and tell me what's the matter.'

Dr Jack wore his professional face and manner.

'Oh, I know what you'll say.' Elana was suddenly racked by big body-shaking sobs. 'You'll blame me, you'll—'

'No, you *don't* know what I'll say, Elana pet. You haven't a clue. I doubt if you've done anything in your whole life that either myself or your mam haven't done ourselves at sometime.'

She looked at him, tears on her cheeks. 'Oh no, Da, not like this. Not like this.'

'You mean your boyfriend lying to you and spending all his time with a married woman?' He smiled at her surprise. If he'd wanted to startle her, he'd succeeded.

'Why, dearest child, it's an old story. A classic tale. We've all had someone who has lied to us, played us the joker. We've all been rejected and betrayed. And if we ourselves have not then we know someone who has and we've suffered with them. Oh, my dear, there's nothing new under the sun, only you knew.' He pulled her to him and sat her on his knee as he used to when she was a child. 'Listen, Elana, your mother and I have watched you over these past weeks and you know our only thought? Our only hope?' She shook her head, feeling important yet babyish at the same time. She pressed her cheek against his lapel. This was her Da and here on his lap was safety and comfort and the answer to everything. 'Well, what we hoped was, you'd stop suddenly and say to yourself, tell yourself, "I'm worth much more than this. I'm more valuable than this. I will not let any man treat me like this any more."' He tilted her chin. At first her eyes dodged meeting his, but he held her chin firmly between his forefinger and his thumb and at last she had to meet his level gaze. 'And you *are*, my darling, you are.' He scrutinised her but she said nothing, loath to give up so suddenly, loath to accept.

'Well?' he persisted.

'I suppose you're right, Da,' she muttered reluctantly.

'You *know* I'm right and you know you'll be happier when

you admit it, painful as that admission will be. And when you let him go the relief will be tremendous. But what you don't realise, my dear, is that he's already gone. You'd never want him back in any event. You'd get him back and then you'd discard him. You can save yourself that trouble.' He pushed her to her feet. 'My, you're heavier now than when we used to have our stories, our talks, remember?'

'Yes, Da. I loved those stories. I adored the talks. You made me feel so grown up,' she told him. 'You knew the answer to everything.'

Dr Jack smiled ruefully. 'If only that were so,' he sighed. 'But for tonight, it's bed for you, young lady, and tomorrow, a long think.'

'Yes, Da.'

'Now off with you. Go.'

After that things were a whole lot better. It seemed there was no point in deluding herself any more. So filled with the confidence and courage her father had instilled in her, she telephoned Gavin and told him she wanted to break off the line. He seemed very surprised and when he wanted to know why she said tartly, 'If you don't know, Gavin Fitzjames, then you're an even bigger eejit than I imagine.' She put down the phone and felt relief sweep over her. The remark spoiled the dignified exit she had intended to make from his life, but it gave her enormous satisfaction, and she suddenly felt free again and much happier.

Chapter Sixty-one

🪁 🪁

'I'm leaving Pierce.' Oriana turned to Gavin and touched his arm a little tentatively. She was not absolutely sure how he was going to react to her plan.

Elana may have thought that Gavin and Oriana were lovers but she was wrong and they were not. In her innocence she had imagined that sex was the attraction. Oriana, a married woman, 'did it' with Gavin. She, being unmarried, did not. What she could not know was that Oriana Powers was still a virgin. Oriana was not going to let anyone know this. It was a shameful secret she carried around with her and now, with Gavin, it could only cause confusion. She knew people would be contemptuous if they found out and she suspected she'd be blamed for not doing her duty to her husband. It was a tangled web and she was caught in it.

Gavin was attracted to Oriana, though she was not aware of the fact, simply because she'd turned him down. They had been sweethearts and at her father's command she'd jilted him. That was humiliating and it had been a great blow to his pride. So when one evening she'd sent for him, begging him to help her, be her friend through the impossible position Pierce had put her in – as she put it – he was eager and curious to see what had happened, and human enough to want to crow a little. And some of that battered pride was salvaged. 'If you'd defied your father and married me,' he'd told her, much to her irritation, 'this would never have happened. Vanessa did it, so you could've.'

She looked at him wide-eyed. 'I wasn't to know that,' she snapped. 'And if I had married you,' she added, 'I wouldn't have this beautiful house.'

Nor, he thought, the maid, the Crown Derby china, the

rubies on her finger and wrist. Those things counted with Oriana.

'How could Pierce do this to me?' she asked plaintively. 'And how could I know he'd do it to me?' She was piteous now. 'If only he hadn't behaved like that. It was so stupid.'

She liked 'if only'. She played that game with him constantly, Gavin realised and had always done so. It never seemed to occur to her that her choices were clear and simple and that 'if only' was a waste of time. She could leave Pierce, her house, all her worldly goods. Or she could stay with Pierce, and shut up. She seemed to want to do both. There was no doubt in Gavin's mind that she stayed with Pierce because she was afraid of losing the house. And Gavin became quite sure on his visits to Foxrock that he would not break up with Elana to become whatever she wanted to this restless, disloyal woman.

She talked endlessly about Ireland not having divorce. Useless for him to name some of the many couples who lived quite happily together 'in sin', as the church called it. She would hear none of it.

'It's not legal,' she said. 'I'd have no rights. And besides, it's against my religion.'

'Suddenly, Oriana, you sound like a fully paid up member of the Church, all devoted and conformist.'

'I don't know what you're talking about,' she replied innocently.

'Oriana, you only ever obeyed the Church when it suited you. You're far too mercenery to be a good Catholic.'

'Oh Gavin, you're horrid. I can't live "in sin" as you call it. We would never get asked anywhere.'

'You're not asked anywhere now!' he told her.

'I know! And it's terrible. And Pappy could help. He got me into this in the first place.'

'*You* got *yourself* into this in the first place,' Gavin told her very unsympathetically. He was enjoying himself hugely.

'I did not! Pappy got me into it! I've told him so. He says he was misled. Anyone could be. He says, Pappy says I must tell Pierce not to come home. He says Pierce has no right to put his feet on the mat. So I've done that. I told Pierce he was not welcome here any more.'

308

Gavin gasped. He did not keel over with delight as she'd imagined. He simply looked at her, thunderstruck.

'Is that what you mean when you say you're leaving him?' he asked eventually, when the power of speech returned.

She nodded.

'So you've thrown the poor bastard out when he's at his lowest and needs you most?'

'Oh, shut up, Gavin. Stop being beastly to me.' She was glad now she had not told him about her being a virgin. She could have had her marriage annulled quite easily if she wanted, because it had not been consummated. But she had held that card close to her chest. How could she know what would happen? Would she still be able to hold on to her beloved house if her marriage was made null and void? She trembled when she thought of being returned to Dundalgan. She did not want to live there again. She was not at all sure coming clean about her real position with Pierce would be to her advantage. And she was pretty sure that he would not publicise the facts. It made him look such an idiot. Feeble.

Gavin was standing up. 'Don't go, Gavin,' she pleaded. She did not want him. He would never be anything other than a hard working GP and she could not contemplate making any sacrifices for him. Why didn't men like Gavin and Leonard Fitzjames – and Dr Jack – realise that there was absolutely nothing wrong in a woman wanting a comfortable life?

'What do you want me to do?' he asked her.

'I don't know,' she cried impatiently. 'Stop talking to me like that. You confuse me.'

She was wearing a deep claret satin *robe-de-chambre*. It had an inset waistband and the satin flared out above and below, emphasising her full breasts and the curve of her hips, her narrow waist. Her hair, cloudy and dark, billowed out mistily around her face. She had, Gavin thought, never looked so beautiful, so desirable. And he had never desired her less. He had understood her marrying Pierce on her father's demand. Her father was a formidable man and Gavin could see how difficult it would be to defy him. It would need a courage Oriana did not possess. But to dump poor Pierce at the first sign of trouble was another matter entirely. He'd simply got his hand caught in the cookie-jar and should expect her to stick by him unless he made a habit of it. Gavin suddenly realised what a shallow lady she was. He'd never really seen it before.

He'd been dazzled by her. Her beauty, her style. He'd not been able to see through to the real person beneath. He left Oriana's house, emerging into the cold clear night air. That was that. He'd laid the ghost of his battered pride. He shook his head as if to rid himself of an encumbrance and got into his car. Oriana's lure had disappeared. She was no longer a question mark from his past, an enigma, a haunter of dreams. She could not come between himself and Elana any more. He could brush away the cobwebs and give Elana the attention she deserved.

Elana! He thought of her with such pleasure, such joy. He'd been so comfortable with her in all the time they'd been together, the laughter they'd shared, the closeness they'd felt, the warmth between them which he'd delighted in and which he knew now was love. He'd confused love with infatuation and the power Oriana had always had over him. And now he realised the truth he hurried home to phone her, to let her know how committed he was to her.

When he got home, however, the phone was ringing. His father Leonard was answering it as his son bounded into the hall.

'Father?'

Leonard grinned at his son and shook his head. 'You're a disgrace, you know that?' He held out the phone, his hand over it. 'It's Elana Cassidy. How can you chase a worthless baggage like Oriana Powers when you've struck pure gold? I'll never understand.' And still shaking his head he relinquished the receiver into his son's outstretched hand and crossed the faded grandeur of the old hall to his study, leaving Gavin to find out that it was too late. Elana Cassidy was dumping him.

Chapter Sixty-two

⦿ ⊚

The rain was torrential. It cracked on the pavement like pistol shots and bounced roughly off umbrellas.

Elana left the Bank of Ireland by the staff exit at the side. She remembered suddenly on a similar day meeting Gavin. She shivered. She didn't have the car and the bus, she knew, would be crowded. Steaming people crushed together to escape the rain, people who usually walked or idled home with stops in coffee shops or pubs were suddenly galvanised into a desperate desire for their homes and hearths and jostled together to struggle on to public transport.

She trudged down College Green towards the bus stop and at first did not notice the car cruising along beside her at the curb.

'Elana? Elana Cassidy?'

She hitched the collar of her coat up around her ears in a vain effort to prevent the water dribbling down her back, then leaned forward and looked into the automobile. The car was a ramshackle Buick and she couldn't think who could be inside. She imagined it might be one of her fellow workers.

'It's you isn't it? Here get in. I'll give you a lift. A dog shouldn't be out on a night like this.'

She got in. It never occurred to her not to. Taking a lift in Dublin was perfectly safe and she was certain to know the driver.

She slid through the open door and found herself seated beside Leonard Fitzjames.

She knew a moment of acute embarrassment. She'd just broken off a line with his son and it flashed across her mind that perhaps Gavin had complained, sent his father to plead his cause.

She looked at Leonard Fitzjames nervously, but he was

311

manoeuvring the car out into the mainstream of the traffic
and was preoccupied. 'It's not this way, Mr Fitzjames,' she
told him. 'I live in Blackrock. It's the other way.'

'I know,' he said, glancing at her, his brown eyes shining
mischievously. 'But I'm taking you for a drink. You're very
very wet. A toddy wouldn't hurt. That is, if you don't
mind?'

She shook her head. 'Of course not,' she replied and her
heart sank. Oh God, it *was* about Gavin. She looked about
wildly for escape but could see none.

'I thought we'd pop into the Bailey,' he said. 'Or would you
prefer the Hibernian?' She chose the Bailey on the off-chance
that some of her friends might be there and if he lectured her
about Gavin she could signal them to rescue her.

He said nothing until after he'd parked the car in Dawson
Street and they crossed the road. He took her arm just under
the elbow and steered her up Duke Street to the Bailey.
He held his umbrella over her and she looked up at him,
charmed despite herself at his protectiveness.

The small entrance bar in the Bailey was crowded but he
managed to get her a seat at a table. He put the evening paper
on the marble top and turned a spare chair for himself against
it, then pushed to the bar to get drinks.

'What'll you have?' he asked over the heads of the crowd.

'Gin and It,' she shouted back and laughed. He nodded
and turned his back and she looked around. There was
no one there she knew. She had never been in the Bailey
before and known no one. She sat, squeezed against the wall,
clutching her hands together in her lap, trying to think of
some way to escape, but could come up with nothing.

She could see Leonard's silver and black hair across the
room. He turned once and grinned at her, his smile flashing
reassuringly.

When he returned with the drinks she gulped her gin, and
while he was settling himself she said, 'If you want to talk to
me about Gavin, you're wasting your time.'

'I wasn't,' he said.

'You see, I've quite made up my mind and I'm not going
to be persuaded to . . .' she paused, put her gin down with a
bang and looked at him. 'What did you say?'

'I said I was not going to talk to you about Gavin,' he

replied tranquilly. He was very relaxed, leaning back in his chair, indifferent to the crowd that occasionally jostled him. His skin was tanned and smooth as if he had just shaved and his hands were steady and calm, loosely clasped around his drink.

'Why did you ask me for a drink then?' It sounded bald and gauche and she blushed at her own question.

He glanced at her, one eyebrow raised. 'Why not?' he replied and she could think of nothing to say.

'I've always enjoyed our dances together, Elana,' he said as she relapsed into silence. 'I've always thought of you as . . .' he paused – 'utterly delightful.' He suddenly looked very serious. 'I don't want to alarm you, but when Gavin told me how he treated you, the thought came to me unbidden, that if I were lucky enough to take Elana Cassidy out on a date, I'd never, ever dream of breaking it, let alone moon after someone like Oriana Powers.' He shrugged. 'He's mad!' he said, then glanced back at her. 'So when the thought had percolated it played around in my head, and then I thought, why not? Why not ask her for a date? This, Elana, is my clumsy way of going about it. I thought, what have I got to lose?'

She digested this in silence, not knowing what to think, how to react.

'Don't embarrass me by saying anything now,' he continued, not looking at her. 'Just think about it. It's all I ask.'

'But why? Why do you want to go out with me? I'm gauche and boring and—'

'Hush, shush! Don't talk like that about yourself. It's twaddle.' He took her hands between his own. 'You ask me why? I'll tell you. My wife died nearly ten years ago. Gavin must have told you. I loved her, Elana. I'm a one-woman man. I missed her terribly. So it never even crossed my mind to go out with anyone else. No one hustled me to remarry. I'm not rich. I've little to offer. An old crumbling house, a pile of obligations, barely enough to cover costs. Certainly not anything like the sort of assets Oriana Powers or the Ardmores have.' He sighed. 'So the avid hordes gave me a polite miss and mothers of eligible girls kept them out of my way. Widows avoided me—'

'Oh Mr Fitzjames, I don't believe that.' Elana was stunned into protesting. 'You're much too—' She stopped and bit her lip. She was going to say much too attractive, but prevented herself, then could not decide why she had cut the sentence short.

'It's true,' he continued, 'and I didn't realise what was happening. I wasn't looking, you see. I wasn't thinking about other women at all. If you'd asked me I'd have been shocked and said I did not want another woman in my life.'

The bar noise had reached a crescendo. There were shouts all around them. Glasses clicked. People pressed in out of the rain. Elana saw now a group with Dom Bradley over in a corner near the door. He caught her eye and waved but she shook her head gently, indicating to him that she was engaged. Happily engaged. She was, truth to tell, utterly fascinated.

Never before had she felt so breathlessly on the verge of something. She hardly dared to take her attention away from the man beside her. She stared at Leonard Fitzjames as if she had met him for the first time, engrossed in everything he said to her, unwilling to miss his words or gestures, the tiniest change of expression. She wanted to go to the ladies' but she did not move.

'Then I saw you at Oriana's engagement party,' he continued, 'and you were glowing with vitality. You were so very much alive and you made me feel young. You made me feel happy just to look at you. I danced with you but even then you seemed to me another admirably delightful young thing, a friend of Gavin's. Then you said, and I remember the exact words, you said, "Oh Mr Fitzjames, I've never thought of you as old", and you meant it! In that moment everything changed.' He was not looking at her but over the heads of the crowd. He was nervous now, she could see, and she waited until he went on, 'I don't know what happened but our relationship, or rather my perception of it, altered dramatically.' She opened her mouth to speak but he protested, 'Oh, I do assure you, you had nothing to do with it. I'm not blaming you, Elana. Your manner was quite proper. In fact if you *had* been flirting I would have run a mile. I would have been terrified. No. You said it so *sincerely.* That's what nonplussed me. You seemed sincerely unaware of my age and my heart lifted and I thought, why not?' He grimaced. 'Then Gavin started dating you and I retreated and called myself

314

a silly old fool. Naturally I bowed out. I castigated myself, blaming myself for even thinking about you in that way.' He smiled at her suddenly. 'I shocked myself by wondering about you so often. When Gavin talked about you I was so interested and I could not help it. Now, please don't be upset. My suit is hopeless, I know, but Elana, think about it, it's all I ask.'

He stood and took her by the elbow. 'Now, knock back that gin and let me drive you home,' he said. 'I've said my piece, so let's go.'

He led her back to the car. There was thunder somewhere over the mountains. He settled her in and drove off towards Blackrock. Neither of them spoke.

When they reached her home he pulled up at the curb and she turned, hesitantly, shyly to him. 'How'd you know which house?' she asked.

He didn't reply. He turned sideways, leaned over and took her face between his hands, examining it very closely.

'You're very lovely, Elana,' he said softly. 'Whatever happens next, at least I'll know I tried.' He grinned. '"Faint heart ne'er won fair lady",' he said, then he kissed her.

His lips were soft, tender and gentle. She felt as if the skin all over her body had been electrically shocked and it was the last sensation she had expected. When Gavin or Dom or Billy Monks had kissed her they had plunged into her like starving savages suddenly presented with meat. Their hard-mouthed tongue-down-the-throat passion had not awakened any response in her at all, only a desire to bite, or pull away. This kiss dissolved her bones, made her melt, while along the surface of her skin and in the sexual recesses of her body such fluid sweetness flowed as to make her breathless with desire. It was a desire to be petted and stroked, embraced and touched and kissed, and to pet and stroke, touch and kiss back.

When he'd finished she was weak. He let her go abruptly. 'Remember that,' he told her, 'when you make your decision. It's how I feel about you.' And he got out of the car and went around it to open her door. Her knees were limp and she did not think they would bear her weight, but he helped her out, pushed her gently towards the house and with a murmured, 'Good night, sweet girl.' He jumped back into the old Buick and was gone.

315

Chapter Sixty-three

ᴏᴥ ᴏᴥ

Elana wished with all her heart that Vanessa was not so far away. From someone she rarely thought about, Leonard Fitzjames had suddenly become the sole occupant of her mind. People at work were irritated by how unusually absent-minded she was. Adele 'despaired of her', Dr Jack worried about her. Dom Bradley, footloose since Vanessa's defection, was a constant and very frustrated escort and Gavin Fitzjames now plagued her with invitations, all of which she turned down.

She thought of his father constantly. She remembered. That kiss lingered in her mind. Her finger tips seemed sensitive to every touch.

Leonard did not phone her. She expected him to but all was silence. He left her strictly alone to make up her mind, without pressure, without pleading his case. He could not have done anything more conducive to arousing her interest.

At last she could stand it no longer. She had to taste him again. After a week of drifting in a cocoon of misty day-dreaming, a week during which she had sleep-walked through her work at the bank, gone with Dom to two cocktail parties and a play, none of which events she had any clear recollection of, she phoned him.

'I'd like to see you,' she told him.

'Sure,' he replied, so casual, so calmly. They made a date for the evening, two days later. He said he'd book a table for dinner in the Brasserie in the Hibernian.

She spent the next two days in an agony of expectation. What would she say to him? What on earth could she, would she say? Oh, if only Vanessa were here. He'd made it quite clear that the ball was in her court and she now felt acutely the burden of the decision she would have to make. She wished he would do it for her. She knew exactly what that decision would be.

She took all her clothes out of her wardrobe and tried to select a suitable outfit. She wished for the hundredth time that her friend was in Ireland to help her. It might not seem so deadly serious then, so very important. She felt that it had been left to her to make a life-and-death decision and finally, the morning of her date with Leonard, she burst into her father's surgery as he was putting his stethoscope into his black bag in preparation for his rounds.

'Da, can I talk to you a mo?'

'Of course, my love. What is it?'

He was immediately available to her and put aside the bag and folded his hands, giving her his full attention.

This was awful. She could not think what to say. Her father's calm eyes encouraged her and after two false starts, a mumbled and mangled sentence, she got it out.

'I'm going out with Gavin's father tonight, Da.'

Dr Jack did not bat an eyelid. 'So?' he inquired mildly.

Suddenly everything was all right. Saying it aloud, his reaction, so matter-of-fact, filled her with joyous relief.

'Oh Da. I'm going out with Leonard Fitzjames.' She plonked herself on her father's knee, eliciting a loud groan. 'Oh Da, he's wonderful!' She had not expected to hear herself saying that. She wanted to laugh, to shout, to cry all at once.

'He's much nicer than his son,' Dr Jack remarked and Elana hugged him, kissed his cheek and cried, 'The brown velvet sheath with the jacket Vanessa gave me!'

Dr Jack looked at her, frowning, 'What dear?'

'What to wear, what to wear,' she sang. 'I was going to wear black because he's older. But no. I'll wear the brown. It suits me perfectly.'

'I'm sure it will, dear,' Dr Jack said and rose and began again to put his stethoscope into his black bag.

She got a taxi from Blackrock to the Brasserie. It was that important, she wanted to arrive looking perfect. She wore her brown velvet, the rich chocolate colour highlighting her pale skin, picking up the gold in her hair. Her heels were high and she wore nylons on her lovely legs.

317

He was waiting at the table. He rose to greet her as the waiter showed her over to him. She could see the excitement in his eyes. The question. The expression reminded her of a child. Eager to please. Anxious and excited at the same time. She was instantly at ease, feeling older and more mature than he at this moment.

'My dear,' he welcomed her. 'Sit here. Let me pour you some champagne.'

'Celebration already when you don't know what I'm going to say.'

He shrugged with a nonchalance he obviously did not feel. 'Celebration. Consolation. Champagne is good whatever the situation.'

She sat beside him in the leather-backed banquette. The waiter put two menus before them and left. She took his hand and found it was trembling. She moved closer to him and said, 'You'll think me a hussy, Leonard –' the name tripped easily off her tongue, she had used it so many times in her head in the last few days – 'but what I want now, more than the champagne, more than the food, more than anything is for you to kiss me as you did that night in the car.'

'But Mrs O'Grady and her terrible daughter are across the room. Think of the scandal.'

'It's dark – well, dim – here.'

'She's watching like a hawk. I don't want to compromise you.'

His voice was thick and she moved even closer. 'I *want* to be compromised,' she breathed and this time she put her hands on his cheeks and her lips to his. And he kissed her again, and she was not disappointed. The warmth spread and trembled all over her skin. It felt like a blossom opening in the sun, the rays piercing her most secret places. It lasted seconds but seemed like hours. When they broke apart he shivered and breathed, 'Oh God!'

'That's my answer,' she said softly.

'Are you sure?' he asked. 'I'm much . . .'

'Older,' she supplied, giggling. 'Oh, let's skip that bit. You are everything I want. Everything I . . . desire. Now shut up, Leonard, about that side of things and let's eat. I'm starving.'

It was suddenly very easy. She felt older and wiser than he

in the area of their suitability, financially and socially. What did all of that stuff matter? She thought of Oriana and Pierce Powers. What she felt for this man was not lust, not romantic airy-fairy love but a deep passion and a desire to grow in friendship with him. Admiration, companionship. Shared experience that included their bodily union as well as their mental and spiritual one. It was like nothing she had felt before, the landscape was too broad, but she knew quite certainly that she belonged with him whatever age he was.

She knew too that he would lead her and that she would follow down the pathways of passion and fulfilment, of friendship and love, with willing abandonment. It was settled. He understood. He looked over his shoulder and she followed his gaze and saw what was amusing him. Mrs O'Grady was glaring with ferocious disapproval at them. She harrumphed and shook her head and they shared a giggle. They smiled at each other in complete understanding then began to study the menu.

Chapter Sixty-four

ఴ అ

Vanessa and Glenn came back to Ireland as quietly as they had left. They did not trumpet their return and no one knew beforehand except Elana and Reginald Crosby.

The first thing Vanessa did was telephone Elana and arrange a meeting. The first thing Glenn did was telephone Reginald Crosby and arrange a meeting. He then telephoned Dundalgan and asked Rosalind if she could meet them and keep their arrival in Dublin confidential. Rosalind burst into tears of joy at the news that Vanessa was back in town and would have promised anything to see her again. She did not even mind it when her son-in-law cut the connection saying, 'Well, Mother-in-law, goodbye now! Have a nice day!'

She was just as glad not to have to break the news to Brendan. A pall of doom hung over Dundalgan and Brendan rarely spoke now unless it was to shout at someone, herself included. She did not like being shouted at so she avoided him as much as possible.

Patrick McCawley and his family had come with the Careys. Patrick, however, was behaving in a very paranoid way, giving them all a hard time. He was, Cessy told Vanessa, 'Scared shitless yer Da'll have him locked up.' No amount of reassurance relaxed him. He insisted on staying in a little bed and breakfast place off North Great Georges Street as far away as he could get from where anyone he knew might be. 'I'm goin' nowhere,' he said, 'until it's all sorted. I'm invisible.' Terrified of emerging from the small room that he and Cessy, heavily pregnant, and little Meg were squeezed into, he awaited Glenn's summons with fear and trepidation.

'Look, we'll send a cab for you and we'll keep it waiting

outside while the meeting is on, Paddy,' Glenn promised him. 'Then if Mr Ardmore threatens legal action, which I don't reckon he will – not when I've finished with him – if he does, you can scarper and grab the cab, pick up Cessy and the baby and your tickets and you'll be gone before the police arrive in Dawson Street.' With that Patrick had to be content and he spent the next few days scuttling in and out of the B & B until Cessy told him the landlady was becoming so suspicious he'd probably end up in jail anyway. 'She was quizzin' me yesterday, hintin' I could trust her, an' if ye believe that ye'd believe anythin', askin' if ye were on the run.'

'Well, don't tell her nuthin',' Patrick said.

'Listen, Paddy, we've got nuthin' to fear, honest,' Cessy told him earnestly, 'Mr Glenn's promised an' I trust him. No one knows we're here an' no one's lookin', but if you carry on like this Mrs Tuberty will get the polis an' you'll end up in the pokey an' *then* the fat'll be in the fire an' no mistake. Once they've got you there Mr Ardmore can sue and they'll throw away the key. So Paddy, let's go out, to Phoenix Park tomorrow, like an ordinary couple, for God's sake. God'n I'm desperate to walk in Phoenix Park again.'

Patrick saw the sense of that and that Sunday he and Cessy and Meg went to Phoenix Park and listened to the band. They ate ham and cheese sandwiches sitting on the grass and drank lemonade and had a Walls ice cream doused with raspberry cordial from a van that played 'I'll be your Sweetheart' even though the military band was ta-ra-ra-ing and boom-booming out marches on the stand nearby. The resultant cacophony was rousing if not melodious but Paddy and Cessy were so relieved to be out and about like human beings again that they did not care. It was wonderful to hear Irish voices, wonderful to hear the language of their homeland, and Patrick was filled once more with courage and hope.

Glenn and Vanessa stayed in the Gresham Hotel in O'Connell Street. The Gresham is one of the best hotels in Dublin but it is up near Parnell Square, on the other side of town from the Shelbourne, and any of the other places that the Ardmores' friends frequented. Glenn and Vanessa felt quite secure there. They did not want their presence in Dublin to be discovered quite yet.

On their first day in Dublin Glenn had arranged a meeting with Reginald Crosby, who had strict instructions not to let anyone know they were in town. Reginald had no intention of breaking his word to Glenn, who represented his only hope of survival.

They had timed their visit to coincide with the AGM of Ardmore & Son. It was autumn and Dublin was drowning in a coverlet of amber, gold, russet and scarlet leaves. The air was crisp and dry and snappy. Cheeks glowed, chestnuts were on sale and apples tempted in the shops. The dusk was long and mysterious and people wore scarves.

Reginald Crosby arrived into the hotel lounge like a fugitive from a Graham Greene novel, a raincoat covering his smart suit, its collar turned up, his briefcase tucked under his arm, the brim of his hat pulled low over his eyes.

Glenn suppressed a smile. 'God, it's turning into *The Third Man*,' he whispered to Vanessa and when she suggested leaving them alone he said no, he'd prefer her to be there. 'You're in on this, 'Nessa,' he told her. 'I'm relying on you to back me up.'

He greeted Reginald, calling him Reggie, and they sat in a secluded corner, drank coffee and talked.

''Nessa's Grandpappy left it in his will that any progeny, the children of his son Brendan, should have shares in the firm. He wanted it to be a family affair, see. And he wasn't too complimentary about his son. He said he hoped that his grandchildren would prove more adept at management as Brendan, quote, "was such a numbskull". That means that Vanessa has shares. And Oriana, of course. And Sitric.'

'Good God, that means he's been less than honest,' Reginald breathed.

Glenn nodded. 'Their father would not consider it worth talking to them about. He'd feel he had absolute right over anything that belonged to his children.'

'But not legally, Mr Carey,' Reginald said with pursed lips. 'Not in the eyes of the law.'

'Exactly. He was breaking the law every bit as much as Patrick McCawley was when he absconded. Though truth to tell, I don't think it would have occurred to him that he was. I think it will come as a shock when he finds out.'

322

'So what does that mean?' Vanessa asked.

'It means you and your sister and brother have voting powers. You have a say in how Ardmore & Son is run. And it means that through you, Vanessa, I have a right of entry. If you'll give me the authority to act for you.' He grinned at her.

She covered his hand with hers. 'Of course, honey. You don't need to ask.'

'Oh, but I do. I'm not like your father. You are a free agent and can do as you wish.'

'I wouldn't know how to start!' she laughed. 'Oh no, my love. You *must* act for me.'

'Reginald will draw up the relevant paper for you to sign half your shares over to me.'

Reginald nodded. 'I'll have it for you tomorrow,' he said. This was more like it. He loved being asked to do things and knowing he could deliver efficiently and quickly. Major planning policy was for others.

'All! All my shares. To you,' Vanessa was saying. 'I wouldn't know what to do with them.'

But Glenn was firm. 'You'll learn,' he said. 'It is not my way to bulldoze myself into power. It is to prove that I can save Ardmore & Son from going bankrupt.'

'Oh, I hope you can, Mr Carey, for that's precisely where it's headed at the speed of light.'

'Now this is what I propose.' Glenn cleared his throat. 'I've written to Sitric and Oriana and I've telephoned Mrs Ardmore. I've invited them to the meeting, tomorrow, Tuesday, and I'd like them all there. But Reginald has written the letters and so they don't know I'm here. Only Mrs Ardmore, Elana and we three know that.'

'Sitric and Oriana won't come,' Vanessa said.

'Oh yes they will. Sitric will come because he's curious. Oriana will come because it might mean money and she's broke. Or to her way of thinking she's broke. I've – we've –' he indicated Reginald – 'informed the shareholders – the Lavertys, Clark, McIlhinny and the others of the date and the time. And we've let your father know. We've told him it is vital he be there. At least, Reginald did. He doesn't yet know I'm involved.'

Vanessa shuddered. The memory of her father still filled

her with dread and the thought of meeting him again overwhelmed her.

Glenn read her thoughts and smiled at her encouragingly. 'I'll be with you honey, so don't worry,' he said and looked at Reginald. 'What I propose, if it's okay with you, is this. You start the meeting as per. Then when you've told them there is no money, the profit is nil, the firm is on the brink of bankruptcy and they've realised the money is about to stop completely, *then* you tell them you have a plan.' He smiled radiantly at them both. 'It's amazing how receptive people are when you tell them there is nothing to gain. Then, as they digest this, you spring the solution. That's where I come in.'

'How will I announce you?' Reginald asked.

'The opportunity will present itself, naturally. You come and get me and I enter with Vanessa and Patrick.'

'And Pappy has a heart attack!' Vanessa muttered dryly.

'From then on it's up to me,' Glenn said.

Reginald gulped. 'You've got guts,' he said. 'Holy mackerel, you've got guts.'

Glenn threw back his head and laughed. 'That's what they say about the Marines. I've left the Corps but part of me will always be a Marine. You ask any Yank about us and they'll tell you – those guys got guts.'

Chapter Sixty-five

౭๑ ๑ఌ

Elana peered around the Gresham lounge. She'd been to many dress dances here with Vanessa and the Ardmores so she knew the hotel well. However, as they did not frequent it in the daytime she was unsure of the exact location of the tea lounge.

She was very excited. She had missed her friend dreadfully and was thrilled at the thought of seeing her again.

When she saw Vanessa at last, tucked away in the corner she let out a squeal of delight and almost ran to greet her. She did not hear Glenn say hi to her. She did not react to his introduction to Reginald Crosby, nor did she notice the small man depart, furtively looking over his shoulder and slipping away in best *film noir* style, hat pulled down even further over his forehead. She did not hear Glenn excuse himself and leave. All she could see was her dearest friend, the friend she had missed so much.

'Oh gosh, 'Nessa, you look gorgeous! Nylons! That suit is sumptuous.' She stared at her friend's navy and white outfit, her two-tone shoes, her neat little handbag. 'Wow. You're glowing!'

'So are you,' Vanessa agreed, mutual admiration alight in their eyes.

They hugged. They stared at each other, touching each other with delighted recognition.

'Gosh, I missed you. I missed you terribly.'

'Oh, it's good to be home, see you again.'

They smiled mistily at each other, then sat, side by side.

'When do you go back?' Elana asked. 'Oh, I hope you're here for a long stay!'

Vanessa put her fingers to her lips. 'Hush,' she whispered,

looking around her as if she feared eavesdroppers. 'It *may* –' she winced delightedly – 'it *may* be for good.'

Elana squealed again, then clapped her hand over her mouth and smothered the exclamation.

'Glenn's left the Marines,' Vanessa explained. 'A lot of guys are going. They've seen enough of action.'

'Yes,' Elana nodded. 'And there's Korea. Leonard says –' she stopped suddenly and then continued, 'So? So what's he going to do?'

'He just wants to settle down,' Vanessa said, frowning and pouring some coffee for Elana. 'He just wants a quiet life with me.'

'But here?' Elana asked wide-eyed. The possibility had never occurred to her.

Vanessa nodded. 'Glenn loves it here. We'd be happy.'

'You are happy, 'Ness. You're glowing. I've never seen you look so good.' Elana scrutinised her friend closely, liking what she saw. Vanessa was radiant. Her skin, her lips, her cheeks were satin-smooth and her eyes were shining with an inner light. She had bloomed. She had lost that tense look so evident in the days just after her wedding to Glenn.

Vanessa became serious. 'I'm very, very happy,' she said. 'I didn't know it was possible to be so happy.' There were tears in her eyes. 'It has worked out like a miracle, 'Lana. I'll never know what I did to deserve such happiness.' She looked at Elana and gave her a blissful smile.

Elana sipped her coffee. Vanessa stared at her friend. 'I've been so busy telling you my news that I haven't asked you. 'Lana, you look *magical*. What have you done? If I look good, you look better. What have you been up to?'

'Let's get all your news first,' Elana said. 'How'd you like America?'

'I wasn't keen on the camp.' Vanessa replied. 'In fact I *hated* it.'

'I know, you said,' Elana began, then she amended, 'No, you didn't say, but I read between the lines.'

Vanessa nodded. 'It was a tough time. I thought I was going to have to live in such places for the rest of Glenn's career. It would have been – well, it would have driven me nuts.'

Elana took her hand. They were silent for a while as the

waitress cleared the table and brought them a fresh pot of coffee.

''S that okay for you, ma'am?' she asked prettily and Vanessa met Elana's eyes and they nearly giggled.

'Yes. It's fine,' Vanessa told her and the girl went. They sat still like sixth formers out on a spree.

'I missed all this,' Vanessa explained. 'I missed the familiarity. Knowing the people. Missing the places that were all part of my existence. I missed the sounds of Irish voices and the saucy back-chat. You know, 'Lana, I was tense all the time in America. Oh, I was happy . . .' She glanced sideways at her friend. She would not speak of her problems with Glenn. It was not appropriate. It was not something she could ever share with her friend and that was sad. But it would be somehow disloyal to her husband. She thought of how friends acquired secrets after they married and were never again as close as before and she thought it a shame. Those oaths they'd taken, so sincerely, to be friends until death, to tell each other everything, to be at all times totally honest with each other, those pledges could no longer prudently be kept and with that loss was a sense of something sacred gone forever. A regretful step further out of maidenhood and into maturity.

'I was happy,' she repeated. 'But I missed home.' She poured some more coffee. 'Mind you, I never mentioned it to Glenn. I wouldn't.' Elana nodded. She knew wives were expected to support their husbands. She would always support Leonard. It was the cardinal rule. Wherever they were, in whatever situation they found themselves, a wife was one hundred per cent behind the man she had pledged her life to. Up the Amazon, in the jungles of Borneo, sharing a sundowner in the humidity of Singapore, or tiffin in the afternoon heat of India, the little woman smiled, uncomplaining and loyal, always at her man's side, a rock, a helpmate.

Elana nodded and Vanessa continued, 'But Glenn is so understanding. He knew I was finding it rather . . .' She hesitated searching for the right word – 'difficult, and he decided he should leave the Marines and settle down in Ireland. Of course I was delighted.'

'What will he do?' Elana asked.

327

'Well –' again her eyes swivelled around the lounge and she lowered her voice – 'you know Ardmore's is going bust?'

Elana nodded. Leonard had mentioned something to her about the old firm sinking quite rapidly and the Ardmores losing all their wealth.

'Well, Glenn has come, charging in like the cavalry to save Pappy and the firm. He's got it all worked out.'

'You must be joking!' Elana looked at her friend incredulously. 'Why on earth would he do that?'

'Well, he'll run the business. He'll get it on its feet and—'

'But *why* would he want to help the man who was so horrible to him? It doesn't make sense.'

'To Glenn it does,' Vanessa said tranquilly. 'It's what he wants.' She leaned over and squeezed her friend's hand. 'Oh, it's so good to see you, 'Lana. Now you *must* tell me what's happening to you. You've been absolutely stumm on the subject and I'm aching to know. Who did you choose? Gavin? Or Dom? Gavin, I bet.'

Elana felt suddenly shy, but she was saved by Glenn's return.

'Hi, girls,' he cried, throwing himself into an armchair. 'Any coffee left?'

'Yes. The waitress brought us a refill,' Vanessa told him.

'It's nice to see you again, 'Lana,' he said. 'Vanessa missed you a lot.'

'I missed her,' Elana rose. 'Well, I must go. I'll call you tomorrow, 'Nessa, if that's okay.'

'Sure. That'd be nice.' Vanessa rose and hugged her friend. 'So who? Who is it?' she said softly in her friend's ear. 'You look so wonderful, either you have a terrific beautician or you're in love. Give me the name of the first, or tell me *who he is*. Gavin?'

Elana giggled, 'No. His father!' she cried, and as Vanessa choked and gasped Elana turned and left the lounge, smiling to herself. At the entrance she turned and waved to her friend and saw that Vanessa had recovered. She was smiling and had her arm outstretched, her thumb upturned and she was winking.

Chapter Sixty-six

✧ ✧

Rosalind sat calmly in the Gresham Hotel lounge listening to the piano music that floated lightly across the room. It embraced the scattered groups of people in the room with the music of Cole Porter and Irving Berlin. Fred Astaire had opened in the Savoy Cinema next door in *The Berkleys of Broadway* and the music he danced to was everywhere. Occasionally Rosalind raised the teacup to her lips and sipped.

It was the afternoon and she was waiting for her daughter and son-in-law to arrive. She had come early. She wanted to relax and feel settled before they told her whatever news they had to impart.

Life, she mused, was very odd. She had always known of her husband's ignorance of the family business, but of course had kept that fact from him. And from everyone. Deep down she had always feared the collapse of Ardmore & Son and the resultant chaos it would bring to all their lives.

Now chaos had come and it had nothing to do with the business. Her daughters had left the nest, left her lonely and frustrated. The servants had left and Dundalgan was beginning to look neglected. It had been run for years with military precision and efficiency, smoothly and comfortably. Venny was wonderful, of course, but she only cooked – she was quite incapable of getting the enormous house clean, and Imelda was a little slow. Venny had absolutely no authority over her and with money tight they could not afford more staff.

Rosalind did not criticise her husband. That was against the tenets of her church, but in her heart she wished he'd been a little less hasty in dismissing not only his daughter but the whole Dundalgan staff in one fell swoop.

Her second grudge was against her elder daughter. Oriana was not behaving well. She had disappointed her mother who, though she adored her daughter, could not but compare her selfish behaviour with the dignity and graciousness of her younger sister, Vanessa. She had thrown poor Pierce out of his home at a time when he should have been able to rely on his wife's loyalty. It showed very poor taste indeed and the whole of Dublin was talking. She had quite ruthlessly divested herself of the husband she had no more use for and who, in most people's estimation, had only stolen in order to accommodate Oriana's extravagance. Rosalind agreed here with public opinion. She knew how greedy her daughter was. Brendan had granted her every wish even as he chastised her. It had done Oriana no good at all. People were also saying that Oriana was chasing Gavin Fitzjames all over town. They were saying that he was running in the opposite direction. It was all most unsavoury.

Rosalind did not know where Pierce Powers was at this moment. It worried her. Not only did his wife refuse to have him home, but it appeared that his family had also rejected him. Only Glenn, the American, the outsider, had had enough Christian spirit to bail him out when he had been in jail. Only Glenn had looked after him in his hour of need.

And now the firm was in dire trouble. Their funds were at a standstill. Dundalgan was going downhill rapidly as all big houses did if they were not cared for constantly.

We were so unaware that anything might go wrong, she thought. That May, when Oriana became engaged, that June when she got married, we never dreamed that we were standing on the edge of a precipice. We thought that our affluence, our comfort would never be threatened. It was a stupid assumption to make. It was always foolish to take security for granted.

What surprised Rosalind most was how well she was bearing up under all this. She had mucked in, learned to make cups of tea. Learned to whip up a light omelette. Learned to sew a little, take up hems, replace buttons – mainly for Sitric. She had learned to take cuttings, weed, make a bed, iron a shirt, do a little dusting and ride a bicycle. This last was the most fun. It gave her a feeling of wild freedom, to speed down the hill outside the Dundalgan gates to the village in her slacks and twinset and collect the papers in the freshness of the morning. To greet a few people. Link up with humanity.

'Morning, Betsy.'

'Morning, Mrs Ardmore.'

'How's the baby?'

'Oh, a little better now.'

At first they had been wary, even a little hostile. What was the grand Mrs Ardmore from the big house doing on a bike in the village?

But they soon got used to her and returned her greetings at first coolly, then automatically, then gladly, pleased to see her.

She was surprised at her resilience, her ability to adapt, her indifference to their change of fortunes. Something that all her life she had felt dependent on and feared losing had proved, when removed, not essential to her happiness. While Brendan ranted and raved, well on the way to giving himself another stroke, she calmly met the challenge with a dignity, courage and good humour she had not known she possessed, astonishing herself in the process.

Sitric cribbed a lot. He said he wanted some money, a lump sum soon. She told him there was none.

'The kitty, Sitric, my dear, is empty.'

'But, Mother, I just need . . .'

'Don't ask, Sitric. Do not ask. Your father is in deep trouble . . .'

'Oh dear! Oh dear! Oh dear!' he chanted sarcastically.

'Don't be facetious, Sitric. At the moment the fate of the Ardmores is in the balance. We may face penury.'

'Oh Mother, how Dickensian of you.'

'You cannot imagine it, Sitric, can you? You've lived in comfort all your life. You have no experience of insecurity. Most young men have to go to work, have to fight for the wherewithal to do the simplest things, like go to the movies. You've had it so easy all your life and you don't realise it.'

'Oh I do, Mother, I do. But it's Pappy's fault and you know it. He's never allowed me to study for anything. He shot down my ambition to become a lawyer, refused to let me go to college – and he never allowed me to have a go at the business. Even see if I was any good at it. He kept me so far away from Ardmore's and when I asked him questions he always refused to answer them.'

This was only too true. Rosalind had to admit that Brendan had brushed away any interest Sitric showed in the family business with impatience and bad humour. With brutal finality he told his son that he was far too stupid to be able to understand the intricacies of the wine trade.

'Know what I think, Mother? I think Pappy is pig-ignorant himself. That's what I think. I don't think he knows or really understands one end of the business from the other. And I think Patrick McCawley was the one who ran Ardmore's and the reason it's going down the hill so fast is because Patrick ran off with Cessy.'

'What makes you think that Sitric?' She'd never seen him so animated and deep down she knew he was talking sense. 'What do you know about it? I'm sure your father didn't tell you . . .'

'Avalan told me the shares—' He stopped abruptly.

'Your Aunt Avalan? When did you see her, Sitric? You never told me.'

'Oh . . .' He waved his hand airily. 'I saw her for a few minutes in the Arts Club the other day.'

'How unlike Avalan.' She glanced at her son, surprised. 'My sister hates going into town. How odd.'

Sitric twisted uncomfortably. 'I think she might have been in about Uncle Simon,' he said carefully. 'She said he was very ill.'

His legs around those glorious thighs, his thoughts almost made him blush in front of his mother, his mistress's sister. But he simply did not feel guilty. He thought of her breasts at his cheek. Her breath harsh in his ear as he fondled her there, and there, and there. He looked out of his mother's window. The trees had an untidy look and the hedges were travelling. He sighed.

Rosalind followed his gaze and read his thoughts. 'Why don't *you* get a ladder and do it?' she asked.

'I'd probably kill them, Mother,' he replied. Then he saw the corners of her mouth tremble. 'Maybe I'll do just that,' he told her. 'Maybe.'

They both knew he wouldn't but she was grateful that he'd

offered. It removed the barrier between them and he kissed her cheek and left her.

Sitting in the Gresham she remembered the conversation, and she thought about her son. He really should have something to occupy him, some work to do, some study to interest him. Glenn and Vanessa's arrival jerked her out of her reverie and brought her back to the present.

'Mother. Oh Mother,' she heard her daughter's voice and she rose to her feet and opened her arms.

'Vanessa, my darling.'

'Oh Mother,' Rosalind embraced her daughter then sat down holding her hand. She noted at once how calmly beautiful Vanessa looked, so relaxed. Her heart rejoiced. Her daughter had lost that tense, tight expression that had worried her mother and was glowing and lovely.

'Hello, Glenn.' She greeted her son-in-law warmly. He was, after all, responsible for the change in Vanessa.

'Hi.' She winced a little but there was a smile on her face. She had missed her daughter too much to be finicky about slang. 'I asked you to come here to meet us because there is something I reckon I need your help with,' Glenn said when they were settled.

Rosalind arranged herself in the chair, checking her skirt, crossing her ankles. 'Well, Glenn, enlighten me please.'

'The thing is,' he said, 'with your help, your permission I I think I can save Ardmore's.'

She opened her eyes wide. 'Why would you want to do that? My husband has not exactly earned, nor does he deserve your help.' Rosalind looked at her son-in-law, perplexed. She was deeply puzzled.

'I'm not one to hold grudges, Mother-in-law.' He leaned forward, his handsome face split by a ravishing grin, which abruptly vanished, giving place to a frown of concentration. 'No, there's nothing to be gained by nursing resentments. You see, I love Ireland. I love your daughter. I've spent enough time in the army. I've come to a place where I have to make a new start. Now, I'll be frank with you. I'm not a rich man. Oh, I have savings and my pension from the Marines. But not enough to start from scratch and give Vanessa the kind of life she deserves. I want to give your daughter all the comforts she's used to. I think I can do that if I take over the running of the firm. The gamble is, can I do it? Don't worry, I'll demand a large fee and shares, some of which I already have in the project, if I succeed. And what have you got to lose? You're going down anyway. You're drowning. Without help, without someone to rescue you the firm will go kaput.'

Rosalind gasped. Shocked, she stared at her son-in-law. 'Good heavens, Glenn, you don't know the first thing about it,' she breathed.

'Patrick McCawley does,' he said – Rosalind gasped again – 'And I've got him with us.' He laughed. 'Don't look so shocked. It will work out, I promise.'

'Patrick and Cessy are here?' she asked, amazed.

'I did not say that. What I said was I had his help. And I've lots of plain common sense. And I'm not lumbered with an overpowering awe of the business, which seems to have overwhelmed most of the staff of Ardmore's. I don't feel reverential about wine. I feel commercial about it.'

Rosalind nodded her head. 'It is the new way,' she said sadly. 'I can't say I approve, but I suppose sometimes it is necessary.' Then she cleared her throat, looking slightly uncomfortable. 'Brendan will never permit this,' she said. 'He'll never allow you to take over.'

'He won't be able to prevent it,' Glenn told her. 'He's never told you, has he, that you have a block of shares in the company? You and Sitric and Oriana. And, of course, Vanessa. She's deeded some of hers over to me. It was in his father's will. But I'm sure he never bothered to inform you.'

Rosalind spread her hands. 'Well, I had some idea that I ... But Glenn, I would never try to muscle into my husband's business. It's not a woman's place.'

'Even if that business is on the verge of bankruptcy? Even if by interfering you could save the family from ruin? Remember you face losing everything.'

Rosalind looked doubtful. 'Well, put that way ... But I don't know what it means,' she added.

'It means you have voting power. I'll not do anything without the democratic consent of the majority of the shareholders.'

She nodded. 'I see.'

'What I plan to do is have all the shareholders at the AGM. They'll be there anyway. And I want you and the family there. I'll put my plan to them and we'll see what happens. If everyone votes that I butt out, then that's what I'll do.'

Rosalind to her astonishment heard herself saying, 'Okay.'

'But don't say anything to your husband yet. If he gets wind of what I plan he'll refuse to appear and then it would not be satisfactory.'

'Would it be legal?' Vanessa asked.

Glenn nodded. 'Yes. But it would not be satisfactory. I'd much prefer if everything was above board so that afterwards I could not be accused of acting behind anyone's back.'

To her vast surprise Rosalind heard herself once again utter the word she had vowed would never pass her lips.

'Okay,' she said.

Chapter Sixty-seven

❧ ❧

He left Vanessa sleeping in the hotel bedroom. They had made love and had taken a long time over it. She had eventually, tired and fulfilled, slipped into a sensuous slumber.

He went down to the bar for a drink. He took the elevator to the ground floor and then went down the short flight of stairs to the bar. As he entered he saw Sitric seated obliquely, half-concealing whoever was with him.

Glenn sat in the farthest corner where he could see but not be seen. As he sipped his Canadian Club on the rocks he tried to decipher what was going on in the corner. He could only hear snatches of the conversation.

'. . . ask me to meet you here . . . madness.' This a female voice, curiously familiar.

'. . . loved me . . . wouldn't care!' Sitric sounded emotional and petulant.

'. . . think . . . deliberately . . .'

'We have to *do* something!' Sitric cried clearly.

They were emotionally involved, there was no doubt about that, and if Glenn was surprised that Sitric's companion was his aunt, Rosalind Ardmore's sister, it did not show on his face. Sitric, on this last statement, turned and stormed out. Glenn caught his arm as he passed. Sitric recoiled as if Glenn had struck him. 'You? Here?' he stammered.

'You look like an old-movie vampire hit by the sun,' Glenn remarked and Sitric rolled his eyes, looked wildly about and fled.

Glenn crossed to the bar and sat down beside Avalan. She was startled but unlike Sitric she retained her composure.

'Glenn, isn't it? What are you doing here?'

'That's not important,' he said. 'Can I offer you a drink, Avalan?'

'How'd you know me?' she asked, a trifle despondently.

'I know a lot,' he said cryptically. 'A drink?'

She nodded. 'Yes,' she said, 'I think I need one.'

She was very beautiful, Glenn thought, like a more mature Vanessa. She was what Vanessa would be like in the years to come. A warmly beautiful, voluptuous woman.

'I suppose you witnessed that little scene?' she asked when he put the glass before her and poured the tonic over the gin.

He nodded. 'I only caught bits and pieces,' he said.

'Enough to make a fair assessment of the situation?' she asked lightly.

He nodded again and she asked, 'Are you shocked?'

He shrugged. 'It's not up to me to make judgements,' he said calmly. 'My track record's not so great.'

She raised her brows and he added, 'In the war. No one who fights and kills in a war has the right to sit in judgement on anyone.'

They both drank for a while in silence, then Avalan said, 'You're going to think this very strange, maybe wicked.'

He smiled wryly. 'Oh, I guess I don't reckon anything you told me could be really wicked.'

'Oh?'

'Naw!' He smiled. 'No, wicked is without love. Where there is love there is always something good.'

'I love my husband. I really do,' she told him.

'But he's all messed up, right?'

She nodded. 'He's in terrible pain. Constant agony. He wants me to . . .' She couldn't finish.

'I guess I can understand that,' Glenn said.

She pulled a handkerchief out of the pocket of her softly pleated blue wool dress. 'No, no. You don't understand. I love Sitric as well. As well as my husband and with the same intensity.' She shook her head, baffled by herself, and Glenn saw there were tears in her eyes. 'Can you believe that? I truly love my husband who is sick, dying. And I love my lover passionately, madly, both at the same time. I horrify myself. Mother of God, I'm utterly bewildered. I don't know what to do.'

Glenn put a gentle hand over hers. 'Don't do anything,' he told her. 'Let it all rest.'

337

She seemed to relax. A tear spilled over her cheek and she absentmindedly dabbed it with her handkerchief.

'Am I evil?' she asked him after a moment.

He smiled reassuringly. 'No,' he told her. 'You're not evil.'

'You won't tell anyone?' she asked fearfully.

He shook his head. 'Of course not. Need you ask?'

She smiled a little tremulously. 'Oh God,' she muttered, twisting her handkerchief between her hands. 'What a mess.'

He said nothing. There was nothing to say. She gulped back the last of her drink.

'I better go,' she said. 'Simon will—' She broke off and turned to him. 'He's suffering so,' she whispered. 'So much.'

'I saw lots of guys like that. Suffering like that.'

'You might come down sometime to Rackton Hall and see him. Tell him that. Fellow soldiers. Comrades in arms.' She shrugged. 'It's such shit. But it might help.'

She stood and he helped her into her pale blue wool coat.

'Sitric will be outside,' she said with a small smile, then looked up at him. 'You are very kind, Glenn. To listen. Not to condemn.'

'I said, I'm not the kind to sound off.'

She held out her hand. 'Thank you,' she said sincerely. 'Thank you so much.' And he took her firm grip, shook hands, and she left, drawing admiring stares from the men as she passed by on her way out of the hotel.

Chapter Sixty-eight

❧ ❧

The six men were seated around the oak-panelled boardroom table. Regan O'Doherty, Barry Blessington, Thomás McIlhinny, Roddy Clark, Geraghty and Vincent Laverty. One by one they had entered, gloomy-faced, and sat down in their accustomed places.

It was a while before they noticed that the huge mahogany table had been extended. Two extra leaves had been added, obviously to accommodate more people. They shifted uneasily in their seats. If rumour was correct they were in for huge financial losses and they felt very fearful as they sat silently waiting for the meeting to commence. The usual joviality was missing.

Each of them was unwilling to admit the extent of their ignorance. None of them knew what was afoot. None of them knew how the land lay. They knew the firm of Ardmore & Son was losing money and its shares were plummeting and they each wanted to desert the sinking ship as swiftly and as painlessly as possible and with as little distress to themselves. But they did not want to show their state of mind. All of them individually had tried to contact Brendan Ardmore but he had been incommunicado.

Thomás McIlhinny plonked a pile of papers before him and he glanced around the table triumphantly. The papers were proof that Ardmore & Son had screwed them out of considerable sums of money on the surefire Vie de France account. He did not know that Patrick McCawley was waiting, even now, in the Connemara marble toilet off the boardroom, waiting in fear and trepidation with Glenn and Vanessa. The scene was set.

When Sitric and Rosalind entered and sat down, calmly, at the table, the men, anticipating Brendan's arrival, were

339

taken aback. The tension rose and they were suddenly acutely uncomfortable. The time-honoured routine had changed. The AGM had unthinkably altered its shape. Mrs Ardmore and her son were in their midst. What on earth were they doing there? Perhaps young Sitric, of whom no good so far had ever been heard, was going to take over? Rumour painted him a dilettante and an idler, but maybe he was going to run the firm. Else why was he here? Why for that matter was his mother here? Perhaps Brendan Ardmore's stroke had incapacitated him to such an extent that he was no longer competent to direct things?

But they kept their speculations to themselves. They were not, in the circumstances, perfectly sure who was friend and who was foe. They stood, nodded formally to Rosalind and reseated themselves, making appropriate remarks about the weather for the time of year. Rosalind sat on one side of the table and Sitric on the other. He wore a grey worsted suit, his black cashmere coat thrown carelessly over his shoulders. He shrugged it off now and as usual tilted his chair, heavy though it was, right back on to its hind legs so that all the men swallowed nervously and wished he wouldn't. His hair kept falling over his cheek and he pushed it back with long nervous fingers, smoking incessantly. He did nothing to reassure the men there that he would be in any way helpful to them in this hour of Ardmore's need. His was not a figure to inspire confidence.

Rosalind wore black furs and a small black pillar-box hat with a veil over her face. But she was a woman and could have no real authority here. The men moved closer together away from Brendan's family members as if they had some contagious disease. They all looked very uneasy at this unexpected intrusion.

Suddenly the door opened and Reginald Crosby entered. They all stared. No one knew who he was. They watched the little man process from the door to the head of the table with fascinated interest.

Nerves had bestowed dignity upon Reginald Crosby. He walked slowly and stiffly to the head of the table, to Patrick McCawley's place, and sat rigidly down. They watched open-mouthed. No one spoke.

Minutes later the door was flung open and Brendan

Ardmore entered. He walked haltingly as if to his execution and took his seat beside Reginald. He looked at him and nodded, then drew his breath to speak. At this moment he saw his wife and son at the table and his jaw dropped as a look of bewildered astonishment crossed his face. The other men in the room stared at him, wondering what his astonishment indicated.

He remained sitting, mouth agape, then stammered, 'Wha . . . wha . . . ?' And Rosalind thought, looking at him, that he was going to have another stroke. However, Reginald was rising to his feet and all Brendan could do was gulp, pour himself some water with a shaking hand and drink it.

'Gentlemen,' Reginald began, 'ah, and Mrs Ardmore—'

'Why is she here?' Brendan asked, regaining to some degree his composure.

'You'll find out in a moment, sir,' Reginald began, 'if you would let me . . . ?'

Brendan stopped and looked at his manager. 'Oh yes, of course.'

'None of you really know me,' Reginald said. 'Perhaps I should explain who I am.'

'Well, we don't really care.' Roddy Clark had a hangover and desperately craved a drink. He had a flask in his jacket pocket but dared not take a drink from it in front of everyone. He was casting about in his mind how to sneak a surreptitious gulp. 'Get on with it, man, heaven's sake.'

Barry and the others didn't give a damn about Reginald Crosby either. They wanted to escape to the golf course at Portmarnock. Only Thomás McIlhinny was keen to be there, desperate to produce his proof of skulduggery, but Reginald was not to be rushed.

'I am Reginald Crosby, Personal Assistant to Patrick McCawley who, as some of you know, left this firm after twenty years.'

'He left?' Thomás McIlhinny shouted, jumping to his feet. 'He *left*? Well, that explains *this*.' He slapped his papers with the tips of his fingers. 'He obviously left with half the firm's profits from last year in his pockets.'

The others had not known that Patrick McCawley had gone. 'What does he mean?' Geraghty asked, pricking up his ears. 'Half the profit?' He'd never liked Brendan and contemplated a row with him with deep pleasure.

Reginald held up his hand. It gave him a great feeling of security to remind himself that Glenn Carey was in the room behind him waiting for his name to be called.

At this moment the main door opened and Oriana burst in. 'What's all this about?' she asked breathlessly. Her face was flushed and she was draped in sables and cashmere.

'Late as usual, Ori,' Sitric drawled and his sister blushed. 'Sit down, sit down,' Sitric continued. 'It's fascinating, really fascinating. I never realised how interesting and challenging Pappy's work was.' His tone was heavily sarcastic. Brendan glared at him. 'I still don't know why we are here,' he finished.

'And neither do I,' Brendan shouted suddenly. 'Who told you to come here, I'd like to know?'

'Pappy?' Oriana looked at her father wide-eyed. He stared at her blankly. Sitric tapped the leather chair beside him. 'Sit,' he told her and she obediently sat. No one answered Brendan's question.

'Mother?' Oriana looked at her mother for direction.

'Sit quietly dear and listen to Mr Crosby,' Rosalind instructed her.

Reginald opened his mouth to continue but once more he was interrupted. 'What did he mean?' Vincent Laverty asked, 'about Patrick McCawley leaving with half the profits?'

'If you could be a little patient, gentlemen and ladies, I'll explain,' Reginald Crosby stated firmly, then cleared his throat and, seeing that he had caught their attention, he continued, 'I am Mr McCawley's Personal Assistant. My duty was to continue as Mr McCawley had, while he was in America. I cannot hide from you gentlemen that the business, Ardmore & Son, is ailing. Nothing to do with Mr McCawley, I assure you, but certainly accelerated by his absence. Market forces beyond our control have unfortunately damaged our trade outlets and only Mr McCawley has the business know-how to rescue us. I tried my best in the year Mr McCawley has been away, but I have to tell you, gentlemen and ladies, I have to admit that my strengths lie not in administration as I have no entrepreneurial expertise, but rather in what my title suggests, Personal Assistant to the Manager.'

342

'What's he blethering about?' Roddy Clark asked unsteadily, then announced, 'My shoe's undone,' and he disappeared beneath the table where he took out the flask, gulped down a slug and wiped his hand across his mouth. No one paid any attention.

Barry Blessington said, 'What he's saying is, he made a mess of it. Failed.'

'That is *not* what I'm saying, sir,' Reginald insisted pedantically. 'But I've obviously not been able to make you understand what I mean. So perhaps I should ask someone else to do it for me.'

'Pain in the ass,' Roddy Clark muttered, then, 'Oh, beg your pardon, ladies. 'Struth, I forgot.'

'Well, who are you going to get to explain?' Brendan asked, exasperated.

'Mr Glenn Carey,' Reginald said, giving up.

Brendan looked at him as if he'd misunderstood. 'Who?' he asked stupidly. Then in utter disbelief he stammered, 'What the . . .'

'Now, dear,' Rosalind said, 'don't distress yourself. Remember what the doctor said. Sit down, dear. You don't want another stroke.'

Brendan glared at her, surprised at her tone. She was ordering him. Never before in his life had she spoken to him like that, as if he were a child. 'You see,' she continued calmly, 'what it boils down to, Brendan –' she glanced up at Reginald, 'I hope you won't mind me simplifying it for my husband – the fact is, dear, we are facing bankruptcy and ruin. I don't think I'm exaggerating, am I, Mr Crosby?' She looked up at Reginald again.

'No, madam, you are not.'

'And that unless something pretty drastic is done, not only the firm, but Dundalgan is in jeopardy.'

'Exactly.'

Brendan looked aghast at this plain speaking. He'd refused to face up to this possibility. He'd avoided the facts that were plain to his staff, and in the last hopeless months he had taken out another huge mortgage on Dundalgan, only to discover that the firm was not bringing in enough profit to make the payments now overdue. He squirmed in his chair, reseating himself as his wife had commanded.

343

'But why did you mention that name?' he asked gruffly.

Rosalind cleared her throat. 'The point is, there may be a way out,' she said, and everyone looked at her hopefully. She marvelled at how accurately Glenn gauged people. What they were interested in, he'd told her, was profit. Not losing money.

'What you've got to understand is that the only one who can help us now appears to be Glenn Carey, Vanessa's husband.'

'I'd rather go under,' Brendan growled, staring at her dumbfounded. Surprise had overcome his instinct to roar abuse and march out.

'I'd advise you to listen to him,' Rosalind said firmly, 'and weigh the position we're in very carefully indeed before you act precipitously. All right, dear?'

'He's here?' Brendan seemed to have trouble with his breathing.

'Yes, dear, he is. In the lavatory behind you with Vanessa.'

'Then the meeting is adjourned,' he said abruptly, rising to his feet.

Rosalind grabbed his sleeve. 'Sit down, Brendan, don't you see—'

'I'm afraid, Pa, if I understand the situation, you'll be ousted if you leave now.' Sitric could not keep the delight from his voice.

His father looked at him uncomprehendingly. 'What . . . ?'

'If you go now, the vote will be taken without you. You'll find yourself out on your ear. No power. No position. No firm.'

'But this is preposterous!' Brendan shouted, his voice returning. 'You cannot do this! It's not legal.'

'I'm afraid, dear, that it is.' Rosalind smiled at her husband. 'I think we ought to take a vote, Reginald, don't you?'

The other men had pricked up their ears and listened to the argument intently. Hands shot up in favour of listening to what Glenn Carey had to say. They were not swayed by loyalty, as Glenn had suggested, when money entered into the equation. These men wanted profit, a return on their shares, and Glenn Carey seemed to offer some hope on that score. Here was a possibility of avoiding disaster.

'You mean he thinks he can save the firm?' Barry Blessington asked.

'Yes. But I have something to say first.' This was Reginald, taking over.

'Oh God, not again,' Vincent Laverty cried. 'Why can't we just get on with the solution?'

'We have to face the fact that no one can run the firm like Patrick McCawley,' Reginald said stoutly.

'That bastard,' Thomás McIlhinny cried, delighted at last to talk about his discoveries of fraud. 'I have here papers that will convict him in any court in the land.' And he drummed his fingers on the papers before him.

'Can you please hear me out, McIlhinny?' Reginald said softly. 'It is, after all, in our interest. We are on the same side. The fact is, and I can't emphasise it enough, we have to have him back with us.'

'After he's ripped us off? After he's . . .' Thomás was beside himself.

'Well, you got a choice. It's all or nothing, McIlhinny,' Reginald said calmly. 'You refuse McCawley amnesty, you lose everything. After all, what he did was to take less than your dividends amounted to for that period. He ran the firm on a pittance.'

Brendan snorted, opened his mouth to speak but Reginald held up his hand. 'No, sir, just a moment. Let's face facts. I don't approve of what McCawley did. I don't condone it. But I *understand* it. We take him to court, we get nothing. He has no money that I know of. We get all the publicity. He'll squawk loudly about how much he was paid for the extraordinary amount of work he did. It is going to shock people, bring the firm into disgrace. Even the judge might think it not unreasonable that he took the action he did. Oh, he'll sentence him and much good that will do you and me. In the meantime the name of Ardmore & Son will be discredited and it will go into the hands of the receivers and we will be in a much worse situation than we are today and with no hope of ever recovering. You don't reinstate him, we are wiped out.'

The men nodded. Thomás McIlhinny made to protest but the others shut him up. Brendan's face showed the war within.

'So, what do we do?' Brendan asked. He sounded helpless. All heads swivelled his way. It was the first time anyone had heard Brendan Ardmore ask for advice. Rosalind smiled. Reginald did not miss a beat. 'Mr Carey is in the bathroom,' he said. 'With Mr McCawley.' Uproar. Sitric rubbed his hands together and grinned. 'So if we are all in agreement, ladies, gentlemen, that it's better to reap the rewards offered by these people than to indulge in righteous indignation, and, by insisting on retribution, end up with nothing, the choice is yours.' He spread his hands and paused, then sat down looking around at them questioningly. 'Let's have a show of hands. Those in favour of the motion.'

All hands were raised except Brendan's.

'Against?' No hands were raised, not even Brendan's.

'Motion carried!' Reginald cried with some satisfaction.

346

Chapter Sixty-nine

⤚ ⤙

Reginald walked to the boardroom door to the marble bathroom and opened the door. Glenn, Vanessa and Patrick McCawley walked out. Glenn took charge immediately. Over the roar of Brendan's 'Get out of here, you insolent puppy!' and the urgent hushing of the others, Glenn said, 'Hi. I'm Glenn Carey. Vanessa's husband.' They were quiet and he grinned at them with his film star smile. Relaxed and charming and paying no attention to Brendan, he walked down the room holding Vanessa's hand in a firm grip and bringing with him a charge of energy and vitality. Patrick McCawley followed him. On reaching the other end of the table Glenn sat down opposite Brendan at the head and motioned Patrick and his wife to sit one on either side of him.

'I've gotta plan,' he said. Brendan sputtered, banged his hand on the table impotently. 'Insolent puppy, get him out!' he shouted, but there was no conviction in his voice, no authority, and once again the others shushed him and generally ignored him. Their attention was on the other end of the table. No one blinked an eye. No one seemed to find it odd that they were quieting the man they had once listened to with respect.

Glenn, without seeming to hurry, said, 'See, it's like this. The firm is kaput. Unless something is done swiftish Sitric here and Oriana, Mrs Ardmore, my mother-in-law, and Mr Ardmore all will be penniless, and you gentlemen will lose a considerable amount of money. Your investment will become null and void. Now, what you may not know is that Oriana, my mother-in-law, Sitric and my wife all have shares in this firm and so have voting power, which means that any voting we have here today includes them. Now, what I want—'

347

'Shares?' Oriana cried. 'What shares?'

'Your grandfather left you shares, Oriana,' Glenn said gently.

'I never knew that. What does it mean?'

'It means, Ori,' said Sitric, 'that you and I and 'Ness should have received quite a lot of money over the years when the firm was doing brilliantly, but now, as it is bankrupt – good as – we won't get a bean. Pappy, dear girl, has been screwing us.'

'Oh my God.' Oriana stared at her father. All her life she had trusted him, loved him. He had been her God. She had obeyed him, even married the man of his choice, believing he knew best. Now he sat before her, unable to run his business, and she had just been told that he was diddling her and her brother and sister. He had been cheating them all these years.

It was not that he had taken money rightfully hers away from her. He had given her everything she needed. It was the deception, the lack of honesty that dumbfounded her. He had been so strict about that, always demanding that they tell the truth, always expecting scrupulous honesty. They had all been beaten when they had tiptoed on the edges of the truth. He had raised his hand to them, hurt them, abused them, and all the time he himself had been offending against the standards he demanded of them. And he was an adult, they children. He was a cheat. She glanced at Sitric and saw the confirmation of disgust in his eyes. There was no mistake. Vanessa looked at them and nodded. 'It's true,' she said, but she was not as surprised and cut up about it as they. She had left her father emotionally a long time ago. She had had time to assimilate the true nature of the man. Sitric had done so too, in his own way, though it was still a shock, but to Oriana it came like a douche of cold water, a shattering of her faith.

'Oriana, don't fret,' Glenn said softly. 'All of us are human. If we intend forgiving Paddy here because that way we'll all prosper, then you can forgive your father doing what he thought was best for you.' He continued smoothly, not giving pause for comment. 'We can change the course of Ardmore & Son under certain conditions.' He held his hands up. 'Now keep cool. Some of these conditions are radical and will shock you. But you've got to look at it dispassionately. See here, I've got a plan and I want to put all my cards on the table. No jerking around.' He had their attention. To a man they settled to listen to him – only Thomás McIlhinny had a last try.

'I've got papers here to show that McCawley here –' he pointed at Patrick who shrank against the back of his chair – 'was stealing.'

Glenn leaned forward. 'Would you like to leave, Mr McIlhinny? Because unless all of us, *all* of us, every man Jack leaves *all* animosity outside this room, then the deal's off. Would you like to go? And I'll declare this firm insolvent.'

They were all quiet. Thomás sat down.

'I take it none of you want that?' Glenn asked. Much shaking of heads. 'So is everyone agreed to that principle?'

A chorus of yea's.

'Gee, that's great. In that case let me proceed. Take notes, Reggie. The minutes.' He cleared his throat. 'You all know Paddy here?' Patrick leaned forward. He looked relaxed for the first time since he came into the room.

'Patrick here is a goddamn genius. Why you didn't pay him more I'll never understand. So I want you to listen to what he has to say. Okay, Paddy it's all yours.'

Patrick was rapidly regaining his *sang-froid*. He stood. Only Thomás glared at him. The others waited expectantly.

'Good morning,' he said. 'I first of all want to say that I did wrong and I'm sorry. You'll never have cause to mistrust me again, as God is my witness. Now the deal is this. I get the salary – not wages – the *salary* I deserve, what other firms pay their men in my position and a share in the future of Ardmore's.'

There were loud murmurs of 'That's a bit rich, coming from him' and 'A salary's one thing, but *shares*'.

'Hear me out,' he pleaded. 'I run the actual business of Ardmore's as I think fit. It will be in my hands to turn it around. Glenn Carey will take over as Manager of the whole enterprise. And, as he says, trim its sails.'

Brendan stood. 'I'm sorry,' he said in a trembling voice. 'This cannot be. I'll not stay here while this . . . this outsider takes all I care for, our family's business . . .'

'He is family, dear,' Rosalind said firmly. 'Sit down. If you leave you'll find your proposed position as President rescinded and Glenn's name voted in instead.'

Brendan sat down abruptly. To his children he seemed smaller, shrunken.

'I'd hoped to keep threats out of this,' Glenn said, looking at Rosalind reproachfully, but Rosalind continued, 'And you'll end as a bankrupt and a pauper. The choice dear, as Glenn said, is yours.'

'But Mr McCawley reinstated won't, *can't* get us out of trouble in time.' Barry cried. 'It's all very well you sounding off, but—'

'I'm coming to that,' Glenn told them. 'See, it's like this. Paddy can put the firm back, but it will take a year or two, and to bridge that gap I've devised a programme of recovery. It's a very ruthless one but it's the only way to save the day.'

'How's that?' Vincent asked.

McIlhinny was sulking over his papers, but listening intently nevertheless. His head was cocked sideways as if at any moment he might change his mind.

'Some of you may not like it –' it was obvious Glenn meant Brendan – 'but it is the only way. I propose to sell the warehouses in Marrowbone Lane and Rainsford Street. Guinness is interested in buying. I sounded them out. They've made a tentative offer already. I suggest we sell the sorting offices in D'Olier's Street. We have a lot of property that's not used. We hardly ever utilise the space we have in abundance. That way we can clear any outstanding debt and turn the whole business around. The real estate in D'Oliers Street is worth a fortune. Quite a few hotel conglomerates have shown interest. Great interest. Then I propose we turn half of the Burgh Quay warehouse into a restaurant and bar. Get Pierce Powers to run it.' He smiled around the table, daring them to object. His blue gaze came to rest on Oriana's astonished face. He smiled at her. 'And I propose we narrow down our imports of the old, expensive stuff. Oh, not cut it too much, but make room for the newer wine markets. As well as the burgundy and the champagne and the expensive ports and sherrys, we could incorporate Californian and Australian wines. They are just beginning to take off and I think we could make a killing there.'

'Did I understand you to say Pierce would . . .' Oriana asked in a dazed voice.

Glenn nodded briskly. 'Sure. He just needs an opportunity to prove himself. Got great talent but no one's ever given him a chance.'

'Mother, I think I'm going to be sick,' Oriana whispered.

'You'll sit there and behave yourself,' Rosalind commanded.

'Lastly and by no means least I want to let out stalls and have an antique market where the offices are behind the Quays. There's money to be made that way. And now I think we ought to vote on it,' Glenn said, rising. 'Either you like the deal or you don't. No arguments – one bit in, one bit out. Not like that. All or nothing. I'll leave while you take the majority vote. If you want me in I'll put my plan into action at once. If not, I'm outa here. Come along, Paddy. We'll leave you to it.'

They rose. Vanessa rose too to follow them but Glenn pressed her back into her chair.

'No. You stay here and vote, honey. It's your right. I can vote too,' he told the collected company, 'but I don't want to be accused of putting pressure on you. And I do not want to be the deciding vote. Paddy and I will wait outside. Reginald Crosby is in charge.'

They all watched until the door closed behind the two men.

Brendan rose to his feet. 'Well, you all heard what that young bounder said.' His voice was much calmer. He had regained some of his composure and his determination to stop Glenn Carey in his tracks had been cemented by the American's plans. Turn him into a common shopkeeper, a property developer, a market-stall outlet. Never! He was no nabob. His profession as a wine import/export merchant was old and honourable and had its roots in the aristocracy. The people in France, Germany and Italy he did business with were, as often as not, noblemen with vineyards and châteaux. To demean himself by selling off his property to hotels and a porter company – for that was what he considered Guinness to be – was out of the question. And the mere idea of becoming the proprietor of a bar and restaurant thoroughly shocked him.

'Yes, we heard. And it seems that young man is about to do wonders,' Barry Blessington commented with delight, visualising the increase in income this could bring about.

351

The others nodded decisively. Suddenly it seemed hope had appeared at the end of a very long and gloomy tunnel. Shares could skyrocket. Money could be made. The American inspired confidence.

'You don't intend to let him take over?' Brendan asked incredulously. He could not understand their attitude, which seemed to him a gross betrayal. At the first bleep of trouble they were deserting him, crossing over to support his avowed enemy.

But the American said he did not want to be elected by a small margin. There were his family. Surely they would stand by him. But Rosalind was looking at him as if he'd lost his reason. So were Oriana, Vanessa and Sitric. And the others. Staring at him as if he were an idiot. It was the nightmare he'd feared most: everyone staring at him because he'd been found out. Unmasked. The little boy in the class revealed as an ignoramus.

'Of course we do,' Vincent said emphatically, glancing around at the others, speaking confidently for them all.

'Let us take a vote.' Reginald Crosby spoke harshly. 'Now.'

'But . . . but . . .' Brendan was spluttering.

'Sit down please, Mr Ardmore.' It gave Reginald great pleasure to issue the order. 'All those in favour of Mr Carey's plan please raise your hand.'

All hands shot up. There was no hesitation on the part of the family. Rosalind, Oriana, Vanessa and Sitric were as quick as the others to vote for Glenn.

'Against?'

One hand rose. Brendan Ardmore saw his lone hand in the air and he cried out to them, suddenly unselfconscious, 'You are destroying me! You are selling out to a goddamned Yankee. This is *my* business and you are taking it away from me. Stop it please. You were supposed to be my friends. All these years I took care of you.' His voice had run down and at the end he was nearly crying, pleading with them.

'Patrick McCawley did, Pappy,' Vanessa cried. Suddenly she was no longer afraid of him. He seemed childish and faintly ridiculous. A blinkered man drowning in self-pity, spurning the lifebelt offered him because of his stupid pride.

Reginald Crosby announced, 'Motion carried,' and Brendan's head sank in defeat on his folded arms.

Chapter Seventy

❧ ❧

Brendan Ardmore sat alone in his study at Dundalgan sunk in gloom. He glanced at the birch rod but did not really see it. Its days were over anyhow. His head throbbed and he wished Rosalind would open the door and ask him if everything was all right in that lovely mellow voice she always used when she knew he was worried or in the dumps. But those days too were over and Rosalind was not on his side any more. She had crossed over to the American camp after that fatal AGM in Ardmore & Son. She too had deserted him.

When they had returned to Dundalgan after the meeting she had walked past him in the hall and started climbing the stairs without as much as a glance in his direction. She was going to her room without a word, something she had never done before in their lives together.

He put his head into his hands. He had truly never thought that she would mind about the shares. The idea had never entered his head. The law, he knew, was that he owned all his wife's property automatically, so what was all the fuss about? But she had let him know she was disgusted with him because of those shares. Yet he had treated her and the girls, and Sitric, with open-handed generosity. He had never been mean, not like Sean Powers. He had given them everything, so what had he done to land himself in this mess?

He shuddered. That goddamn American. Everything had been all right until he had blundered into their lives. He remembered Oriana's engagement party. Oh, if only they could go back to that May day. He'd telephone the American Embassy and tell them not under any circumstances to send the two sergeants to the Country Club, then none of these problems would come to plague their lives. Tell them to phone a message to the Country Club, have the Ambassador paged, goddammit. Tell the manager to take a message, the doorman not to let them in. Anything, anything to have stopped that fatal meeting.

He turned and twisted it in his mind but the answer always came up the same. He'd lost. The American had won. Brendan groaned. This guy, this smiling foreigner was now leader of the pack. He was top dog at Ardmore's. He would rule the roost and would commercialise their name and degrade the noble business that they had run so respectably for so many decades. What Glenn Carey said now, went.

And he would leave Brendan behind, a defeated man, the object of scorn and pity. Brendan let out a bellow of rage that echoed through the house and made Rosalind shudder in her room and shake her head and sigh. But she did not go to him. No one would go to him any more. There was no one to terrorise, no one would run away from him in fear. No one at home and no one in the office.

What was there for him to do now? He'd explain to Rosalind. She'd understand about the shares eventually.

He looked out of the small window. The lawn, sloping down to the river was ragged and unkempt. Someone had mown one half of it and not the other. Rushton Byrne's loving hands were sadly missed. In fact on this awful day of truth and dare he had to admit that the whole Byrne family were a terrible loss. He wished he could smell Sive's rabbit pie, or her beef and dumplings or her rich lamb stew. He wished he could count up the days and work out which pudding would be served today. Lush berry pudding. Gooseberry fool with meringue. Three-layered chocolate mousse – white, milk and dark with a hint of orange – tarte tatin, apples runny with toffee juices and a thick dollop of cream.

The new cook, Venny, was uninspired. She gave them rice pudding and tapioca. Food for an invalid. And now, according to Rosalind this morning, Venny intended to return to Vanessa and Glenn, whence she had come, which he'd never have allowed if he'd known. So even Venny would be going.

Brendan Ardmore turned and looked up at the portrait of his father. 'What can I do now?' he asked helplessly. But as in life his father did not help him and there was no reply. Only lonely silence.

Chapter Seventy-one

છે જ

Upstairs in her room Rosalind sat on her chaise and pondered. She could vote about things now. She also had money and that gave her clout. She felt very good inside and wondered what that feeling was precisely. Then she thought it was probably power. She had a little power now. She did not have to wheedle everything she wanted out of Brendan, she did not have to coax him any more.

Dundalgan was in a mess. She would get it decorated. Tell Brendan to have the repairs done. She would hire a reliable staff and pay them over the odds. The days of resentful servants were over.

She had no doubt that Glenn would make a huge success of the business. Everyone liked him. He would inspire loyalty and effort from the workers. Some of his ideas made her shudder, but beggars couldn't be choosers. Apparently Ardmore & Son were going into the laundrette business. That was according to the latest reports. And the business of leasing land to stall-holders down on the Quays. Glenn had told them that they were branching out in all directions. Ardmore & Son was no longer a dignified old establishment where morning-suited employees walked haughtily between rows of packers and sorters. It had joined the hustling, bustling modern world.

Still, Rosalind did not really mind all this diversification. It did not impinge on her social world. People might query the shopkeeper aspect of Ardmore's but Rosalind was confident that she could carry that off. She would make a joke of it, treat it as an amusing nod to the new decade. After all, the fifties had arrived. And having money gave her the power to give the best parties, to entertain.

She looked around her room. She loved this room. In it

she could nurture her spirit and nourish her soul. Oh, she had so much to look forward to now that she had shaken off the terrible yoke of Brendan's authority and control. She had so much to be happy about. She smiled.

She was going to be a grandmother. Vanessa had told her after the meeting and Rosalind was ecstatic. How wonderful it would be. A child. And if it took after either of its parents it would be the most beautiful baby ever born.

She fully intended Vanessa and Glenn should come and live here in Dundalgan. The house was huge and there was plenty of room for all of them. She had a feeling that after this day Brendan would decline. His prime was over, his day was done. He'd become a grumpy old man that no one listened to.

And she was now, or would be soon, free to do all sorts of wonderful and exciting things that heretofore, because of Brendan's refusal to even consider her suggestions, she had not had a chance to.

She opened her purse and took out a sheet of folded note-paper. She opened it up and smoothed it out. There was the list. She had written it so long ago and then had put it firmly away when she had seen that she had no hope of realising these ambitions. She looked at it now and a new hope sprang to her heart. Travel. It was headed 'Travel' followed by a list of the places she intended to visit with the money she would get when she sold her shares to Glenn. Paris. She'd see for herself the Sacré Coeur, Notre Dame and the cafés, drinks on a terrace at a marble-topped table. Oh, the joy!

Italy came next. Rome, the Vatican and an audience with the Holy Father. Rosalind touched her scapulas. Oh, that would be bliss for sure, ensure her entry into Heaven when she passed on. Which she had no intention of doing until she had seen the Sistine Chapel. The Colosseum. Spain. Madrid. The Prado. Oh, how the names enchanted her. They sounded like magic.

She would go somewhere new each spring and autumn and Brendan would just have to learn to do without her at those times.

She gave a little giggle. She hadn't felt like this since she was a little girl. Certainly since before she had married

Brendan. It was going to be such a joy. The whole world lay before her. She thought fleetingly of India, discarded it, then drew the idea back in. She thought of the teeming masses in bright saris and the golden temples where the yellow gods sat endlessly with fingers raised and eyes turned inwards. Her eyes glowed and she stared at herself in her mirror and whispered, 'Why not? Why on earth not?'

She was going to take a course in Art History. She was going to get books and read and learn. She would study the great masters and try to understand the new. She was going to do that wisest of all things, she was going to say 'I don't know. Teach me.'

She was going to take a cookery course as well. There was an exotically named place in Switzerland that was advertising Cordon Bleu cookery classes during the summer vacation and she was going to apply and Brendan would just have to lump it.

She thought of him now with both compassion and contempt. He'd let them all down. Those men he despised like Dr Jack and Leonard Fitzjames had always had integrity. She'd never understood that. They had integrity and therefore they were free.

Well, now she was too, and she intended to make the most of her freedom. She touched her hair, glancing at herself in the mirror. Perhaps she'd get her hair cut and styled. She might even have a rinse. You never knew. Perhaps. Oh hell, definitely.

Chapter Seventy-two

ৎৎ ৩৩

Pierce was living these days in one room in Crumlin. Rejected by his father, evicted by his wife, receiving a small salary, he spent most of his time in a lather of fear. He drank too much and smoked too much and spent his time in terrified contemplation of a poor and lonely future. Oriana demanded every penny he earned, and God knew that wasn't much, and he found he had precious little to live off.

He spent most of his free time in the dim interior of Lawlor's sipping Guinness followed by chasers of Jameson's best, when he could afford it.

He could not think what to do. He had been prepared to follow in his father's footsteps and that goal having been removed he floundered, a fish out of water. He was grateful for the work given to him at Murphy and Callaghan, but knew that they had no intention of allowing him to rise to any kind of importance. He was grateful but he saw no future there. It had dawned on him rather belatedly that Brewster Callaghan did not intend his advancement, having proved himself more Christian-minded than his father. He was content, and Pierce was in a dead-end.

Oriana had damaged his self-confidence to a degree that he believed himself utterly useless, and suicide had not been far from his thoughts. His wife's ridicule and rejection had sapped his energy and left him indifferent to his future.

And so he sat each evening under the amber lights of Lawlor's pub, sipping his Guinness, tossing back the Jameson, desperately seeking oblivion.

'Hiya, old buddy!' The American voice beside him, the friendly hand on his shoulder startled him. He turned around and there on the stool beside him sat his American brother-in-law. Pierce stared at him indifferently. He resented the intrusion in an abstract sort of way. He had just reached that gloriously numb state when his nerves had been anaesthetised and he had not a problem in the world. It would not last long, this utterly transcendental euphoria, and he wanted to enjoy it while it lasted. He did not want to be interrupted by this vital American breathing energy and toothpaste breath into his ear, spoiling the effect and the aroma of the whiskey.

'What you want?' he asked thickly.

'I want to offer you a job,' Glenn said quite seriously. Pierce choked and spluttered on his whiskey, looking at the American in amazement. 'You kidding? You daft?' he cried, when he could get the words out.

Glenn smiled. 'Oh no. I'm not daft,' he said. 'I'm serious.'

'I'm a thief, Glenn. Didn't you know? You been in America, you didn't hear about me?'

'I was the one bailed you out, remember? I want to offer you a job.' He nodded to the barman who refilled Pierce's glass and poured a paddy for Glenn.

Glenn settled himself on the stool beside Pierce and leaned his arms on the bar. He stared at his brother-in-law ruefully. 'You'll have to cut down on the sauce. And you must never, ever, think of stealing from me. I'd have them lock you up and throw away the key. But I don't expect you to.' He drank some of the whiskey. 'See, I believe that you did it for a reason, not because you are fundamentally dishonest. Anyhow, I'll soon find out. Patrick McCawley needs good men. Men who'll be loyal. We want someone to run the market, let out the stalls. Hey, let me set it out for you and you see what you think.' He grinned at Pierce. 'You might not *want* the job. You might be happier where you are now, without a challenge, doing your nut here every evening in the gloom.'

Pierce shook his head. That was not what he wanted at all. He stared hopefully back at Glenn. He reminded Glenn of a puppy he once had, so eager to please.

'See, I'm converting and letting out at least half of the warehouse space on the quays.'

'What warehouse space?' Pierce asked.

Glenn tapped his forehead. 'Oh, I forgot, you don't know. I've taken over Ardmore's,' he said mildly.

Pierce hooted incredulously, stared at Glenn in disbelief. 'Over our father-in-law's dead body.'

'Oh no. It's true,' Glenn replied firmly.

'I can't believe it.' Pierce shook his head in bewilderment.

'You better believe it. Old Brendan see doesn't know diddly-squat about running a business. Never had the humility to ask. Patrick McCawley did it all for him. When Paddy left, well, Brendan was up the creek without a paddle. And I promised I'd rescue it,' he finished triumphantly.

'Well I'll be . . .'

'Already it's been turnaround time. I've sold off a lot of property. We're afloat again.'

'You serious?'

'You betcha!' Glenn smiled at the bewildered Pierce. 'Brendan Ardmore said I'd make a balls of it –' he grinned widely – 'so I'm damned if I'll have him proved right. Now we're out of the red, bills paid, money trickling in, but I want it to *flood* in. Heck, I want a deluge.'

'Great, sounds great.'

'I have to make a go of it. You wanna help?'

'Geez, I'd love to see the look on his face an' we come out tops.'

'We will, Pierce. Make no mistake about that. Thing is, will you help?'

'Sure I will. How though? How?'

'Easy. I want you to run the market, leasing and letting, keeping a tight control over variety and seeing there's no funny business. I thought we'd run it like the Portobello Market in London.'

'Not like Moore Street? Veggies and fruit?'

'No. *Not* like Moore Street. I'm thinking silver, antiques, jewellery, pictures. Artifacts old and new. Artisans working on the spot. I'd leave that to you. Make a go of it.'

'You know, Glenn, I'm sure I could.' Pierce's eyes gleamed. 'Yeah, yeah, I could. Just think. A job again. Money in my pocket.'

'You betcha. And no funny business?'

'No funny business!' Pierce smiled for the first time in ages.

Glenn put out his hand. 'Then it's a deal?'

'A deal!' They shook hands. Glenn tossed the last of his

drink down his throat and stood. 'Okay,' he said, satisfied. He walked to the door. Pierce called after him, 'And, Glenn?' The American turned. 'Thank you.'

'Oh, don't thank me,' Glenn laughed. 'Just get on with it.'

'You betcha,' Pierce cried, imitating Glenn. 'You betcha!'

Chapter Seventy-three

~ ~

Simon was dying, slowly, painfully. Avalan had lost weight and looked drawn.

'Have you ever helped anyone to die, Doctor?' she asked Dr Jack, who hushed her and put his finger on his lips.

'I cannot permit you to talk that way,' he told her. 'Oh God, Avalan, I'd like to, but it's against the law. And my oath. Dear woman, you must understand.'

They both turned to the bed as Simon cried out in agony. His shallow breathing was a constant terrible wail, a worn-out scream of protest.

The family, all except Brendan who was totally preoccupied with his own dilemma, came to pay their respects. Dr Jack did not allow any of them in to bid Simon farewell, except Glenn. He felt it would distress them too much, for Simon's dying was horrifying. And the patient was locked into his own dark world of suffering and did not see that they were there. It would benefit no one.

Rosalind came first. She held her sister tightly as Avalan wept. 'Oh Ros, he's in such torment. It isn't fair.'

'He'll reap the reward in Heaven,' Rosalind told her calmly and Avalan looked as if she might hit her sister.

'Well, it's true, Ava. The more we suffer in this life the higher and happier our place in Heaven.'

'And who told you that?' Avalan asked angrily. 'Have you a direct line to the Almighty that he passes on such ludicrous information?'

Rosalind's eyes flickered in surprise. She had not seen anything at all ludicrous in what she thought of as loving consolation. 'Don't blaspheme, Avalan. Simon's in God's hands.'

'Then I wish God would let him go,' Avalan cried, eyes flashing fire.

'You don't mean that, dear,' Rosalind said calmly.

'Oh yes I do,' her sister insisted. 'God, if there *is* a God –' Rosalind gasped horrified – 'God's managed this so badly that if He exists, then I do not want to know Him.' She looked at her sister piteously. 'If He is there, dear, why is He allowing this awful agony to drag on? Simon never hurt anyone in his life.'

Rosalind's face was stubborn. 'He killed Germans, didn't he? I'm sure the wives and mothers of those dead boys wouldn't agree that he'd never hurt anyone. *As ye sow so shall ye reap. Those who live by the sword shall die by the sword.*'

'Rosalind, you are my sister and I love you, but I want you to go now. Please leave.'

Rosalind left. She was glad to go. She hated hearing those terrible groans, that awful screaming that every so often shattered the peace of the home. It troubled her too that such pain could be prolonged, that sweet Simon should be asked to suffer so. Still, she reminded herself, Canon Tracey had told her that only the chosen few were given the privilege of extreme suffering and such agony guaranteed swift entry to the Heavenly Hosts. But she did not want, at this moment, to be close to death and pain. She had set her feet on a different path and she was not going to allow anyone or anything to spoil it for her. She had spent her whole life in service and now she had shrugged off the shackles and the world lay before her, waiting to be explored. She could not help Simon, make it easy for him or relieve his pain. Nor did Avalan appreciate the only consolation she could think of giving. Her sister didn't want her around so she shrugged her shoulders gratefully and left.

Oriana came. She too had lost weight and if Avalan had not been so utterly absorbed in her husband's illness she would have enquired into the reason for the girl's pinched face and restless eyes.

Oriana had discovered that the husband she had cast aside was now working for Glenn Carey and that he was rising, and rising, making a spectacular success of the undertaking and a great deal of money into the bargain.

Dublin, until then, had sold antiques solely in auction rooms or exclusive antique shops off Grafton Street. The advent of a market of stalls selling silver and lace, pictures, china and jewellery had proved irresistible to the public and the premises on the quays buzzed with activity. Oriana had gone there herself to see, but overcome with shame had not had the courage to actually go in and look around. She'd been a complete fool, she knew that. She'd been selfish and greedy and unsupportive. In her own defence however she told herself that she'd been frightened. She persuaded herself, sometimes with feverish intensity, that her father had been right. That the beatings were justified as they produced her happiness, her well being. What she'd seen at the AGM had opened her eyes and the adored Pappy had fallen from his pedestal. Oriana found herself alone, illusions shattered and nothing to put in their place. She was very lonely.

She had come to Rackton Hall hoping Aunt Avalan would help. Aunt Avalan always had answers and Oriana had dreamed of a solution offered, a plan of campaign suggested. But she found Avalan distraught and totally preoccupied by her husband's condition. She went away, back to the empty house in Foxrock – once her dream, now a reminder of her isolation. She returned having neither given nor received help.

Sitric came and stayed. He held her hand and that helped. He sat silently beside her, undemanding, a staunch, loving presence, and in a moment of lucidity Simon smiled feebly at them both and whispered, 'Italy.' He knew their dream. How he divined what they had never told a soul was a mystery. But it seemed he gave them his blessing. He was so far beyond her now, as if he was in another dimension, and he suddenly howled as the pain viciously attacked him again and he screamed under its merciless onslaught. Sitric found the animal sounds of the dying man unbearable for any longer than short periods. He would go into the rose garden and try to repossess his soul and his equilibrium, sitting on the stone bench there, surrounded by living nature in all its glory.

Vanessa and Glenn came and heard the terrible struggle above. Vanessa covered her ears with her hands and left the house. Glenn and Avalan went into Simon's room. They were there for a long time.

Vanessa wandered into Avalan's rose garden and sat beside Sitric. They sat there until dusk lowered a mantle of darkness

364

over everything, until the stars began to wink and blink and dance in the depthless navy-blue sky and the moon began her journey across the heavens.

'I'm praying for God to release him, Sitric. He's suffered enough pain,' Vanessa said, her voice tremulous.

'I wish I had the courage,' Sitric whispered.

Vanessa looked at him, her eyes wide. 'What do you mean?'

'Put him out of his misery, what do you think I meant?'

Vanessa digested this. She thought about it and nodded. 'Then why don't you? It would be a kindness.'

'He's Avalan's husband. I love Avalan. It would come between us some day.'

Vanessa was doing her best to understand. Her brother's beautiful face was bathed in silver light. He looked carved in marble. None of them had ever known or understood him, except, she supposed, Avalan.

'Remember Pappy caning us?' Sitric whispered in the dark. 'Remember the pain?'

Vanessa nodded. 'It was the humiliation,' she said and her brother nodded too.

'All pain is humiliating,' he said. 'It's the loss of dignity. It's a terrible thing. An outrageous thing. Like Simon's pain. Not to be borne.'

Vanessa leaned over and took Sitric's hand. She held it softly between her own.

Suddenly an enormous silence fell over Rackton Hall. The earth seemed to hold its breath, the trees were still. The birds were silent and for a second there was no sound at all.

Then the ordinary noises recommenced. The birds called to each other their night-time greeting. The stars blinked once more. The river bumbled and danced and sang over the stones and smooth black rocks. A branch cracked and a nocturnal animal scuttled through the leaves.

'He's at peace now,' Avalan, in the house, said with infinite relief.

'I hope you can live with this,' Dr Jack said to Glenn. His tone was not condemnatory, it was a genuine hope.

'I'm a soldier,' Glenn replied calmly and Dr Jack nodded.

'You want to see him, Doctor?' Avalan asked.

Dr Jack shook his head. He looked tired. 'No. Not just

now. I'd like a brandy while I write the death certificate,' he said.

Glenn stared out of the window while Avalan poured the doctor his drink. Then she joined Glenn at the window. The doctor sat at the desk and wrote. There was silence. Outside they could see the rose garden bathed in moonlight. Sitric and Vanessa sat side by side holding hands. Avalan took Glenn's hand in her own. 'Thank you,' she whispered. He remained silent a moment.

'What will you do now, Avalan?' he asked eventually.

'I'll go to Italy with Sitric,' she said.

'Are you afraid?' he asked.

'Very,' she replied softly. 'But all life is risk and risk is frightening.'

He nodded and they both watched Vanessa and Sitric rise and begin walking back to the house.

'You are quite a guy, Glenn,' Avalan whispered as they gazed out on the ones they loved walking up the gravel pathway. 'Vanessa and Elana called you "the lovely American". It suits.'

He smiled at her a little sadly. 'It hurts too,' he said. 'Taking responsibility.'

'Being grown up,' she added and again he nodded.

'Let's meet them,' he suggested and took her arm and together they went downstairs.

Chapter Seventy-four

⁊ ⸺

Elana looked at her father, noting his pallor. He was tired. The look in his eyes said, 'please let me rest'.

'Sit down, Da. I'll get you a cup of tea.'

'Oh God, Elana, please not a problem. I'm bushed.'

'Not really a problem, Da, more an item of news.'

'Simon Rackton died tonight.'

'Merciful release, from what Vanessa told me.'

He nodded and sighed. Yes. He supposed that was accurate. A merciful release.

'Da?' She sounded apprehensive and he looked up.

'Mmm?'

'I'm . . . that is, I want your approval.'

His eyes became keen. 'Marriage?' he asked.

'Mmm.' She nodded.

He realised for the first time how radiant she looked, how she sparkled and shone, how diamond-bright her eyes were. He took a deep breath. He knew what was coming, and he knew too a moment of fierce jealousy. But his face didn't change and he realised in an instant that if he wanted to keep that special relationship they had, that trust and spontaneous love, he'd better accept what she told him now without reservation.

'Leonard has asked me to marry him,' she said.

He smiled at her.

'Do you love him, my darlin'?'

'Yes, Da.'

'Does he love you?'

'Oh yes, Da.' She had been pulling off his shoes, hunkering down. She laid her cheek on his knee.

'I feel complete with him,' she said, then looked up at him, her eyes full of dancing lights. 'You know, Da, I always cracked the whip with the others, with Dom and Gavin and Billy. I said go and they went, fetch and they obeyed. I realised recently that until Leonard I simply had no respect. I ordered the young lads around and now . . . oh, it's so wonderful to look up to someone. To want to be guided by them. He's like you, Da, and if you tell me I have a father-complex I'll kill you.' She laughed, looking at him with shining love.

'Maybe you have,' he said gently.

'So what? I'm happy with a man like my Da and unhappy with crass idiots like my brother—'

'Hey! Steady on!'

'No, Da. I mean it. He makes me happy to be alive.'

He tilted her chin. 'And when you're forty, he'll be seventy.'

'I'll face that, Da, when I get to it. No one can foretell *anything* in this life. Look at Avalan Rackton and Simon, God rest him. The perfect couple. They were so suited, so beautiful, so in love. Who could have guessed what would happen to him?' He nodded. What she said was true. 'And look at Pierce and Oriana,' she continued. 'Mr Ardmore chose him as the right man for his daughter yet it was a disaster.'

'No need to give me an argument. You have my blessing, love.'

'Thank you, Da. Now off you go and kip.'

'You'll have to win your mother over,' he warned her.

'Oh, Ma'll follow your example. She always has. And he's insisting on phoning you and making a formal bid for my hand. Isn't he old-fashioned? Oh, Da, he's gorgeous.'

Dr Jack smiled. That would be difficult. Interviewing a man his own age who was asking for his daughter's hand in marriage. But he'd do it if it made Elana happy. Life was all about compromise.

'Oh Da, I love you so.'

And looking into her glowing face he knew that that was why he did it. To hear her say that to him, wholeheartedly. Oh yes, it was worth it. He rose and stretched and yawned.

'Love increases love, doesn't it?' she asked. He nodded and she continued, 'I love you and mother more because I love him,' she said. 'Oh Da, isn't life wonderful!'

Chapter Seventy-five

ও ৩

They began to congregate in the little Wicklow church an hour before the service. Simon had not gone out and about much; he was not a great socialiser. He had always been a quiet, private man, yet they came from all over. Hundreds of them came to bid farewell to the kind and loving person Simon Rackton had been.

Rosalind and Brendan were first to arrive. Brendan kept his head lowered, his face away from everyone. His face and neck had broken out in a nasty rash of red lumps and flaking skin that covered him in an itchy mass. He looked old and tired and defeated. Rosalind knelt and whispered, 'And if Glenn and Vanessa greet you, greet them back. I don't want to find myself in the poorhouse because of your stubbornness.' She used a hectoring voice, the old respect gone. She wore no hat and her hair seemed to have lost its grey. It was cut short and was a soft nut-brown and curled around her head in a very fetching way. People thought she was looking very well indeed.

Vanessa and Glenn came into the church with Sitric and Avalan. Vanessa was big with child. A grandchild. Rosalind's heart lifted whenever she thought about it. The family whole again. Their baby stood a very good chance of being beautiful, she thought, not for the first time. They were a gorgeous couple. Standing there in the shaft of sunlight Vanessa glanced up at her husband and exchanged a look of such passionate and radiant love that a fierce little pain seized Rosalind's heart.

They walked up the centre aisle, arm in arm, Vanessa's face full now of apprehension as she neared her father. 'Hi Mother. Hi Pappy.'

Brendan glanced sideways at them, not meeting his daughter's eyes. Rosalind nudged him. 'Harrumph,' he said and nodded. It was a start.

Rosalind, satisfied, kissed her daughter and squeezed her son-in-law's hands. 'It's nice to see you,' she said.

'Mother, you look great,' Vanessa noticed her mother's hair. If she was surprised she did not say so. 'You look lovely.'

'Thank you, dear.'

Rosalind was surprised to see her son with her sister. She had decided that she did not understand men. She had come to the conclusion that Sitric was beyond her comprehension and that the best way to deal with him was to let him do what he wanted. He really was a very nice boy. She was pleased he was being so sensitive and sympathetic to his aunt in her hour of need. So kind to help her in this dark time.

'I'm taking Avalan to Italy, Mother,' he told her as they greeted each other. Avalan, looking remote and empty, as if she was a robot, touched the coffin, then knelt in the front pew reserved for her.

'Can you afford it, Sitric?' Rosalind asked. 'It's very considerate of you, but it will be very expensive.'

'I've sold my shares to Glenn,' he said. 'He gave me a very good price and insisted I keep a few. He said that in a few years they'll be worth a fortune. With the money he gave me I'm all sorted out. We're set. I've always wanted to go to Italy,' he added. 'So has Avalan. And it will do her good to get away. We'll be company for each other.'

'Wouldn't you prefer to go with people your own age?' she asked mildly.

He smiled. 'Oh Mother, you know me. I was *born* old. Something to do with Pa.' He glanced sideways at his father but Brendan was looking down at the floor. 'I'd rather be with Avalan than with anyone else,' he said and knelt beside Vanessa and Glenn.

'I wish he wouldn't be so forward,' Rosalind whispered to Brendan. 'Calling her Avalan like that. Trying to be modern. It's Glenn's influence. Calling people diminutives and cutting out their titles without asking.' She sighed. 'Oh well, time marches on and I suppose we'll have to get used to it. She *deserves* to be called "Aunt". I'll have to speak to Sitric about it.'

Brendan didn't reply. He was mentally racing around in circles. Who was looking at him? What were they thinking?

His humiliation and defeat were on show in this public place and he wished himself a million miles away. He would not have come to the funeral at all only Rosalind had threatened him. She had never done that before. She was getting out of hand. And she said that people would talk more if he *didn't* go. They'd say he'd lost his bottle. People, she told him, would say he couldn't take it. They would despise him even more if they felt he couldn't stand up to his son-in-law or accept his take-over with equanimity.

He looked fearfully about. He would brazen it out, show them he did not care and then the laugh would be on the other side of their faces.

Margaret and Jonathan D'Alton came into the church. He could feel himself cringe. He sank on to his knees and buried his face in his hands as if in prayer. They genuflected and went to the altar and pressed Avalan's hand, their faces studies in sympathetic concern. Then they turned to Brendan and Rosalind. He had no choice but to look up.

'Oh Brendan. Rosalind. Good morning. We're so sorry for your loss.' Margaret was kissing Rosalind. Jonathan echoed his wife. Then he cleared his throat. 'It was so sad it had to happen,' he said. 'And after the good news.'

Here it came, Brendan thought, and darted a fierce little glance up at Jonathan. 'What do you mean?' he asked, trying to sound casual.

Jonathan shook his head, but his smug smile proclaimed insider information. 'I've been talking to your son-in-law.'

Brendan's heart lurched despondently. 'Oh,' he muttered. If only the earth would open up and swallow him!

'Oh come on, Brendan. Don't be shy. Take a bow. Glenn told us how you'd saved the firm, and how you'd asked him to carry out your Great Master Plan.'

Brendan was dumbfounded and very nearly blew it. 'What on earth are you talking about?' he gasped.

'Now, now, Brendan.' Jonathan tapped the side of his nose with his forefinger. 'We *know*! The market. The restaurant. Great ideas. Very clever of you. Glenn told us *all* about it. Must say, Margaret didn't think you had it in you to come up with such a *modern* plan.'

Brendan looked for irony, saw a little lurking in the depths of Jonathan's eyes and realised with relief that it was not because he did not believe Glenn, but rather Brendan's concept that startled him.

'Margaret loves the market,' Jonathan continued. 'Got a lovely painting there last week. Sheep on a mountainside. A bargain. We enjoy going there, browsing. Must say, I never thought you would have had such an original idea, but Glenn assures us it is all your doing. Congrats, old chap.'

Then he genuflected, blessed himself piously and moved over to take his place on the left of the altar.

'And it was really Christian of you to give Pierce Powers a job,' Margaret whispered as she made to follow her husband. 'Showed up Sean Powers. Serves him right. He shouldn't have dumped his own flesh and blood like that. One should always be loyal to the family.' She glanced at Rosalind, 'I hope Oriana will have as much charity as your husband, Rosalind—' she could not resist this parting shot as she moved away to join her husband.

Brendan sat down abruptly. He was very confused. He could not understand the man. Glenn. What were his motives? Why wasn't he boasting of the success of his ideas? Why would he allow his sworn enemy to take the credit? No, *give* him the credit. Hand it over to him. Why? Brendan shook a bewildered head and tried not to scratch his face. He turned and saw Glenn smiling at him reassuringly and he gave him a tight little smile in return.

At that moment Elana and Leonard Fitzjames came up the aisle and took their places beside the Careys. Elana and Vanessa hugged each other.

Brendan shook his head. He'd never understand. It was yet another bafflement. Why on earth, he wondered, would Elana Cassidy choose to marry an old man with no money when there were so many rich young lads available? Stupidity, he guessed. Or perhaps Leonard had got her in the family way. He stared at the couple, pondering. Leonard held her hand and Elana looked up at him with an expression strange to Brendan but very like the way Vanessa looked at Glenn. No one, he was quite sure, had ever looked at him like that. Except maybe Oriana when she was a little girl. Oriana had sometimes had that look of adoration on her face.

As the thought entered his head he caught sight of his eldest walking up the aisle alone. She was wearing a *haute couture* outfit in black Moygashel and fox and she stared at him coldly and did not return his smile.

He felt suddenly very sick. He half rose. 'Oriana!' he cried, turning to her, but she averted her face and all he could see was the brim of her wide hat. Everyone was looking. Rosalind caught his arm and pulled him back down beside her. 'It's all right, dear. She'll get over it,' she said.

Pierce Powers entered and Oriana, turning from her father, noticed him. She turned to him, but he did to her exactly what she had done to her father; he gave her an icy stare and walked to the other side of the church and knelt down with the D'Altons. Oriana dropped her head on her hands and Brendan could see that her shoulders were shaking. He stood up. Rosalind looked at him, perplexed.

'What are you doing, dear?' she asked sharply. She was blocking his way.

'Let me out,' he cried, suddenly oblivious of others. She stood up obediently at his command. It was automatic after years of practice. He stumbled by her, then walked past the pew where Vanessa and Glenn, Elana and Leonard and Sitric sat. Behind them Oriana knelt alone at the end of the pew. 'Move over,' Brendan told her. She looked up, at first cold-faced. Her eyes were red with weeping but she stared at him angrily.

'I'm sorry,' he said. Her eyes widened. It was difficult. He'd never said it before, at least not since he was a small boy. Then he'd said it all the time.

Now he looked at Oriana and said, 'Sorry.'

She melted. It seemed to her that her bones became jelly and the great weight she had been carrying had been lifted by her Pappy. He had always carried her loads and she gratefully handed the burden over to him. She sank into his arms and turned her face to him and said, 'Pappy. Oh Pappy.' He held her while she wept. He would fix it. He decided he knew exactly what he would do. He looked across the church at Pierce. The boy was, of course, watching. He lifted an arm from about Oriana and beckoned him. Pierce hesitated, then rose and went and knelt behind his wife and father-in-law. Brendan relaxed, content.

The priest had come on to the altar. No one paid

373

any attention to Oriana crying. Everyone cried at funerals. Rosalind Ardmore was crying, but she did not look sad.

'They're raking it in,' Jonathan D'Alton muttered to Margaret. 'Who would ever have thought it. A while ago there I thought that the Ardmores were wiped out. It's amazing. I'm glad because I haven't lost a golf partner.'

'An' Pierce Powers is a big-shot now. An' him a jailbird. But you can't cut him or we'll be refused entrance to the restaurant and the market and I'm mad about that market. It's great.'

'Think he'll go back to Oriana?' Jonathan asked, watching the touching little scene across the aisle.

'Sure to.' Margaret glanced sideways to where Pierce sat gazing fondly at his wife's back. 'Brendan'll not give up that easy. He'll sort it, never fear.'

'If anyone treated me the way she treated him I'd kill her first,' Jonathan said.

'Don't be silly. He's mad about her. But then he's a fool. She's a fool. They're well suited,' Margaret said crisply.

'Why's she crying? I didn't know she was so fond of her uncle.'

'Don't be daft, Jonathan. She doesn't know *how* to love. No,' she whispered as the priest intoned the requiem mass, 'she's crying for effect. She wants to get back where the money flows. It's the only place she's comfortable. She dumped Daddy and hubby when they couldn't or wouldn't cough up. Now they are both in the money again and she has to find a way back into their lives. And their purses.'

He smiled at her. 'You're a very observant woman, Margaret, and I think you are right.'

Avalan was not crying. Her heart felt like a stone. It would dissolve in Italy, but not before. Simon was at rest. That was all that counted. Her beloved husband was at last at peace.

They would travel to Italy next day. Sitric would accompany her to Tuscany and there they would find an agreeable villa. They would stay. Soon they'd be forgotten. People would occasionally wonder where the aunt and her nephew were, how they were doing, but it would be a fleeting query forgotten as soon as uttered. They had no close friends, either of them. They had not been tied to others.

Rackton Hall was being sold. Glenn Carey told her he

could sell it to a hotel chain that was investing in Ireland. They had bought some Ardmore land in Dublin and were interested in buying the prime site in Wicklow. She told him to accept. She offered him a percentage of the sale price but he refused. 'I've been cut in already,' he told her, 'on the Dublin deal. This is the sugar. I've also asked for shares in the hotel. They want, you see, to create one of the best golf courses in Europe. That will bring me in a tidy sum and I won't have to lift a finger.' Then he smiled at her. 'Be happy,' he said and took her hands and kissed her cheek.

'You don't think I will be?' she asked.

'I think we get back what we put out,' he said. 'I wouldn't presume.'

'You be happy too,' she had told him and he nodded.

'I will. Oh, I will.' he said. 'But then, you see, it doesn't take much to make me happy.'

Avalan looked at the coffin now. 'Goodbye, sweet man,' she whispered. 'Dream peacefully.' Then she smiled at Sitric and he smiled back.

Vanessa and Elana glanced at each other.

'Happy?' Vanessa whispered.

Elana nodded. 'Very.'

'Who would have thought?' Vanessa mused, indicating Leonard, who was kneeling.

'He was there all the time, Ness, under my nose. I *always* felt just perfect with him.'

Vanessa took her friend's hand. 'Life's wonderful,' she said.

'Then enjoy it. We mustn't waste any time. It's too valuable.'

The two girls stared at the coffin. Death seemed an alien and frightening concept to them at this moment when they both felt so vitally alive.

Elana whispered, 'Remember the poem we did at school, "Golden Lads and Girls all must, As Chimney-Sweepers, Come to dust."?'

'Oh Elana,' Vanessa looked at her friend reproachfully.

'We won't waste it,' Elana said. 'Will we?'

The priest was leaving the church. He went ahead of the coffin. Two little altar boys followed, swinging censers out of which the incense poured. Avalan, supported by Sitric, came after. Rosalind fell into place beside Vanessa and Glenn. Elana and Leonard came next, pausing to allow Brendan and Oriana to walk out of the church before them. Brendan handed his daughter to her husband and Pierce took her arm as they left. Jonathan nudged his wife who smiled smugly at him. Elana took Leonard's hand and Glenn put his hand under his wife's elbow.

'We'll call it Simon, if it's a boy,' he said.

'What a wonderful idea, Glenn. Simone if it's a girl. Oh, Glenn, I love you so,' she said softly.

'Yes, the way you fixed everything,' Elana said.

Glenn grinned. 'Positive,' he said. 'Not wonderful. Positive. You can always get some good out of a situation if you try hard enough. And *I* gain. Don't forget that. This is for me too.' He smiled at them and the four of them went out into the sun together.